SEX LIFE

SEX LIFE

A Novel by Bruce Cook

M. Evans and Company, Inc. • *New York*

Library of Congress Cataloging in Publication Data

Cook, Bruce, 1932-
   Sex life.
   I. Title.
PZ4.C76915Se [PS3553.O55314] 813'.5'4 78-13487
ISBN 0-87131-263-8

Copyright © 1978 by Bruce Cook
All rights reserved. No part of this book may be reproduced or transmitted in any form without the written permission of the publisher.

M. Evans and Company, Inc.
216 East 49 Street
New York, New York 10017

DESIGN BY DENNIS J. GRASTORF

Manufactured in the United States of America
9 8 7 6 5 4 3 2 1

PROLOGUE

DETECTIVE SERGEANT JOSEPH MELANIPHY of Tenth District Homicide switched off the ignition and sat for a while in his car. He had already spotted the building he was headed for —just ahead of him and across the street. He could hardly miss it. There were already two cruisers and a police van there. A uniform cop was posted at the door to keep out the curious crowd of five or six who had gathered outside, mumbling earnestly to one another, asking the same old questions.

Rather deliberately, he fished out a cigarette from the crumpled pack on the seat beside him and lit it, realizing as he did that he was merely delaying what lay ahead. For a job he liked, it sure gave him some bad moments. This was always one of them—viewing the premises. When it came right down to it, he didn't like being around dead people.

Well, he could put it off, but he couldn't make it go away. Melaniphy jerked open the door and extricated two hundred pounds on a five-foot-nine-inch frame from behind the wheel of his car.

"Sergeant! Hey, sergeant!" It was the cop at the door.

"Yeah?"

"The medical examiner's people want to know when they can move the deceaseds."

"After I view the premises." The cop ought to know the routine by now. What was he, a rookie?

"Yeah, well, they're pretty anxious."

Melaniphy slammed the car door contemptuously, hitched up his pants, and buttoned his suit jacket, taking his time about it all. He took a long look at the windows looking down on the street and noted the face of the old woman—second floor right front of the building he was headed for. A busybody, observer of the human scene. He would look in on her himself.

As he was crossing the street, using the saunter he sometimes affected to signal his authority, it occurred to Melaniphy that he had parked his car in Evanston and was now walking over to Chicago. The little sidestreet ran right down the city line. Why couldn't the murder have happened in Evanston for a change? He had a sudden, wild fantasy then, asking himself if it might not be a good idea to start dumping some Chicago bodies in Evanston, Skokie, Park Ridge, and those other rich suburban jurisdictions where murders never happened. Let them shoulder a little of the load for a change. Melaniphy, who often had such bizarre notions, knew enough to keep them to himself; they were unbecoming to a sergeant of detectives. What he didn't know, or chose not to recognize, was that it was this fantastic turn of mind that made him a good detective. He was as professionally thorough as the next man, but he often played hunches, and they often paid off.

The little crowd parted for him on the sidewalk. Melaniphy decided that the cop at the door, who looked quite young, really was a rookie and was instantly disposed to be merciful. Still, something had to be said.

"Upstairs, sergeant. Second floor rear."

"Terrific. You working for the Cook County Coroner or the Police Department?"

"Police Department."

"Remember that, would you?" Melaniphy sauntered past the kid and through the door.

"Uh, sergeant," the rookie called after him, "you got a handkerchief by you? It smells pretty bad up there."

Oh, Jesus, thought Melaniphy, with sinking heart, it's going to be one of those, is it?

It was, all right. They were all out in the hall—a couple of uniform cops, one of Melaniphy's Tenth District detectives named Klezek, the police photographer, and a guy from the medical examiner's office—a regular conclave. Melaniphy caught a whiff of what lay ahead as he approached them. He didn't like it.

"You guys all done?"

"Just waiting on you, sergeant," said the medical examiner's man.

"Terrific. You move anything?"

"Is the Pope Irish?" asked the me's man. Smartass. He looked like a Jew.

Melaniphy pushed past them and opened the door. The full force of the smell assaulted him as he stepped inside the room. He grabbed for his handkerchief, flicked it open, and brought it up to his face. Melaniphy hadn't had a cold in years. He kept it with him for just such emergencies as this. The handkerchief made it a little easier to breathe but not much.

The bodies were in full view from where he stood—the nearest lay on the bed: a male adolescent about thirteen or fourteen, face down, a belt tight around his neck, fecal matter around the buttocks, cause of death obviously strangulation. Melaniphy stepped around the bed for a closer look at the second body. It lay face up—or what was left of the face was up. Blood had coagulated over it. The nose was broken—flattened would be more accurate—and the yawning, slightly askew position of the jaw told Melaniphy it had been broken. His eye moved down the male body—a man about forty, he told himself—noting the darkly mottled and swollen skin that indicated the time of death as at least five days ago. The sternum was crushed, the thorax dark with a large bruise, and the rib cage on the right side dented. The man had been beaten and stomped to death. The male organ was intact—Melaniphy was mildly surprised at that—but it, too, showed signs of having been belabored by a heavy boot.

There were surprisingly few signs of struggle in the room. Whatever had happened had happened fast. But it was hard to get a fix on exactly what it was that had taken place there. The man was evidently beaten to death first, and then the kid was strangled. Or maybe the assailant knocked out the man, strangled the kid, then went back and stomped the man to death. Any way you tried to figure it, the sequence of events was puzzling, because it took time to do the kind of number that had been done on that guy on the floor. Why didn't the kid just jump and run away? Maybe he knew the assailant. Or maybe there were two or more involved.

Melaniphy took a quick turn through the room. There wasn't much to see. There were the clothes they had been wearing—the kid's in a pile at the foot of the bed, the man's folded neatly over a chair. He checked the label in the Glen plaid worsted suit and saw it had come from Marshall Field's Store for Men, about what he had expected. The wallet had been thrown down on the floor, open, and was ostentatiously empty of money. Technically, a robbery, but this hadn't been done for money. It had been done for fun.

After one last look at the bodies, Melaniphy headed out the door, glad to reach the hall at last. He waved the handkerchief in front of his nose, fanning the air, panting from having held his breath for nearly a minute. "Whew," he managed at last.

"Pretty bad, huh?" said one of the uniform cops. "It was the smell roused the neighbors."

Melaniphy nodded and cocked his head toward the door. "You get all the pictures you need?" he asked the photographer.

The photographer nodded.

"Then take them out."

The medical examiner's man picked up the body bags from the floor and led the two uniform cops back into the room. Melaniphy and Klezek moved a few steps down the hall, and with a nod to them both the photographer made for the stairs at something less than a run.

"You got ID's on the deceaseds?" he asked Klezek.

"On the man, yes. It's all over the wallet on the floor. No. I didn't move it. Didn't have to. Name's John Francis Gawlor. Good address in Evanston—an apartment building right on the lake." Klezek grimaced slightly and shook his head. "How does it look to you, sergeant?"

Melaniphy almost laughed. "How does it look to me? Shit, it looks just like your run-of-the-mill, garden-variety faggot double homicide. That's how it looks to me." He gave a sudden, savage kick at the wall and loosed a chunk of decaying plaster. "Jesus," he muttered tightly, "that poor, fucking little kid."

"You mind if I smoke, ma'am?"

"Well, I'd really rather you didn't. I don't object personally, but I don't have a single ashtray here because *I* don't smoke and none of my friends smoke. And the smell of those things is, well, it's just awfully hard to get rid of. You understand, I'm sure."

"I understand."

The lady in second floor right front had turned out to be just about as Melaniphy expected her to be. She was about seventy, maybe a year or two or more, powdered, rouged, and wearing a wig. There was something querulous, almost hostile in her manner when she had answered his knock. She had held him there for over a minute while she studied his Chicago Police Department identification, allowing at last that it looked like the real thing. When at last she took the chain off and let him in, she explained grudgingly that sometimes badges were fake. "They do that on the TV all the time." Her name was Mrs. Potter. She had lived in the building five years.

As Melaniphy was tucking away his cigarettes and asking himself just how direct he really ought to be with her, Mrs. Potter leaped in and took the initiative. "He's dead, isn't he? Murdered?"

"Who's that, ma'am?" Playing coy with her.

"Oh, you know. *Him.* The one down at the end of the hall."

"What was his name?"

"His *name?* How am I supposed to know that? That's your job, isn't it?" She hesitated a moment, then added, "Besides, he didn't live here. Nothing on the bell at all."

"No?"

"No! He just came and went, you know, came and went. It was obvious he was using the room for, well, immoral purposes."

"I see. How long would you say this was going on?"

She groaned and looked away for a moment, glancing out

the window where he had first seen her only minutes before. "I'd say about six months, maybe seven. I'm sure you could get the exact date from the landlord—our *absentee* landlord. Honestly, they let anyone in this building. They don't care. A woman just isn't safe."

Melaniphy took out a small pocket notebook and doodled on it with a ballpoint pen as though he were taking notes. People like Mrs. Potter were reassured by this. It meant they were being taken seriously. "How often did he come?"

"Oh, I don't know."

"Once a week?"

She smiled deprecatingly, a sneer really. "More often than that. You could count on him every weekend, a couple of times then. And during the week, too. He must have been around here two or three times a week steady." She let that sink in. "It was funny, too, because he didn't look like that kind of man."

"What did he look like?"

"Oh, I don't know. I only saw him once or twice up close and a few times in the daylight—or in the *early morning* light, if you know what I mean." She sighed. "Well, what did he look like? Just ordinary, but well off. I remember that one time there was something kind of funny about his eyes, like he wasn't paying any attention to me looking at him at all, like I wasn't even there. He sort of looked right through me. I guess all he had on his mind was that floozie he was with."

Melaniphy stared at her for a moment. "Uh . . . floozie? You mean a woman, don't you? He had a woman with him?"

"Well, *you* can call them women, if you want to. I believe you men have got some other names for that kind. Listen, *he* didn't care what sort he took back there with him. Loud, some of them so drunk he had to hold them up. If you ask me, it's a disgrace to call trash like that *women*." She leaned forward then, lowering her voice to just over a whisper. "He even took some coloreds back there. I know he did. I saw one of them with my own eyes."

Sergeant Melaniphy was confused. If his twelve years as a detective had taught him anything, they had taught him that things were not always as they seemed. Yet he had learned, too, that there were certain patterns of conduct that you could trace in behavior. And the reasonable conception he had formed of John Francis Gawlor as a sparrow hawk, a pederast, simply didn't tally with what Mrs. Potter had told him. It bothered him a little. If he had taken time to think it through, he would have admitted that it disturbed his personal sense of sexual identity. A man didn't suddenly turn from whoring to chasing little boys, did he? Jesus, he hoped not. Because if that were the case, then there was danger that half the men he worked with might go the same route.

To satisfy his uneasy curiosity about Gawlor, he put an extra man on the case, just for the day, when he went back to the station. Nothing major. He had Pernell go down to Eleventh and State and run Gawlor through Vice records to see if he might come up with anything, and then check Missing Persons for the kid. Klezek and his partner, Moskovsky, continued the canvass of the building Melaniphy had begun with Mrs. Potter. After that, they would return to the premises and, with the bodies removed and the windows wide open to dissipate the smell left behind, the two detectives would go over the room carefully with men from the crime lab to look for physical evidence. And Melaniphy? He headed north to Evanston to find out what he could by going through Gawlor's apartment.

What struck him first about it, once he had been let in by the building superintendent, was that he had never been in a place that was kept so neat and clean. It wasn't that the apartment didn't look lived in. There were pictures, books, mementoes of all kinds around the living room, but there was not even a suggestion of clutter to their arrangement. There was an almost symmetrical order to the furniture, and as the afternoon sun streamed in, the polished wooden surfaces of tables and the oiled teak in a couple of the chairs fairly gleamed as they caught the light. There was hardly a mote of dust to be seen anywhere.

"The maid sure does a job on this place," Melaniphy commented to the superintendent.

"Mr. Gawlor didn't have no maid in here."

"He didn't?"

"I'd know about it if he did."

"I guess you would."

The superintendent was obviously reluctant to leave him alone in the place, and technically Melaniphy had no right to be here. He was outside his jurisdiction. He supposed he should have stopped by and gotten an Evanston cop to come with him; but what the hell, that would have taken time—and besides, he had no use for those suburban cops anyway. The less contact he had with them the better. Well, he would just have to put up with the guy following him around and come back later with a court order for a more thorough search.

There were only three rooms—the living room, which he walked through quickly, only noting the family photographs on the wall; a good-sized kitchen that was just as polished and sterile as the rest of the place; and a spacious room that had served as a combination bedroom and study. This was more promising. He went to the big old mahogany desk that stood near the window and began rummaging through the drawers, bringing chaos out of order. In the top left-hand drawer, evidently reserved for personal finances, was a pile of paycheck stubs from an advertising agency on Michigan Boulevard. He took down the name and address in his notebook and did a bit of quick calculation in his head, coming up with an annual income figure for Gawlor of well over $50,000. Not bad, thought Melaniphy, with a twinge of bitter envy.

The wide middle drawer yielded a sheaf of letters separate from the others there. The return on them was identical—Patricia Gawlor from an address in Des Plaines, Illinois. Wife? Ex-wife? Anyway, Melaniphy decided she must be the nice-looking woman who gazed out at him from the gold-framed picture on the desk; she looked like a wife. And the two pretty teen-age girls, each smiling from her separate gold frame, would be their children. He opened one of the letters and glanced over its contents. It had to do with the disposition of property in Wisconsin and was couched in rather formal prose—except for the last paragraph: "Jack, I want you to know that the girls and I really do miss you. The checks are welcome, of course, but you'd be welcome, too. Believe me. Easter perhaps? If you'd care to make it a family occasion, we'd love to have you." Easter was well over a month past. Melaniphy found himself wondering if Gawlor had made it out to Des Plaines then. Somehow he hoped he had.

In the back of the top drawer he found a small key and an address book. He waved the address book at the superintendent, who hovered disapprovingly nearby. "I'm taking this along," he said. "It's evidence."

"Well, I . . ."

Without waiting for the superintendent to formulate his response, Melaniphy began tugging drawers open, giving them only a cursory inspection until he came to the one—bottom right—that was locked. He inserted the key, twisted it, and tugged open the drawer. As he expected, it contained Gawlor's trove of pornography. He threw a pile of the magazines up on the desk. "Take a look," he said to the superintendent. "That's the kind of stuff Gawlor was into."

Actually, it appeared to be pretty mild—most of it straight sex, though there was also a little S-M and bondage. None of it, he noted, was homosexual in appeal. Funny. He turned and quickly strode over to the bureau next to the bed, leaving the superintendent free to peruse at will. Which he did. Melaniphy had successfully created a diversion.

Banging his way one by one through the bureau drawers, Melaniphy found nothing but clothes, well laundered and neatly arranged, until he opened the top drawer. There, next to two cartons of cigarettes, one opened and one unopened, was what he had been looking for—matches, a nice, neat pile of matchbooks. He grabbed them out of the drawer, and with a glance back at the superintendent, who was paying him no attention, he pocketed them all.

He walked casually back to the superintendent. At last the man looked up. "Well, what do you think?" Melaniphy asked.

"This is really something. My wife won't let me keep this stuff around the house."

"I'm not surprised." He decided to go fishing. "But *he* was living alone, wasn't he?"

"Oh, sure. He was divorced or separated or something.

But he was proud of his kids, always talking about those girls." The superintendent nodded at the pictures on the desk.

"What kind of a guy was he, anyway?" Not a very professional question, but Melaniphy was curious.

The superintendent shrugged. "Oh, I don't know. A nice guy, really. Always had a good word for you. Not like some of the people in this building, I can tell you." He frowned his concern, then added philosophically, "Well, you know what they say. The good die young."

All the way out to Des Plaines he asked himself why in the world he had let himself in for what lay ahead there. He could just as well have sent Klezek and Moskovsky. He hadn't been out on one of these next-of-kin notifications since he had made sergeant. Why should he put up with it when he no longer had to? A good question. Why was he prepared to put up with it now?

Melaniphy had to admit that there was something about this case that fascinated him. Not the crime. If he had ever seen a homicide that was a piece of shit, it was this one. Even this early he felt fairly confident they would make a collar. It was just a matter of plugging into the right network, making connections, and then leaning on people until they came up with the right man.

No, what fascinated him was the victims—or one of them, John Francis Gawlor. Who was he, anyway? What was he *about*? If there was any element of mystery to this case, then it lay in fixing the nature of the man in the middle of it. Mystery—what a crock! Melaniphy wouldn't have dared to say the word aloud back at the station. Yet as a kid, the very idea of mysteries to be solved, puzzles to be worked out, had absorbed him for hours, days, years on end. Through high school he had read every detective novel he could put his hands on—Nero Wolfe, Father Brown, Lord Peter Wimsey, Sherlock Holmes, all of them—and ultimately, it was because of them that he had decided to be a cop, a detective. It was the only ambition he had ever had. And then, of course, discovering the reality of police work, all the shit-work and drudgery of it, had come not just as disappointment but as a real shock. Yet he had survived the disappointment and withstood the shock and eventually became a real detective—and a good one. That was because he learned at last to follow routine investigative procedures and leave the mysteries to Nero Wolfe. But had he put all that behind him? No. There were mysteries, dammit, and John Francis Gawlor was one of them!

The house he had been looking for was not far from Touhy, the road he had taken out, and it lay just off the approach to O'Hare Airport. A couple of miles away and a few hundred feet up, the planes followed one another down at intervals in stately procession. The kids on the little suburban lane down which he drove paid no attention to them. They went on doing the things kids always did—wobbling along on bikes, playing catch, bickering, fighting. You always knew where you were on a street like this.

The Gawlor house was the last one on the block, a brick split-level no different from the rest. As Melaniphy walked up to the door and gave it the once-over, he decided the window frames and shutters could use a coat of paint and the roof looked like it needed a little work. Maybe those welcome checks weren't coming as regularly as he had supposed. His knock on the door was answered by a pretty blonde girl about seventeen years old, one of those in the pictures. She looked expectantly at him but said nothing.

"Is this the Gawlor house?"

"Yes, it is."

"Is your mother at home?"

"No, she's not, but she ought to be back any minute." There was a momentary pause, and Melaniphy realized she was embarrassed about something. Then she said, "I'm not supposed to let anyone in."

"That's all right. I'll wait in my car for a while, okay?" Without waiting for a reply, he turned and hurried away from the door. Jesus, the last thing in the world he wanted to do was to sit around and make small talk with the dead man's daughter.

Just as he was opening the door to his car, a station wagon came down the street and wheeled into the Gawlor driveway. The woman at the wheel, red-haired and about forty, with a face now familiar to him, gave him a curious glance as she passed by. As she got out of her car, Melaniphy gave a reassuring wave but stood his ground. The girl he had talked to at the door came running out of the house, said something to her mother, and ducked into the car to pull out two bags of groceries. Mrs. Gawlor walked over to Melaniphy, looking a little uncertain.

"You wanted to see me?"

"Yes, I did." He popped out his CPD identification and held it up for her to see. "You are Mrs. John Gawlor, aren't you?" He knew she was, but this was procedure. "Wife of John Gawlor, 1280 Sheridan Road, Evanston?"

She nodded. "Well, ex-wife, I guess. We're divorced."

"Uh, I wonder if you'd like to sit in the car and talk. It's kind of public here."

Without a word she circled around and got into the front seat. As Melaniphy squeezed behind the wheel, he noticed that Mrs. Gawlor's hands were trembling. Otherwise, she seemed quite composed.

"Is this what I think it is?" she asked suddenly.

"What's that, Mrs. Gawlor? What do you mean?"

"Has Jack been arrested?"

"No, your husband—your ex-husband's dead."

There was no immediate reaction. He waited. Then she blinked rapidly three or four times and said, "Oh, God. How?"

"It was a . . . a homicide, Mrs. Gawlor. His body was found this morning. He'd been dead five, maybe seven days."

She frowned and looked away, as though concentrating hard on what she had just been told. And then: "You mean he was murdered?"

"That's right. You, uh, assumed he had been arrested. You mind telling me why?"

She stiffened slightly at that. He noticed there were tears in her eyes. "Well, I don't think that I—"

"Mrs. Gawlor, your husband is dead. He's been murdered. You're not going to help him, holding anything back. Now, we've got an investigation going. I expect you to tell me anything that can help us. Now, that's about as clear as I can make it, isn't it?" He'd lean on her if he had to, but he didn't want to do it.

"I—I understand. It's just that I . . ." She hesitated, then moaned as though in physical pain. "Oh, *God!*" The tears came then, rolling down her cheeks, as she began sobbing uncontrollably, gasping and gurgling. She hid her face on her knees, but the muffled sobs continued. Melaniphy pulled out his handkerchief, then remembering when he had had the thing out last, he sniffed at it and, with a sigh, pushed it down into her hand. It took her a minute or two of blowing and wiping before she was back under control. Now, Melaniphy thought, comes the hard part.

"Look," he said, "maybe I'd better explain some things. They'll probably have it all over the newspapers, so if you're prepared for it, it will be better for you—and your kids— anyway. In the same room with your husband's body, there was also the body of a boy about thirteen or fourteen years old. He'd been strangled. Both his body and your husband's were nude. The obvious conclusion is that they had been . . . engaging in sexual activity." He paused, waiting for some reaction. She wasn't looking directly at him but staring out the windshield at nothing in particular. At last she nodded, so he went on: "Now, what I'm asking you, Mrs. Gawlor, and what you've got to tell me, is whether or not you'd been given reason to suspect him of . . . well, this sort of behavior in the past. I mean, what we need are names, Mrs. Gawlor, places he went to, anything at all that we can go on."

"Nothing," she said. "No, nothing at all. I can't help you. I don't know anything at all about that."

"This *can't* come as a complete shock to you."

"I, well . . ." she hesitated. "No, not a complete shock. No."

"Well, for Christ's sake, isn't that why you were afraid he'd been arrested?"

She turned then and faced him for the first time in several minutes. There was something in her eyes, a kind of absolute seriousness, that commanded absolute attention. She was ready to talk. Melaniphy was ready to listen. "For a long time my husband was having problems," she said, "and if I tell you I didn't know, and don't know now, exactly what kind of problems they were, I hope you won't think we had one of those marriages where nobody talks, because I think we had a good marriage for a long time. I think—well, I know—these were sexual problems. There were indications. But he *couldn't* talk about these problems, whatever they were, and he got—oh, I don't know, sort of desperate. And so we split up. I wanted to help him, but I couldn't. I didn't know how. He wanted to make the separation final, and so we got a divorce. I really didn't want the divorce. But after that, the few times I saw him during the last six months or so, he frightened me a little. He seemed like a man who was absolutely walking the brink. Oh, he was cheerful with the girls and nice to me, but I know that man, and I could tell that there was something very, very wrong. So now you come to me today, and I can see that it's an official visit, and I thought, 'Jack's in trouble with the police.' It could've been anything. Absolutely nothing would have surprised me. And so if I guessed that my husband had been arrested, well, that's why. All I can say is that for a year or more he's been a desperate man. I mean he *was* a desperate man. It's all over now, isn't it?"

Melaniphy nodded. "Okay, Mrs. Gawlor. Thanks for your cooperation. The Coroner's Office will be in touch with you about official identification of the remains. If you could pick up dental records or come up with some physical marks or scars it might be helpful. You might have some trouble recognizing him."

"How . . . ?"

"It looked as though he'd been beaten to death."

"Poor Jack. Poor, poor Jack." She hesitated. "Will that be all?"

"That's all, Mrs. Gawlor."

She opened the door and jumped out of the car. Melaniphy watched her as she started for the house. He was about to start the engine when he saw her stop, turn, and come running back to him.

"What's your name?" she asked. "I don't even know your name."

"Melaniphy. Sergeant Joseph Melaniphy. I thought you saw it on the ID I showed you."

"No, well, it doesn't matter. I just wanted to tell you one thing, Sergeant Melaniphy, something you've got to understand."

"What's that, Mrs. Gawlor?"

She stared at him for a moment, as though trying to find the right words for what she wanted to say. And then at last she said, "My husband was a very good man." Looking as though she were about to start crying again, she turned and ran for the house.

Melaniphy started his car and drove off down the street.

He sat smoking on the front steps of the old three-flat on Catalpa where he lived with his family. He had gone out at dusk, just after dinner, as the two younger girls started wrangling about whose turn it was to do the dishes. Thinking it might be good to get away from that, he had gone out to have a cigarette by himself and was now on his third. The streetlights were on. It was dark. From the sidewalk, you would only know he was up there on the top step from the red glow of the cigarette he held cupped in his hand as he puffed on it at regular intervals.

Melaniphy owned the building. This wasn't so much a monument to lower-middle-class Irish thrift as it was a souvenir of the years he had spent on Vice down at Eleventh and State. He had been on the take, of course. Who wasn't? But after he bought himself a couple of suits and taken Kate off on a vacation to Florida, the money no longer meant very much to him, so he began putting it away in a bank account he opened in her name. And by the time he had transferred to Homicide, he had enough socked away to buy the three-flat they were living in when the owner died and it came up for sale. There was no money in Homicide, but he liked it better—maybe that was *why* he liked it better.

There were, however, other perquisites that came his way

as a Vice cop that he never really tired of. Women. They were hookers and B-girls, mostly, and he never kidded himself that he was especially favored because of his good looks or personal charm. He was just there, on the scene, part of the milieu. The hookers paid him off with what they had to offer, and the B-girls because he wasn't as bad as the last conventioneer who had grabbed at their leg and vomited on their dress—or maybe because the manager had given a nudge and said to take care of the cop. It was all done in the spirit of good fellowship—no arm-twisting by him and no demands of any kind from the women. They were all in this together, and wasn't it a pain in the ass? This was their unspoken comment. Nothing more.

But all that ended, too, when he transferred to Homicide and was moved out to the north side; and he found it harder to give up than the money. He began going out at night, cruising his old turf, looking for the girls who before had been so willing to give him what he wanted. Well, they weren't so willing anymore, and it left him frustrated, angry, and on a couple of occasions even willing to pay. And then he realized he had gotten hooked. It had become kind of an addiction, certainly a habit. He was no longer quite in control, and he didn't like that. But he dealt with it, handling it as he might any other problem, nursing himself back, easing himself around the corner, until he had once more established a kind of working equilibrium. He hadn't put himself out of contention altogether. When something came his way, and he had the desire, he was more than happy to accept a warm body as a gift of fortune. That was the important thing, though —when *he* had the desire, not when the desire had him.

Melaniphy inhaled deeply on his cigarette, and then held it up carefully to the streetlight. He saw that he had an ash nearly an inch long on it. He wondered what the record was. He wondered, too, why he had been recalling all of this out here on the steps tonight. And then he realized it was because of John Francis Gawlor—Jack, Mrs. Gawlor had called him. She said he was a desperate man. Melaniphy was sure he knew that feeling.

The door opened behind him. He turned to the sound, and

the ash fell off his cigarette. It was Kate, his wife, already in robe and slippers, the girl he had gone to St. Gregory High School with just a few blocks away, the woman he had married before she was a woman and before he was a man.

"You coming in, Joey?" she asked. "It's getting cold out here."

"Yeah, I'm coming in." He took a last draw on the cigarette and flipped it, live, out onto the sidewalk.

"Job getting to you?"

"Yeah, you might say that, Kate. You might say that."

As he rose heavily and dusted the ashes from his trousers, he found himself reminded of Mrs. Gawlor running back to the car to tell him her husband was a good man. Melaniphy wondered if, knowing all there was to know about him, Kate would say the same. He thought about that a moment and decided that yes, he guessed she would. That made it easier to go back into the house.

CHAPTER ONE *1952*

IN THE SPRING of 1952, during his senior year in high school, Jack Gawlor suddenly started to travel the city. Until then, he had lived in Chicago all his life—except for those first three and a half years in Fort Dodge, Iowa, where he was born—without getting much outside his neighborhood. He knew his way around the north side well enough and would travel downtown to go to the movies every once in a while, but until that spring, he had never gone west or south, or walked alone down those dark streets where the buildings smelled of rot and the people smelled of ruin.

How did it begin? He just jumped on the 22 streetcar one Friday night in May at the corner of Foster and Broadway, intending to jump off again at Lawrence. If he had done that, he would have spent the same sort of Friday night he had for the past three years—meeting Eddie and Parker and the rest of them at the Greek candy shop next to the Uptown Theater, going to a movie, hanging around afterward at any one of a dozen places where the remainder of the evening would drain around them in swirling eddies of bluster and boredom. It was always the same. He knew that, and that may have been why, when the streetcar rolled on by the Uptown and came to a halt at the corner, he remained where he was seated and waited for it to move on again.

Or was it because of the woman who got on at Argyle? He remembered her for weeks afterward—in her late thirties, with a cloth coat over a black dress that might have been a waitress's uniform. She smiled at him in a peculiar way as he sat pushed against the window, and she took a seat nearby. What kind of a smile was it? Had he had the good sense and experience to read it rightly, he would have known it said nothing more than that she was tired and had a bad life and that the only pleasure she got out of it was the little she was able to make for herself with her body. Do I look good to you, kid—at my age? Christ, I hope so. Because if I do, then I just might look good to somebody else, too, and I might make it through to Saturday morning.

But Jack thought she was smiling at him, *for* him. He wanted to think that, of course, for like any other boy of seventeen, he needed desperately to be taken seriously as a man. He watched her closely from across the aisle. She looked Italian, didn't she? or maybe Jewish. Perhaps she wanted him to move over and sit down next to her and start talking. That was the way it was done, wasn't it? He was still studying her and trying to decide what to do when the streetcar pulled away from Lawrence Avenue, and a woman came staggering down the aisle under the weight of two shopping bags and collapsed into the seat next to him. Trapped! He couldn't very well move over and sit next to her now, could he? He could think about her, though—and that he did, beginning a long, involved story which began with him sliding into the seat beside her and ended, of course, with the two of them in her bed.

"I have so much to teach you," she would tell him.

"I'm so willing to learn," he would say.

The fantasy involved him so completely that he hardly even noticed when the object of it, the woman who had boarded at Argyle, got off at Belmont. What did it matter? He would just ride on the streetcar a little farther and try to think the thing through to a satisfactory conclusion. That, however, was always difficult because he was a little vague about what happened when both parties were lying side by side and had dedicated themselves to a successful completion of their labors. He had only a general, clinical, diagrammatic notion of what happened next—and fantasies demanded particulars, specific images, precise data, none of which he himself was able to supply. Well, what was the use? He rode on glumly, realizing with a start that he was near north, almost downtown now. He looked around him and, for the first time since Lawrence

Avenue, gave some attention to the new passengers who had settled in the other seats up and down the aisle. You could tell most of them were headed for the Loop—couples, Mexicans, and a few greaseball Poles, out for the first big night of the weekend. Some of the guys were no older than he was, you could tell, but they wore suits, ties, and Mr. B roll-collars, the standard weekend greaseball uniform. And the girls? No telling how old they were, for they seemed so much alike with their sculptured hair, pancake makeup, and stiletto heels—fourteen or thirty-four, they looked the same. Funny how quiet they all were, murmuring in pairs, humming with a kind of secret anticipation for the glories of the evening that were to come. He wondered why it was he never felt like that on Friday night. Maybe they knew something he didn't.

They all got off at State and Randolph, and for an instant he was tempted to follow, but he knew there was no place in their night for him. And so he blessed them off to their movies and mambo palaces and settled in to see a little more. He was beginning to enjoy this new role—Jack Gawlor, public investigator, rider through the city, explorer of the night. If he waited and watched, he might find something to write about in his journal when he got home.

Minutes later South State Street, that double-block stretch of penny arcades, bars, and burlesque houses, materialized magically beyond the windows of the streetcar. He started, at once invited and intimidated, as patterns of exploding neon reeled slowly by—and he quite unexpectedly realized he had reached his destination. He had ridden by here before but never really looked it over—as he intended to do now. Jumping off at State and Harrison, he sidestepped a drunk sitting on the curb and stood for a moment, his hands plunged in the pockets of his jacket, staring curiously at the pictures outside the burlesque theater on the corner. In them, nearly nude, full-bodied women stood in various attitudes of ecstasy, like icons to be worshiped, saints of the flesh. Jostled and bumped by the crowd, he drew himself reluctantly away and patted his wallet, just to make sure it hadn't been lifted from him as he stood and looked. He walked, peering into the crumpled faces of those he passed, glancing into places along the way—into the bars with their doors open revealing only darkness that dared entry, and into the bright arcades with soldiers and sailors in front and dirty movies in the back.

So he made his way as a tourist, motivated mostly by curiosity, looking benignly on the squalor around him as so much local color, until he crossed Congress Street and found himself in front of another burlesque house, the Gem. There a pitchman held forth loud and long on the sensual joys that lay just inside the door. Jack stopped and listened, almost amused at the spiel, and then he realized the pitchman was talking directly to him.

"Stage show's just beginning, kid," the pitchman said.

"Can I go right in?"

"All you have to do is pay your money and get a ticket."

Then the pitchman shifted his attention to three young sailors in from Great Lakes. He came on strong, singing a song older than he was by a millennium or two, a pitch that would have outpimped Pandarus—of girls! girls! girls! of white thighs and soft breasts, of Oriental delights in a sultan's harem. They stopped. They listened. They paid their money and went right inside. The pitchman turned to Jack with a frown. "You still here, kid? I thought you wanted to see the show!"

Well, why not? Jack said nothing. He simply nodded and bought a ticket from the frowzy fifty-year-old blonde at the window and marched through the doors. He found a place near the sailors and sat down. The curtains were drawn across the small stage, and the small crowd of men sat waiting, quietly expectant. They waited, and waited a little longer, until a hunched figure came snaking through a tunnel beneath the stage. It turned out to be the pitchman from outside, now come back to sell candy and dirty books to this somnolently silent male congregation. He addressed them as sports. He appealed to their sophisticated nature and promised them power over women from the erotic wisdom contained in the little booklets he waved before them now. Jack was almost convinced. But as the pitchman passed among them, so few bought the candy and the picture books that Jack quickly understood it was not the thing to do. He glanced at the sailors, decided they were no older than he was, and somehow felt reassured by that. This might be their first time, too. And then at last, four men came out through the same tunnel, bringing their instruments into the pit immediately before the stage, and began to play a kind of overture. The show began.

You couldn't say that Jack reacted in any single way to what he saw there that night. Instead, a great jumble of responses came flooding over him, one after the other and sometimes all at once. Well used to the fast, high-stepping precision of movie musicals, he found himself snickering when the graceless four-girl chorus line limped onstage, hopping where they should have strutted, bouncing indifferently on the upbeat and the down. Their ineptitude embarrassed him, and at the same time their quivering, vulnerable flesh touched him with something between pity and desire.

The comedians—the pitchman again, playing straight to a spluttering, splattering character with a bawling lisp named Willy—did routines so dim-witted, corny, and obvious that Jack could see the punchlines coming the moment they began. But at the same time there was something kind of freeing about the pure and magnificent vulgarity of their performance. The jokes were grandly crude, the kind that Jack could never make. He found he was laughing at them in spite of himself.

And the strippers? Each one was different, each said something—or several things—new to him about herself, her sexual aura. He made up stories for them all. It was easy. He understood instinctively that this was why they were up there on stage—not as dancers or entertainers, for even the best of the five who appeared were only passably talented; and not, primarily, to present their bodies as naked as city ordinances and local custom then allowed—although that was part of the package, of course. But no, each of them was there as a character in a story, an actress in a play—only *you* wrote the story, *you* directed the play. And that, Jack understood, was what all of it was about—the bumps, the grinds, the subtler touches and self-caresses—just so much physical detail to stimulate the imagination. When Bebe Perry appeared, bouncing around with her head a mass of tight blond curls, her face aglow with a kind of dim-witted sweetness, and then proceeded shyly to remove piece after piece of her clothing right down to pasties and G-string, she incarnated the remembered Shirley Temple letch of every old man, as well as the rickety-rack cheerleader fantasies of all the young. And when sinuous Jet Carroll exploded across the stage, her mane of black hair aflutter, only to begin throwing her clothes off recklessly, she became the woman that every man there dreamed about and dreaded, the aggressively sexual Salome he could only hope to satisfy.

Jack dreamed about her. Waking, he dreamed about them all. In fact, he rushed home to dream that very night—took the subway and the el because it was faster—pretending to himself he didn't know why he was in such a hurry.

"You're early." Jack's mother greeted him almost accusingly as he came into the apartment. She was sitting in the chair with a book open before her.

"Yeah, well, it was pretty boring. I cut out after the movie."

"Before you could make the usual round of taverns, I suppose."

"Oh, come on, Mother."

"Don't come-on-mother me. I've smelled that beer smell on your breath before. Just tell me I haven't."

"All right, sure. Once. Once you did. And that was after a party." He came up close to her. "You want to smell now?" He made a threat of it.

"No." She lowered her eyes to the book. She was sulking. She seemed to be sulking most of the time.

"Okay, then." He left her and on his way back to his room looked in on his father. George Gawlor was where he expected him to be and doing what he expected him to be doing. Jack's father was a rather abstracted man, gentle enough but with too many rough edges to be much good in social situations—not even the very basic ones involving him with his son. He painted—without any real gift and without benefit of instruction, but nevertheless with a great deal of simple pleasure in the work that Jack had come to respect. It had all started a few years before when Jack's mother had decided her husband needed a hobby. She had forced upon him one of those paint-by-the-numbers sets, and under her supervision he had reluctantly set up on the sunporch to give it a try. To his surprise, he found he liked it well enough, but he soon decided he could do a better job and have a lot more fun if he didn't have to pay attention to all those numbers. He bought a couple of canvases, some extra tubes of color, and simply began painting on his own. The remarkable thing was the way he had kept at it. Painting was soon more than a hobby—it was a way of life for him. He would come home during the week from that job in the accounting department of Armour and Company that he so hated, eat his dinner, and then head straight for the sunporch. His wife came to resent all the time he spent out there, but he pretended not to notice—and kept right on painting.

"Hi, Dad. How's it coming?"

"Oh, I don't know, Jackie. What's your opinion?" George Gawlor leaned back from the canvas for a better look at it himself. He regarded his efforts critically—a covered bridge in Vermont painted from a calendar photo—but seemed generally encouraged by what he had done so far. Although the colors were still thin on the canvas, and some of it was barely sketched in, there was a nice strong feeling to it. It was all worked out in a series of planes and angles that Jack liked a lot.

"I think it's pretty good," Jack said quite honestly. "I sort of like the shapes inside of it, if that makes any sense."

"Oh, yes," his father said. "Yes, it does." He was silent for a moment, regarding the painting himself. "I have to admit I kind of like it, too." He turned around and smiled rather shyly at his son. "Of course, it's not finished. I might still manage to spoil it like I did the last one."

"No, you won't."

"You going to bed? I'm about ready to call it quits myself."

"Going to shower first," said Jack. "I won't tie up the bathroom too long, though."

Jack grabbed up his pajamas, rushed into the bathroom, and locked the door. Having successfully staked his claim, he leaned back and relaxed on the stool and began undressing slowly, just letting his mind wander. But instead of returning immediately to the Gem, as he had expected to do, he found himself thinking instead about his mother and father. They were a strange pair—even Jack understood that now. Tonight was typical. She in the living room, reading who knew what pious tract, he on the sunporch painting pictures of color photographs of places he would never see. They occupied the same space, even the same bed, but they came face to face surprisingly seldom during the day. Jack had no brothers and sisters. He had come to wonder seriously how it was he had come to be born. But that had been back in Iowa. Maybe things were different between the two of them then.

According to his mother, everything was different there. When he was younger, she had talked about Iowa so often and so glowingly after they had moved to Chicago that he came to think of himself as somehow deprived because he had been unable to grow up in that faraway Eden. After the war he began making trips back to Iowa with her every summer—and then he didn't think that anymore. He didn't think anything at all except how glad he was to be living in Chicago and not Fort Dodge—although he had the good sense to keep his preference to himself.

His mother hated the city. Her family name was Mincher, and they were hard Baptist stock, unyielding and unamused. Although they had never risen very high, they knew their worth, for they knew they had riches piled away where moth and rust would not corrupt. Grandpa Mincher was a farmer who had worked himself to death at an early age—though not before he had sired six children and instilled in each of them a desire to get ahead and a contempt for those who did. His oldest daughter, Rowena, married George Gawlor, a man of uncertain background and no particular religious persuasion, in a desperate bid to escape the hardships of the Depression, which for the fatherless and landless Minchers were very real indeed. George had a job as bookkeeper at the local meat-packing plant, and she supposed that any man who had a white-collar job in those hard times must be bound for glory. She believed that in spite of his Irish name, she might make a true Christian of him. And, by her standard, she did: he consented to accompany her to church every Sunday—and, as a result, he hadn't missed a week since they had been married.

It turned out, however, that George Gawlor wasn't bound for glory; he was simply bound for Chicago. Dutifully and fearing the worst, she accompanied him, her hand clasped tight to their three-and-a-half-year-old son. Chicago satisfied her, confirmed her worst Baptist fears. It was boozy, whory, and overrun with dark-complexioned people who spoke English in such a way that it was difficult to understand them. She stayed, endured it all, but she never ceased complaining. Nor had she ceased lecturing her young son on all that was wrong with Chicago. She had him convinced so early that what she called "drink" was bad that until Jack learned just what it was she meant, he felt a little sinful asking for a drink of water. About women he was even more sorely confused. For the day that he brought a word home from the alley, she sat him down, and in a voice so solemn that she frightened him, she gave him an account, only a quarter of which he understood, of what it was that women did to men. He got the distinct impression, however, that it was a very bad thing and only excusable when the man and woman involved were married. Because of this thing, he understood that women were not to be trusted. There lay the difficulty, of course, for wasn't his mother a woman? Of course she was. And would she do this bad thing? Surely not. The problem was still more or less unresolved, as far as Jack was concerned.

His father was peculiarly absent through all this. A vague man who went humming tunelessly through the apartment, he often seemed not to be there at all. He had never apparently thought it necessary to supplement his son's knowledge—or, more likely, had been too shy to do so. What Jack knew he had gotten from his friends at school—mostly from Parker, who was a mine of information, not all of it completely reliable. It was Parker, too, who had fixed him up with girls on the few dates he had had in high school. Somehow that was something he just couldn't manage on his own. He continued to wonder why.

Jack stood up and looked in the bathroom mirror, as

though searching for the answer to that particular problem there. But it wasn't to be found. He looked ordinary—no better nor worse than most, more like his mother than his father perhaps, but less like either one than simply like himself. No, if he had problems with girls—and there was no doubt that he did—then the problems were all inside of him. He knew that. But he didn't really seem to be able to do much about it. He seemed, like his father, to have too many rough edges. Small talk was beyond him. Girls didn't want to hear about the books he had read, nor about the things he had written in his journal—and so he was left speechless, mumbling inanities in the back seat while Parker held forth in front.

There was a tentative knock on the bathroom door. "Jackie? Jackie? I thought you said you'd be through in just a little while."

"Oh, right, Dad. Just getting in the shower now. I'll be right out."

Not waiting for an answer, he switched on the water full-blast, took a moment to test it for temperature, and then jumped inside. It was warm, not hot, just right. As it steamed up the space between the shower curtains, Jack directed his mind purposefully back to the spectacle he had witnessed earlier at the Gem. He soaped up his genital area quite lavishly, and then he closed his eyes and concentrated on what he had seen. He had discovered masturbation one day in the shower not so very long ago and had practiced it there ever after. It was comfortable and private, and of course, all the evidence ran right down the drain afterward. He found himself thinking of Bebe Perry, that bouncy and effervescent would-be cheerleader. As he gave himself completely to his mind's eye, recapturing each nuance of movement, each flutter and flounce, he found, to his surprise, that on Bebe Perry's body the face of Joanie Benson had begun to appear, merging with it, then superimposing completely. He accepted that as a mystery of the occasion, glad for the unexpected opportunity to be on intimate terms with the captain of the cheerleaders. He had suffered after her for a year or more, casting dumb looks her way from the sidelines at football games. Here and now, erect and slippery with soap, he was able to express himself to her at last.

Another night Jack took the elevated B train to the end of the line and wound up out on the south side at Jackson Park. The car he had been riding in emptied in seconds, and he was left sitting there wondering what to do. Should he cross over and ride the next one back the way he had come? He stepped out onto the platform and considered. No, he hadn't come all this way to do that. He would have to get down and walk the pavement a little to satisfy himself that he was really out here on the south side now. And so he plunged down the stairs at the far end of the platform and at the bottom of them found himself just a few steps away from Sixty-Third Street.

That was where he walked, hiking west under the el tracks, listening to the train he might have caught rumbling away overhead. The farther he went, the more it looked like any street on the north side—shops closed for the night, windows well-lighted, a steady stream of auto traffic in either direction. But why shouldn't it? How could the south side be any different from the north?

He got the answer to that when he had walked over a mile and began to notice more people on the street than earlier. Black people. Negroes, as he thought of them. He glanced after them curiously, aware that they seemed to take no notice of him whatever. He stood for a moment outside a Pick-a-Rib barbecue joint, staring in fascination at the clamorous activity inside. And then, a little farther down the way, he came upon a place that stopped him cold. His ears had given him early warning. Music. He heard it nearly a block away, a thin line of jazz over a steady impact of percussion. And then just ahead of him, he saw people starting through a door, and when it opened, the music swelled forth in a great rush and roar. A sign above him said this was McKie's Crown Propellor Lounge.

He stopped, hung outside the door, and listened, transfixed and nodding—not so much in time with the music as in protracted agreement with it.

And he was still standing there nodding when a black police squad car rolled up and stopped at the curb just opposite the entrance to McKie's. Jack saw the car but ignored it. It had nothing to do with him, after all.

"Hey, kid. Come over here."

There could be no doubt that the cop leaning out the squad car window meant him. Jack walked over, more curious than apprehensive. "What is it?" he asked.

The cop had his uniform hat off and was nearly bald. He stared up at Jack with flat, unsympathetic eyes, looking him over. "That's what I want to know, what-is-it. What're you doing hanging around here?"

Jack shrugged. "Listening to the music."

"Yeah, sure. You can't go in there. You're underage."

"I'm not going in. I'm just listening."

"Let's see your ID."

Jack pulled out his wallet, puzzled. What could he show him? "I've got a library card." He offered it to him.

"Jesus. A library card. The kid's got a library card, Artie." There was a snicker from inside the squad car. "Let me see your draft card, kid."

"I haven't got one."

"How come?"

"I'm not eighteen yet."

"Jesus. Okay." He grabbed the card from Jack and held it out to read it. "This says you're a long way from home. How come?"

"I don't know. Just walking around. Exploring."

The cop handed the card back indifferently, letting it fall just short of Jack's outstretched fingers so that he had to bend over to scoop it up. "Well, go explore someplace else. You want my opinion, it's pretty stupid to go walking around a spade neighborhood this time of night—anytime, for that matter. Now you go up to Cottage Grove and catch a streetcar home. You got carfare, haven't you?"

"Sure." Jack hesitated. "You mean I can't just stand outside and listen if I want to?"

"Not if I say move on—and that's what I'm telling you now. We're going to circle the block and we better not find you here. If we do, your ass is in a sling." The cop nodded with finality at that. The interview was over. He rolled the window part-way up and with a word to the driver, the squad car pulled away.

Jack watched it go, his lips pursed in annoyance, wondering for a moment just what he ought to do. But only for a moment. In the end, he did just what the cop had told him to do.

A few days later, he sat with Parker in a back booth of the Walgreen's drugstore near school and told him about the incident. Parker was impressed.

"Really, Gawlor? Come on, you didn't make this up, did you?"

"Why would I do that?"

"I don't know. Maybe you read it in a book or something."

"Well, I didn't."

"No shit." Parker shook his head and meditated for a moment on what he had just heard. Then he returned to Jack and regarded him for a moment, clearly puzzled. "Only thing I don't get is, what *were* you doing way out there on the south side?"

"What do you mean, what was I doing? Just what I told the cop. Exploring. I go places and look around."

"Well, is that . . . fun, or interesting, or something?"

"Sure."

"I don't know. It sounds pretty weird to me." Parker paused, thought over what he had said, and added, "It might be okay, though. Maybe I'll come with you sometime. Or better yet, why don't you come with me to Maxwell Street some Saturday?"

Jack shrugged. "Well . . . sure. I don't know. Maybe."

"You'd like it. It's really neat. They sell all this hot merchandise there and everything. Anything you want to buy. No kidding."

"Well, maybe."

Three nights later, a Friday, he rode the A train to

the end of the line, all the way out to Englewood. This time he didn't wait for the car to empty before making up his mind what to do. He left with the rest of the passengers—it was early enough in the evening so that there was a good-sized crowd of late commuters—and found his way down the stairs in the direction of the street. He suddenly had a peculiar feeling that he was being watched. He turned around, sweeping the faces behind him, half-expecting to find the policeman from Sixty-Third Street among them. But there was nobody like that there. About the only one who seemed to be taking any interest in him at all was a middle-aged man with a red face and watery eyes who happened to be looking in Jack's direction. The man smiled tentatively and nodded.

Jack thought the man looked familiar, and then realized he had been sitting across the aisle from him on the el train just a few moments before. It was funny. The guy just wasn't the sort you noticed—or remembered for very long. Jack double-timed down the stairs, bouncing down them two at a time until he came to a knot of people lined up at the transfer machine. As he squeezed through them, trying to work his way out to the street, he felt a little pressure on his arm from behind. He whirled around and found the red-faced man there.

"What is it? What's the matter?" Jack was suddenly alarmed. He squirmed ahead almost desperately, trying to get away from the man.

"You dropped something back there. Some money." The man again smiled his uncertain smile and nodded vigorously, as though confirming what he had just said.

"I did?" They were through the crowd now and Jack stepped off to one side and began patting his pockets. He plunged a hand into his jeans and grabbed up the single and handful of change he was carrying.

"This five-dollar bill? Didn't you? I thought it came out of your pocket just as you stepped off the train. Anyway, I picked it up off the platform right behind you." The man was speaking with such unnecessary earnestness that it occurred to Jack he might be lying. Why should he do that? "Isn't it yours?"

Jack shook his head. "No, not mine." He shrugged and began moving away. The man moved right along with him, keeping pace as Jack headed for the street.

"You're pretty honest, I must say. You know it's not often you find such honest people. Not in this town, anyway."

"Is that right? Well, uh . . ." Jack trailed off uncomfortably, not knowing quite what to say.

"Why, I'll bet you're not from here, are you? You've even got a tiny bit of an accent, haven't you? Where are you from? Someplace down south?"

It always irritated Jack when people thought that. He didn't sound funny. He sounded like everybody else. "No, I've been here most of my life."

"Oh, come on. Where were you *born*? I'm terrific on accents. Let's see . . . I'll bet . . . Missouri. Right?"

"No. Wrong." How could he end this?

"Oh. But I'm close, I'll bet. Where *were* you born?"

"Fort Dodge, Iowa."

"There! You see! How close can you get? Iowa! That's terrific."

Jack didn't see anything terrific about it. He tried walking a little faster, but the man with the watery eyes matched him stride for stride.

"Where are you headed in such a hurry?"

Clearly he had to have a destination of some sort. He invented one: "I'm going to my uncle's. For dinner. I'm, well, I'm sort of late."

The man came to a sudden halt. Quite involuntarily, Jack stopped, too. Why? He couldn't imagine why he had done it. But once he had stopped, he couldn't just walk off, could he? How did he get in these situations, anyway?

The man regarded him with enormous sympathy. There was something abject, almost doglike in the look. "Gee, that's a shame," he said at last. "Well, I just had the feeling that you were really an exceptional person, and I'd like to get to know you better, you know? I was going to say, why don't you let me take this five dollars I found and take you out to dinner? I know a nice Chinese place that's not so far from here . . ."

He trailed off hopefully, then added: "I think of the money as yours, anyway."

"No, I'm . . . I'm sorry. I have to go."

"Your uncle. Of course."

Jack began backing off. "But thanks anyway. It was nice of you to ask." Always the young gentleman.

"Maybe some other time?"

"Maybe. Goodbye."

Jack turned and all but ran from him. He felt sort of desperate, afraid to look back, half-certain that if he did he would find the man close behind him in pursuit. He hurried blindly down to the end of the block, turned a corner, and only then felt safe enough to venture a glance over his shoulder. Nobody there. Relieved, he slowed his pace and tried to think his way back through the whole encounter, asking himself how it had started and when. The guy was obviously a queer. Had Jack encouraged him or what? Had there been something in the way he had looked back on the stairs that told the man that Jack might be ready for some kind of an approach? Had their eyes met across the aisle on the train? He couldn't remember. Was there something about Jack that invited that kind of attention? He hoped there wasn't. He hoped to God there wasn't.

There was nothing to do but continue on his way. He took a long trip around the block, slowing gradually to a leisurely stroll, breathing easier the farther he went. Just give the guy time to catch a bus or walk wherever it was he was headed, then Jack would hop back on a northbound A train and get the hell out of there. When at last he had made the circuit, he had the foresight to approach the elevated station from across the street. He went cautiously to a proper vantage point in the shadows and stood for a long moment inspecting the area around the entrance to the el station closely. He decided at last it was clear. He ran across the street, paid his fare back to the north side, and then went up the stairs three at a time to the waiting train. It was only there and then, as he sat pressed against the window, that it occurred to Jack that this must be the way that girls feel. Pursued. Sought after.

A little uneasy with all the attention. No wonder they always acted so crazy.

The next day, Saturday, he went with Parker to Maxwell Street. It was nothing special. Jack bought a shirt and had his fortune told by a Gypsy woman ("Long life, love, and a large family"). Parker bought nothing at all but kept asking Jack if all this wasn't really neat. Jack assured him that it was. But it also stank of fish, and the sellers at every stall were loud and all of them acted like they were angry. People pulled at you and pushed you from every side. It wasn't like going places at night when you had the street all to yourself. He knew he couldn't explain that to Parker, so he didn't try.

The family went driving on most Sundays. Jack hated listening to his mother hold forth, wrangling with his father's silences; nevertheless he went along nearly every week because it was about the only chance he had to drive the family car. His father took the el to work every day, and so the Ford remained in the garage during the week. Occasionally there were Saturday shopping expeditions far enough afield to require the car, but the only regular outing it received was on Sunday. Jack, who had had his license for less than a year, was trying to pile up enough hours behind the wheel so that he might at last begin to feel comfortable driving. It never occurred to him to ask if he might take the car out alone— nor to his father to offer it.

His mother, of course, did not drive. It seemed to Jack that she belonged to an entire generation of women who did not drive, who did not smoke or drink, and who didn't even smile very much either. She rode in the back seat, coldly alert and erect, critical of most of what she saw, yet always holding back a few words of praise to spend as soon as they left Evanston heading north. Time was when Evanston came in for a blessing or two—but no more. She said it had "changed," and she certainly knew, for there was no more avid nor knowledgeable connoisseur of the North Shore than Rowena Gawlor.

She had been studying it on such drives for years. She

knew real-estate values as well as the professionals. There were whole sidestreet blocks of Winnetka and Wilmette that she knew house by house. It had always been her wish to live in one of them. She made that plain—just as she made plain her disappointment that George Gawlor had never allowed her wish to be granted. She never brought it up, never offered it as an accusation, but there could be no doubt that in failing to provide one of these old marvels left over from the Gilded Age, he had fallen short of the mark she had set for him. The judgment was there in hints, omissions, little indiscretions, and conclusions left undrawn. A sample:

"Just look there, George. You see that nice old white house? The one with the big porch? Just seven years ago we could have had that for twenty thousand dollars—or it could have been had for that, I suppose I should say."

"You can say it any way you like, Ro. The fact is seven years ago I wasn't making much more than five thousand a year."

"We just never seem to be able to save a thing, George, no matter what your salary is. I wonder whose fault that is?"

"Nobody's. We get by. That's all we ever have done. That's all we ever will do."

"Some of us think otherwise. Some of us like to think there's a brighter tomorrow in store for us."

Silence.

"George, I don't mean to criticize, but you used to be a real hoper, a real fighter. I don't know what ever happened to you . . . And there you go sighing again. You're *always* sighing like that. What in the world is that supposed to *mean* anyway?"

Silence. Then at last: "Nothing, Ro."

"Well, that's the loudest nothing I ever heard. Oh—George, George, look! You see that gray three-story? Now, that's an absolute castle. Now, that, *that* I distinctly remember was just thirty thousand five years ago. Can you *imagine?*"

Jack listened to this conversation and drew no particular conclusion from it, since he had been hearing one like it every Sunday for as long as he could remember. He simply drove on, enjoying the feel of the steering wheel in his hands and the firm rumble of the tires beneath him. One thing did puzzle him, though: Why was his mother always talking about what things *used* to cost? He supposed it had to do with missed opportunities or something.

On a Friday night the week before his high school graduation, Jack walked up to the Greek place next to the Uptown to meet the guys. It was the first time he had gone there in weeks. There had been too many other places to go, too many things to see. One night he had gone to West Madison Street and walked Skid Row, glad when he got there that he had started out early, because for the first time since he had started these investigations he actually felt a sense of potential danger around him. He went back to the Gem. They had an Indian there named Princess La Homa, who wore a full headdress and sang "Blue Moon" before she stripped. She wasn't a very good singer, but otherwise she was all right. He went to Bughouse Square and listened to hours of impassioned oratory delivered from atop packing boxes and milk crates.

If you had asked Jack just why he made these excursions and what he hoped to accomplish by them, he would have told you that it was all part of learning to be a writer. He looked upon them more or less as field trips, part of the educational process. For the record, he had decided to become a writer after looking at an article about Ernest Hemingway in a magazine. That was about a year ago. At that time he had only read one novel by Hemingway, and that one because he remembered he liked the movie they made from it a lot. The book was different. He didn't like it as well. But, after all, it was nothing he had read *by* him that persuaded Jack, but rather what he read *about* him. For if being a writer meant living the glamorous life described in the article—travel, hunting, fishing, loving, fighting—then Jack was even willing to begin putting words on paper. In fact, the only real writing he did was in a journal that he had begun a few months before. A book from the library had informed him that every writer kept one. That was good enough for Jack. He went out and bought a thick spiral notebook which he kept well hidden in his room between entries. He thought of these night forays into the city as so many trips down the shaft to mine material for his journal.

What had brought him out that night to the Greek place was something special. Because it was so near graduation, Eddie Banks's father had let him have the car for the evening. As soon as Parker had heard about that, he began promoting a trip out to Calumet City. He talked it up so loud and long that by the time that Friday night rolled around, he had persuaded another whole carload to come along. Calumet City was Chicago's little Las Vegas, a suburb on the Indiana line with a split personality. In its residential areas, it was an ordinary middle-class bedroom community, predominantly Catholic, where the usual gangs of children ranged helter-skelter over sidestreets, and mothers stood bored in hair curlers watching them from their front lawns. Cal City's business district, however, was something quite different. It was three solid blocks of honky-tonks and strip joints, with half a dozen locked-door gambling parlors scattered among them, at least one whorehouse, and a small army of free-lance hookers who plied both sides of the street. Like Cicero, it was an institution left over from the old Capone days.

Jack had never been there. Somehow he had been absent on the two earlier occasions that Parker had organized these expeditions. He was ready tonight, though—primed, curious, and almost eager for the night ahead. Parker was there in a back booth with Gus Karras, who was to drive the second car, and Karras's big buddies, Calder and Swiggett. They were ready to go, just waiting on Eddie. All of them but Calder had played football together on a team that had won just a single game during the entire season—the worst record, the coach grimly informed them, in the forty-year history of the school. They stuck together not so much out of friendship as out of the feelings of guilt they shared. They had been there. They had suffered together. They knew they were worth something, even if nobody else seemed to think so.

Karras, the quarterback, was always replaying the old games, trying to get them to come out different. They never did. "You know how many passes I had dropped against Taft?"

he asked suddenly, just as Jack was sitting down beside him.

"You mean me? Do I know?"

"I mean anybody. I was just counting up last night, and you know how many? Seven. Seven goddam passes. I'm not talking about off by a yard or a foot or any of that shit. I mean in the hands and out."

Parker shrugged. "Yeah, well . . ."

"Now, don't get me wrong, Parker. I don't mean *just* that one you dropped in the end zone. I mean, that one was straight over the head, and you had a defensive halfback hanging all over you. I mean, Gettelman dropped three with nobody around him."

"Yeah, shit, Gettelman," said Calder, properly disgusted.

Jack thought back. "Let's see, this is the Taft game we're talking about, right?"

"Right."

"The way I remember it, the big thing in that game was the three interceptions they made on you in the last quarter, Karras."

"Aw, shit, I was getting desperate."

"We all were," said Jack. "Leave it alone, why don't you?"

A momentary pall settled over the table. Karras was headed for a small college in Wisconsin and still had hopes for college football. None of the rest of them did.

"I got to give you credit, though," Jack added, taking the sting out of it. "You could really throw."

"He sure can," Swiggett agreed loyally.

"Hey, come on," Parker exhorted, "let's not even think about that shit tonight. Let's think about where we're going." He wiggled his eyebrows comically and rolled his eyes. "Sexy ladies! Naked dancing girls! Neat, man."

"Yeah, hey, I hear they strip all the way in Cal City." Calder had lowered his voice as though it were a secret.

"Nah, I'll bet they don't," said Swiggett.

"You mean I'm going to drive all the way out there, and I don't even get to see snatch?"

"You'll see plenty," said Parker. "Don't worry."

"Here comes Eddie now," said Calder.

Jack turned around and saw him swaggering down the narrow aisle, his thick trunk and stubby legs all but filling the space completely. He was wearing a wide lascivious grin, as though he had tuned in on them early.

"He's ready," Parker said. "He's *ready*!"

Eddie held up the car keys. He didn't even bother to sit down. "You guys all set?"

"What kept you?" Karras asked. "We been waiting."

"Aw, I had to gas up the car and that shit. My father's really not too excited about me taking out his new Buick. I had to practically swear on the Bible I wouldn't get a dent in it."

"Gee, a Buick," said Calder. "A four-holer?"

"Three. But it's new."

"Neat."

Parker looked around the table and cautiously drew a folded sheet of paper out of his jacket pocket. He pushed it over to Karras. "Now, here's the directions on how to get there all written out."

"I got a map."

"You won't need a map if you just do it like I wrote it down."

Karras unfolded the paper and began reading. He nodded. "Okay."

"The important thing is don't miss that diagonal right near the Lever plant. It smells like shit there and they got a big box of Oxydol on top of it, so you can't miss it. But if you do miss that right and you keep on going, you'll wind up in Hammond. And that's breaking a Federal law."

"What?" Karras asked sharply.

"Sure," said Parker. "Crossing a state line for immoral purposes."

Jack and Eddie laughed, but Karras was unamused: "More of your shit."

Parker slid out of the booth. "Just follow the simple directions, and we'll all meet at the Riptide."

"Where's that?" asked Calder.

"Believe me, you can't miss it. The Riptide you definitely can't miss."

With Eddie driving and Parker navigating, they made good time there. Even so, it took them nearly an hour and a half, all the way across Chicago and out the other side, then along the industrial South Shore with its steel mills and oil refineries, and finally off along polluted Lake Calumet, where the only lights for miles were the headlights of oncoming cars. Then at last into Calumet City, through a few residential blocks, and down a corridor of bright lights and brilliant neon: Broadway. Jack was amazed. Way out here on the prairie, miles from the Loop, was South State Street all over again—re-created; more than re-created: tripled in vast garishness, vulgarity, and volume.

Parker glanced back at him. "Really something, huh?"

"Really something," Jack agreed.

They inched along in heavy traffic. Eddie was conscientiously keeping his eyes on the car just ahead, obviously mindful of the heavy responsibility that he had assumed, determined to protect this Body by Fisher—with his own, if he had to.

"Where are we going to park?" Eddie asked suddenly. This looked hopeless.

"Don't get nervous, man," Parker spoke up reassuringly. "We can put it on a sidestreet. I know where to go. But . . ."

"But what?"

"But I think maybe one of us ought to go into the Riptide and nail down a table. It's coming up in the next block." Parker turned quickly to Jack in the back seat. "How about you, Gawlor? Why don't you jump out at the corner and see what you can do?"

"But I've never been in the place! I don't even know if they'll let me in."

"Are you kidding? This is Cal City. Now here . . . here, we're coming to a stop. Go get us a table."

Reluctantly, wanting to stay on and argue against it a little longer, Jack ducked out the rear door on the curbside and watched the green Buick pull away. What else could he do?

He thrust his hands into the pockets of his jacket and made his way along the block. The men he met along the way were not in the same sad shape as those on South State, not a wino or a drifter among them, and no soldiers or sailors either. No, they looked like millhands and refinery workers from the immediate area, older men in twos and threes, loud and boisterous, out for a little action they couldn't get at home.

The Riptide looked like the other places up and down the street, though perhaps a little bigger than the rest. There were the same livid, tremulous neon above the door and the usual sexy pictures out in front. He stood for a moment taking it in, then plunged inside.

It was dark, of course, but not so dark that you couldn't see your way around the place. His eyes went immediately to the small stage that projected out among the tables in the center of the room. There a woman with flaming red hair was gyrating earnestly to the steady boom-boom-boom of a band hidden behind a curtain. She danced as though transported, oblivious of the audience that craned up around her, all of her concentration directed inward, upon herself, at her own muscular body as it twirled and pumped recklessly around the narrow space. She wore a black merry widow and hose, but even half-covered she seemed more naked than the girls at the Gem. Something told him she was in a different league altogether.

"You want to sit down, or you just going to stand and look?" It was a tough little waitress, chewing gum, not much older than he was.

"Uh, sit down, sure, only . . ."

"What?"

"There's going to be two more, maybe six in all."

"Three I can handle. I don't know about six. Look, I'll put you right here, against the wall. Maybe I can push a couple of tables together. Maybe not."

He accepted her terms—what choice did he have? She put him at the table she had pointed out and took his order for a beer. He sat forward and concentrated on the red-haired woman on the stage. The merry widow was coming off. He was almost sorry to see it go. But go it did, after two quick tours of the stage and a brief duck behind the curtain.

He barely noticed when the waitress came back with his beer. She had put him fairly close to the door, so that by dividing his concentration a little he was able to keep watch for Parker and Eddie. That wasn't so easy to do. The redhead demanded total attention. She was dancing now with her breasts exposed. They were not small but so erect and taut that they were like packages of muscle quivering on her chest. And the nipples on them were so red that he wondered if she had touched them up with lipstick. He had heard once that strippers did that. But most of all, he was fascinated by her profound self-absorption. It wasn't just those pats, and touches, and long shimmering caresses that she delivered to her body. Most strippers did that; it was part of the routine. She went beyond that into a world all her own—eyes shut so that he wondered how she found her way around the stage, her fingers probing her pubic area so actively that he wondered if taking off her clothes here before this male audience were not somehow an act of masturbation for her. He had heard that women did that, too.

It was hard for him to take his eyes off her, but from time to time he did, checking the door and the new arrivals. A waitress would meet them and escort them off to some distant corner of the darkened room. The tables on either side of him were still vacant, so if Karras and his buddies came soon, they could still push them all together and make a party of it. But where were Parker and Eddie?

About the fourth time that he glanced over to the door, he saw a cop standing there. That was a surprise. Somehow he had the feeling they didn't have cops in Calumet City. But no, there he was, and he was looking straight at Jack. Now what was he supposed to do? Jack forced himself to look away for a long moment or two—he must have counted at least to ten—and then glanced back to find that the cop was headed over in his direction. He fought back the impulse to jump up and run away. No, play it cool, look indifferent, just hope that he walks right on by.

He didn't. He stood before Jack's table, confronting him,

staring down at him. He was short and stocky, no taller than Eddie but about twenty or thirty pounds heavier. He was smiling at Jack crookedly.

"How old are you, kid?"

"Uh, nineteen?" Why did he say nineteen? That was still under age. If he was going to try to bluff it out, he should have said twenty-one.

"You better come with me."

He pretended for a moment he hadn't heard. That, of course, was the final, desperate ploy: ain't nobody here but us chickens. But the cop was not so easily deterred. He simply stared on at Jack impersonally and completely without sympathy. "You hear what I said?"

Without a word, Jack rose and followed him out the door. Outside, on the sidewalk, the cop turned around and looked him over. He seemed distinctly disappointed with his catch, but he wasn't about to let him go. There was a squad car double-parked in front of the Riptide. He pointed to it and said, "I'm taking you into the station."

Just then, as Jack stood stricken, unbelieving, and miserable, Parker and Eddie came walking up and saw him there in front of the club.

"Hey, Gawlor, what's the matter?" Parker yelled. "They all filled up or what?"

Jack turned to them. Maybe they saw the awful look on his face, or perhaps then they noticed the cop standing there beside him. But suddenly, instantaneously, both of them understood the situation.

"Oh, Jesus," said Parker.

"Is there anything we can do?" asked Eddie.

The cop heard him. He whirled and faced them furiously. "What you can do is get the fuck out of here. You go inside, and I'll come back and get you. I promise you."

The two looked at each other and shrunk back. The cop pushed Jack in the direction of the squad car. "Get in the back," he told him. Jack did as he was told. There was no other cop inside, and that surprised him. He could just jump out and run, couldn't he? No, he realized, he couldn't.

They moved out into traffic. From the back seat Jack

watched in amazement as the cars massed on the street moved off to the left and right, opening the way before them. And then he realized, as he noticed the weird light bouncing around them, that the squad car had its dome light flashing. The cop was treating him just like a real prisoner.

A quick right and a left, and they were in front of the police station. The cop switched off the engine and turned around to Jack. "Empty your pockets," he said.

"You want to see my wallet?"

"I said empty your pockets."

Jack straightened his legs across the floor of the back seat and strained to scoop out the contents of his front pockets—keys, bills, and change. He handed them over, and then he pulled out his wallet from his hip pocket and added it to the pile. A moment passed as the cop went through it all. Finally, he raised his gaze to Jack and looked at him in disgust. "Three dollars and fifty-seven cents? How long did you expect to stay here on that?"

"I don't know. A couple of hours."

"Big spender." The cop shook his head. He had bad teeth. He was showing them now in a grimace which he intended as an ironic smile. "Okay, out. We're going to call home."

This was terrible. Jack wondered if there weren't something, *anything,* he could say now to talk the cop out of it. He turned to him just outside the door of the station and opened his mouth to plead. But then, looking at the mean rage in the man's face, he knew that nothing he could ever say would matter. Jack shut his mouth and marched into the station.

Inside, the place was flooded with bright, harsh light. It smelled of Lysol and cigar smoke. There were two other cops there, sitting at desks in the rear. One of them, the cigar-smoker, had his feet up before him and his hands clasped behind his head. He nodded as they entered. The other was paging through a magazine. He didn't even look up.

The cop, his cop, held up Jack's wallet. "Your phone number in here?"

Jack nodded.

"You sit down there." He pointed to a bench near the

door. "Don't even think about running away. Because if you do, we'll get a fugitive warrant issued, and when we get you, we'll throw the fucking book at you." He grinned at him. "We just might, anyway."

He left Jack and sat down at a nearby desk. Glancing back at the two in the rear, he picked up the telephone and started dialing. Jack sank back onto the bench and watched. There was nothing he could do. He burned so with embarrassment that what he felt was something close to physical pain.

He sat there on the bench for almost two hours. After making the phone call, the cop had come over and told him that his father was coming to get him, and that if he didn't show up, Jack would be tossed in the drunk tank with all the perverts. The cop left then, calling back to the cigar-smoker to keep an eye on the kid. Jack was left to his fears and shame, considering the possibility that his father might not find his way, wondering what in the world he could say to him if and when he did arrive, fearing—and this was somehow the worst —that his mother might come along and confront him right there in the station.

Time crept. After about half an hour, the cigar-smoking cop roused himself at last from his desk and ambled over toward Jack. Up close, he looked much younger than Jack would have supposed—not yet thirty, but already round in the face and gone to fat in the middle. He had his mouth set in something like a sympathetic smile. "Where'd Siemonowski pick you up?" he asked.

"At a place." For a moment Jack couldn't even remember the name of it. "Uh, the Riptide."

"Underage?"

Jack nodded. He studied the cop's face for some reaction but could detect nothing there. The bland smile remained fixed. "Look," Jack said at last, "how bad is that? How much trouble am I in?"

The cop looked at him a long moment with something new in his eyes: amusement. Then he shrugged and walked away.

After about an hour, Siemonowski returned. Jack half-expected him to have Karras, Calder, and Swiggett in tow. But no, he was alone. Parker and Eddie probably waited around and warned them away. Why did it have to be Jack who got caught? He felt suddenly a victim—or worse, one singled out by fate, or God, or whatever, for special abuse. Maybe his mother was right.

"Not here yet, huh?" Siemonowski regarded him almost indifferently. Even the malice that was there earlier had now disappeared.

"No. But it's a long drive, all the way from the north side."

"Well, he better show up pretty soon. Because if he doesn't, we book you and you go into the tank." The threat was delivered matter-of-factly, with no special emphasis, all done more or less according to formula.

For all that, it had its effect on Jack. He had been aware for quite some time of noises emanating from behind the big room where he was sitting. Occasional yells and groans that at one time rose to a kind of crescendo and were capped by a sustained nasty laugh. That was when the magazine-reader had at last risen and walked through a rear door to quiet things down. And he had done just that. Things had settled somewhat by the time he reappeared and returned to his reading. Only an occasional muffled sound, barely audible to Jack, came through the door after that. Whatever happened, he didn't want to be put back there.

Siemonowski went back to talk for a while with the two other cops. As far as Jack could tell, nothing much was said. They laughed a little among themselves, and Jack got only occasional snatches of what was being said. The telephone rang. Would that be his father? Evidently not. Siemonowski took the call and then rushed off with the cigar-smoker close behind him. As he passed Jack at the door, he said tersely, "Your old man better be here." And they they were gone.

Not long after that, George Gawlor did step through the door and looked curiously around the station. When his eyes came to rest at last on Jack, he nodded and said mildly, "Well. Glad to see you're okay."

Jack barely had time to tell what had happened before Siemonowski and the other cop came bursting through the double doors supporting a thickly built man taller than either of them. The big man was rubber-legging it all the way

—whether because he was drunk, or because of the blows he had taken to his head, Jack couldn't tell. Probably a bit of both. The two cops dumped him in the nearest chair, and Siemonowski called to the one in the rear, "Got a customer for you, Addrisi. I think he's a paisan, so you'll want to take good care of this one." Then he turned around and saw that Jack's father was there. "Book him D and D," he said to the other cop. "I got business." He motioned toward the door, and George Gawlor started, with Jack following after them. Siemonowski whirled on Jack and snarled, "Not you. You stay here."

Jack did as he was told, sinking down again on the bench as they disappeared outside. He had nothing to do but sit and watch the blood trickle down the face of the man slumped in the chair. But in no more than a couple of minutes Siemonowski and his father returned. Jack stood up expectantly and looked from one to the other.

"Okay," said Siemonowski. "You can go."

Jack fought the impulse to run through the doors a free man. He stood his ground and said to him, "My stuff. My wallet and stuff?"

"Over there on the desk." He pointed indifferently and walked away. Jack went over and scooped up his wallet and keys but found no money there. He glanced at his father and saw him fluttering his fingers, urging him along. Jack nodded, and with one last look back, walked out of the place.

Outside, he turned to his father and said, "He took my money."

George Gawlor laughed abruptly at that. "Well, I guess he did," he said. "He took a little of mine, too."

"Is that what that was all about?"

"What else could it have been about?"

Without another word between them, they walked to the car. There his father handed over the keys and said simply, "You drive. I'm a little tired."

In less than a minute Jack had them on Broadway, headed through the bright lights out of Calumet City.

"Which one of these place was it where he picked you up?" his father asked. He seemed merely curious.

"The Riptide. That one right there."

His father turned and took a good look. But all he said was, "Mmmm. Interesting."

They didn't say much more than that during the drive back home. Jack fought back the impulse to ask his father how much he had had to pay Siemonowski. It wasn't fair to ask—and besides, Jack wasn't really sure he wanted to know. After they reached the Outer Drive his father dozed off. He roused himself somewhere around the Oak Street turn and sat up a moment and took stock of the situation. "I guess we're getting there, aren't we?" His voice, muffled and indistinct, was almost lost in the hum of the road.

Jack glanced over at him. "It shouldn't be too long."

"Oh, by the way, you don't have to worry about what's waiting for you back home. I told your mother you had car trouble. That's all. She'll be asleep." Jack's father himself was again asleep a few moments later.

When at last they pulled up in front of the building, Jack had to shake him awake. They ascended the stairs together, veterans of a long hard night. His father looked at the living-room clock as they entered and nodded. "Well, two-fifteen," he said. "That's not so bad, considering.

"No, I guess not."

"How about a glass of milk?"

"All right."

They went into the kitchen. Jack got down the glasses and his father poured. The taste was too familiar to notice, but it felt good going down.

"You know, Jackie," his father began, "you haven't caused me much trouble, and I'm grateful for that. I don't know how helpful to you I've been over the years. I'd like to think a little bit, anyway. But on any straight trade-off, I'd certainly say I come out way ahead."

"Well . . ."

"What I'm trying to say is that you're going to be out there on your own pretty soon, away from us. Now, there's a lot that can go wrong in your life—and maybe it will. You never can tell about life. I wish I had some good advice to give you, Jackie, because this would be the time to do it, I guess. All I can think of to tell you now is just don't get scared too easily." He hesitated, looked away, and then: "I got scared, and look what happened to me."

Jack was puzzled. He couldn't see that anything very much had happened to his father. But maybe that was what he meant.

*

Melaniphy sat brooding at his desk. A kind of unfocused, slow-burning anger smoldered inside him. He had been feeling this way all day, and he knew why. It was this damned thing with Gawlor that had him turned around. He found it hard to concentrate on the dozen or so other current files on his desk. Why should some stupid faggot homicide mess up his routine? That's what had made him angry.

He had resisted the temptation to keep an extra man on it. It was Klezek's baby now. Melaniphy would keep a hand in, but he would depend on Klezek to keep the case cooking. He knew he could count on him. Detective Klezek was a good man.

A uniform cop came into the squad room. Unless he was new, he wasn't from here. Melaniphy prided himself on knowing them all.

The cop went to Moskovsky, whose desk was nearest the door. There were a few words muttered between them, and then Moskovsky turned and pointed across the room at Melaniphy. The cop nodded his thanks and headed over.

"Sergeant Melaniphy?"

"That's me."

He stuck his hand out. "My name's Phil Parker. I'm from Chicago Avenue." Melaniphy took the hand and gave it an indifferent squeeze. Parker looked about Melaniphy's own age and was still a patrolman. Well, what the hell.

"One of Captain Quigley's boys, huh?"

"Yeah, I guess so. Though I don't think the captain would put it that way exactly." Parker smiled deprecatingly and shrugged. It was all done so automatically that it was almost like a tic.

"What can I do for you?"

"I understand you're the man to talk to on the Gawlor case."

"Well, maybe. Actually it's Detective Klezek's file, but I..."

"Sure, I know." Parker hesitated. "I just wanted to ask somebody about it."

"Ask? What?"

"I knew him, Sergeant. I went to high school with Jack Gawlor. We were, well, we were pretty good friends back then."

Melaniphy indicated the chair at his desk. "Sit down," he said. He studied Parker, wondering if he had any real answers, the kind that Melaniphy was after.

Parker was about six feet tall and gone to fat. As he collapsed into the chair his gut sagged out and over, obscuring his belt completely. Melaniphy caught his eye and realized, as he did, that Parker's glance had, until just then, been shooting every which way around the room. You would have called him shifty-eyed, if he weren't a cop. Maybe you would anyway. "This must've hit you pretty hard," Melaniphy suggested.

"You better believe it, Sergeant. I hadn't seen him for years, about ten years, but even so, something like this . . ."

"It really hits you where you live—is that it?"

"That about says it, Sergeant."

Ah, Melaniphy, he congratulated himself, you eloquent devil, you. "Well, what was it exactly you wanted to know, Parker?"

"I guess I just wanted to ask if there were any leads."

"Leads? Sure. There are always leads. But as of now it's still an open case." He let that sink in and added, "Wide open."

Parker nodded. Again his eyes went wandering around the room. This guy bothered Melaniphy. Could Gawlor have been anything like him? Melaniphy doubted it.

"How did you happen to know him in high school?"

"Oh, I don't know. How does anybody know anybody in high school? We were from the same general area and in a couple of the same classes. But I suppose that mostly it was because we played football together."

"Yeah? He play much drop-the-soap in the shower?" It was a remark calculated to give offense—or at least to get a rise out of Parker.

Parker looked at him steadily—really for the first time. "I'm glad you brought that up, Sergeant," he said, "because I wanted to talk about it, but I didn't exactly know how. I heard it was going down as a faggot homicide, and that's the part I just absolutely can't understand about Jack. There was absolutely no hint of any of that stuff with him. I mean really *no hint. He may have been kind of shy with girls— but who wasn't back then? I mean, shit, I remember he almost got into trouble just before graduation when we all went off to Cal City and a local cop picked him up for being underage."*

"I didn't know they did that in Cal City."

Parker smiled and shrugged again. That same tic. "It was just a shakedown." He paused, considering, then: "But, I mean, Cal City. Does that sound like a queer?"

"I don't know," said Melaniphy. "What does a queer sound like?"

CHAPTER TWO *1956*

THEY WERE REALLY MOVING. The idea was to stay on 66 as long as you could, even taking the swing west toward St. Louis, before you turned south again for Little Egypt. You stayed on 66 so you could barrel-ass down the broad, divided highway and make up in advance for the time you would lose on those meandering secondary roads that lay ahead. That was how Wooley explained it to Jack, shouting over his shoulder from behind the wheel as he passed the pint of I. W. Harper to Deke in the seat next to him.

Jack liked them both. He thought of them as fabulous characters. When first he got to know them, they were just the hillbillies down the hall, bawling, badmouthed disturbers of the peace who regularly shattered the reasonable tranquillity of the dormitory on study nights with their Hank Williams and Lefty Frizzell records played full blast with the door to their room flung wide open. Then one evening Jack passed their door, looked inside, and caught Wooley looking out.

"Hey, good buddy."

Did he mean him? Jack wasn't sure. He'd never even talked to the guy. How could he possibly be his good buddy? He was about to move on by when Wooley slewed his huge hand in an arc, beckoning him inside. Without quite knowing why, he went in. It was like stepping over the border into another country. They spoke English, sort of, though with inflections and expressions Jack had never really known before. And the stories they told! Fabulous stories of Williamson County—about the Klan wars and the Shelton Gang and Charlie Birger. Jack heard them for the first time that night, drinking from the jug of wine when it passed to him, careening back to his room three hours later, really drunk for the first time in his life.

The funny thing was they never ran out of stories. Or if they repeated one, it was so embellished with digressions and incidental interpolations that it became new again with rich and abundant details. Wooley told them best. Robert Lee Wooley had, at six-feet-four and about 270 pounds, come to the university to play football. During spring practice of his sophomore year, he had mangled his knee and lost his athletic scholarship. He stayed on, however, interested enough in the academic process to wish to prolong it. He attended classes, took tests, and would even do a paper now and then, though he drew the line at regular nightly study. Even so, he managed to limp through into his senior year with a low-C average.

Deke, short for Wilbur Deacon, was in most ways different from Wooley—slight, dark, and country cool. He played the sardonic commentator to Wooley's gusty yarn-spinner. In him, there was a flickering malevolence that Jack came to recognize only gradually. The more he drank, the brighter it burned, sweeping like a searchlight, indifferently illuminating all and everything with scorn. On this day, on the drive down to Herrin, he had been in top form, drinking better than half the pint of I. W. Harper, discoursing savagely on the subject of women.

"Ain't one of those little cunts in Champaign worth the trouble it takes to fuck them," he declared darkly at one point. "I tried them all—sorority girls, dormitory girls, town girls—ain't I, Wooley?"

"Goodness knows you done your best, Deke."

"And they just flat ain't worth the trouble. Know the big problem with them, Gawlor?"

"Uh, well . . ."

"They want you to talk to them. The town girls you have to tell how goddam pretty they are." Deke twisted around in the seat and shook the pint bottle at Jack. "I mean, they can just be absolute pigs, taking ugly pills three times a day—and they still got to hear that."

"I guess so."

"And the ones at the university, they have to hear how pretty they are *and* how smart they are. You got to tell them how goddam much you admire them all the time. It ain't enough for you to talk to them, *they* have to talk to *you*. They got opinions on everything, don't they? You been there, ain't you?"

"Well, I've dated, if that's what you mean."

"*Dated*? Sheeeiittt!"

Deke swiveled back around, took a swig from the bottle, and stared sullenly out the side window for a moment. Jack found himself wondering just what he could say to convince him that he, too, had had some experience. Or why should he try? After all, he didn't *mind* talking to girls, and he liked it especially when they talked back. There was this blonde, Pat Faraday, in his Creative Writing Workshop—he had begun walking her from class and had eaten lunch with her a couple of times. It wasn't that she was really so great-looking, he guessed, but he could talk to her. Wasn't that worth something? Deke evidently didn't think so.

Wooley cocked his head back in Jack's direction. "You'll have to excuse my friend here. He gets carried away sometimes. Deke's got the idea that the female of the species is good for one purpose and one purpose only."

"Aint it true?" Deke yelped. "Think about it. Ain't that what they were made for?"

"Well, sure," Jack ventured. "Biologically, maybe. In a way, that's what we're all made for."

"Now, that's the first goddam true thing I've heard from you, Jack, old buddy."

"But not *just* that."

"Horseshit."

"Like I say," said Wooley. "You'll have to excuse him."

"Horseshit."

Deke sulked for a few miles more, and the silence hung heavy in the old Frazer. The car was Wooley's. It seldom ran on more than most of its cylinders, and the musty smell inside it bespoke years in a farmyard before Wooley bought it, but the Frazer made the trip regularly from Champaign to Herrin, and that was all he asked of it. They were home boys, Wooley and Deke, and they could no more have survived permanent separation from their native corner than Jack could have endured staying on at home in Chicago. He didn't wonder at that, however. As it was described by them Herrin and surrounding Williamson County had taken on the luster of a Camelot, a kind of heroic never-never land where passions flared and violence ruled. Strange he thought Chicago so much tamer by comparison, but on the one hand he was dealing with experience and on the other, with myth. There could be no doubt which had the more powerful appeal for him.

"Know what's wrong with you, Jack?" Deke again.

"No. What?"

"I'll just bet you never had any black pussy, have you?"

"Uh, no . . . I haven't." That was true enough. Black *or* white.

"Aw, come on, Deke," said Wooley. "You going to start in on that again?"

"Well, why not? If the boy's never tried it, he just flat doesn't know what he's missing, does he?"

Wooley shrugged his broad shoulders.

Deke swung completely around in his seat and for the first time offered Jack the bottle of I. W. Harper he had until then been hoarding as his own. Jack accepted it and dutifully took a careful swig. It burned all the way down, but he managed not to cough as he handed back the pint.

"Now, what I'm trying to tell you is this," said Deke, lowering his voice so that it became almost inaudible over the rough roar of the engine. "You're just never going to know what real pussy is until you try some black stuff. A nigger woman really knows what it's for. She does it. You get a sample of that, Jack, and you'll know how a real woman's supposed to behave."

"Well . . ."

"You're not—you know—*disgusted* by the idea, are you?"

"Oh, no!"

"Well, then, Wooley, I think we owe this boy a visit to Ma Hammer's, don't you?"

"If you think he's up to it, Deke."

They had talked about Ma Hammer's place before. It had been around since the thirties, a back-country roadhouse with rooms in the rear where a small harem of black women imported from St. Louis and Chicago had provided carnal service to most of the male population of southern Illinois at one time or another. It was presided over by an old black queen of a woman who was known simply as Ma. She was severe, cool, and direct with her customers—anything but the blustering good-time madame of legend. "You don't mess with her," Wooley had told Jack, "because if you do, she's liable to call Junior, and then you truly will be sorry." Junior Hammer was a sure-enough pimp, but nobody had ever summoned up the nerve to call him that. His mother had raised him at her place as a young prince, and as a prince he spent his days and nights, taking his ease, bestirring himself only to enforce the rules of the house on those rare occasions they needed enforcing. Jack had been fascinated to hear Ma Hammer's described as it had been to him—yet at the same time it seemed somehow forbidding. He couldn't imagine himself in such a place. The thought of it intimidated him a little.

The rest of Williamson County certainly did not. In fact, by the time they at last arrived in Herrin and took their first run through the place, Jack found himself a little disappointed by what he saw there. It could have been any one of a dozen towns he knew between Chicago and Champaign. This was no Camelot, no shining city, but just an old coal-mining and farming community in the secondary stages of decay. People on the street seemed to walk a little more slowly than they did other places. They waved at Wooley and Deke and greeted them by name. And even Deke grew appreciably more expansive and relaxed as he viewed these familiar surroundings.

"Ain't no other place like it, is there, Wooley?"

"You can say that again, Deke."

At that point, Jack began seriously to doubt all that they had told him.

They took him on a brief tour of the sites of the town's past glories. They pointed out the corner where once stood the cigar store in which Ora Thomas had shot down Glenn

Young, the local general of the Ku Klux Klan. They drove out a winding country road and halted almost in the driveway of a rundown old farmstead. There Wooley nodded at the shingled frame house and murmured almost reverently, "That's the Sheltons' old place. That's where it all began. I've seen a photograph of the whole gang—Carl, Bernie, Earl, Roy, all of them—posed out in front of that house with their tommy guns and BAR's and all. The place looked just like it does now." Jack looked at the house, noted its peeling paint and leaning porch, and the legend of those country mobsters instantly diminished in his estimation. The Sheltons may have run everything south of Danville, but they sure could have taken lessons from the Capones and the Accardos in the art of gracious living.

It didn't even help much when, on the way out to Deke's house, they took him past the location of the old Shady Rest roadhouse. "That's were Charlie Birger's old place was," Deke explained. "The Sheltons tried everything to get him out of there. They went after him with an armored car. They bombed the place with an airplane. Finally it just blew up. People think they hired some miners to dig under it and plant some dynamite beneath. Whatever they did sure worked, though, because they blew the Shady Rest just as high as the courthouse tower." Jack surveyed the site. Well, there it was—a couple of walls half overgrown with weeds in a grove of poplar trees. So what? It looked just like any other country ruin. It could just as easily have been burned down by Mrs. O'Leary's cow.

They drove off and let Deke out five minutes later at a comfortable, middle-class, suburban-style dwelling on the outskirts of Marion. Wooley promised to come by for him about eight that night and brought Jack up to sit beside him in the front seat. As they drove away together, Wooley glanced over and smiled tentatively at Jack. "You don't want to take what Deke says too seriously," he said.

"About what?"

"Oh, things. He gets kind of carried away sometimes. He's more wish than be."

Wooley's parents were a surprise. Jack expected, had always assumed, they would be farm people. But they were not. Wooley drove back into Herrin, to the other side of town, wound his way through a couple of sidestreets, and turned up a long, looping driveway that led to a pillared house that would have looked impressive anywhere. In Herrin it seemed absolutely palatial.

Jack, who was a little confused by this, looked inquiringly at Wooley when at last they came to a halt before the broad porch.

Wooley looked almost rueful. "My father manages stuff for the Peabody Coal Company around here."

"Oh, I see."

Before Wooley could explain further, his mother burst out of the house with a small, elderly black man close behind. "Bob*by*," she wailed, "how many times have I *begged* you not to park that smelly old wreck in front of the house? William"—she turned to the black man—"do drive it around the back and unload it, won't you?"

"Right away, Mrs. Wooley."

He hastened to the driver's side just as Wooley was getting out. A flicker of a smile passed between them, sufferers together.

"How're you, William?"

"Oh, fine, Mister Robert. How you gettin' on?"

"Can't complain."

As Jack stepped out of the car, Mrs. Wooley met him with hand outstretched. "How do you do? I'm Bobby's mother. You must be his friend from the university. If I were to wait for him to make a proper introduction, I'm afraid we'd be here all day."

"Well, yeah, I guess so. I . . . my name is Jack Gawlor."

"So *very* pleased to meet you, Jack. I want you to know you're very, very welcome here. We don't see many of Bobby's friends—just that boy from Marion." That last added with a wrinkle of her long, straight nose. Jack could tell that on appearances alone he had scored high.

"Aw, Mom," Wooley groaned, "don't start in on Deke again."

"I didn't say a word, and I don't intend to."

"That's good."

"I'm just *so* pleased to have such a nice-looking young gentleman here. Let's leave it at that, shall we?" She smiled from one to the other in a way that Jack had seen before only in the movies. "But please, come inside. I'll show you your room, Jack. I'm *sure* you'll want to wash up after your drive here in *that* thing." She led the way. Jack followed dutifully, noting with some slight embarrassment that beneath her cocktail dress she had the best pair of legs he had ever seen before. He heard the car start and accelerate raggedly as William drove it around to the rear.

Tom Wooley was in his own way just as much a surprise to Jack. He didn't get home until just before dinner and when he arrived, he appeared as a country gentleman—in an MG, dressed in extra-large Harris tweed and flannels, a pipe clenched in his jaw, and with a martini in his hand supplied magically by William. Still, that did not do him justice. He was something of a diamond in the rough, a tough-talking self-made man of the old school who had risen from the pits above ground to management. He must have married the boss's daughter somewhere along the way, for he deferred to her as sovereign to sovereign. That, at least, was how it seemed to Jack as he chatted with husband and wife before dinner and during, stretching to please them with charm he had never really possessed. He found himself on his best behavior with them, trying at once to satisfy Wooley's father that he was vigorously masculine and to reassure Wooley's mother that he was a young man of cultural aspiration and some attainment. He satisfied them both by telling them he wanted to be a writer. He cited Hemingway as his model. To that Mrs. Wooley said, "Oh, dear," but remained attentive. Mr. Wooley simply nodded in approval. During all this, Jack omitted looking directly at his friend, and just as well, too, for he felt waves of disapproval emanating from that corner of the table. He was performing, carrying on for their approval. He knew that, and it bothered him a little. He sensed it bothered Wooley a lot.

"Well, now, Jack," said Tom Wooley gravely, just as black Harriet was serving dessert, "I understand what you say about

Hemingway, but there's a man with just a world of experience. Why, he's hunted and he's fished the kind of game that can kill you. He's been to war two or three times. Most of what he's written about he's lived—or so I've heard. How do you propose to write like Hemingway if you haven't had Hemingway's experience?"

"Well, get it, I guess."

"Oh, my." Mrs. Wooley glanced at Jack and then suddenly away, as though something she glimpsed distressed her terribly. "Harriet, do tell William we'll be taking our coffee in the living room, won't you?"

"Yes, ma'am. Sure will."

And that is what they did—coffee in the living room and cognac for Jack, Wooley, and his father in snifters. Jack had heard of cognac, of course, but he had never before drunk any. He wasn't sure quite what he expected—something sweeter, he supposed. He saw it was okay to sip it. It was warm in his mouth, but it didn't burn going down. He decided he liked it.

Wooley remained quiet. He was not sulking but seemed oddly reserved, ill-at-ease in his own living room. Jack found it all a little hard to understand. There was, thank God, no more Hemingway talk. Instead they listened to Tom Wooley hold forth on the iniquity of unions in general and the United Mine Workers in particular. It wasn't exactly a tirade, but it did seem a set speech and was delivered with force, vigor, and conviction. Jack had never heard his own father talk like that.

When it was ended, Tom Wooley quaffed off the measure of cognac that remained in his snifter, signaling the end of the occasion. "Bobby . . . Jack," he nodded at each of them, "you boys enjoy yourselves now. Just don't do anything I wouldn't do. Heh-heh-heh."

"Oh, *Tom*." Mrs. Wooley, who had remained quiet and attentive through it all, rolled her eyes in mock exasperation. She rose then and smiled at Jack. "Really," she said to him, "don't pay any attention to Tom. He pretends to be such a rounder, but he's really just the sweetest old homebody ever was."

Tom Wooley threw his arm around his wife's shoulder and squeezed her to him. "Just look what I've got to keep me here." She laughed gaily, and the two walked out of the living room arm-in-arm, calling their goodbyes after them, advising Wooley not to be *too* late.

"Je*sus*!" Wooley said softly nearby. "Don't you fall for that shit now."

"What do you mean?"

"Well, if I have to tell you, I guess it won't do any good."

Jack was irritated at that. "I like them," he said defensively. "Don't you? I mean, they are your mother and father."

"Oh, I like them well enough. But not when they're putting on their goddam act."

He didn't know what to say to that, and so he said nothing. Jack just shrugged and, taking his brandy snifter with him, got up for a closer look at the hunting prints that lined the far wall of the living room. They were sort of like cartoons, but really, really old.

"Jack?"

"Yeah, Wooley?" He turned around and saw him sprawled where he had left him on the couch, staring.

"You really believe that stuff?"

"What your father was saying about the unions?"

"No, I mean before. About being a writer and getting experience and all."

"I guess so, yeah. Sure."

"Well, are you so damned hard up for all this experience you have to go shopping around for it? Couldn't you just sort of let things happen to you?"

Jack was annoyed. Who was Wooley to tell him how to live his life? Who was he especially to instruct him on what you did to be a writer? "Well, it seems to me," Jack said, drawling out the words rather disdainfully, "that you and Deke are doing the shopping for me. Isn't that what this trip to Ma Hammer's is all about?"

Wooley leaped up from the sofa, waving his big hands in agitation. "Quiet about that, will you?" he rasped in a loud stage whisper. "That's a name you just don't say in this house. My mother'd have a fit if she heard that."

Jack lowered his voice. "Well . . . isn't it?"

Hovering uneasily close by, unwilling to settle back on the sofa, Wooley continued in a whisper: "Yeah, well, I wanted to talk to you about that, old buddy. Now, Deke he talks a better game than he plays. If he runs true to form he's going to get you there—you know where I mean—and just leave all the doing up to you. I've never known him to do more than drink beer there and bullshit with Junior."

"Well, what do *you* want to do?"

"I was figuring we might meet a couple of girls I know after they get off work and go out and have some fun."

"You mean ditch Deke?"

"Not exactly." Wooley hesitated. "No, hell, I don't mean that at all. Don't worry. I'll explain things to him."

"And no Ma Hammer's?" He wasn't going to let Wooley off quite so easily.

"Shhh! Come *on*, Jack."

"Sorry."

"Well, sure. We can go by there and sort of look it over, if you want to. Have a couple of beers and then get on to other things. How does that sound?"

On the drive over to Marion to pick up Deke, Jack congratulated himself that he had managed to strike a good face-saving bargain. Nobody could accuse him of chickening out now. Not even Deke, who was already out on the porch and waiting when they pulled up to his house. He was in rare high spirits when he jumped into the car.

"By God, Wooley, we're going to do it!"

"Yeah, well, we'll go over and take a look, anyway."

"You ready for Ma and Junior and the girls, Jack?"

"Just as ready as you are, Deke." That should put him on notice.

The way Deke was whooping and hollering, Jack half-expected to be driven direct to Ma Hammer's. But no. They set out for Carbondale and wound up at a drive-in just beyond the teachers' college, where Chuck Berry blared from six loudspeakers, and the satin-uniformed carhops were bouncing to the beat as they moved back and forth from car to car. Jack watched them, fascinated. They had more style and spirit than those lumpy milkmaids who car-hopped in Lincolnwood. He had never once seen any of them cut a cute little side-stepping caper like the one the skinny brunette used when she bopped up to the window on Wooley's side. She wasn't so terrific-looking, but she did have style. He had to give her that.

"Hah, Wooley. Hah, Deke." She gave Jack just a glance.

"Hey, Cathy, how they hanging?"

"You just watch yourself there, Mr. Foul-Mouthed Deacon. I'll call the manager on you."

"Aw." Deke winked at Jack.

She leaned close to Wooley and asked confidentially, "Y'all looking for Sharon?"

"Might be. Where's she at?"

"Inside. She's waitressing tonight."

"I might just walk in there and say hello to her."

Cathy giggled. "You might, huh? You might? Well, ain't that a surprise! Y'all eatin'?"

"Naw, just Cokes," said Wooley. "Three Cokes."

"Just Cokes, just Cokes," she mimicked. "That's all you ever order is just Cokes. I swear I don't know how you ever got so big." She turned and started to go, then ducked back suddenly. "I'll tell her you're here."

"You do that."

She left, and Wooley turned to Jack. "I've got this little friend here I like to look in on every once in a while. No big deal. I'll just say hello and be back in a minute." He opened the car door and hauled himself out from behind the wheel. Tucking in his shirt, he ambled as casually as his size would permit around to the front of the place and inside. Jack watched him through the glass as he made a circuit of the booths, waving here, shaking hands there, calling out a word of greeting across to the other side. At last Wooley came to the goal of all this apparently aimless meandering. He stood, hands in hip pockets, talking with steady concentration to a blonde girl who was at least a foot shorter than he. She was dressed in the same brief satin uniform that the rest had on, but she wore it better, filled it out as a woman should. Even at a distance, Jack could tell she was pretty in a soft, melting, feminine way. He could also tell that she had the biggest breasts he had ever seen on a small woman.

"Ain't she something?" It was Deke, staring just as he was, his eyes narrowed in appraisal. "She's why Wooley keeps coming back home practically every weekend."

"Really?" Jack was surprised without quite knowing why.

"You didn't think it was to see his mommy and daddy, did you? Old Wooley, he won't talk about it much, but he's really stuck on that girl. I can tell. Would you believe she just turned sixteen? God *damn!* Look at the tits on her. Think what she'll look like when she's a grown woman!"

Cathy thrust her head through the open window on the driver's side. "I heard what you said, Deke. Honestly, you are a dis*grace!*"

"Oh, I'm not so bad. If you just got to know me a little better."

"Huh. That'll be the day." She turned to Jack, smiling at him for the first time. "He talks like that all the time, doesn't he?"

"No, not all the time," he conceded.

"See? See?" Deke crowed. "I told you I wasn't so bad."

"Just most of the time," Jack added.

Cathy cackled in response. "There. Just what I thought."

"Thanks a *lot,* good buddy."

"Well here's your Cokes. Wooley already paid for them. You know, Deke, you really ought to take some lessons from him. That big old boy really knows how to treat a girl."

"Yeah," Deke said lewdly, "he knows what they're for."

"Oh, *you!*" She backed out of the window only to bob back an instant later to say to Jack, "Pleased to meet you." Had they met? He wasn't sure. Anyway, he watched her go as he sipped at his Coke, realizing then she was the girl Wooley had in mind for him. She was hopping along to Gene Vincent now.

"That girl is so hot for my body she can't hardly stand it," Deke said with profound conviction.

"*Her?*"

"Sure. Can't you tell?"

A moment later Wooley emerged and moved much less leisurely than before back to the car. He jumped in and started it, practically peeling rubber as he backed up and shot out of the drive-in lot. It was simple exuberance. Wooley was happy.

"Jesus, Wooley, watch it! This Coke is spilling all over me."

"Oh, sorry, Deke. Guess I got kind of carried away."

"I guess you did."

Jack had seen it coming and put the cap back on the paper cup. With them now out on the road, he discreetly rolled the back window down and dropped the Coke. He never wanted the thing, anyway.

Now they were on their way. They sped down winding back roads through a moonless country dark so thick it was like driving through deep, deep ocean. Deke, momentarily subdued, lapsed into silence, but Wooley took up the slack, bawling out as much as he could remember of Hank Williams's "Kaw-Liga" into the night air.

"When you going to learn the words to that song, Wooley?"

"Just about the time you break down and admit you missed the boat on Cathy."

"Missed the boat? Are you kidding? All I got to do is snap my fingers for her."

"Well, time was that might have been true. But now I wouldn't be surprised if some good-looking stud like Jack might beat your time with her."

"Aw, shit."

"Hey, Jack." Wooley half-turned to address him in the back seat. "What'd you think of her anyway?"

"You mean Cathy? The carhop? She's okay. The girl's got some style."

"Hear that? Jack knows quality when he sees it. He just might look in on her later on tonight himself."

Deke was silent. "No, he won't," he said at last. "Not when he gets a whiff of that nigger pussy at Ma Hammer's."

Jack knew they had arrived when he saw a red neon sign

ahead in the shape of a hammer. That was it. That was all. No legend of any kind. He was impressed. Even though there weren't many cars around, Wooley drove around to the rear to park. Nobody said anything about that.

Inside, it was dark. But it was different from the outside darkness they had just left. There were shapes, tones, a constant tremor of movement through the place, though the only discernibly visible spot in view was the bar at the far side of the room, all mirrors and bottles. That's where they headed.

They ordered three beers and had barely gotten them poured when Junior Hammer came over.

"Hey, Wooley, how's my man?"

"How you gettin' on, Junior?"

"Can't complain. Can't complain. Stayin' in shape. That's the important thing, isn't it?"

Junior looked like he stayed in shape. He was nearly as tall as Wooley but much leaner. Even wearing a suit and tie, as he was, there was taut muscularity evident in his movement as he pretended to relax with the three white boys that seemed positively feline. Not alley cat; jungle cat. He himself wasn't much older than they were—twenty-five, at the most. There was something elegant, not just in his appearance but in his manner, as well, that took Jack by surprise. He seemed totally in command of himself, and perhaps of them, too.

"You remember Deke," said Wooley. He's been by a couple of times."

"Sure, sure. How you doin'? Glad to have you back."

"And this is Jack Gawlor. He's at the university. From Chicago."

"Hey, Chicago. The big town, huh?"

"Well, yeah, I guess so."

"And you came all the way down here just to check us out?"

"I guess you could say that. Yeah."

"Beautiful. Hey, Gineen." Junior waved a long arm off into the room behind him, and Jack turned to look. It was now just possible to make out the dozen or so figures, mostly female, that were scattered in twos and threes at tables around the room. One of them rose and obediently moved forward to the bar. She was a tall girl, probably as tall as Jack, sturdily built with wide shoulders. Almost athletic. Glancing back at Junior for some hint as to what was going on, Jack found him leaning over and listening intently to what Deke was whispering in his ear. Jack didn't like that, especially when Junior nodded, glanced in Jack's direction, and broke into a laugh.

Up close Gineen looked pretty and was somehow less imposing physically than she had seemed at a distance. She was quite dark but had a long nose and thin lips. White features. She reminded Jack a little of a girl from his home room in high school whose name he now couldn't recall. Except for the color of her skin, of course.

Gineen gave him a long sidelong glance but didn't smile. He realized he was sweating heavily and wondered when he had begun. Was it really so hot in here?

Junior rested a hand easily on her shoulder. "Gineen, child, I just wanted you to know how famous our little place here has got." He spoke in a sly, bantering drawl to her that was subtly different from the way he had addressed the three of them a moment before. "Now, this is Jack. He came all the way down from big old Chi town just to visit us here because we so famous. Ain't that right, Jack?"

"Sure. That's right. All the way down." Jack glanced at Wooley and Deke. They were trying hard not to laugh. That annoyed him.

"Gineen," Junior continued, "you from Chicago, too, ain't you, child?"

She looked at Jack again without smiling. "Yeah," she said, "I am." Her voice was as flat and unexceptional as the words she chose.

"Well, why don't you two get yourselves together and kind of, you know, compare notes?"

At that Wooley and Deke burst out laughing. Junior joined in, too. What was so damned funny, Jack wanted to know. Hadn't they brought him here? Wasn't this their idea in the first place?

"You want to dance?" he asked her suddenly.

"Ain't no music," she said. It was simple fact.

"Well, we'll fix that," said Junior. "We sure enough will." He went directly to the jukebox near the bar, tossed in a quarter, and began punching buttons.

"Come on," Jack said to her and, with a look back at Wooley and Deke, took her hand and led her to the tiny dance floor nearby.

The music started. It was, as he would have wanted it, something slow—King Pleasure's "I'm in the Mood for Love." He took her in his arms with greater authority than he felt and, holding her close, began to dance. They moved easily across the floor together, and he was fully aware that they were being watched closely by everyone in the room. Let them look. He wanted them to. She was following well, so he whirled her once or twice and even did a dip. She pulled back then and smiled at him tentatively.

"You pretty good dancer," she mumbled.

"You, too," he said.

The girl pressed herself against him yet managed to move with him remarkably well. She was nearly Jack's height, so that when they began dancing around the floor like Siamese twins attached at the pelvis, he found that her crotch fit against his exactly. He felt her push and grind against him until he began to swell.

"You gettin' hard."

He said nothing. Looking back to the bar, he found Wooley and Deke still staring. Junior had left them. And as the last record ended, he excused himself and left Gineen near the jukebox, then made his way over to the two at the bar.

"I'm ready to go when you are," he told Wooley.

"You just going to walk out on that girl after you got her all worked up?" Deke joked.

"Give me a few minutes," said Wooley. "I just ordered another beer. You want one?"

"No, I haven't finished this." Jack sipped at it politely and then set his bottle back on the bar. Wooley could sure drink a lot of beer.

Deke smirked at him. "Junior told me to tell you that if you ain't crazy about that one, there's lots more where she came from. He thought maybe you might be interested in something a shade lighter."

"No, she's just fine."

"Well, what're you doing here then?" Deke asked testily.

"Aw, leave him alone," Wooley grumbled.

"You ain't gonna do it, are you?" Deke persisted. "Come all the way out here just for the ride, didn't you?"

"Well," said Jack, "so what if I did?"

"I'll tell you so-what. It looks to me, Mr. Jack Gawlor, like you just never have, and you never will."

"Deke! shut up!" Wooley urged.

"No, let me finish." He turned to Jack. "Just look at you—twenty goddam years old, and you're still saving it. Saving it for what, I want to know. You think yours is better than anybody else's, you can't stick it just anyplace? Listen—"

But he didn't listen. He had heard enough. Jack pivoted on his heel and marched away from the bar. It so happened that the direction he took brought him back to Gineen, who was still standing where he had left her by the jukebox, regarding him curiously. He fished some change out of his pocket and dropped it in the machine, then punched two or three buttons at random.

"You want to dance some more?" he asked her.

She looked at him directly and countered, "You want to dance some more or you want to go in back?"

He turned and looked back at the bar and saw that Wooley had slid off his stool and was beckoning him back. The music started again. He turned to Gineen and found her looking indifferently away. "Let's go in back," he said.

They went. Without so much as a nod, she led the way to the far corner of the room and to a door he hadn't noticed before. Down a long, ill-lighted hall he watched her hips sway tautly and was reminded with a start of just where they were headed and why. Somehow he had misplaced that in his effort to demonstrate that he was not so easily intimidated, that he was just as much a man as Deke or Wooley or any of them. But now something more would be required of him. He was suddenly very uneasy.

Light flooded in at the end of the corridor. They came

upon an open space, a kind of vestibule, where a ponderously fat black woman sat in a well-stuffed easy chair with a magazine open in her lap. Jack saw that she had a copy of *Time*, and he realized immediately that this was Ma Hammer. The woman in the chair looked up at him appraisingly and, apparently satisfied by what she saw, replaced her glasses and nodded at Gineen.

"Same place?" Gineen asked.

"You know where to go, child. Treat him right now, hear?"

They started past her, but suddenly the woman reached out and fastened onto Jack's arm. He was startled and reflexively shook loose of her.

She fixed him with a look. "Just wanted to say, young man, I run a good clean house. You got nothin' to be afraid of from any of my girls." Again she nodded and this time picked up the magazine from her lap. Gineen led him away to a nearby door. She opened it, and he followed her inside.

Nothing to be afraid of? What did she mean? Oh, God!—it suddenly struck him—*disease,* of course! He hadn't even thought about that. And why not? He didn't have a rubber with him or a pro-kit or anything. He just never thought about practical stuff like that because, well, there was never any need to. Now what was he going to do?

He turned to Gineen as though expecting she might supply the answer and, to his amazement, found her undressing. She was shucking off the red sweater she had been wearing and now reaching behind her to unclasp her pink brassiere. She shook loose of it and looked at him oddly. "Ain't you gonna get undressed?" she asked. If not, if that was his kick, then clearly it was okay with her. She just wanted to know.

He looked at her breasts. They were larger and rounder than he had supposed they would be. The deep brown nubs on them invited him to touch them, but he held back, waiting for an invitation to do so. None came.

"Undressed? Oh . . . oh, sure." He began tugging at his clothes, casting them off in one direction, then another. But suddenly he stopped, having thought of another embarrassing detail. "Look," he said to her, "I don't have a lot of money with me. How much will this . . . ?"

"Don't worry. It's all tooken care of."

"What? Who took care of it?"

"Your friend. The little one. Now come on over here and let's get you washed off."

Obediently he went, not knowing quite what to expect. She took him to a wash stand in the corner. Jack looked at it and noticed the picture of Sam Cooke pasted to the mirror above it. He was shocked but not surprised when she reached into his shorts and pulled out his penis. Nobody but he had ever touched it before. And not even he handled it with the rough, casual assurance that Gineen did. She held it up to what little light filtered into that corner of the room and looked at it closely. She squeezed the head a couple of times and, satisfied, ran water, soaped it down, and then rinsed it. As she was drying it with a ratty old rag of a towel, she regarded him critically and said, "You pretty soft. Get on the bed, and I'll suck it some, make it hard."

Without another word, she finished undressing. From the bed he watched her. Once, in Cicero, he had seen a stripper go all the way, but she was old and fat and white. There had been no hint in her body of the supple muscularity he now saw in Gineen's. It was as though the two women belonged to separate species. All they had in common was the patch between their legs. He studied it curiously, noting the coarseness of the hair there and dimly perceiving the ripples and tucks of the skin beneath. There it was, the thing he had thought about all these years, tried so hard to imagine—and imagined so imperfectly. It seemed strange to him still —a strange, dark, secret place.

"Take off your underpants," she directed him.

He did as he was told, but just as she was going down on her knees before him, he said, "Look, how about sitting up here on the bed with me?"

She looked up at him suspiciously. "What for?"

"We could talk."

"Talk?" She was puzzled. Reluctantly she rose and sat down beside him. He was suddenly overwhelmed by so much nakedness next to him. Feeling a kind of surge, he reached out to touch her nearest breast, holding it in his hand from the bottom, as though weighing it.

"You like my tits? You want to play with them a while?"

"No, let's talk." Even though he felt his fear beginning to abate just a little and his penis at last beginning to work its way up, he removed his hand from her breast and touched her hair tentatively. It was thickly set in heavy waves around her head. Jack felt it somehow imperative that he make some sort of personal contact with her before he did this thing. Somehow he had to get to know her.

"Talk about what?"

"Oh, I don't know. You really are from Chicago, huh?"

"I said I was."

"What high school did you go to?"

"Phillips."

"When did you graduate?"

"Didn't."

"Oh. Well . . . that's too bad." He didn't know what else to say.

"You something, you know that?"

"What do you mean?"

"You come in here asking me all this shit. What you want to know all this shit for?"

Jack hesitated. Could he really explain? "I'd . . . I'd like to get to know you before we . . . you know . . ."

She moved a little way from him on the bed and stared at him oddly for a moment. "Then, man, you better start fucking me right now, because there ain't no way in the world you ever get to know me."

He looked at her and knew what she said was true. But before he could say a word, she threw herself back on the bed, drew up her knees, and spread her legs. Her eyes were open, and she was staring up furiously at the dirty ceiling above them. It seemed now that it was all up to him, and so he tried. His penis was half-erect and almost hard, and so he mounted her and blindly tried to insert it into that dark place below. He fumbled and pushed with increasing desperation. Finally she grabbed him roughly and stuffed him inside her like so much sausage. He began lunging and thrusting away at her in what he supposed was the proper manner, but nothing happened. And he could tell that nothing was going to happen. He felt himself shriveling inside her. At last he stopped.

"You through?"

"Yes."

She pushed him up and out of her, jumped out of bed, and began throwing on her clothes. His time was up.

Not long afterward, over a weekend, Jack wrote a story about it. Or not so much a story as a masturbation fantasy—the way it seemed to him it should have been. In his version, Gineen responded warmly to his questioning, revealed herself and her miserable life to him, grateful that a man had come along at last who cared enough to ask. He had comforted her, and then, as naturally and innocently as our primal ancestors, white Adam and black Eve had made love. They did so in sweeping flights of poetic prose, fluttering on wings of metaphor, soaring together to a perfect climax that left them both dewy-eyed with marvel that such beauty could be created in the midst of such squalor. There the story had ended. There was no mention in it that afterward Jack had been unceremoniously dumped by Wooley back at his house so that he and Deke could return to pick up the two girls from the drive-in. Jack realized then he had made himself taboo, at least for that night, by going off with Gineen. And that was probably what Deke had intended, for he had apparently decided at last to give Cathy a tumble. But eventually Jack got his revenge, for in the story he wrote Deke and Wooley were reduced to comic characters, nothing more or less than oafish adolescents who had no real notion of the power and majesty of sexual love.

Jack was proud of the twenty pages he had written and thought them the truest and toughest he had ever done. He handed them in to the Creative Writing Workshop and after class asked Pat Faraday to the movies that Friday night. They saw *La Strada* and talked about it afterward—about the poignant sadness of Giulietta Masina, the brutality of Anthony

Quinn, the mystery of their relationship. It was marvelous. The kind of talk Jack had always hoped to have with a girl. Inspired by it, he grew bold when he said good night and told her he had never had such a terrific time. They kissed, and he found her receptive, more than receptive, almost passionate. Jack and Pat made plans to meet again. Tomorrow night? No, that was out. Her best friend, a music major, had bought tickets to a Budapest String Quartet concert at the theater, and she had promised to go with her. What about Sunday? Well . . . all right. Another movie? Why not? *Rebel Without a Cause* had just hit town, and that James Dean was pretty interesting, wasn't he? Kind of like Brando or maybe Montgomery Clift, a real actor. It was a date then? Swell.

And so they went to the movies again, and again they talked over drugstore Cokes afterward—though this time not so long nor so passionately about the picture. Instead they began to discuss writing in the high-minded way that people in creative writing workshops often do—talking about honesty and the particular truths they wished to tell, about the writers they liked for themselves—Jack had to admit he had never read Jessamyn West—and those from whom they felt they might learn.

Walking Pat back home, Jack remembered that she was from Robinson, over near the Indiana line. She had informed him with a pained expression on Friday night that her father was the Ford dealer there: he was not to blame her for that. It took him a while, but at last he had put Robinson together with James Jones, the novelist. He lived there, didn't he? Hadn't Jack read an article in *Life* about the writers' colony there and Jones's terrific house? He asked Pat about him. What was he like? Did she know him?

"Are you kidding? I wouldn't want to." She was suddenly most emphatic.

"Really? Why not?"

"Well, he's a pretty unsavory character, I guess you could say. And . . . have you read that book of his?"

"Well . . ."

"Don't you think it's pretty crude?"

"Well . . ."

He changed the subject as quickly and artfully as he could, though not before Pat had told him in no uncertain terms just what she thought of *From Here to Eternity*, the foul language and all that sex. "I don't want you to get the idea, Jack, that I'm a prude, because I'm not. It just seems to me that sex is something beautiful, and that's the way you should write about it." Well, of course. Who could argue with that? Not Jack. It did make him a little uneasy about the story he had just handed in, though. What would she think of that? He'd sort of been thinking of showing it to her when he got it back. Now he decided that was out.

And then, at her door, the long, lingering goodnight. They talked on in the shadows between kisses, and as though to prove to him that she was, as she claimed, no prude, she allowed the hand that he had timorously placed on her cashmere breast to remain for a moment or two before she pushed it gently away. "Not now," she said, "please." A minute or two later she left him, brushing his cheek with one last kiss, leaving him a little dizzy with desire. Not now? That meant some other time, didn't it? He hurried back to the dormitory to masturbate. But there in bed in the darkened room, no vision of Pat Faraday came to him—none, in any case, that was of any use to him then. He thought instead of Gineen. He thought back to the soft roundness of her breast and the weight of it in his hand. He carefully remembered the details of her body—her wide shoulders, the lean angularity of her hips, the fuzzy black patch between them. And then, as he alternately caressed and squeezed his penis, he once again told himself the story he had written. As it grew hard and erect, he relived an experience he had never had.

The next week he came into the Workshop a little apprehensive. He just wanted to get that story from Goldman, the teacher, tuck it away, and get out of class with it. David Goldman, rumored to be working on a novel, had published a few short stories, most of them in established literary magazines. One, however, had appeared in *Esquire*. Jack ran across that one and read it, realizing when he did that it was the first time he had ever seen anything in print by someone he knew personally. That made him feel funny. The story was about a voyeur, and he thought it was pretty weird, not at all the sort of thing he expected from the careful man in tweeds who spoke so tentatively and wrote on his manuscripts in such a small, precise hand.

Goldman bustled into class that day, briefcase in hand, and unloaded a good-sized sheaf of manuscripts from it. He removed his glasses and looked down the long table at the dozen students seated around it.

"You've been busy," he observed. "A lot of work to go through today, some of it successful and some of it, for various reasons, not quite so successful. We won't get through it all, but I think we should look at a little of both. As usual, I'm not so much interested in whether a piece of writing is good or bad—and I'd like you to keep your comments as nonjudgmental as possible—as I am interested in whether or not it is successful or not on its own terms. Does it work? If not, why not?"

With that, they began. Jack hoped—prayed!—they might get through the hour without looking at his story. It was customary for each of them to read his own work aloud, and Jack wasn't sure he could do that—especially not in front of Pat Faraday. As luck would have it, hers was the first piece they considered, a tedious little sermon on the subject of jealousy in the form of a conversation between home-town friends. Jack listened respectfully as she read it in a faltering voice, but he found himself wishing that it was better. Oh, it was written well enough. There was a certain colloquial quality to the dialogue, an anecdote was cleverly sketched out as background and occasion for all this talk—but talk it remained, tendentious and moralistic, and not a story. That was Jack's opinion. He kept it to himself. Those who spoke up had much harsher things to say.

They listened to another story, a rather old-fashioned piece of ersatz Faulkner about a deer hunt, written and read by a tight-lipped young man who had, in the past, been fiercely critical of the work of others in the class. It fared better, but Jack suspected this had less to do with the quality of the piece than it did with the general fear of reprisal.

Goldman must have decided that the writer was getting off a bit too lightly, for when all had had their say, he added in his halting way, "It's possible, isn't it, that even though the story is, as we all seem to agree, successful on its own terms —that its own terms aren't its own terms? Or is that too obscure?" He flashed a quick smile to indicate that of course he was just joking and cast his eyes immediately downward at the pile of manuscripts before him. "This next one," he began, clearing his throat, "is even longer than the last. And because there is, I think, quite a lot to be said about it, I'm going to ask that it be read now. If there's some time left over, there's one more we might want to discuss." He looked up then, straight at Jack. "Mr. Gawlor?"

With sinking heart, Jack reached out and took the sheaf of pages that was passed down the line to him. He glanced at Pat and found her smiling encouragingly at him. His mouth was dry. His throat was tight. Yet he had no choice but to begin reading.

Somehow he got through it. There was little shuffling of feet once he was under way, and there were even a few appreciative chuckles for the considerably embroidered antics of the Wooley and Deke characters at the drive-in. At one point, just when he had begun his gentle questioning of Gineen, he looked up as he turned a page and caught Pat's glance. He saw, to his consternation, that her blue eyes had filled with tears, and for a moment he found it difficult to continue. When at last he did, he had another surprise waiting for him on the next page. As he approached the erotic climax of the story, he felt a slow, steady tightening at his crotch. It added a little to his embarrassment, but not even that stopped him. Jack managed to read on through to the end.

"Let me congratulate you, Mr. Gawlor," said Goldman, as soon as Jack had finished. "Those who write such stories are not always able to read them." He let that sink in, then looked around the table. "Comments?"

Although a lot was said, not much of it was very critical.

Even the tight-lipped imitator of Faulkner praised the "authentic feel" of the piece. Pat Faraday, of course, said nothing. And so it was left to David Goldman to pronounce upon the story. That he did at some length, saying after the usual hesitations, that he had never read a piece of student work that had so much right and so much wrong with it, all at the same time. "What's right with it is evidently apparent to you all. What's wrong with it—what's *inconsistent*—" he emphasized the word, smiling around the table "—is its conclusion. Somehow it seems forced, unconvincing. The natural flow of the writing—and there is certainly a flow to it up to that point—is interrupted, and there's a sudden shift to a kind of forced, lyrical tone that to me, at least, just doesn't seem right. All of which means that the final part reads to me like so much bull . . . well, leave it at that—so much bull." This got a light laugh from the class. Goldman fidgeted a moment until it had subsided.

"Now, the final thing to say about this story is that it's very good that Mr. Gawlor wrote it, for now, I hope, he's gotten it out of his system. Everyone—every young man, at least—must write a sexual intercourse story before he can get on to other things. You must accept that as an immutable law of nature. All right, now he has written it. Now he can do something else."

Jack had no idea how he was supposed to take that, and so he simply nodded his understanding—perhaps his assent, as well. Before they could go on to the next piece, the hour was up and Goldman dismissed them. Jack grabbed up his pages and ran for the door.

"Uh, Mr. Gawlor." It was Goldman, of course. "Could I have a minute with you?" Jack had no choice but to retrace his steps.

"Yes, Mr. Goldman?"

"I really don't want you to get the idea that I'm dismissing your effort. I thought that it—most of it—was really very well executed. I'm just interested in getting you through this phase and on to other things." He nodded. That was all.

When at last Jack got through the door, he found Pat waiting for him in the hall. Her eyes were dry, and she was smiling bravely. Even as he opened his mouth to apologize to her, she began to speak and continued as they rushed along together.

"Look, Jack, I don't care what Mr. Goldman said. He's not some kind of absolute authority, you know. I mean, he says himself that his opinion is just another one in the room—except that he gives the marks, of course."

Jack stopped and looked at her. They had just stepped outside and he now found himself blinking in the bright sunlight. "Wait a minute. What are you saying?"

"That I think it was good," she declared. "That I think it was all good."

"Even the end of it?"

"It was the best part," she said, almost defiantly. "You remember what I said about the way all that should be written about? Well, the way you did it *was* beautiful."

He managed to wangle Wooley's car the next night. On the pretext that there was a really terrific old country restaurant that was always too crowded to go to on weekend nights, he had persuaded Pat Faraday to go out in the middle of the week. What Jack really had in mind was a really terrific old country motel out beyond Chanute.

The restaurant really wasn't so bad. Wooley had given him directions there and cautioned him to ignore everything on the menu except steak and chops. Deke, who pretended a new respect for him after the visit to Ma Hammer's, had told him about the motel. And so, as Jack and Pat sat over the remains of sirloin and lamb chops, sipping coffee, they talked again about the class. Pat had borrowed Jack's story overnight so that she might read it again herself. It lay on the table between them.

"You know," she said, "there's one thing that bothers me a little about what you've written."

Uh-oh, he thought grimly, here it comes. "What's that?"

"I don't know quite how to put this, Jack, but that whole side of life, that whole . . . experience, it just seems so important to you."

"You mean to the guy in the story."

"Well . . . yes."

"And you think he's me."

She looked at him rather warily. "Not exactly, I guess. But you did write it."

"Look, if I wrote a story about a murderer, would you think I'd killed someone?"

"Oh, come on. It's not the same thing at all." She looked at him then with some intensity, hesitating a moment before at last she resumed: "I feel like I'm over my head with you. I'm not exactly a little country girl, Jack, but I know I haven't had the experience of . . . life that you have."

He was flattered. Nobody had ever said anything like that to him before. But he also realized she had thrust a dilemma upon him. If he were to deny her notion of him, he would surely disappoint her, and, on the other hand, if he were to let it stand . . .

"Jack, let me ask you a favor as a friend. We are friends, arent' we?"

"Sure."

"I want you to take it easy with me. Don't . . . push me. You understand, don't you?"

"Yes."

"And you'll do it—what I ask?"

Suddenly he was seething with frustration. How did it happen that he—and apparently only he—always found himself backed into such corners as this one? He had been taken as a friend so often, confided in, put on his honor. And all for what? Just to keep him at arm's length, under control, to make a eunuch of him. Girls did this instinctively with him. Why? How?

He sighed and said at last, "Sure. Of course I will."

She smiled brightly. "Maybe I'd better be getting back to the dorm. I've got some history to read."

They stood up and started to go. He could forget about the motel tonight. He knew that. Probably forget about it forever with Pat Faraday. Suddenly he thought of Gineen and decided that her way was best. Just do it and don't ask any questions. He wondered if he could persuade Wooley to take him down there again.

Pat paused at the door of the restaurant. "Oh, Jack?"
"Yes?"
"Your story is back there on the table. It wouldn't do to leave it. This *is* a family place, after all."

Wincing with annoyance, he glanced at her and concluded she was trying to be funny. Then he went back to fetch the typescript.

When he came back from classes the next afternoon he found Wooley waiting for him at his door. There was something wrong. Jack could tell it just looking at him. Wooley leaned up against the doorjamb casually enough, but his face wore an expression that Jack had never seen on it before—jaw set, brows knitted in a frown, eyes coldly regarding him.

"Hi, Wooley."

From his hip pocket Wooley produced a sheaf of pages and handed them to Jack. "Here," he said, "you left this in the car." It was the story.

"Oh . . . thanks."

"I read it."

So that was it—of course. Jack waited.

"I thought it was bullshit. Total bullshit. But it told me one thing, old buddy. It sure told me what you think of me and Deke."

"Oh, Wooley, it was just a story."

"More bullshit." Wooley heaved himself up to his full height and glowered down at Jack. "If I wasn't so much bigger than you, I'd kick your ass all over this hall. Better be goddam glad."

With that, he turned and walked away. Jack just watched him go. From that time on Wooley and Deke kept the door to their room closed. Once in a while, when he walked by, Jack could hear those same Hank Williams records playing very softly inside.

*

"*Are you ready, Mrs. Gawlor?*"

"*Yes, well, I guess so.*"

The medical examiner's man looked at her soberly. He was all concern and sympathy. On the telephone he had promised he would make it as easy for her as he could—and she was sure he had tried to do just that. She had sat with him in the little cubicle that did him for an office and listened carefully as he took her step by step through the process. In the course of his five-minute lecture, she found out that Dr. Stern—that was his name—was just out of medical school and had taken this job in the Cook County Coroner's office for just a year in order to decide if he really wanted to be a pathologist, after all. And had he made up his mind? No, not yet. "The trouble with me and pathology," he had told her, "is that I'd really rather work with live people than dead tissue." Under the circumstances, Pat found it difficult to laugh at that, as he clearly had intended her to do. She decided that Dr. Stern wasn't cruel, just young, very young. Whatever he did, he had better put in some work on his bedside manner.

Moments later he had conducted her down the hall to the examination room. Consulting a chart, he had walked to one of the drawers in a corner of the room. There he had stood poised for a moment grasping the handle of the drawer and asked her if she were ready. When she said she was, he seemed to feel obliged to postpone the moment with a caution: "Now, about all we did was clean the blood off, Mrs. Gawlor. Don't expect to recognize him, exactly. If I were you, I'd look at the color and texture of the hair and the shape of the ears and stuff like that."

She nodded, took a deep breath, and said, "All right."

He gave the drawer a tug. Although it was obviously heavy, it slid smoothly and easily on its roller bearings.

Nothing young Dr. Stern could have said would have prepared her for what she saw. She tried to do as he had suggested and did not look directly at the face. Instead she made an effort to focus tightly on the hair—that brown-blond color was right, and it was wavy, almost curly, the way Jack's was. But then, shifting down to the ear nearest her, her gaze tracked over the bloated, broken pulp which was all that was left of the face. It didn't even look human. The features were swollen so that they seemed to merge together into a kind of crudely sculpted papier-mâché mask. But the color was the worst of it all. It was a kind of gray-yellow, like the underbelly of some crawling creature. Ever afterward she would think of it as the color of death.

"Oh, God," she said. She gulped and felt suddenly dizzy and was afraid for a moment that she might faint. She hadn't expected this.

Dr. Stern slammed shut the drawer, took her by the arm, and led her off to a bench against the wall where he sat her down. He hovered over her solicitously for a moment without speaking. Then at last he cleared his throat and said, "Well, what do you think?"

"What do I think? I don't know what to think."

"Can we say it's your ex-husband?"

"You can say it's anybody you want to. Just don't make me look again."

"Okay. But don't worry. It's him." He sounded so positive, almost cheerfully certain.

"You know that?"

"Well, there was wallet identification. The fingerprints checked with army records. And we even ran a dental check."

"If you did all that, then why did I have to come down and look?"

Dr. Stern smiled rather sheepishly, as though he had somehow just been caught out. He made a vague gesture with his hand. "Just a formality," he said.

CHAPTER THREE *1958*

IT TOOK MONTHS for Jack Gawlor to find his way into the little bar across from the Gutleutkaserne in Frankfurt. In the meantime he learned a great deal about the city, the part of it American soldiers saw, that he found somewhat frightening and very dismaying. He tried not to let it show. The approved personal style that spring season, 1958, was college-cool: sit back, sip your beer, and take it all in. Be a camera like Isherwood or a tape recorder like Hemingway—but get it, keep it, and file it away for future reference. Yet what was he to do with such raw material as he had gathered? The crushingly dull bar talk of the whores in crude, accented English, those conversations that began nowhere and circled back to it again—what use would these ever be to him? The pictures he had of GI's in PX mufti wobbling back to the barracks in the dim first daylight at the end of a long night of drinking—weren't these only worth forgetting?

What frightened him was the thought that this might be all he would ever see of Europe—that the year and a half he had here might be squandered in furtive small talk with whores he was too timid to proposition, that he might himself wind up like his roommate, Brownie, quietly and inconspicuously drunk every night by eleven. Herbert Brownell Packard, III, B.A., Amherst 1957, was a fat and charming fellow who drank to excess, though it was never clear why. He did most of his drinking at the bar across the street from the barracks that Jack had taken pains to avoid. It was the name of the place that had kept Jack away—the Chicago Bar. Had he come so far to go home again? But no, it was nothing like home. What it suggested to him was another crass GI joint, even louder, more brawling, and whore-ridden than the rest he had visited.

But what Jack found, when at last Brownie brought him over, was that it was not like that at all. Naturally because there were soldiers in the place, there were also a few whores. But there were fewer of each than Jack would have expected. Dark and dank but only slightly disreputable, the Chicago Bar's greatest charm turned out to be its proprietor. He was a Polish Jew named Jake. Brownie waved him over as soon as the two of them had settled down on barstools and introduced Jack.

"A little empty tonight, Jake," Brownie commented sympathetically.

Jake shrugged. "The end of the month. It could be worse. Just wait until Friday night, and then it is full."

"What happens Friday night?" Jack asked innocently. It was still the end of the month. The soldiers would still be broke.

"Friday night Gertrud comes." Jake fluttered his hands and suddenly waxed poetic. "Then nobody is lonely. Smiles bloom like flowers when Gertrud comes. I want that nobody should be lonely by me. It is a terrible thing to be lonely."

"Terrible," Brownie agreed.

"So. Good. You drink. We talk later." He moved away, the perfect host, to greet newcomers at the door.

"What was that all about?" Jack asked.

"I guess you'll have to come back Friday to find out," said Brownie.

But he proved more communicative on the subject of Jake. His name was Lakov Schtetler. He was from Poland originally and had come to Frankfurt from Lodz by way of Auschwitz—first to Berlin, where he had spent five years bribing his invalid sister out of Warsaw, and then here to Frankfurt, where he put together enough capital to open up this place. The two of them, Jake and his sister, lived across from the Palmengarten, the old Rothschild estate, in a high third-floor apartment from which they could see every corner of the botanical gardens.

"Have you been up there?" Jack asked.

"Oh, no. But I met them once in the park, Jake wheeling his sister, and afterwards he told me all about it." The sister, Leah, was paralyzed from the waist as a result of a beating she had received in the last weeks of the war. She only left the apartment to be pushed through the Palmengarten in her wheelchair and to go with Jake to temple on the high holy days. "It was weird," Brownie said. "She wouldn't talk to me, wouldn't even acknowledge I was there. I asked Jake about that, and he said she wouldn't talk to anybody, only to him sometimes when she would ask him about things before the war. Then I asked him what she did all day, and he said she just sat and thought about the things that had happened to her."

Jack leaned forward, fascinated. This was the closest he had gotten to history since he had come to Frankfurt. "*What* things?" It came out with a kind of urgency that even surprised him.

"That's what I asked him. You know what he said? 'Are you such a little boy you can't imagine for yourself?'" Brownie paused, gulped at his beer, and then went on to say that it was the only time he had ever known Jake to speak with anger or annoyance at anyone. "But we get along," he said. "Jake's a nice man."

Jack did return on Friday night with Brownie, drawn out of curiosity and an attraction to the European *schmerz* that he now imagined pervaded the place. His job as a clerk-typist in the Northern Area Command G-4 office left him plenty of time to fantasize between requisitions, and his mind played over that scene Brownie had described in the Palmengarten and returned again and again to Jake's sister, sitting in the apartment, staring silently out the window, remembering the unimaginable. But was it? Could it be imagined? Was it wise to try? About all he could come up with were images of the naked dead, stacked like cordwood, waiting for burial, and the emaciated living dead walking among them—photographs he had seen in *Life* magazine at the end of the war. Was this the reality of it?

No, there was more, he was sure. Because he wanted somehow to make a record of all this, these speculations and uninformed intuitions, he sat down one night and wrote a long letter about Jake and his sister to Patricia Faraday back in Robinson. She was the only one he knew who wouldn't simply dismiss all this as "morbid." He was proud of that letter. It was the best piece of writing he had done since he left college. He was certainly glad he kept a carbon for himself.

On the appointed night he sat with Brownie at the bar, watching the place fill up, just as Jake had predicted it would. Whoever Gertrud was, she packed them in. There was even a sprinkling of Germans in the crowd, which was much quieter and well-behaved than he had seen before in Frankfurt. Even the GI's were on their best behavior. One of them down the bar asked Jake when Fräulein Trudi would show up, and Jake, the professional host, was affably reassuring. "She is here soon," he said. "Sometimes she keep us waiting but always okay at the end—uh?"

Jack was quite unprepared when Trudi actually appeared a few minutes later. He hardly noticed her—a small, frail-looking woman who moved with a little difficulty from the door to the bar. When she pulled off her coat and handed it over to the barman, Jack saw that she wore a brace on her left leg. Although that leg was a bit thin and wasted, it was straight enough; the right leg, equally straight, was much stronger and was nicely shaped. How old was she? It was hard to tell. As she passed, walking down the bar (throwing her braced leg out and around just slightly every second step), Jack guessed her age as about his own—twenty-three, or perhaps a little older. But in another minute she had reached the little piano platform at the back of the room. Jake appeared then and, without a word, lifted her up to the bench. And as she sat down, a single hard red light flashed over her, and she suddenly looked about ten years older.

"Is that her?" Gawlor asked. "Is that Gertrud?"

"Fräulein Trudi," Brownie answered. "Just listen."

He did listen, and what he heard was less an entertainment

than an education. Hers was a voice quite apart from all others he knew—dry, mordant, filled with ugly wisdom, but never simply sad. It was a voice that came from some narrow room beyond despair, one in which the doors and windows had long before been shut against every sort of intrusion. The songs she sang were the right ones, the only ones, for such a voice. She borrowed extensively from the Dietrich repertoire, as she did from Lenya's, and she also did a few Piaf songs—"Padam-Padam" and "Milord"—faking the French when she had to, her head cocked to one side, mouthing those phrases she could remember in a raw whisper; and failing that, throwing her head back to deliver the rest in an unearthly crooning moan.

Jack was quite overpowered. It wasn't until she finished seven or eight songs and pushed back from the piano in a dramatic attitude of stiff attention that he came to and began to applaud. And when he did, he went on so long and loudly that he extorted an encore from her. She glared out in his general direction, threw out a little arpeggio on the piano, and began to sing "My Man" in English. It was broad and full of burlesque the way she did it, full of dramatic pauses and crescendos, and yet at the same time Jack felt it was very moving. He thought he had never heard it done quite so well.

More applause. But Trudi did not wait to acknowledge it. She rose quickly from her bench and, with two fast, faltering steps, moved to the edge of the platform. For an instant it seemed certain she would fall, but quite suddenly Jake was there, his hands at her waist, lifting her down. Together they moved off to a table in the rear of the room and sat down, both a little wearily, in adjoining chairs.

"Well," said Brownie, a little pompously, "I take it you liked her."

"Liked her? She's great!" Then Jack sucked in his breath with sudden resolution and pushed off the barstool. "And I'm going to tell her so right now." Brownie grabbed at him vainly as he wheeled off and started off for the corner where she sat with Jake.

He presented himself to them and without warning presented an impromptu speech about this marvelous experience he had just had. He would have gone on to compare her with Dietrich and Piaf, but in the middle of it he was suddenly aware that those at the tables around them had suddenly grown quiet and were listening, too. He faltered and paused, and Trudi turned angrily to Jake and began speaking in German, gesturing toward Jack. Then, just as he was about to resume, she looked directly up at him and said in clear, expressive English: "Go away, you Amee asshole."

Suddenly the tables around them exploded in laughter. There was even sporadic applause from a few. It was too much for Jack. He turned and rushed headlong out of the place, barely noting on his way out the sick smile of sympathy that Brownie offered from his barstool.

He got drunk that night and for the first time in Frankfurt he went with a whore. It wasn't as bad as it had been that first time at Ma Hammer's—or rather it was bad enough but in a different way. He couldn't *do* anything. She kept telling him to take it easy, but how *could* he take it easy when the damned thing simply wouldn't work? He had wakened with an erection every day of his life for the past five years. They came upon him unexpectedly in class at college, while riding the elevated downtown, even once when standing inspection for a visiting colonel at Fort Benjamin Harrison. And now—now that he needed it—where had all that God-damned virility gone to? Just disappeared completely.

"You want to rest, Schatzi?"

"No."

"You drink too much. That's all. You sleep a little and you see. It come up for you."

"No," he repeated angrily.

Suddenly he felt sick. He jumped up and ran for the sink in the corner—the toilet was out in the hall, and it was too late for that—and he had time only to fix himself above it, a hand on each side of the basin, before his head ducked and he began retching up the whole miserable night. It all came out, and afterward he wasn't sure whether he felt better or worse for it. He turned on the water and tried ineffectually to push the mess down the little drain.

"I clean up, Schatzi. Don't worry about it."

"I have to go."

"So?"

He staggered to the chair where he had thrown his clothes. He began clumsily trying to pull them on, nearly toppling as he balanced on one foot and then the other to get on his pants. He scooped in his shirt. In his condition the tie was beyond him. He pushed it in his pocket.

"Schätzlein, I got bad news for you."

"Huh?"

"You still gotta pay—hundert mark, like I said."

He plunged into his pocket and pulled out his bills, throwing an assortment down on the floor beside the bed, and then he made for the door.

"You try. I try. Maybe next time it work better."

"Sure. Next time." Somehow he made it down the stairs and to a cabstand not far away on Friedrich Ebert Anlage. He must have gotten past the MP at the barracks gate, but he didn't remember any of that. All he remembered was Brownie saying loudly in his ear, "I tried to stop you, didn't I? I tried to tell you about Trudi."

Jack was in bad shape the next day. He slept the morning through, and only barely made it into the messhall at the end of the chow line at lunchtime. Brownie was nowhere in sight. He had only himself for company as he stared sullenly at the cup of coffee before him feeling guilty about the night before. It wasn't so much that he had at last gone with a whore—paid money for what he more or less felt he had coming to him—but that once committed he had made such a bad job of it. Was this what sex would be for him? Long periods of unfocused desire punctuated only by such minor catastrophes as that one last night? Others seemed to manage. Why not him?

Yet at the same time he found himself recalling in fragmentary detail whatever he could of the experience. There were images of a slender, almost frail body, yet with skin that was white, toneless, and slack. He remembered the pubic patch, black and mysterious. And finally, the smell of her, old sweat mingled with 4711 cologne. It revolted and at the same time fascinated him. Try as he might he couldn't remember her face—or rather when he tried, he kept mismatching Trudi's face, from the Chicago Bar, with the whore's body. It was funny, wasn't it, the tricks that memory played?

When he returned to the room in the barracks, half-intending to lie down and sleep some more, he found Brownie waiting for him, just returned from the PX where he had bought a new album. He heard "That'll Be the Day" blaring out through the open doorway down at the end of the hall. When Jack stepped into the room, Brownie held the album up, *The Buddy Holly Story*, and turned the volume of the phonograph down to where it was just barely possible to communicate over the din.

"He's dead, isn't he?"

"Yeah. A real tragedy. Buddy Holly, Big Bopper, and Richie Valens all down in the same plane. Rock-and-roll may never be the same." This was Brownie's rebellion against Herbert Brownell Packard II. Jack often wished he had found another avenue for it. But then if he had, Jack would have had to buy a phonograph of his own on which to play his Stan Getz and Billie Holiday albums.

"Look," said Brownie at something less than a shout, "don't feel too bad about last night. It's happened before."

"You mean Trudi?"

"Sure. I don't know what her story is, but she hates everybody. Us most of all."

"Us?"

"U-S. Americans."

"Oh. Well, if it's happened before, why does Jake put up with her? Why doesn't he fire her? It must be pretty terrible for business."

"He doesn't want to fire her. Trudi's his girl."

"His girl?" For some reason the idea was particularly hard for Jack to grasp.

"I guess you'd really say she was his mistress."

The word hung awkwardly between them for an instant until Jack picked it up and repeated it. "Mistress?"

"Oh, you know. She comes in a few nights each week, and she sings some songs, but she leaves whenever she wants to.

And—well, Jake takes pretty good care of her, that's all. She's got an apartment in Sachsenhausen, I hear, that Jake paid for, and I don't know if you noticed, but she dresses pretty well. He just takes pretty good care of her, that's all."

"Oh," said Jack, a bit weakly, "I see."

"Besides," Brownie added, "she's not so bad for business. *You'll* be back."

Brownie was right, of course. Jack went back a few nights later in the middle of the week. He neither expected nor wanted Trudi to be there. He wanted to talk to Jake. Before, the proprietor of the Chicago Bar had interested him as a survivor of Auschwitz, a man with an invalid sister and a wartime past. Now he fascinated him as the Jew with the German mistress.

As it happened, that night he went there alone. Brownie was someplace else, and it was just as well. Jake saw Gawlor come in, and came over quickly to the bar where he was sitting. He was the very picture of humility as he stood there, abject, downcast, his hands clasped before him in an attitude of penance. "I must speak with you," he said in a voice so quiet it was barely audible.

"Sure," Jack said. "Certainly." How could he refuse him?

"Please," Jake said, stretching out a stubby arm toward a nearby table, "we sit over here. I will talk to you in private."

He was making a bigger thing of it than Jack wanted him to. Once at the table, he began by begging his pardon for the "sad thing" that happened the other night. He said he wanted everyone to be happy in his place and that when such sad things happened, it made him, personally, feel very bad. (This Jack could believe.) And it also made Fräulein Gertrud equally unhappy. (Of this he was not quite so sure.) He must have read the disbelief on Jack's face, for he was quick to reassure him: "Oh yes, it is true. I am a very dear friend of this lady, and she is very sad about this thing. She cry about it. You must believe me." And then he began suddenly to stammer, as though he had said something that he shouldn't have.

So Jack believed him, more or less, listening as Jake told him about "this lady" and instructed him in the ways of artistic natures such as hers. He was to understand that such people are not like others. They are so sensitive, so subtly attuned to the atmosphere in which they create their art that when there is some change—any change—it frightens them, disturbs them, makes them strike out like some wild beast in the jungle.

Jack thought that over and said, "She didn't seem frightened to me."

A slight smile played on his lips. "Well, maybe you are right this time. But still, she is *bothered* by you."

"By me?"

"*Ja,* sure. You are too *nice* to her. She does not understand that, and so—" He made a quick motion with his hand in imitation of a cat striking out with its paw. "You see?"

Jack laughed very hard then, unable to help himself. "Yes," he said at last, "I guess I do."

They were good friends after that. Jack came and went, not just another patron but one especially favored, a friend of Jake's. The two of them shared Trudi like a secret, one that is hinted at, touched upon, yet never quite articulated. That, however, did not prevent Jack from thinking about Jake and Trudi. He thought about them a lot, too much really. Did she take off the brace to make love, or simply throw that dead leg off to one side, rigid in its steel frame? What would it be like to feel the coldness of the thing against your thigh?

One night, very late, when there were not many left in the place, Jake told him that he would have married Trudi long ago if it were not "for the conditions of my life."

"What do you mean?" Jack asked him. "What's keeping you from marrying her?" It was unkind to be so blunt. He regretted it immediately.

"I have a sister," Jake explained, mentioning her to him for the first time. "She is by me—and sick, you understand. How can I marry while my sister is by me? These two cannot live in the same house, believe me. They are too much alike. Both know too much hate. Both have too much to remember."

Jack accepted that. He decided that yes, Jake would have married his Fräulein Gertrud if things were only different. His intentions were honorable. There seemed to be something profoundly familial about the man. You could see it in the way he mixed with the patrons. He loved them all—not perhaps as sons, but as nephews in some nepotistic, incestuous oriental court—he, the chamberlain, and Trudi, the empress.

She reigned over them all as a sort of lurking presence. She was only there *physically* about three nights out of seven, and yet in a way the place was more hers than it was Jake's. It was most alive when she was present, yet quieter and better-behaved. There was a subtle and intricate protocol governing conduct when she was around. It was, for instance, wrong to notice her when she entered the room: the proper attitude was to look and then look casually away. All this was in deference to her brace. When she ended her set, it was then time for applause—though again, not too much, for that displeased her.

All this annoyed Jack a little. He resented the rules and the royal treatment she received—and yet he kept coming back. Why? If nothing more, to hear her sing, for she was very good at that. One night, apparently as a whim, she did all her songs in English. And toward the end of the evening it seemed to Jack that she began to sound a little like Gertrude Niesen, doing "I'll Be Seeing You" in that plaintive voice of hers. He mentioned it to Brownie, sitting beside him, who, in answer, just stared at him blankly. Jack decided that a rock-and-roll connoisseur like Brownie probably had no idea who Gertrude Niesen was. Probably nobody else in the place did, either.

And he kept coming back because of Jake, who had singled Jack out especially to be his friend. They talked at length when the place was empty and business was slow. Little by little, Jake told Jack everything about his sister that Brownie already told him—though not much more. The holy days were especially important to her, and although they weren't to him—he had spent one whole evening railing at the God of his fathers who would let such things as Jake had seen happen—he was obliged to take her to and from the temple and sit with her through the services, for she could never have managed by herself.

Nevertheless he kept the Chicago Bar open. To do any differently would not only be hypocritical, he declared, it would also be bad for business. That was how it happened that just before Rosh Hashanah, he took Jack aside one evening and told him that he wouldn't be around for a few days and why. The bartender would have no trouble during the week, and for the weekend, Jake had taken on an assistant to help out. All this had been arranged already. There were, however, a few more details to be attended to. He said he wanted Jack to take care of Trudi—sit with her, lift her up to the stage and down, and then take her home in a taxi at the end of the evening.

"But, Jake," he said, "I don't even know her." He hadn't said a word to her since that awful night a few months ago.

Jake nodded vigorously. "*Ja,* sure, that's right. But *I* know you. You are *my* friend. That is why I want you to take care of her on Friday night. All you do is be nice and take her home in a taxicab when she is through."

"But—"

"Please give me no arguments. Arguments I get plenty of from other people. From you I want some sense." Jake had a strange expression in his eyes. To Jack he seemed almost too serious about it. "Do this for me."

And so Jack shrugged his assent and agreed to fill in for Jake the next Friday. He decided that Jake lived in mortal terror of being cuckolded. Could he trust no one else? In a way, Jack was flattered by that, but it made him uneasy, too. He didn't like being put on his honor.

When Fräulein Trudi came in that Friday night, Jack was waiting in his usual place at the bar. She marched past him without a glance, carefully maintaining her haughty air. But when she came close to the platform Jack suddenly panicked, realizing that Jake would have been there to lift her up. He started toward her then, as did three or four others from different points in the room. But she made it on her own, reaching up with her single strong leg and then pulling the braced leg recklessly after it. She teetered for one perilous moment on the edge of the platform, and then recovered, turning to throw an evil glance directly across the room at Jack.

She sat down at the piano and opened her set with "My Man," her put-down song. It was done as before, with all the same pauses and crescendos, and yet somehow she did it even more broadly and viciously than she had that first night. After that, a standard set for her—a little Kurt Weill, some Cole Porter, and some Piaf. But this time, when she finished, Gawlor was right there, ready to lift her down as the applause rang lightly around them. Trudi was standing before him on the platform, yet she was so short that her eyes were almost on a level with his. He thought for a moment that she meant to push him aside and jump down. But she stepped forward quickly and allowed herself to be lifted. She was very light. For no good reason it occurred to Jack that the brace she wore was very likely as heavy as the leg it supported.

"You are Yakov's friend?" Her tone was flat but with just an edge of sarcasm to it, as though it amused her to think that Jake might have a friend.

Jack nodded quite seriously and stepped aside so that she might make her way to the table. "He asked me to—"

"I know all that," she interrupted sharply. "Here. Hold the chair for me and then sit down yourself. We will talk. Yakov always talks to me, so now you talk to me, too." When she was settled, she sent Jack off to get her a drink, a Steinhäger. "Don't worry," she called after him, "you don't buy my drinks. I *earn* my drinks here."

Jack did not object when the bartender poured out an extra for him, nor did he make any gesture toward paying for it. He felt as though he were earning his drinks that night, too.

Back at the table she called out "Zum Wohl!" and waved her glass to the room at large before tossing down about half of it. At the same time Jack began sipping his.

Trudi leaned over toward him then, as though conspiring.

"Well," she said in her hard little whisper, "how you like my singing now?"

Jack numbled something about her sounding pretty good to him.

She laughed. "I remember one time you try to say something better than that. Only I don't let you. I be mean to you that night. Very often I be mean." She shook her hair lightly, a gesture of gaiety, he supposed. As Jack looked around him, suddenly everyone in the place seemed to have just looked the other way. They had all been staring, and he didn't like that. "You think now I sound like Dietrich? Like Piaf?" She was looking at him obliquely from the corner of her eyes. He found it was hard to return the look.

"No," he said. "You sing some of their sings, but you sing them your own way. You sing like yourself."

She smiled scornfully. "That is good only if I like to be myself. Sometimes I don't."

But then Jack remembered Gertrude Niesen. "Once, not so long ago, you sounded to me like somebody else, another singer. It was the other night when you sang everything in English. You remember?"

"I remember. Who do I sound like then?"

And then he told her about Gertrude Niesen—who she was, the kind of songs she used to sing, and tried quite unsuccessfully to describe the particular plaintive quality of her voice. Throughout all this, Trudi gave him all her attention. Her suspicion softened to curiosity, and then deepened into wonder. It occurred to Jack that probably nobody had ever talked to her seriously about her singing before. She was listening like a child. She looked almost pretty to him.

When he had finished his little recital, she nodded her appreciation and asked, "Why don't I hear about this other Gertrude now? What happen to her?"

"I don't know," he said. "I think she's dead."

And then she was back in character, cackling in nasty amusement at that. "First you tell me I sing like somebody, then you tell me she is dead. You think that's nice to hear?" She shoved her empty glass toward him. "Here," she said, "get me another drink. Also a cigarette."

He did as he was told, and when he returned she gestured impatiently for the drink, took it, and threw it down. "Please," she said, "I'm thirsty." She reached across and took the half-filled glass from in front of him. "I drink too much. Smoke, too." He lit the cigarette for her. "But it make no difference. Pretty soon I be dead like the other Gertrude, the one who sing like me." She thought about that a moment, then shuddered slightly. "When I be dead, his sister, she will be glad. You know Yakov has a sister?"

Jack nodded, looking around him, wishing miserably that she would keep her voice down.

She resumed, much louder than before: "The sister know about me, and I know about her." Leaning close to him, she stared at Jack so intently for a moment that he knew she was not drunk. And then at last she did drop her voice. "She say I been whore. So what? Sure I been whore. How she thinks I meet her brother?"

A strange sort of anger seemed to be building inside her. Jack was afraid she would soon begin shouting again. He wondered if it might not be best to try to get her to leave. "Look," he said in a whisper, "wouldn't it be a good idea to go home now?"

Then he became aware of something hard and cold against his leg. The brace. She smiled at him suddenly—or at least the corners of her mouth turned up—and she leaned forward and said, "Okay. I don't sing no more now. Not no more tonight. If you want to take me home, I been ready to go. Yakov said you take care of me. You show me you can take care of me better than him."

This wasn't turning out at all as Jack had expected. He had hoped to be able to simply put her in a taxi and send her away. He would tell Jake something about her getting ill and then let the two of them sort it out between them. Besides, there were other nights when she had sung only one set. Why not tonight?

"Well, I'll take you to a taxi, anyway."

"Ha!"

She pushed back noisily from the table, as though to signal to all around her that she was on her way out. Jack would gladly have crawled out if he could only have hidden from their eyes.

"Come on," she snarled. She moved out in the rapid, leg-throwing hop that was so peculiarly her own, and Jack —embarrassed, unhappy, miserable—followed along close behind.

At the door he saw that there were cabs lined up, as there usually were, at the Gutleutkaserne gate. He waved one over and in one awful moment tried to compose the speech he would make to send her on her way as he held the cab door open. No speech was made. As the taxi pulled up, she simply looked at him coldly and said, "Get in." And he got in.

She gave the driver an address, and he pulled away. She glanced over at Jack. "You got a cigarette by you?"

"No, I . . . I just smoked my last one back there."

"That's okay. We be there soon. I got plenty by my place." They drove across the bridge, over the Main, to Sachsenhausen. Jack had heard that this bridge used to be called the Hermann Goering Bridge, named after the Reischsmarschall. They didn't call it that anymore.

"Yakov was the big Amee pimp in Berlin," she said in a quiet, conversational tone. "I been his cocksucker. He send me around to all the Amees to suck their cocks. They like that. Amees don't know they got them till they have them sucked." Jack found himself nodding at that as though she had just stated an interesting political opinion. What, he wondered, was the matter with him, anyway? What was he *doing* here?

"A real German man," she resumed, "he don't like that. Afraid somebody bite it off." She laughed sharply, as though remembering something specific. "You afraid I bite it off?"

"I, well . . ."

"You afraid." She sat out the next few minutes quietly until at last the driver pulled up before a doorway on a dark street.

"Maybe . . ." He cleared his throat. "Maybe I'd better leave you here."

"No," she said quietly. "Upstairs." He paid the driver and

followed her through the doorway and slowly up the stairs.

Quite simply, he was afraid. He had no precise idea what lay ahead of him. Somehow he feared the worst without knowing what the worst might be. Was this what it meant to be a man? To carry it off with a swagger and a joke? If it was, then it would never work for him, for he was certain that he would always be afraid.

She unlocked the door. Although he was cold sober—what had he drunk? half a Steinhäger?—he had no clear and continuous memory of what followed. There was a dreamlike quality to it all, a sense that what was happening was not really happening to him but rather to some third party very much like himself, a young man of the same age and general description who had lain down on a bed beside a human-shaped, white-skinned member of the wolf family. *Lupus horribilis*. Would he survive her? He wasn't sure.

The problem he had this time was not the same one he had had before. In a way, there was no problem at all, for his member stayed up and up and up through all manner of twisting and turning, and for nearly an hour of shuffling and panting. Toward the end of it, he found the perspiration dripping off his body and onto hers, and he looked down into her face and all he could see, somehow, was her open mouth, her thin lips pulled back and her sharp teeth exposed. It was the mouth of an animal, a wolf. He was still afraid of her.

It was only then that he became aware for the first time of the coldness of the steel brace pressed against the outside of his right knee. She had better control over the leg than he would have supposed. They had shifted and turned a number of times, and he had forgotten about the brace—forgotten? put it out of his mind—until this moment. It was as though she had touched him with it to remind him of it. Or perhaps to get his attention.

She groaned slightly, and then in a tone that was at once muffled and husky yet peculiarly distinct, she said, "Off." Just that. It was the first word she had spoken since they had left the taxi. He withdrew from her and toppled off to one side. They lay side by side for minutes, saying nothing. Their breathing eased. He glanced cautiously at her and found her staring at him.

"You like all the rest," she said. "All the Amees need a cocksucker to make them come." She grabbed him roughly, and he twitched involuntarily. She laughed and squeezed him a little.

"Don't," he said. "Please."

She laughed again. "It was a long time before Yakov find out I could make money with my mouth some other way. You like me to sing?"

"Now?"

"Sure, now. What you like to hear?"

"I—I don't know."

"Okay, Amee. I sing a song to you. My own song. You never hear this one before, but you hum with me if you want to. You know how to hum?"

"Yes."

She nodded, satisfied, and slowly slid down his body until he lost sight of her. He felt the not-quite-unexpected sensation of moisture on the head of his penis, yet it was a more delicate touch than ever he would have supposed that it would be. A mere grazing, and then another, and then another, and then a sudden barrage of soft fluttering touches. Was it what he had expected? No, he had seen those teeth, that wolflike maw of hers, and what she was doing to him had nothing to do with that. This was different—different from anything else he had known before.

When he left, there was no going back, no returning to Trudi or to Jake at the Chicago Bar. He knew that. A kind of knowledge had been communicated to him. He knew something more now than he did before—more, really, than he wanted to know, more than he was prepared to deal with. Walking through the empty streets of Sachsenhausen, he tried to think all this through and couldn't. Maybe tomorrow he would have some perspective on all of it, or next week, or next month. But right now he was confused and was still a little afraid.

Tomorrow he would write Pat Faraday a long letter. He

couldn't tell her any of this in specific detail, of course, but if he found some way to discuss it in, well, philosophical terms, then she might understand. More important, he might understand, too.

As it turned out, Jack never wrote that letter. Instead, the next morning he went to work, just about as he always had at the Northern Area Command Office in the I. G. Farben Building, only to be summoned down after an hour to the Red Cross office and informed that his father had died. Coronary. It was all just as sudden as that. The gray-uniformed functionary ushered him brisky into his cubicle, sat him down at the desk, and briskly told him the news. "You'll want a leave, of course," he added.
"I—yes, I guess so. Sure." Jack wasn't certain how he was supposed to react. Obviously he wasn't supposed to cry. That was okay with him. He didn't feel like crying.
"Unfortunately, you don't qualify for an emergency leave. If your father were seriously ill or dying . . . You understand, of course."
"Well, no, not exactly."
The man seemed a little embarrassed at having to go into the details. He cleared his throat nervously. "It's like this. Dying is an emergency. Death isn't."
"Oh."
The Red Cross man then offered him a wan smile. "You do qualify for compassionate leave, though."
And so it was that a week later Jack found himself on a troop ship in the middle of the Atlantic, steaming slowly in the direction of America. Although he wouldn't have admitted it to anyone else at the time, and bitterly resented not being whisked off by airplane as he would otherwise have been, Jack gradually came to accept the distinction made by the army as legitimate: Death was no emergency but a condition, a state, something you eventually got used to. And he had to admit, too, that it wouldn't be so terribly difficult getting used to his father being gone, for the man had occupied so small a space for so long. And that angina attack just before Jack went into the army had served as

fair warning, after all, that his father wouldn't be around forever. Jack supposed he would miss him most as a kind of buffer, a bit of necessary insulation between Jack and his mother.

He thought about that as he stood one day with a vast company of returning soldiers along the rail watching the dolphins jump along about two hundred feet to starboard. You either played poker or you watched the dolphins. The thought of going back to his mother didn't cheer him much. Of course he wouldn't necessarily be living at home once he got out of the army in a year's time. But even so . . .

At that moment, as his eyes wandered off over the monotonous Atlantic horizon, Jack began to think seriously for the first time about getting married. To Pat Faraday, of course. He could talk to her, couldn't he? And wasn't that what was wrong with most marriages today—that people couldn't talk to one another? That's what the magazines all said. He hung over the rail, thinking it over—not so much weighing the pros and cons as trying it on for size. Did it fit? Was there some sense to it? He fantasized a bit, bringing Pat into domestic focus, trying as best he could to picture himself in such a situation with her. It came, all right. And how did it go? Books and records in the evening, discussions at the dinner table—all this together with a sneak preview of the sexual routine he visualized for their future. Yes, what would that be like? Not so much one glorious orgasm after the next as something comfortable and steady. He thought of Trudi and the episode just behind him in Frankfurt, and he admitted to himself the value of the kind of life he saw with Pat.

The idea took hold of him during the next few days. The slow, almost somnambulistic pace of life aboard the troop ship seemed to encourage reveries of this kind. And Jack's response to the overwhelmingly masculine environment in which he was temporarily trapped was to concentrate on this hypothetical relationship with Pat, to daydream it to life, to fantasize it to fruition.

By the time he disembarked in Brooklyn, he had himself convinced: "What-if" had become "when." He stood in line that night at Fort Hamilton with a great handful of change in his pocket, waiting for a telephone. And as he waited, he rehearsed the conversation that was to follow—Pat's side, as well. Yet, as things will happen, when at last he reached the phone and got through to her in Robinson, Illinois, nothing came out quite as he intended, neither her part nor his.

He began, of course, by telling her how it was he happened to be back—about his father's death and so on. He wanted to get through that part as quickly as possible. But no—Pat wanted to talk about it.

"Oh, Jack, how?"

"Heart attack. It . . . it wasn't totally unexpected. He'd had one a year ago. You remember? I wrote you about it."

"Yes, I remember." She sighed audibly into the receiver, "You must feel just terrible. I know how I'd feel if it were my father. How's your mother taking it?"

"Oh, pretty well, I guess. I got a letter from her just before I left with all the details. The funeral and so on."

"But you haven't called her yet?"

This was it, he told himself. He was on his own from here on out. "Uh, no," he said. "I wanted to talk to you first."

"You did? What about?"

"Look, I know this might not be the greatest way to discuss this—over the phone, I mean—but I wanted to give you some time to think this over. I'd like to come down to visit you there in Robinson—I mean, if it's okay."

"Well . . . sure." She sounded puzzled. "It's okay."

He plunged ahead: "So we can talk about getting married."

"Oh, Jack . . ."

He waited almost patiently, but she said nothing more. Oh, Jack? What was that supposed to mean? Finally he spoke up, merely prompting her: "Yes?"

"Well, I'm just overwhelmed."

He laughed nervously. "You mean overwhelmed in a good way or a bad way?"

"Oh, good. Yes, believe me. Good!"

They left it at that. Jack explained he would be back for a couple of weeks and then would return to Germany. They agreed that he would come down to visit and when. And at last he hung up, hoping the thing had somehow got itself said, realizing that now it had all suddenly become quite important to him.

The old neighborhood looked good to him. He hadn't supposed that a year away would make much difference in how he felt about his corner of Chicago—but it did. He found himself straining to remember what lay around each corner as he turned it, noting each little change in the commercial facade—a new Japanese restaurant opened here, a Plymouth agency switched to Buick there. It was a strange feeling for Jack. Like it or not, this was home.

As he turned on to Foster Avenue, he saw that the Greek candy shop was gone, the one where he had stood all those years at the magazine rack sneaking looks at the girlie books—*Wink, Titter, Beauty Parade,* and all the rest. *Sic transit gloria mundi*—he had just had that one translated for him by an ex–Latin major in his office at the Farben Building.

And then, at Foster and Glenwood, he pulled up for a red light and glanced out at the bus stop and saw somebody he recognized—a round, heavier-than-plump female figure topped by an amiable, big-nosed face peering anxiously up Foster, looking for a bus. It was Gus Karras's kid sister, Stella, no mistaking her. He honked lightly on the horn to catch her attention and waved her over. She looked curiously in the open window.

"Jack! Are you out of the army or what?"

"Just on leave. My father died. Hop in. I'll take you downtown if that's where you're headed."

She opened the door and settled in with surprising nimbleness. Jack guessed she must weigh well over two hundred—and not much over five feet tall. He had always liked her, though, because she seemed to look up to him—and she had the prettiest eyes. Maybe she had a crush on him or something.

"I knew about your father. My mother saw it in the paper. She always reads the obituaries."

"Parents do that. I guess it's the age." He looked at her and decided he ought to say something on the occasion. "I wasn't here when he died or for the funeral or anything—so it's not like he's dead, just not around, you know?"

"You get used to stuff like that," Stella said almost coldly. "It doesn't take long." He remembered then that her own father was dead. About three years ago. He had heard that from Gus one night when they chanced to meet outside the Uptown theater.

Stella glanced back and saw Jack's suitcase in the rear seat. "Where are you going?" she asked. "Back to Germany or something?"

"Well, yeah, eventually. But not right now," he explained. "I'm on my way down to Robinson, Illinois."

"*Robinson?* What's down there?"

"A girl named Pat Faraday."

"Oh."

Jack threw Stella a grin and decided to tell her about it. "I'm trying to talk her into getting married."

He felt her eyes—those pretty eyes—upon him, so much more intense than he had expected. He kept his own on the road ahead. "Well," she said, after a moment's delay, "you shouldn't have any difficulty at all."

"Well . . . thanks."

"Only—Jack?"

"Yes?"

"Are you sure you really want to? You used to talk about writing a lot. To my brother. I remember listening one night on the front porch. I thought the only thing boys ever talked about was football."

There was such intensity in her voice. Jack didn't know quite how to respond. Finally: "You . . . you remember that, huh? That's . . . nice." It was all he could think of to say.

"Of course I remember. You were going to get all this terrific experience and write all these terrific books."

"Well, I'll still write them."

"Not if you get married." She sounded so certain. It annoyed Jack, made him almost angry. He couldn't understand.

What had he done to rate this? He had the feeling that without intending to, without even knowing quite how, he had managed to betray this big-nosed fat girl sitting beside him here in the car. "You'd better let me off at the next corner," she said with some finality.

*

When Klezek at last came in, Melaniphy waved him over. He had been downtown to the lab to pick up the report on the clothes that Gawlor and the kid had been wearing. The team that had gone over the room had turned up nothing of interest except, under the bed, a used tampon. It also turned out there was menstrual blood on the sheets. Which didn't really lead anywhere but made you wonder.

"You want to see the report, sergeant?"

Melaniphy shrugged. "No, just tell me what they turned up. Anything on the kid?"

"Nothing much. Levi's, Sears shirt and underpants. No keys, no wallet, a five-dollar bill and thirty-five cents in change in his pocket, and a pack of Wint-o-Green Lifesavers."

"Come on. I could have told them that much just going through the clothes. Didn't the lab come up with **anything?**"

"Well, yeah. They said the pants were dirty."

"Terrific. They didn't look so clean to me, either."

"No, what I mean is, they said there was soil ground into the fabric on the knees and along one of the legs. But it wasn't from around here—kind of a red clay. They said the kid was probably from someplace down south."

Melaniphy nodded. It seemed a good bet. All you had to do was check out the Trailways depot on Randolph, and you'd spot a dozen a day coming in just like that kid with the belt around his neck. Runaways. No money. No future. They might wind up just the way he did.

He studied Klezek and wondered if such thoughts ever occurred to him. Somehow he doubted it. At thirty, Klezek was still unmarried and was apparently satisfied to remain that way. He was a smart young guy and a good detective who had already picked up two departmental citations. He was a cinch to make sergeant in a year or two. The only fault that Melaniphy found with him was personal: Klezek never dug beneath the surface, never once seemed to trouble himself about the right and wrong, the good and evil, of what he saw and touched. He was fairly mechanical about what he did, and mechanically he was perfect. In a way, Melaniphy envied him.

"What about the medical report on the kid?" Melaniphy asked.

"About what you'd expert. Death by strangulation. Perforated rectum."

"Jesus. We're pretty casual about it, aren't we?"

"Why not? It's all over for him, anyway. The way it looks to me, he's better off dead."

Melaniphy studied Klezek for a moment and finally shrugged. "Maybe he is. Who knows?"

And maybe he was.

CHAPTER FOUR *1962*

JACK LOOKED AROUND and found his daughter back at the water fountain for the fourth time. She was crouched in a giggle with a finger over the spout squeezing out a jet of water in a long arc. "*Carol!*" he shouted. But she continued to giggle and squirt. He ran over and jerked her away from the fountain, then stood her firmly in the sand six angry steps away. Of course she started to cry immediately.

"Carol, will you *please* stop that? What's the matter with you, anyway? I told you the last time you did that to *leave the fountain alone*. Now, why don't you mind Daddy?" How do you talk to a three-year-old kid, anyway?

In answer, her mouth puckered and from it suddenly exploded a series of wails, each louder than the last. He looked around him miserably. It seemed that the hostile eyes of every mother and baby-sitter in the playground were focused precisely on him. He knelt and pulled out his handkerchief and waved it in exasperation at his daughter, hoping to distract her. A man always seems such a bully with a little girl. He asked himself why. It wasn't at all like that with a boy, was it?

"Carol, please," he said, "*please* stop crying." At last the wails subsided, and he held up the handkerchief to her face. "Here. Blow your nose." She made a production of it, as she did most things, trumpeting forth three long blasts that seemed almost comically loud coming from such a little girl.

"Are you all right now?" he asked her.

"I think so. Daddy"—she threw her arms around his neck—"Daddy, can I have a drink of water?"

He lifted her up and brought the red-eyed, tear-stained

face up close to his own. "Honey, how many drinks of water have you had in the last ten minutes?"

"I don't know," she said reasonably. "I can't count."

"Well, you've had four, Carol."

"Is that a lot?"

"Yes," he said in a deep, serious voice, "that's a lot. Now, I don't mind how many times you go to the fountain, if you'd just *drink* the water instead of squirting it all over every place."

"But can I have just one more *real* drink?"

"All right, all right." Beaten, Jack hauled his daughter back to the fountain and bent down with her so that she might drink. Then, after she had gulped and glugged to her satisfaction, he pulled her up to him and wiped her face with his handkerchief, the same one with which she had blown her nose a moment before. "That should hold you for a while, shouldn't it?"

She nodded very seriously. "Yes, Daddy. Thank you very much for letting me have a drink of water."

Jack was secretly amused at that. She could be quite the little lady when it suited her. "Would you like to go back and play on the swing some more, Carol?"

She shook her head. "Could we go back and see Mama now?"

Jack sighed. He knew that it was quite natural for a three-year-old girl to show some preference for her mother, but all the same, it was annoying to be cast constantly in the supporting role. At times—times like today—he felt like nothing more or less than a stand-in for Pat. "No, honey," he said. "Mama won't be back from the doctor's for at least another half-hour, so let's just stay here and have a good time until then."

"Is that a *long* time?"

"No, not so long."

"Okay." She thought about that a moment. "Let's go down to the lake."

"All right, then, let's do that, honey."

Jack slid her down his leg to the ground and took her hand. Together they started off through the sand, by the swings and the slide, around whole packs of screaming, jumping, brown-bodied little animals, and on past their huddling female attendants. It was early September, the Saturday before Labor Day. Of course it was warm, but there was a whisper of fall in the cool breeze that blew unsteadily from the west. Fall, thought Jack, that was something to look forward to, wasn't it? For one thing, it would mean an end to this damned, insufferable heat. For another, there was the baby—due, the doctor had assured them, on September 7. How could he be so damned sure about the date? Doctors seemed to take a lot upon themselves—and obstetricians most of all. But it didn't matter. What interested Jack most about the new baby was not the date of arrival but rather its sex. He frankly hoped it would be a boy. Somehow he always felt at a loss with Carol, never knowing quite what to say or do to please her, always bringing tears and anguished appeals when he so much as raised his voice to her. Her mother was a little like that, too. Pat turned out to be made of much softer stuff than he had supposed. He had found it was impossible to disagree with her emphatically even on a matter of taste without risking tears. She seemed to take everything so personally. Maybe all women were like that. He didn't know.

Touhy Beach was public, just about as public as it could be. As Jack led Carol down to the lake, they threaded their way through sprawling tangles of bodies, male and female, big and little, and detoured around ramparts of sand thrown up by busy children. At the water's edge it was quiet and calm. The only ripples in the water's surface were made by a gang of children about Carol's age splashing knee-deep close to the shore.

"Would you like to go in the water?" he asked her.

"Yes. I want to."

"Well, sit down here and I'll take off your shoes." Without a word, she dropped down on the sand and Jack knelt and pulled the sneakers from her feet. "Now, don't go out any farther than those boys and girls right there. I'll stand right here and watch you."

"Okay, Daddy." Carol ran off into the water, slapping the ripples as she went, making ripples of her own.

He looked up and down the beach. The strip of brown sand stretched about half a mile in either direction. There must have been over a thousand people there, stretched out, milling, jumping, and running, into distant black dots. Too many people, Jack thought. Then he thought of the baby due within the week, and he decided there was room for at least one more in the world, especially if the baby turned out to be a boy.

Carol had caught them by surprise. They were living on the economy in a one-room-share-the-kitchen apartment on Schwindstrasse in Frankfurt when Pat got sick the second week in December. It being late fall and the weather especially foul, they told themselves she had a light case of flu—no fever, just vomiting and a general queasiness. She dragged herself around the little place for a few days, loudly uncomplaining, until the landlady, Frau Bernhard, took her aside and suggested in her comical half-English, half-German patois that Pat's morning malady might be of quite another kind. When a trip to the army doctor confirmed Frau B's diagnosis, both Jack and Pat found themselves a little overwhelmed. It wasn't the immediate financial burden of a child that frightened them. Pat had wangled a job as a GS-3 secretary with an Army Intelligence outfit in the I. G. Farben Building, they received modest monthly checks from Robinson, Illinois, and in a pinch they knew they could probably even get along on the army dependents' allowance, as so many others did.

No, what intimidated them both and plunged Jack into a secret bout of despondency was the thought that this was to be the end of all the plans they had made for after the army. They had planned to stay over in Europe—in London or Paris, or maybe even Spain, where it was cheaper—getting by somehow as Americans did then while they conscientiously pursued their joint vocation and simply wrote. With that in mind, they had been banking the checks from Robinson and even putting away some of Pat's pay. Now, it seemed, all that was out of the question. If only they had been a *little* more careful!

Carol's arrival cheered them both. Even Jack was ready to view the future more optimistically in the moments when he watched Pat feeding her, and afterward walked around with her on his shoulder coaxing a burp from her, and especially when the two would then hover over the crib, proudly fascinated at what they had made together. These feelings, old enough in themselves but altogether new to Jack, sustained him on the return to Chicago. They made it possible for him to rush out immediately and land a reasonably well-paying job writing copy squibs at a catalogue house. They had even allowed him to make the switch, a year later, to a Michigan Avenue advertising agency, when for years he had made bad jokes about aspiring novelists who wound up writing headache-remedy commercials at ad agencies.

It was funny, though, as Carol became less a baby and more a little girl, he gradually lost contact with her and even felt in a peculiar way threatened by her. Women seemed to rule his life. His responsibility to Pat had increased incalculably now that she was not just his wife but also the mother of his child. Carol took more time and attention than he was often willing to give her—especially now with Pat pregnant. And, of course, the required weekly visits to his mother exacted a toll from him in annoyance and suppressed anger that he found increasingly hard to pay. He felt himself changing. He saw himself bumbling along in this same way, Dagwood-fashion, for the rest of his life—and he hated it.

"Watch me, Daddy! Watch me!" It was Carol squealing at him. He stepped forward and gave her a wave, then she performed some bit of nonsense that involved kicking her legs high in the air and bringing them down—splash-splash-splash—again and again. Some of the kids around her moved away. A few splashed back.

"Take it easy, Carol."

"Okay."

She settled down, and Jack was glad of it. The last thing

in the world he wanted was for her to get in a fight with one of those kids. He had had to separate her a couple of times from adversaries in the playground. There were recriminations from the mothers and screams from the kids, altogether a bad scene. It was funny. She was quite the little lady, but not so much that she wouldn't kick and fight with the boys when she felt threatened, or even greatly displeased.

He looked idly around him at the blankets, piled clothes, and sprawled forms ranged along the water's edge. It was the same at every beach, he supposed—children and old people were everywhere. It was as though everyone between the ages of twenty and sixty were barred from public beaches. He felt like an intruder—and an overdressed intruder at that.

Jack looked back to locate Carol in the melee of splashing children. As he did, he became aware of the drone of music behind him. Something in the constant and familiar sound of it told him that he had been hearing it for quite some time without really listening. It sounded like the Coasters and some hit of a few years back that he couldn't quite remember. He turned around and saw a girl of about high-school age dancing to the tune that whined out from a miniature portable radio at one corner of the blanket. The girl hardly moved her feet at all. Her dance was an easy sway to the heavy rhythm, a rough bargain struck between her soft body and the jagged pounding of the music. Her arms pumped vigorously, and her hands fluttered in graceful embellishment. Somehow her hands fascinated him. Jack guessed her to be about sixteen—not full-grown but certainly no longer a child. She was blonde like Carol, and even in her tight black bikini, she looked a little like he imagined his daughter would look when she was that same age.

At opposite corners of the blanket, swaying and clapping hands in rough approximation of the rhythm, sat two boys of about the same age or maybe a little older. They were thin, crooked, and acne-faced. Jack looked away quickly when he realized one of them was watching him intently. There was something bold in that look, as though he were being sized up, evaluated.

He looked for Carol in the water and found her watching

him. When their eyes met, she waved, laughed, and went back to her splashing game, knees up and full of life. Well, he thought, let her splash. All that vigor comforted him somehow.

Behind him the radio droned on. Then suddenly he heard a laugh. He was sure it was the dancing girl, and he almost turned to look, but he caught himself just in time. What was she doing with boys like that, anyway? You could tell they were tough kids, punks with greasy hair and dirty minds. What was it that made kids like that? Broken homes or something, he supposed. Or maybe it was just in the air, like nuclear fallout. Well, things might get better before Carol grew to be sixteen. With a man like Kennedy in the White House, you had the idea that somehow everything was going to get better. But he caught himself: that was pretty naïve, wasn't it?

In spite of his intentions, he turned around for another look. He decided that what really fascinated him about the girl on the blanket was her resemblance to Carol. Yes, surely that was it. As he saw her now—head bent and her face slightly averted as she talked to one of the boys (where was the other one?)—it seemed almost as though he were looking at his own daughter, as she had been a few minutes before, digging intently in the playground sand. The hair and those soft, round cheeks, the serious expression—why, she was Carol all over again, older, almost a woman. But was this how his daughter would wind up? Bouncing around on a beach blanket with a couple of punks? Not if Jack had anything to say about it.

Turning away, he found himself looking once again into the thin, cracked face of the boy missing from the blanket, the one who had smirked at him before. The kid was no more than six feet away and was looking directly at him. His face twisted into a smile, and he nodded in God only knew what secret understanding.

Burning with something like embarrassment, Jack turned away and took a step or two toward the lake. He called for Carol to come in.

Then there at his side was the kid. "Got a light, mister?"

The pimple-pocked face dangled an unlit cigarette from its mouth.

Jack muttered something in assent and fished out his cigarette lighter. Fumbling with it for a moment, upset and awkward, he managed at last to produce a flame. The kid sucked at it through his cigarette, puffing out great billows of smoke until at last he straightened up with that same smirking smile and a careful wink. "You get the picture?" he asked. "She's a crazy kid, mister. Do anything you ask her to."

Jack was silent for a moment, fighting for control, trying to think what to say or what to do.

"You get the picture?" the kid repeated. "It ain't going to cost you too much either, if you want to make a date."

Jack might have hit him. Afterward, he wished he had. Yet instinctively he knew that if once he were to begin, he might not stop until the kid were unconscious or even dead. So what do you do in a situation like that? You walk away from it—as fast and as far as you can. Which is what Jack did, all but running over to Carol, who, of course, was still in the water. Unmindful of all but escape, he splashed out to her and hauled her out of the water. He set her down on the sand, grabbed her by the hand, and began walking quickly away with her.

"Daddy, not so fast."

But he continued on, and she was forced to run just to keep up. Once she stumbled, and he pulled her up, dangling her for a moment by the arm, and then started off again.

"Daddy, *please!*"

But why punish her? He stopped and looked down at her. "Okay," he said at last. "I'm sorry." And then, as he raised his eyes from her they were drawn irresistibly back to the blanket and the girl. All three of them were there now, standing up and looking his way. And all three wore identical expressions—that same insinuating smile, as though they knew his secret. He fought back the impulse to run. He turned, and taking Carol loosely by the hand, walked slowly and deliberately away.

It seemed that it took them hours to cover the three blocks home. Jack's shoes squished with each step he took, and his pants legs, wet above the ankle, flapped noisily against his legs. He got an amused glance or two along the way. What did he care? Let them laugh. He felt he had learned something about himself, though he was not quite sure what.

When at last they arrived at the apartment, he was surprised to find Pat still away. He glanced at his watch and decided she wasn't late yet. Maybe, if she were feeling well enough, she had taken the car and done some shopping on the way home. Well, it was just as well. It would save him from explaining his wet shoes and pants to his wife. There was no way he could have told her about that girl and her pimp. This saved him a lie. He sent Carol off to watch television and went into the bedroom to change.

Jack had barely pulled on a dry pair of pants when the telephone rang. He went hopping out to the hall, zipping up his fly, and grabbed up the receiver just ahead of Carol.

She stared up at him expectantly as he said his hello.

"Mr. Gawlor?"

"That's right."

"This is Mrs. Berglund. At Dr. Garber's office?"

"Oh . . . yes." An alarm went off inside his head. "My wife—is anything wrong with her?"

"No, well, no, I guess not. Nothing that's not being taken care of, anyway."

"Please. What is it?"

"Well, she went into labor right here in the office. No mistaking. It was the real thing, all right. Well, Dr. Garber told her that she was to have her husband—that's you—drive her straight to the hospital. Then when he found out that she had driven here on her own—"

"She wanted to," Jack interrupted. "She wasn't due for a week. She—"

"When the doctor found *that* out, let me tell you, he was *very* displeased."

Big deal, Jack thought. Big fucking deal. But all he said was, "Is she all right?"

"I'm getting to that. Then her water broke—right in the office!—and Dr. Garber had no choice but to drive her there himself."

"So what are you telling me? That she's at the hospital now? That she's in the delivery room?"

"Well . . . yes."

He hung up on her.

"What's the matter, Daddy?" Carol looked scared. Maybe he did, too.

"Mama's gone to the hospital to have the baby. We've got to get some of your clothes together and take you over to Grandma's in a hurry. Go see if you can find some things while I call a cab. For Christ's sake, Carol, hurry up, *please!*"

And his daughter started to cry again.

There really wasn't much to talk about. There never was in hospitals. You just walked up and down the hall until she got tired of that, and then you sat together on the bed and listened to the silence. That was the way it seemed to Jack during the last couple of days, anyway. These nightly visits to Pat strained them both, left them wondering why they should be such strangers away from home. Did they have a marriage or an apartment?

Jack looked at his watch. "Well, it's almost time to go."

Pat frowned. "Would you like to walk down for one last look?"

"All right."

He helped her up off the bed and held her by the arm as they went slowly down the hall together. There were other couples there, moving past them just as slowly and speaking, if at all, in the same hushed tones.

"Everyone's so damned solemn," he remarked.

"Yes, isn't it true?"

They rounded the corner and came to the nursery at last. There a whole platoon of raw, red recruits was laid out for inspection. Three couples were clustered to view them through the wide glass. Jack and Pat pushed up to one corner and stared intently at the nearest crib. It contained a lump of flesh no different from the rest.

"Isn't she beautiful?"

Beautiful was not exactly the word that leaped to mind,

but Jack nodded and gave Pat's arm a squeeze. "Sure, she's your daughter, isn't she?"

"Flattery will get you nowhere." She hesitated. "What do you think we ought to name her?"

"I thought you'd about settled on Nancy."

"Well, you ought to have some say in it. Is there a family name, or something that you'd like better?"

"What about Patricia?"

"No. One's enough, I think. I hate juniors."

"We can't very well call her Rowena."

Pat laughed. "No, I guess not."

"Nancy's fine. How about Nancy Jean?"

"Nancy Jean Gawlor—that has a nice sound to it." She turned from the glass and started away as Jack moved along beside her. Turning to him suddenly, she said with unexpected vehemence: "Well, at least we got that settled. Your visit's not a total loss."

"Hey! What's that supposed to mean?"

"Oh . . . nothing. It's just that—oh, Jack, I want to go home so badly. I just want to get out of here and have us get on with our lives."

"That's what I want, too. It won't be long. Day after tomorrow, right?"

"I know. But it seems like a long time to me." She had stopped just opposite the elevator, where a whole crowd of male visitors were awaiting release.

"Look," he said, forcing a smile, "why don't I walk you back to your room?"

"No. I'll say goodbye to you here. I—" The elevator arrived. The doors opened. "Go on, please."

He kissed her rather roughly on the lips and joined the other men. All the way down to the main floor, not a word was said by any of them.

During the drive back home, Jack found himself looking forward to a drink. It wasn't often that he did, but tonight he really felt like he needed one. Maybe with a good stiff scotch, he could face the future. He supposed he wanted just what Pat wanted—to get on with his life. But somehow he wasn't so sure about that. He was uncertain if he really wanted to go where his life was taking him. That had occurred to him earlier that evening when his mother had asked him if, with another child, they might not soon be thinking about buying a house. That was at dinner. Carol sat between them, taking it all in.

"No," he had told her, "it's a pretty big apartment."

"But a house is so much nicer." She had leaned over to Carol then, and making a conspiracy with her, she had asked in a loud stage whisper, "Wouldn't *you* like a nice, big house in the suburbs?"

"Where's that?" Carol had asked.

"Come on, Mother. Please."

"If it's the money, I can help you there. Your father may not have made much, but he was well insured."

She had seen to that, hadn't she? Jack thought bitterly about all those Sunday drives into the North Shore. That was what this was all about, wasn't it? Dead, his father was worth more to her than he ever was alive. She would realize her ambition yet. She would have that house on the North Shore or know the reason why.

So he felt that a drink was in order when at last he arrived at the building on Chase where they had lived for the last year. It was a big apartment—there was no doubt about that. He let himself in and began switching on lights, moving from room to room, unhappily intent on cheering himself with light and liquid warmth. When he pulled the bottle down in the kitchen he found there was only about half an inch at the bottom of it, and he wondered suspiciously if Pat hadn't done a bit of afternoon drinking.

Jack poured what remained of the scotch into a tumbler, then added ice cubes and a splash of water. He sipped at it tentatively and then went off to find a book to read. Instead, he remembered the copy of *Playboy* in his briefcase and settled down in the living room with it. The drink tasted good. As he perused the magazine, first looking over the skin layouts as he always did, he found his mind wandering—returning to that girl on the beach the other day. The incident had shaken him. Now he wondered why. After all, he pretended to some sophistication, a certain cool. Was he to be so easily intimidated by a sixteen-year-old? Why, some of the girls in the pages of the magazine were probably not much older, and even better looking, but none of them got to him the way that she had. He guessed it was that supposed resemblance to Carol. Thinking back, he wasn't really sure that they did look all that much alike. Well, what did it matter?

He put her out of his mind and started on a short story by Graham Greene. That was why he had bought the magazine in the first place, wasn't it? After a few minutes, his attention flagged. He gulped at the scotch and finished it off. Then he got up from his chair, suddenly agitated, wishing there were more liquor in the house. A look at his watch told him that the liquor store down at Jarvis had closed ten minutes before. If he wanted a fifth, he would have to jump in the car again and drive over to Morse or Howard. Well, why not? He tossed the magazine aside, and, grabbing his windbreaker from the closet, headed out the front door.

Having bought a fifth of Vat 69 at a liquor store on Morse Avenue, and then having assured himself that he was merely going out for a pleasant evening drive to relax a little, Jack headed straight for Old Town and a bar where he had heard you could find a little action if you were interested. He had heard that at the office. That was all they ever talked about there. Action.

The name of the place was Chumley's, and it was done up in English-pub style, complete with Bass Ale and buxom barmaids. Jack liked the look of it well enough. But Chumley's was the kind of place where it seemed like everybody present must be working in public relations or advertising—kind of phony—including himself, he supposed realistically. It was the last night of the Labor Day weekend, and they were packed two-deep at the bar and shouting at each other over the roar of the jukebox.

He ordered a scotch on the rocks, got it after some delay, and then pushed up against the wall at the end of the bar to survey the room. From there, it looked to him as though the room were in a kind of chaos. It wasn't just the noise, but the flailing of arms, the bobbing of heads, the grabbing, the punching of fingers into shoulders and chests. This was Chicago, all right, rowdyism raised to a level of virtuoso performance. The original classless society. Jack wondered what he was doing here—in this place, in this city—and wished he were away. New York? Why not? He'd start watching the ads in *Printer's Ink* and *Advertising Age*.

His eyes had passed over her the first time he looked up the bar because she was turned to the guy next to her and was apparently deep in conversation. He supposed she was with him, but maybe not. For when Jack's eyes moved back down the bar, he found her looking directly at him—not just up, or in his general direction, but right at him. She was brunette, black-haired really, with high cheeks and a narrow, pretty face. Her eyes were more than pretty. They were deep and dark and frank in their interest. In him? Why him? Nobody had looked at him quite that way before, and it bothered him a little. In the end, he looked away from her, unable to match the intensity of her gaze, uncertain just what it meant. There was something else in that look. She looked at him as though she recognized him, but he knew he had never seen her before. If he had, he would remember. Rather than cast timorous little glances her way, he half-turned from her and tried to figure out what to do next.

He should, of course, walk right over and strike up a conversation. That was how it was done, wasn't it? And clearly she was ready at least for that.

Why not? He pushed away from the wall and started over in her direction—only to meet her halfway there, heading in his.

"Well," she said, "hello."

"Hello, yourself."

"I was just off to the ladies. I hope you weren't making for the door?"

"Not me. May I buy you a drink?"

"What a nice idea. An old-fashioned. I'm old-fashioned." She smiled prettily at her attempted witticism, and, touching his arm, moved past him.

So she was old-fashioned, huh? The hell she was. He went

to her place at the bar, the only empty stool there, and ordered the drink. He got the once-over from the guy on his left, the one she had been talking to. Jack acknowledged the attention merely with a nod of his head and remained aloof, staring off coolly toward the rear of the place where Miss Beautiful-Eyes had disappeared. Too bad about you, buddy.

She did have beautiful eyes, didn't she? When she reappeared his own went to them, and once again he was arrested by the intensity of their gaze. It was as though there were nothing between her and him, just the two of them alone there.

Almost simultaneous with her arrival, the barmaid came with her drink. Jack tossed a couple of bucks onto the bar, trying to appear casual about it.

"Well, I'm back."

"So I see." He clambered off the barstool and made room for her. As they exchanged places, he allowed himself to look over the rest of her. A little wide in the hips but abundant and nice. B+.

But let him give credit where it was most due. "You have nice eyes," he said. Putting it mildly.

"I'm told they're my best feature," she said, casting them downward. "What do you think?"

"Well . . ."

She picked up her drink and gulped at it. "Do you think———?"

Somehow Jack got none of that. She seemed to be indicating the rest of her face. Whatever she said, however, was lost in the general uproar.

"*What?*"

"Never mind," she shouted back at him.

"Maybe we could go some place quieter?"

"Another nice idea. And I know———."

"What?"

"I *said,* I know just the place."

It turned out to be her own, a small brownstone apartment across North Avenue on one of the sidestreets just inside the Old Town Triangle. They walked there, she telling him little about herself, but pumping him with all kinds of questions.

Where did he work? How did he like advertising? What kind of writing would he rather be doing? That sort of thing. Not terribly personal perhaps, but almost solicitous in their evident concern. She kept him so busy talking about himself that he barely had time to reflect on the strangeness of all this. Why should she be so interested in him? Why was all this moving forward with such amazing swiftness?

But he talked on, pleased at the opportunity, expanding a little each time she moved those dark eyes his way. Looked at now obliquely, as they flashed and flickered at him under the streetlights, there was perhaps something familiar about them. Who was she?

"I don't even know your name."

"Names don't matter."

"Oh? What does?"

"People," she said. "People matter."

An admirable sentiment. Jack expatiated upon it windily for nearly half a block until at last she slowed to a halt and indicated the walk-up entrance just off the sidewalk. But still he wondered who she was and why the mystery.

He kissed her as they stepped inside her apartment, and she shut the door behind them. She went at him voraciously, chewing at his lips and sucking at his tongue, as though she meant to devour him from the inside out. Again, he was unprepared for such intensity. There was something almost desperate in the quality of her desire. Could he possibly match it?

As it turned out, no. But it really didn't matter, for after his own faltering gesture at the door, she took the lead. He had set in motion a scenario that moved with gathering momentum by its own force and energy. Getting free, once it was underway, would have been about as easy as jumping from a train hurtling along at top speed—and probably about as safe.

Before he quite knew it, they were in her bedroom, throwing off clothes in the dim moonlight that streamed through her windows. They managed to undress nearly without breaking their embrace, shucking, pulling, wiggling free, until at last their moving hands had nothing more than skin and hair beneath them. Together they tumbled onto the bed. He covered her with his body, kissing her, tasting her, giving himself completely to the job at hand. Yet not as completely as she. She grasped and beat upon him, made choking, gasping noises that made him wonder for a moment if she were somehow suffocating under his weight. But no, they drove on together, relentlessly to the edge and over, tumbling down and down, he moaning slightly and she making gurgling sounds deep within her throat. Panting, they lay together like that for a while afterward. At last he withdrew from her and rolled over beside her, his breath now coming in deep, heaving sighs. His mind was beginning to work again, and as it did he began to puzzle his way back through this whole experience. There was a fantastic quality to all this that frightened him a little the more he thought about it. The question was whether she was his fantasy, or he was hers.

He heaved himself up on an elbow and regarded her for a moment. Her face was obscured in the shadows, but her body was revealed to him in the moonlight. It wasn't quite as he expected it to be, a little heavier in the thighs, a little thicker through the middle. Give it a B, perhaps, or even a B—.

"You like what you see?"

"Very much," he lied.

"Good," she said. "I like pleasing you."

"Why?"

"Well . . ."

"No, I mean *really* why. Why me? Why the suddenness of all this? Why—"

"You're full of questions, aren't you?"

"I suppose I am. Is that bad?"

"Not necessarily." She moved on an elbow and faced him. Those eyes. "You want to know why?"

"That's right."

"It's because I know you."

"You *know* me? But . . ."

She switched on a lamp beside the bed and leaned over to the nightstand on which it rested. From out of a drawer she pulled a picture. She held it back from him.

"You're Jack Gawlor."

"Yes, but . . ."

"I said names aren't important. I believe that. I hope you do, too." She hesitated. "But . . . but this is who I am. Who I was."

She dropped the picture on his lower abdomen, almost hitting his penis. He picked it up and sat up, frowning, to hold it to the light for a better look. It was an old high-school yearbook picture. The girl in it was moon-faced and had a huge bent proboscis of a nose that covered half her face. He recognized her, all right. The eyes were unmistakable. It was Gus Karras's kid sister.

"That's me," she said, "before my nose job and a hundred pounds heavier."

"Stella Karras."

"That's right. I'm glad you remembered." She leaned forward and stared, letting him have a good look at her as she was now, he supposed. But with the light behind her she was not all that easy to see. Only her eyes were immediately evident, and those he felt upon him rather than saw. "Did you think only Jews got nose jobs?"

"No, I guess not." He sighed and handed the picture back to her. She held it for a moment and studied it before returning to the drawer in the nightstand. He got the idea that she must keep it there so that she could look at it every night.

"You were always nice to me," she said. "I always remembered that about you. When I saw you tonight, well, I wanted to be nice back for all those other times."

He thought about that for a moment. "There couldn't have been so many of them."

"Enough."

Suddenly he felt naked—and of course he was. "I think I'd better get dressed," he said.

"If you want to," she said. "Or you can spend the night here, if you want to do that."

"No, I think I'd better go." He slid out of the bed and began gathering his clothes together from the floor. He felt foolish, awkward, dumb. He looked up at her from the foot of the bed and found her gazing at him. That furious intensity was no longer there in her eyes now. Maybe she was disappointed in him, he didn't know. He wouldn't blame her if she were. She seemed beautiful, more truly so than at any time he had looked at her during the evening. He gave special attention to her nose. What could he say? It fit her face. Not too small, as they often were, but right. Whoever had done the job had done it right. But the way she looked now had nothing to do with the size of her nose or the shape of her face. It was her—*within* her. She was in charge of herself in a way he felt he would never be. She knew who she was. Jack envied her.

"You know," she said, as they looked at each other across the length of the bed, "the last time I saw you, you said you were getting married."

He nodded. "That's right. Yes, I remember."

"Are you still married?"

"Yes."

"That's not an accusation. Just a question. I was, well, I was curious."

Jack managed not to see her again, except for one occasion a few weeks later. The lunch they had, though not especially memorable in itself, was part of a day he would never forget.

Stella had called him a couple of times at the office. That bothered him a little. He was trying to bring some order into his life and found himself feeling guilty each time he looked at Pat or the baby, Nancy. You had to be some kind of monster to go out and do what he did when your wife was in the hospital having your kid, didn't you? That, Jack felt sure, would have been Pat's judgment upon him. The trouble was, he didn't *feel* like a monster. He felt ordinary—except for a certain flickering interest in Stella, a peculiar sort of respect for her. He had no real wish to continue the relationship with her—if that was what you called it—but she didn't seem to want that either. When she had called, she told him she was just keeping in touch and talked only briefly. No fuss. No muss. Because of that, he was moderately surprised when she called again one morning about ten-thirty and said she wanted to see him. Could they have lunch together that day? He saw no reason to duck it, and so he suggested a time and a place and even found himself looking forward a little to the meeting.

Only minutes after that, Tommy Corcoran ducked his head into Jack's doorway and asked him to drop by his office in a few minutes.

"I can come now if you want."

"No. I've got to make a phone call. Give me five minutes." He nodded and disappeared.

Jack owed him a lot. As copy chief at Barton and Bradley, Tommy Corcoran had taken a chance and hired him when all Jack had to show for his year at the catalogue house was an unimpressive collection of copy blocks in men's clothing and household appliances. Before Jack had brought his samples out, the two of them had talked at length about the advertising business and Jack's possible future in it. Tommy seemed to sense his misgivings and began to do a selling job on him. Why should he do that? Jack guessed that the big red-faced Irishman must like him. Tommy, it seemed, had come to Chicago many years before from Dubuque, Iowa, and when he heard that Jack had been born in Fort Dodge, it appeared to make a big difference to him. From then on, Jack was his boy—that is, right up to the moment Jack whipped out his samples. Tommy's face crumpled perceptibly. He turned over page after page, and Jack watched the smile fade from his face.

"You're underwhelmed," Jack said. "I can tell."

"Well . . ."

"They keep us on a pretty tight leash there."

"I know they do. It's just that, well, I wish I had something that could give me a better idea of the kind of writing you're capable of." He tossed the assorted sheets back across his desk at Jack and looked at him hopefully.

Jack sighed. "Well, I brought some other stuff along. I didn't *really* think I ought to just throw it in with the catalogue copy because it's a lot different from that stuff."

"What is it?" Tommy asked.

Jack brought up his briefcase, opened it, and dug out a sheaf of papers. "I've got these stories I've written."

"Stories? You mean *fiction*?"

Jack damned himself for even having thought to bring them. Advertising people weren't interested in such stuff as this. He could have saved himself a little trouble and a lot of embarrassment if he had just left the stories at home.

But Tommy Corcoran beamed at him. "You don't mean it? So you want to be a *real* writer? Well, that's the way I started out, too, Jack." He thrust out a big hand across the desk. "Let's have them."

Jack handed them over.

"Mmm. Some of them in type. A published author, no less."

Jack shrugged. "Little magazines."

"Little magazines, big magazines. There's nothing like seeing your words in type."

"I guess not."

"Look, I'll keep these for a day or two. If I think they stink, you'll get them back in the mail with a polite note so cold it'll freeze your blood. If, on the other hand, I enjoy them as much as I expect to, I'll be calling you up for another visit. That suit you?"

Of course it did—and it should have, for Tommy was back on the phone the next day, asking if Jack could drop by. He hired him as a junior copywriter. In ten months, Jack was a copywriter, pure and simple, with accounts of his own and the start of a growing local reputation as the kind of writer who could zip and zing with the best of them—even with the old pros like Tommy Corcoran. Tommy himself had passed the word on Jack. All that Jack was, he owed to him.

He looked in on Barbara Hanson after a decent interval had passed. She was a pert, pretty Swedish girl from Wisconsin, who had been Tommy's secretary for the past year or so. The rumor around the office had it that he was bedding her down.

"Tommy free? He wanted to see me."

She glanced down at the telephone on her desk, with its row of buttons, and nodded, satisfied. "He's off the phone now. Go right on in."

Jack did just that, shirtsleeves up and necktie askew, collapsing on the sofa just to the left of Tommy's desk. With a pencil behind his ear and a cigarette in his mouth, he looked every inch the no-nonsense professional. That was the way he wanted to look around the office.

"What's up, Doc?"

"I don't like it when you say that. It always makes me feel like Elmer Fudd."

"You're not Elmer Fudd."

"Th-th-that's what I keep t-t-telling myself."

Whenever you talked to Tommy you had to put up with a certain amount of this. Although his jokes were bad, most of them were at his own expense. Jack would have liked them better if they weren't quite so bland and humble. They made Tommy seem a little fatuous, and that distressed Jack. He was a decent man and good at his job.

All right. Fun was over. Tommy fixed Jack with a peculiar look. "You trying to get me fired or something?"

"What do you mean?"

"This copy on the Consolidated Airways ad. You've got to be kidding."

Jack blinked. He had expected this, but it wouldn't do to let Tommy know that. "What's wrong with it?"

"What's *wrong* with it? Jack, boy, look, if you think this is the kind of copy we're going to let out of this shop, then let me tell you, there's more than twenty-odd years separating us."

"Come on, Tommy. Be specific."

"Here, this, right here. You know damned well what I mean." Tommy fumbled for his glasses, jammed them on his nose, and read: " 'It's a big country. New England . . . the Gulf Coast . . . the Missouri Valley . . . North, South, East, West. And it takes a big airline to tie it all together. That's our job at Consolidated—getting people from one section of this big country to another so they can visit or do business, or maybe just take a look around and talk to people. You just might think of us that way—Consolidated Airways, the airline for sectional intercourse.' " Tommy pulled off his glasses and faced Jack expectantly.

"So?"

"You're on the level with this? 'The airline for sectional intercourse'?"

"Why not?"

"Well, I think it should be clear why not. There's an obvious double meaning there. It's dirty."

Jack shrugged. "I don't know about dirty, but sure, there's a double meaning. It wouldn't be funny otherwise."

"You call that funny?"

"Don't you? If somebody said it at lunch, wouldn't you laugh? I don't mean break up—but kind of chuckle?"

"That's conversation. This is advertising. Look, you seem not to have grasped a basic truth about this business, Jack. What we do here has the client's name on it."

"I think Consolidated will buy it. I think they'll love it."

That brought Tommy up short. He thought about it a moment and shrugged. "That bunch, who knows? The way they dressed their stews up in short skirts and colored panties, well, they probably would go for it. But what does that prove? I mean, we've got a reputation of our own to uphold. Don't you see that?"

"I'm not sure I do, Tommy. You said yourself what we do has the client's name on it. So doesn't that mean we ought to give him what he wants?"

Tommy sighed. "Look, Jack, you haven't been in this business half your life the way I have. Maybe if you had, you'd know that sometimes the really important thing you do is to protect the client from himself. Not to let him do something he'll be sorry for later on."

"I don't think Consolidated will be sorry for it. I think it'll sell a lot of tickets. I think it'll make them the talk of the industry."

"Women will hate it."

"Seventy-five percent of air travelers are men—and they're the ones who buy all the tickets."

"You've got all the answers, haven't you?" Tommy was showing considerable annoyance. This was the closest thing to a fight the two of them had ever had.

"Basically," said Jack after a moment, "you think it's immoral or something, don't you? That's really your objection to it?"

Tommy's eyes flickered for an instant down toward his desktop. There, arranged in gold frames before him, were the pictures of his six children; his wife was oddly missing from the group. "Jack, let's just say that I think that there are standards in this business, and copy like this doesn't meet them. There's no way in the world you're going to get my initials on this copy sheet." He held it out to him.

Jack sighed and stood up to accept it. "Okay, Tommy. I guess we just had what they call a frank exchange of views."

"I guess we did." Then he added in a lighter tone, "Look, maybe we could get together in the afternoon and kick around some ideas for a fix."

"I suppose so. Around two?"

"No, I've got a late lunch today. Make it after three."

"Okay."

Jack strode out of the office with the offending sheet in hand, and, as he passed Barbara Hanson's desk, he happened to exchange glances with her. She looked slightly amused. Maybe Tommy had read it to her and asked her opinion. The thought annoyed him considerably.

Back in his own office, Jack sat sulking for a period of minutes. Tommy and his goddam Catholic hangups! Why should Jack be made to pay for them? On the other hand, he should have known better than to try to sneak it past him. Deep down, after all, he knew as surely as he knew anything what Tommy's reaction would be. Maybe he should have taken it upstairs to Art Carstens, the account executive for Consolidated, and enlisted his aid. That would have been better all the way around. Well, it was too late now. He couldn't very well go behind Tommy's back. But he'd know better next time.

Jack glanced at his watch and decided he might as well leave for his lunch date with Stella. He could amble down Michigan Avenue instead of doing his usual sprint. He wouldn't get any more done this morning—and besides, it was a good day for ambling. Late September. The really bad days of summer were past. As Jack struck out northward from

Ohio Street, he was aware that in a few months' time he might not even want to take this six-block walk. It was best not to fight that wind on Michigan Avenue during the winter months. Let him enjoy it while he was able.

And enjoy it he did. There was nothing quite like a walk down the Avenue in September to set the blood coursing. The girls in their new fall dresses paraded by him as the breeze wafted off the lake, prettily disturbing their hair and playfully lifting their skirts. He was struck by the infinite variety of women. Although there seemed to be a distinct Chicago type—wide-hipped and thick-legged—there were enough of the rest to lend variety to his dreaming. And dreaming, after all, was what this was all about. Was Stella his type? For that matter, was Pat? He liked to think he had no special preference among women, but rather appreciated whatever it was that each one had to offer—the essential she. Did each have an essence? Something secret that made her special? He'd like to find out.

Jack turned down the sidestreet and walked the half block to the restaurant where he was to meet Stella. He glanced at his watch and saw that he was a few minutes early. He debated taking a walk around the block but then decided to go in and grab a table and get a drink. The brief bout with Tommy Corcoran had left him a little on edge.

"Perfect rob roy on the rocks with a twist." It was really just a scotch manhattan, but he liked the fussy sound of it, and so he had made it his drink. The waitress, a middle-aged, rather matronly type, took his order glumly and marched off without a word. He wondered what her secret was. Probably she had none. So much for his fractionally formulated theories.

Lighting a cigarette, he sat puffing as he watched the place fill up. Mostly men. It was remarkable how few mixed tables he could count—and how few women, except for the waitresses and hostess, there were to be seen at all. What about all those girls on Michigan? Where would the eat? At Woolworth's, he supposed. He vaguely grasped the notion of sex as a kind of class difference, and the thought pleased him.

Stella arrived almost simultaneously with the waitress. He

kept the woman long enough to order another drink ("Whatever you're having"), then sat Stella down opposite him at the table. "You're early," he said.

"You're earlier."

"Okay. You got me. I wanted a drink."

"Trouble at home?"

"No," he assured her hastily. "At the office. It's not very interesting, though."

"Try me."

Well, why not? He considered a moment, then launched hastily into a fairly objective account of his difficulties with Tommy Corcoran. He concluded with a rote recitation of his Consolidated copy. "There," he concluded. "What do you think of that?"

"What do you mean? What am I supposed to say?"

"Whatever you think. For instance, do you think it's funny?"

"I suppose so, yes. Mildly."

"Dirty?"

"Come on. I don't even know what that means anymore."

He looked at her, slightly shocked at her frankness. Well, she could hardly play coy with him, could she? Yet it was this about her that intrigued him most and forced his admiration. Except for the whores in Germany, he had never met a woman before who didn't at least pretend to be "nice"—dreary and transparent as such pretense often seemed.

In the end, he simply mumbled something about it not meaning much to him, either, and let the subject drop. The waitress saved the moment with Stella's drink, and the two then began talking desultorily about people they had known back in high school and what happened to this one, that one, and the other. It was the kind of time-filling talk that usually bored him—and he knew this wasn't why she had asked to meet. Still, she had apparently kept contact with everyone—partly through her brother, Gus, who was now married, selling insurance, and living in Hoffman Estates—and Jack found himself listening attentively all through drinks and lunch, if nothing more, fascinated at the sameness of the fates she described. They had all seemed so different in school yet they had all turned out so much alike—all except for herself and for him. Was that what she meant to communicate to him by this endless recitation of marriages, children, jobs, and divorces? He hoped so.

"I was wondering," she asked after a momentary lull over coffee, "what happened to your friend, Parker? I forgot his first name—the one who used to say everything was 'neat'?"

Jack laughed at that. "Yeah, he did say that a lot, didn't he? Actually, his first name was Felix. That's why everybody just called him Parker."

"My God. Felix."

"Yeah, well, he's a cop."

"Really?"

"He was at Summerdale station. You remember where they had that big scandal with the cops fencing stolen goods and all?"

"Sure. Of course I remember."

"I ran into him right after that. He was on suspension while they conducted their investigation. He said he was pretty clear, but he knew all about it. Everybody did."

"What does 'pretty clear' mean?"

"I didn't ask him. Anyway, he's back now. At Chicago Avenue, I think."

She hesitated, studying Jack a moment. "He didn't seem like a policeman."

"I know."

"You didn't seem much like what you've become, either."

"What *I've* become? What do you mean? What exactly have I become?"

"Well, you're married and you've got two kids. You're a copywriter in an ad agency. I'd say you'll be in the suburbs within five years, Jack."

There had been so little reproach in what she had said to him up to then that he was quite unprepared for this. He was irritated, of course, but interested. He always liked talking about himself.

"What makes you so sure?" he asked her at last.

"Well, I'm not sure. But that does seem to be the direction you're headed."

"All right. What's wrong with that? A lot of different people head in that direction. They're not *all* alike out there in Winnetka."

"Maybe not. But I think you're too much like me to be very happy out there. Or in that kind of life."

"What's that mean?"

"Think about it."

He eyed her skeptically. Was she trying to pull him away from Pat? He wouldn't have thought so until a moment ago, but now . . . "Just where is it you think you're headed?"

"Oh, I know where I'm headed," she said. "That's why I wanted to get together with you. As I said, I want to stay in touch, Jack, and I'm leaving town next week. Moving away."

"Yeah? Where?"

"California," she said. "Los Angeles."

"Why there?" He supposed that he meant why not New York.

"Well, several reasons—but two principally. First of all, a job was offered to me, and I accepted. There's been a curious lack of curiosity on your part about me—who I am, what I do. I guess you must have assumed that I'm a secretary, or something—but I'm not."

"All right," he took the cue, "what do you do?"

"I'm an economist at Standard Oil. I'm good at what I do, too. So good that Union Oil out in Los Angeles has hired me away. It's a terrific opportunity, and it came right out of the blue."

Jack didn't know quite what to say. It was true. He was sort of surprised, all right, but he didn't want to show it. "Well, that's . . . terrific. I'm really glad for you, Stella. Uh, you said there were two reasons you were moving out to California. What's the other one?"

She smiled and leaned across the table. But without lowering her voice, she said, "They fuck more out there, Jack."

When he got back to the office he sensed immediately that something was wrong. There was a small group muttering in earnest tones in the reception area. He looked at them curiously but nobody waved him over, and so he continued down the corridor. About halfway to his own office, he met Charlie Newell coming out of his. The forty-year-old copywriter said nothing, but looked at him sadly and simply shook his head. Jack stopped and stared after him. What was going on here, anyway? He almost ran after him to ask, but Charlie had seemed on the verge of tears. Perhaps it might be best to find out from somebody else.

He went straight to Liz Meyer. She was the office manager, up from secretary, and seemed to have the goods on everybody. Jack leaned into the open doorway of her office and started to speak, but then he saw that Liz's eyes were red and she was sniffling into a handkerchief clutched tightly to her nose. He stepped into the office and sank uninvited into the chair across the desk from her.

"Isn't it *awful?*" she asked.

"What's awful? What's this all about?"

"You didn't hear about Tommy?"

"What about him?"

"He's dead."

Jack stiffened at the impact. It seemed to hit him almost physically, as though he had walked into a lamppost or bumped into a door. He leaned back into the chair, feeling slightly stunned, and looked at Liz for a moment before he could say anything. At last he asked, "But . . . how? How did it happen?"

Liz blew her nose loudly and leaned forward almost eagerly, suddenly ready to tell all. "*Well . . .*" she began, "I guess you'd heard about him and Barbara?"

Certainly Jack had heard. In fact, he had heard it from her as he sat in this very chair a couple of months ago. But he didn't say that. He merely nodded.

"It seems the two of them were in a room in a hotel up on State Street just, well, you know, doing what comes naturally, I guess. And I suppose it was just too much for Tommy's poor old fifty-year-old heart. He had a coronary right there, you know, during . . ."

Jack nodded again to relieve her of any obligation she may have felt to finish the sentence. The two sat quietly and regarded one another across the desk.

"And Barbara had to call the ambulance?"

"Yeah, the poor kid, but he was dead already. I don't know if the cops gave her a rough time. I don't think so, though. One of them phoned in to tell us about it. They said they were taking her home."

Jack didn't know what to say. In the end, all he could do was shrug and shake his head. "Poor Tommy," he said at last.

She nodded quite soberly, as though he had made an especially profound comment. "Yeah," she agreed, "you never know. You know?"

He decided he had had about enough of this and got up to go. Just tell me if there's anything I can do."

She looked puzzled at that. "Oh," she said, "okay."

Back in his office, he sat at his desk for a while and thought about Tommy and the whole sad, squalid situation. What a way to go, he thought glumly. Maybe his wife will be able to keep the details quiet. Probably. As for Barbara, she would quit or be fired or something. They certainly wouldn't let her stick around the agency as a reminder of the way Tommy checked out. Jack reflected on that a moment, then opened the drawer in which he had tossed the Consolidated copy. He reread it, then picked up a pencil and in a rough approximation of Tommy's florid script, he wrote the initials TJC in the right-hand corner of the page, and finally he circled it the way that Tommy always did. He held it away for a moment and studied his handiwork. Certainly it would pass. Who would challenge it?

He jumped out of bed, groped around on the top of the dresser in the dark for his cigarettes, and lit one. Not knowing quite where else to go, he returned to the bed then and sat down. The cigarette glowed brightly as he inhaled on it. It was the only light in the room.

"Jack?"

"What?"

"I'm sorry."

"Oh, don't say that, Pat. There's nothing to be sorry about. It's just that, well, it's obvious certain things don't appeal to you."

There was a prolonged silence. And then at last: "I guess not."

Jack took another drag on his cigarette and asked himself how people managed to get into situations like this. By getting married he supposed. He had a sudden vision of husbands all over America, sitting just as he was at the foot of the bed and smoking in the dark. He turned to her, or where he supposed she was, and asked, "Don't you ever think about things and want to try them?"

"No."

"Why not?"

"I . . . I guess I'm just old-fashioned." Stella's joke. But Pat meant it.

Carol sat beside Jack at the long table in the back room where he had his typewriter set up. Pat was out shopping, and the baby was asleep. On a weekend afternoon the baby-sitting usually fell to him. But it didn't matter, because inside the house Carol wasn't much trouble, and as long as she stayed asleep Nancy was no trouble at all.

Carol claimed to be writing a novel. She had asked Jack yesterday what he was doing as he sat hunched over the typewriter and he had muttered back to his three-and-a-half-year-old daughter that he was writing a novel. Well, that was good enough for her. She would write one, too. That was how it was with her. She picked words up everywhere.

Jack glanced over at her and was reassured to find her doodling furiously on the sheet of paper he had just given her. It was old page one of chapter three. She had written MAMA in bold capitals, and beneath it she had drawn a face circled with an abundance of spiral curls. Jack saw little resemblance.

Carol looked up and caught his eye. "Look at this," she said, holding out the page for him to see.

He saw nothing special in it, so he simply shrugged and said, "Look at what?"

"This is my novel."

"Looks all right to me," he said, hoping to dismiss her with a little easy praise.

"But look at this," she said, pointing at the face she had just drawn. "This is a picture of Mama."

"Oh . . . yeah."

"Isn't it *good*?"

Jack happened to think it foolish to gush over a child's work simply because it was a child's. He felt there were, after all, objective standards. "It's all right," he said to her at last, "but you've got both the eyes on one side of the nose. Picasso can do that, but he learned how to draw the other way first."

"What way?"

"The way things look, the way they are when you see them."

Without another word she put down old page one of chapter three and began to study the portrait intently. Gratefully, Jack returned to new page one of chapter three and reread what he had written: "Nothing but the inevitable phantasmagoria of white thighs and pink-tipped udders, endless and ghostly. . . ." It didn't look right to him at all. It looked . . . what? Written—terribly overwritten. "Phantasmagoria"—that was right out of Faulkner, wasn't it? Not even the words were his own.

Because of Stella he had hauled out this beginning he had made at a novel a couple of years before. She had goaded him into it, asking him when they parted after lunch if he thought he would ever get back to writing again—"real writing" was how she had put it. But why should it matter to him what she thought of him?

Tommy Corcoran's death may have had something to do with it, too—for hadn't Tommy continued to tell himself and Jack that one of these days he was going to get out the typewriter and write a novel that would let everyone know what life in the ad game was really like? But now, dead at fifty, he would never write anything of the kind. Jack feared that he may have inherited Tommy's fate along with most of his accounts. Charlie Newell was the new copy chief. Jack had the feeling he wouldn't last long at the job.

"Daddy?"

Although his fingers weren't exactly flying over the keys of the typewriter at that moment, he was irritated by Carol's interruption. He turned to her with a scowl, hoping to intimidate her into silence. "What *is* it?" he barked (woof-*woof*-woof—can she understand that?).

But she was unimpressed. "Who's Picasso?" she asked.

He was caught off guard—a legitimate inquiry and a pedagogical opportunity. Leaning back, he explained, "Oh, he's a man who draws . . . and paints . . . pictures." So far so good. "Lots of people like his pictures, and they pay him money so they can keep them."

"Are they good pictures?"

"Well, lots of people think so. Sure—sure they're good pictures?"

"Do you have any?"

"Any what?"

"That man's pictures."

"Not me. Maybe if we ever get about a million dollars I'll get one. There are a bunch of them I'd like to have."

Carol was nodding seriously, almost solemnly at him. This was the expression she wore whenever money was mentioned.

Jack suddenly remembered the book. "But, listen," he said, "I've got some pictures of his pictures in a book. Would you like to have a look at them?"

"Sure, Daddy! Sure I would." She jumped from her chair and followed him in a hop and a dance to the bookcase where, after a brief search, he pulled out the promised volume.

With just a glance at the book, he saw a chance to make his point. "Look," he said, holding it up for her to see the dust jacket. "Both eyes on one side of the nose. But over here"—flipping it over for her to see the woman in white on the back—"is a picture of a lady that really *looks* like a lady. See? He can draw *both* ways."

"Can I see the book?"

"All right, if you're careful not to tear the pages. There are lots of pictures in there."

She accepted the book, taking it gingerly in her small hands with a great display of caution. She looked down for a moment at the lopsided woman on the front of the dust jacket, and then she nodded soberly in judgment. "I like this one best," she said. "It's super."

He was offended at that. "*Super*? Where did you pick that up? Kids don't say that anymore."

"Well, *I* do."

"Okay," he said, "big deal. You sit down and look at the book and let me do some work."

They sat down again at the long work table, side by side. Carol began leafing slowly forward through the pages. In spite of himself, Jack grew interested and was unable to return to new page one of chapter three. He looked at the pictures as she turned past them one by one, and he found himself wondering what in the world Carol might think of this gallery of monsters and satyrs. But none of them seemed to make much of an impression until she came to *Guernica*. There she stopped to look, to study, her round brow tight in a frown.

At last her face relaxed as she turned to him with a smile. "I like this picture," she said. "Look at that crazy horse. This one's keen."

"*Keen*?"

"Sure, keen."

"That's another one of those words you use," Jack said accusingly. "I know where you get those words. You get them from television, that's where." He stopped, groping for some way to make her understand. "Listen, kids don't really talk that way except on commercials—*super*, Mommy! *keen*, Daddy! That's just some copywriter's idea of the way kids talk."

She glowered at him. Carol had learned to glower only recently, and she was quite self-conscious about it. She thought she looked terribly fierce. He turned away from her, still irritated, and hunched glumly over the typewriter.

"Hey!" she cried indignantly, "if I get *those* words from television, where do you get all *those* words?" Jack turned to find her pointing with both hands, one toward the sheet in the typewriter and the other at a little pile of manuscript on the desk.

Where indeed? She had him, and he knew it.

Then slowly and with resolution, he took hold of new page one of chapter three with its inevitable phantasmagoria of white thighs and pink-tipped udders and pulled it from the typewriter.

"Here," he said to her, "do you want to write another novel?"

✶

When Klezek told the receptionist at Barton and Bradley that he was from the police and showed her his badge, all she said was, "Oh."

She looked at him oddly, as though she had never even seen a cop before and weren't quite sure how she should respond. He thought they hired pretty smart girls in these Michigan Avenue places, but this one was acting like a complete yo-yo.

"It's about John Gawlor," Klezek prompted. "He did work here, didn't he?"

"Oh, sure." She paused. "He's dead, huh? Killed?"

"Yes. Homicide. Murder."

Her brows knit with concern at that. "Gee, that's awful."

"I'd like to talk to some people who knew him—maybe his boss. Are Mr. Barton or Mr. Bradley in?"

"There's no Mr. Barton or Mr. Bradley. They died a long time ago—or I guess they did. The one you want to talk to is Mr. Van Dellen. He's the president."

"Fine. Just tell him I'm here."

"He's not in. Not back from lunch yet. He should be in before three, though. He has an appointment then."

Klezek glanced at his watch. Back from lunch at three? Some life. "Well, it would be nice if he could squeeze me in then." He hoped she caught the irony. He had certainly thrown it.

"Oh, sure. He'll want to help. We all do." She was silent for a moment, then brightened perceptibly as she said, "You ought to talk to Liz Meyer."

"Who's she?"

"Well, she's the office manager. But she knows everything about everybody here."

"I guess that's the lady I want to talk to, then."

When Liz Meyer emerged from the complex of offices, she went straight to Klezek and offered her hand. This was more like it, he thought. She was a tall brunette, a little past her prime, perhaps, but still worth a look. But even better, from Klezek's standpoint, she practically oozed intelligence and *efficiency. It took her less than thirty seconds to ascertain what he was after and how she might help. She invited him back to her office and, leading the way, called back to the receptionist, telling her to ring the office just as soon as Mr. Van Dellen came in.*

Once Klezek had settled into a chair, Liz Meyer held back and very pointedly shut the door to her office behind them.

"I think a degree of privacy is called for," she said.

"Good idea," Klezek agreed.

She took the seat opposite him and leaned forward at her desk, ready to talk. "You want to know about Jack Gawlor?"

"That's why I'm here."

"Well, I don't know exactly where to begin. When you've worked with somebody for years . . ."

"Sure. I know. I guess I'm just after general stuff. I mean, what was he like? Did he get along with people?"

"Oh, yes. He was vice-president and creative director of this agency. You don't get that far by stepping on people's toes."

"I guess not. But sometimes you make enemies."

"Well, all right," she conceded. "And on the other hand, he wasn't exactly a yes-man, either. He was very good at what he did. He could write copy, and he got to be very good at concept stuff, too. Some people think he wasn't quite as good at television as he was at print. But I think he was just plain good. He was very important to this agency. He'll certainly be missed."

Klezek waited. None of this was very helpful, really, but Miss Meyer seemed to think it was of some importance. He hoped it would lead someplace else, so he simply smiled at her encouragingly. The idea was to just keep her talking.

"I suppose you want to know about his private life and all that?" she asked.

"It would help."

"I don't know that there's much to tell, really. He kept that pretty much separate from work—except once about ten or twelve years ago. There was this copywriter who worked for him, Joan Baggot or Bagley—Bigley, that was it—Joan Bigley. It was pretty plain to everybody that they had something

going, then all of a sudden she just left, took a job with another agency—McCann-Erickson, I think—and it was all over. At least as far as I could tell. Of course he was married at the time. This was years before his divorce." She paused and thought for a moment. *"He changed after that. I'd never really thought about it that way—you know, cause and effect—but he definitely did change."*

"After his divorce?"

"No. After that business with Joan . . . Bigley."

"How did he change? What do you mean?"

She wrinkled her nose in concentration. It was rather an attractive gesture, Klezek decided. For a babe who was looking forty in the face, she was really not so bad. *"Oh, I don't know,"* she said at last. *"In this business, one of the things you learn pretty early is to watch your ass—if you'll pardon my French. Jack got pretty good at that. He became sort of more careful and calculating, somehow. You might say he lost his innocence or something. He sort of withdrew."*

"I'm not sure I follow that, exactly."

She leaned forward earnestly. *"Well, he began to keep pretty much to himself. He always did from then on. He became almost secretive. He was—"*

Her telephone rang. She nodded to Klezek as she picked up the receiver. She listened, spoke a word or two of assent in response, and then she hung up. *"That was Van Dellen. He's back. He'll see you now."*

"Can we finish up later on?"

"How much later?"

Klezek considered a moment. What the hell? Why not chance it? *"After work?"*

"Why not?"

CHAPTER FIVE *1966*

JACK DIDN'T KNOW quite what to make of Miss Joan Bigley. There was something charged, intense, electric about her. When he hired her, nearly two months ago, he had at first suspected that she was sending out signals specifically to him. It was the way she sat forward in her chair and concentrated on him as he told her about the job that had struck him as remarkable. Nobody had ever looked at him quite like that—not eagerly exactly, nor certainly invitingly, but appraisingly, almost as though she were offering him a challenge. Was the challenge sexual? Was that why he had hired her? No, it was because her background was good, her copy samples showed a real flair, and she had had just enough of the right sort of experience to move right into the Consolidated Airways and Breeze Cigarette accounts, which was where someone was needed. Strange as it seemed to hire a woman to write copy outside the usual female specialties (toiletries, household items, and so on), he had decided she was the one for the job and had never once regretted it.

The only problem with her—and it was not his alone—was this live-wire intensity of hers. It was as though a kind of magnetic field had formed around her into which you ventured at your own peril. She had a way of asking awkward questions—as she had that morning a week ago when the two of them had sat down with Ray Dibble, Consolidated's ad manager. He had spent nearly fifteen minutes mumbling vaguely about the new image they had in mind for their stewardesses and just how it might best be communicated to the air-traveling public.

". . . or not so much a brand *new* image," he concluded

weakly, "as maybe the same old Consolidated Girl idea with a little more oomph behind it—if you get what I mean. Maybe we could, you know, *imply* a little more."

Dibble had looked from Jack to Joan hopefully, as though trying to decide if he would really have to be more specific than this. Obviously he wished not to be. Jack would have attributed Dibble's reticence to the fact that a woman was present, if he had not had a dozen such conversations with him in the past. For a guy who was basically pretty dirty-minded, Ray Dibble always had a hell of a hard time getting to the point.

Jack was about to speak up himself, when Joan leaned forward and fixed Dibble with a look. "Now, tell me if I'm wrong, Ray," she said. "But what we're talking about fundamentally here is a Playmate image—that's Playmate as in *Playboy*?"

"Well, uh, yes, but of course I'm not suggesting we use any, well, nudity in the ads."

"No, no, that's not what I'm talking about at all," she said agitatedly. "Look, let me be specific. What you want to say is that these are nice girls who put out pretty regularly. Isn't that right?"

For a moment there was silence as Dibble studied the grain of the wood in the table before him. "That's putting it awfully baldly, but . . ." He looked up at her and smiled almost timorously. "I hope that doesn't offend you, Miss Bigley . . . Joan?"

"It doesn't offend me at all. I just want to get things straight right from the start."

That's how she was. You could be frank with her. She preferred it that way. One day she had pursued Jan Van Dellen up the hall and asked him if it were true he had asked Jack to keep a tighter rein on her at client conferences. When he conceded that it was, she told him that she would appreciate it if he voiced criticisms directly at her and not to her immediate superior. "It's like you're holding him responsible for me, and . . ." Van Dellen looked at her with those cold, blue Dutch eyes and blinked once or twice before she completed her sentence: "Well, I just don't think it's fair to blame me on anybody." Van Dellen let out with that bleat that did him for a laugh and agreed to try it her way.

It wasn't that she got away with a lot because she was a good-looking girl. There were plenty of those around the office who had long since been intimidated into docility. No, if she got away with a lot, it was because she was good—damned good—at what she did. Everybody knew that, and she knew they knew it. But was she presumptuous? Did she take too much upon herself? Jack didn't think so. She acted like a man—and that's what shook them up, the Jan Van Dellens and Ray Dibbles of this world. For his part, Jack rather liked her for it.

God knows she didn't look like a man. A little under medium height, she seemed taller because she was so erect in her bearing and had a way of looking you right in the eye. She had a lean, taut figure that Jack especially admired from the rear, and a face with expressive, mobile features that always let you know, moment to moment, second to second, just where you stood with her.

For instance, now. Joan Bigley sat across the desk from him, searching his face as eagerly as a child, for his reaction to the Breeze Cigarette copy she had laid before him just a moment ago. When he had done these scenes with Tommy Corcoran, and later with Charlie Newell, he always played it pretty cool. He would toss the copy down and stare off into the distance, hands clasped behind his head, making every effort to look bored. It paid not to get too emotionally involved with your work—or at least not to let it show. Now that Jack was copy chief, he wondered if it might not be possible to communicate this to her without deflating her, robbing her of her enthusiasm. She was very good, but she wasn't perfect —how could he make her understand that?

"I like this," he said.

Their eyes met. She looked at him sharply, searching his face. "But not enough," she prompted.

"Well . . ."

"Come on, Jack. Give it to me. You know how I hate people to be considerate."

"Okay." He took a moment to study the sheet before him.

Where to begin? "Now what you've got here is accurate," he resumed. "It's pertinent. It's stating the facts on tar and nicotine . . ."

"But?"

"Why go so far in that direction?"

"Well, it's important. I mean, it's an advantage. Breeze has got an edge there, and I think it's the kind of information that people who smoke really ought to have."

"But is it the kind they want?"

"Come on. What does that mean?"

"Think about it," Jack urged. "Why do people smoke?"

"Oh, I don't know. For the way it tastes. Because it's a habit."

"Okay. But not for how healthy it is? How terrific it makes them feel?"

Joan shook her head in annoyance. "No," she said. "No, of course not."

"All right, let's bring it closer to home," Jack suggested. "You smoke. Why did you begin?"

"Me? I?" She laughed. "Well, that goes back a while. After all, I was only about fourteen or fifteen when I started. But, sure, I guess I know why I began. I wanted to be grown-up. I had all these grand fantasies about how great smoking was and how I'd look doing it."

"What makes you think other people are any different? Sure, it's a habit. Sure, they like the way it tastes. But basically it's a fantasy—an image they have of themselves. Bogart and Bacall. 'Does anyone here have a match?' " He camped the last line outrageously but got no smile from Joan.

"Bogart died of throat cancer," she reminded him tersely.

"Did that put a dent in your habit?"

She frowned at him. "No."

"So okay. You're right. You owe it to the folks out there to let them know the good news on tar and nicotine. But that's not the whole story, just sort of an aside. Remind them why they smoke. Give them a shot of fantasy. You're not selling cigarettes, you're selling a way of life."

"That sounds like something I'm supposed to write up on my wall."

"Just so you remember it." Jack hesitated. He wondered—would she think he was smarting off or getting personal or what? Well, what did it matter? "Look, I've always found that a good fantasy life is about the most helpful asset when it comes to writing copy. How's yours?"

She leaned back and regarded him for a moment as a grin spread across her face. "Terrific," she said at last.

Pat blinked nervously, as though she weren't quite certain what he had meant. But it seemed to Jack that it should all be clear enough.

"Fantasies?" she asked.

"That's right. You know—the dreams you have when you're awake."

"Well . . . sure. I suppose I have them. Yes, I guess everyone does." She smiled at him a little uncertainly, as if to ask if he might not be satisfied with that.

He wasn't. He asked himself why it was that of all the people he talked to in the course of the day the one he seemed to have the least understanding with was the one who was supposed to be closest to him. Were all marriages like theirs? He wondered about that—wondered if it weren't true that in time they all drowned in dullness and boredom. Couldn't she surprise him, shock him, just *once*? He was determined that she do it.

"What kind?" he asked. "I've always been curious about that—whether women think about sex the way that men do."

"Oh," she said, lowering her voice to a whisper, "you mean *sexual* fantasies."

Jack laughed abruptly. "What did you think I meant? Dreams of success? Dreams of riches or something? A mink coat? Is that it?" He shook his head, momentarily overcome by her naïveté.

Pat looked at him rather miserably. "Please" was all she said, but he knew she was asking more than that he be fair with her. Clearly, she felt threatened by him, by this whole conversation. She wanted desperately to be left alone.

But Jack persisted loudly: "No, what I meant was sex—

S-E-X. That's what I'm talking about. There's a lot of it going around lately—or haven't you heard?"

"Oh, yes, I've heard," she said. "And so will your daughters if you don't keep your voice down."

Jack glanced down the hall toward the living room. Although he couldn't see the girls, he knew they were there. Fred Flintstone was yammering loudly at Wilma. Jack's two daughters, seven and four, would be stretched out on the floor before the television set, oblivious of all and everything until it came time to change channels. It was as though they had had prefrontal lobotomies. Would vegetables eavesdrop?

Pat stood up from the table and began gathering up the dinner dishes. Jack followed her movements closely through the whole routine of stacking and scraping, aware all the while that his wife was concentrating so carefully on what she was doing just to avoid looking at him. Was he really so intimidating? Probably only to her. A feeling of tenderness for her welled up in him, and with it came a sense of shame for having made her so acutely uncomfortable. He reached out and capped a hand gently over her forearm, lightly restraining her. When she looked up, he saw there were tears in her eyes.

"Hey," he said. "I'm sorry. But I really think we ought to talk about this."

"Oh, Jack, you always want to talk about things."

"Too much?"

"Sometimes. Yes."

"I don't know but what you're right," he conceded. "But, look, I do think it's necessary to talk about what's important, and fantasies *are* important. They're dreams, Pat. We live by our dreams, too, you know."

Pat swiped awkwardly at her eyes with the back of her wrist. "Don't you think *I* know that?" she asked fiercely. "It's just that, well, I don't have this big thing about sex that you have—that you seem to think I *should* have. Maybe some women do, but I *don't*. Now, I don't know if you think that makes me frigid or something, but that's just how I am."

Then quickly she picked up the pile of dishes and marched

with them to the sink. She turned on the water full blast and began slamming them helter-skelter through the steam and into the dishwasher. He waited her out, aware there was no sense trying to talk to her now. How Jack hated these crises in the kitchen! There was something so ineffably crummy about such scenes of high drama played out over pots and pans, half-picked bones, and the remains of salad. It reduced their lives to the level of characters in the George Price cartoons. Or was he playing Jackie Gleason to her Audrey Meadows? Yet somehow or other the third act always seemed to be staged right here, didn't it? Maybe she planned it that way.

At last she finished and turned to him, relatively composed. She nodded, as though to say that things were now again under control. He nodded back.

"Look, Pat," he began, "you're probably right. I seem to have sex on the brain or something."

"I didn't say that."

"Okay. Whether you said it or not, it's true. But you said you do have dreams . . . fantasies. So maybe they're *not* that particular kind. Okay. What kind are they?"

She looked at him as she dried her hands very deliberately on a dishtowel, then tossed it aside. "I only want what's best for us," she said. "Those are my dreams."

"Sure, Pat, I understand. I—"

"Listen," she interrupted, "if you want me to be specific, then I'll tell you. I remember I was thinking just the other day that it would be great if you were to go back to your writing—you know, at night, the way you used to do. And you just suddenly wrote a best-seller. Wouldn't that be terrific for you? for me? for the girls?"

"*That's* your dream?"

"I can tell you're not very excited by it."

"Well, it's very—I don't know—it's very flattering, sort of altruistic of you. But . . . well, it's not going to happen. We both know that. I just don't have time for that stuff anymore." Suddenly he was on the defensive. Why did he feel it necessary to make excuses to her? Why should he?

She took a step or two toward him and shrugged eloquently. "Jack, I know that. We're not talking about what's possible or what's likely to happen. We're talking about dreams."

Now he was annoyed. He knew he shouldn't be, but there it was. "Well," he said, "if that's your idea of a fantasy . . ."

"Yes, that's my idea of a fantasy." Pat sighed. "Pathetic, isn't it?" She walked on past him and down the hall to the living room, where Fred Flintstone was ranting at Barney.

On the drive back to the office, as Jack threaded his way along the Northwest Expressway at a steady sixty-five, he and Joan found themselves whooping with laughter as they blurted out lines from the afternoon-long meeting they had just sat through at Consolidated. They were giddy, half-high with the the fun of success, coming down by stages from a client conference that had gone completely their way from first to last. Not only was Ray Dibble present, but his boss, as well—Calvin Ross, the director of marketing for Consolidated—and several other interested parties from the seventh floor. That was where the conference took place—the executive conference room on the seventh floor. Art Carstens had been a little uneasy going in—but then, account executives were always uneasy, always afraid the client might react negatively to anything new. The " 'Solid' Girl" campaign that they presented that afternoon was fresh and sexy and about as certain to cause a stir in the ad business as it was to boost ticket sales on Consolidated—which was to say . . . very!

But that, for Jack and Joan, hadn't been the best part. As far as they were concerned, the most fun of all was sitting there and listening to Ross, Dibble, and their associates perk up on cue and say all those bright and corny things in appreciation that company men always said. These were the lines they were quoting back and forth to one another as they sped along on the Northwest, all the way from Mannheim Road to Belmont.

Like, "Golly, that should make them sit up and take notice, shouldn't it?"

Or, "You think we can get away with that?"

And this, from tough, sardonic, Cal Ross himself: "If I didn't know this was going to sell a lot of tickets, I'd think you people worked up this routine just to entertain us."

For some reason it all seemed just terrifically funny.

By Belmont, however, the two had settled down and were making every effort to put on sober faces for their reentry into the office.

They were quiet for minutes. Almost downtown now. Jack glanced over at Joan and found her stretched back comfortably on the seat, head against the cushion, eyes closed. He wondered for a moment if she were asleep.

But no. She shifted, opened her eyes, and turned to him. "That was great," she said. "One of the best afternoons of my life."

"Winning sure beats the hell out of losing, doesn't it?"

She laughed a different laugh at that. More of a chuckle. "It sure does," she agreed. And then, with a sigh: "Well, back to reality, I guess."

Jack glanced at his watch and decided they could afford to tarry a little. "Well, maybe not *right* back. We could have a drink to celebrate before we go back to the office."

"Sounds good," she said. "The Lower Depths?"

"Where else?"

It was a place on the lower level of Michigan Avenue, just north of the river and a number or two south of the building in which Barton and Bradley was situated. The Lower Depths was a hangout for working ad people and the editors and reporters of the *Chicago Tribune* nearby. It must have been the cheap drinks that brought them in, because it certainly wasn't the big, scowling picture of Gorky behind the bar.

The two of them sat at a table in back, and Jack played waiter for them, bringing her old-fashioned and his rob roy from the bar. They drank ritually to their triumph, then sighed almost simultaneously, and dropped back in their chairs. It felt good coming down. In a few minutes he would have eased back into low gear.

"This was a good idea," she said.

"It'll be a few minutes before they send out a search

party." He hesitated, trying to remember—and then it came to him: Stella. "Old-fashioned," he said. "What's in one of those things, anyway?"

"Oh, bourbon, bitters, and a lot of fruit salad. Want a taste?"

"No. I was just curious. Somebody I used to know drank old-fashioneds."

"A lady?"

"Why? Is it a lady's drink?"

"Not especially. It was—I don't know—just the way you said it."

He studied her for a moment, trying to assess her interest. "Am I as easy to read as all that?" he asked at last. "As a matter of fact, yes, it was a lady."

She merely nodded.

That annoyed him a little. She seemed almost too knowing. "That doesn't seem to surprise you."

"No, it doesn't. Should it? I expect that you would have known some ladies at one time or another in your life. Probably still do."

Until she said it, Jack didn't realize that that was precisely what he had hoped to hear from her. She regarded him as a sexual being, a man, and not some sort of neuter figure with a label—the Boss, the Copy Chief, or whatever. Her estimate of him was even generous. There had been one other woman, just one, a year and a half after Stella—a typist named Laurie for whom he had briefly felt an attachment. It ended when, finally made unhappy by guilt and the difficulty of arranging meetings, he had attempted to break things off with her. She continued to make demands on him, and so he had no choice but to get her fired. It had not been all that difficult. She was a sloppy worker.

"What about you?" he asked. "Frankly, if you don't mind my saying so, I'm surprised you're not married. Never have been, have you? Not divorced?"

"No."

"Am I getting too personal?"

She laughed. "Not at all," she said. "As a matter of fact, I kind of like getting personal with people. I love hearing all their dirty little secrets, and I don't mind telling mine in return."

It was his turn to laugh. There was a rough-and-ready quality about Joan that he liked very much. There was, he admitted to himself, quite a lot about her that he liked. "That's honest," he said.

"Oh, I'm honest. It's one of my better qualities—and perhaps one of my worst." She hesitated, then: "But no," she said, "since you ask, I've never been married, and I never intend to be."

That took him slightly aback. "Well, that sounds very final."

"I mean it to be. Oh, I'm not saying it couldn't happen, but it's not in my plans. It would only get in the way of work."

He had heard about career women—wasn't that what they called them? But he always thought of the term as a euphemism for the kind of women that nobody wanted—those who were making the best of a bad deal. He couldn't imagine one of them not wanting to be married—combining a career with marriage, certainly. Why not? But *choosing* work over marriage? It seemed almost perverse to him—acting against nature. Maybe—and this was the first time the thought or anything like it had ever occurred to him—maybe she was a lesbian or something. Was that what she was trying to tell him? "You think work is that terrific?" he asked at last.

"You think marriage is so great?"

"Ouch," he said. "That hurt. But . . . well, I am surprised, though. You don't seem, uh—how shall I put it?—down on men."

"That's good, because I'm not."

Jack looked around him a little uncomfortably. A couple had just pushed past them and taken a table nearby. The place was beginning to fill up. He felt it might be best if they cut this short. It was the sort of conversation he would rather nobody overheard. He drank up and put the glass back down on the table. There was a certain finality to the gesture. Would she understand it was time to go? He looked at her inquiringly. "Are you . . . ?"

"Am I celibate? Is that the word you're looking for? Not me. I'm no nun."

Again, in spite of himself, Jack laughed. There was simply no telling what she might pop out with. "No, that was *not* the word I was looking for," he said. "I was about to ask if you were ready to go. That's all."

Joan lifted her glass and gulped back most of her drink. "Ready, boss," she said.

On the way up in the elevator she touched his hand. Just that.

He collected his messages at the reception desk on the way in. Joan left him there with just a nod. He glanced at his watch. It was just on five. The place would be clearing out soon, and that suited him. He would take about an hour to answer a few calls and clear off his desk and then be back home by six-thirty or so. Halfway down the hall he met Liz Meyer.

"Well," she said, "I hear it went like gangbusters."

"Art tell you?"

"No, Joan. She just dropped in on me."

"Well, it went just fine."

Liz lowered her voice to a whisper: "I guess sometimes she does sort of pop off, doesn't she?"

"Whatever she had to say this time must have been just right," Jack declared, "because the meeting couldn't have gone better."

"Wonderful," Liz said and smiled as though she meant it. "And you're the man who made her over? Just like in the story?"

Jack thought a moment. She must have in mind Henry Higgins of *My Fair Lady*. The Pygmalion man. "You mean Dr. Frankenstein?" he asked innocently.

She laughed and brushed at him in mock annoyance as she started on down the hall.

People liked Joan. In a way, that was quite remarkable because there could be no doubt that she intimidated some and challenged the rest. Even Jack himself was at times made to feel a little uncomfortable by Joan—times such as a few minutes ago downstairs. But the general feeling around the agency—and he had done his best to foster it—was that she was coming along just fine. And why shouldn't they think that? It was true.

Jack took the trouble to pull the door to his office shut behind him in hope that it would discourage the usual casual interruptions. It also made him feel a little more at home. He liked his office. It told him a little about himself. For instance, the fact that Jack had had Tommy Corcoran's sofa hauled out when he took over from Charlie Newell meant to Jack that he was less willing than either one of them had been to make visitors comfortable. People tended to hang around a little too long when they could stretch out in cushioned comfort. He kept it a little darker, too—perhaps to give the impression that he was burning the midnight oil, no matter what the time of day. And the place was neater. Although he had always been a clean-desk man, Jack's desire for order had become practically a mania since he had taken over as copy chief.

Just now, as he settled in behind his desk, he took time to divide the telephone messages into two separate piles and then began dialing his way through those that seemed to require immediate action. It must have taken him about forty minutes or so. In any case, he had finished with his telephone calls and had just started through his in-box when a knock came at the door. "Come on in," he called out, a little annoyed at the interruption.

He was surprised when the visitor turned out to be Joan, and more surprised still when she closed the door behind her.

"What did you—"

She raised a finger to her lips, signaling silence. He frowned at her, puzzled, as she took a step or two over to the desk. The finger she had raised to her lips had remained there. But now she pulled it away, turned it toward him, and slowly wiggled it in his direction, beckoning him from his chair. He began to understand.

Rising quietly and carefully, he stepped around the desk and over to her. He stopped about two feet away. The silence between them was peculiarly charged. Her eyes had been moving around the small room, as though she were sizing it up, but now they came to rest on Jack. She looked him straight in the eye, and what he saw there surprised him.

If the look she had given him had been purely erotic, it would have seemed altogether appropriate to the moment. There was a certain boldness in her eyes, but that was always there. Wasn't it the challenge in them that he had noticed when they first met? No, there was something more, a kind of humor, a merry, conspiratorial quality that made him wonder if she might not burst out laughing in a moment. It made him wonder, too, if he had not perhaps misjudged the occasion. Perhaps it was no occasion at all. Her ostentatiously silent entrance may have been no more than an elaborate preface to a particularly juicy bit of gossip. Suddenly he was very, very glad he had stopped with some space between them and had not laid hands on her. He may have saved himself some embarrassment. At least that.

But, no. Joan had not come to gossip. She reached across and touched his belt buckle. He didn't quite understand. Was she asking him to undo it? Frowning, he shook his head, trying to convey not refusal but perplexity. But still she said nothing. Instead she slipped finger and thumb under the belt buckle and tugged at his zipper. All at once his fly came open, and she plunged her hand inside. He felt himself swell instantly to her touch. She didn't handle him roughly, but there was nothing timid in her movement either. When she squeezed him, as she did five times at easy rhythmic intervals, she moved gently but firmly, all the while keeping her eyes fixed on his, and all the while, too, showing him that same sly look of amusement. Jack realized with a start that she looked as though she were having fun. Was that what this meant to her? Fun?

Joan pulled with one hand, using the other to separate his clothing and open the way. His penis popped out. Involuntarily, he looked down at it. Rising from her cupped hand the red, swollen head of it strained up rigidly and returned his gaze. It was startling to see it from this angle and in this light. With her hand positioned as it was, he was reminded what it was like to masturbate. Was that what she had in mind for him? That could be risky.

He pulled her to him. "People are still around," he whispered in her ear. "Somebody might come in."

She pressed her cheek against his, and he caught the scent of her—soap and cologne over something deep and slightly rank. Then she whispered in his ear: "I know they might come in. That's what makes it fun. Shhh!"

She released him, took a quick step back, and hiked up her skirt. He looked and saw what she was showing him. She was wearing stockings and a garter belt but no pants. There at the junction where they might have been, her pubic bush blossomed, a dark flower that seldom saw the light. She grasped his hand, opened it, and carefully pointed his first three fingers. Taking them, she brought his hand down and wiped them slowly back and forth across her vulva. It was wet, or not just wet but viscous and sticky. She was ready.

But was he? Oh, there could be no doubt that physically he was ready to go. His penis was almost painfully erect—pushing, straining in the only direction that it knew. But could he? Now? Here?

Once more she brought his fingers across her, then took them up to her lips and kissed them. "Are you going to do something about that?" she whispered.

That was Joan, wasn't it? Always the challenge, always the dare.

He pushed her down gently across the desk. Her legs came up. She grasped her ankles. To enter her, he had to stand very tall, even a little on tiptoe, but as he plunged inside, he had the satisfaction of hearing her catch her breath suddenly, as though to tell him that he was a little more than she had bargained for. That, of course, was what he wanted to believe.

A few more thrusts, and he understood that there was a fundamental difficulty involved with across-the-desk sex: his knees were thumping against the walnut panels below. It was ridiculous, of course, but somehow he couldn't make it work right here.

He bent low and kissed her, oddly aware that it was the first time. And as he did that, he probed carefully below with his penis, temporizing, getting the feel of the track inside her and trying at the same time to decide how best to deal with this problem.

The telephone rang.

In a panic, Jack grabbed for it, fumbled the receiver, and nearly knocked the rest of it off the desk. At last he managed to get a firm grasp. He panted a moment in alarm before he was able to get the word out: "He . . . hello?"

"Jack? It that you?" A man's voice. He knew it, recognized it, but was so rattled that for the moment he couldn't think who it was.

"Of course it's me."

"Sorry. You sounded different. Look, I was just calling to make sure you were still around." Now Jack had the voice. It was Art Carstens. "I was about to come down to talk about that meeting this afternoon."

Again, panic. "Oh, don't do that!"

"Why not?"

"Uh, I was just leaving."

"Well . . . okay. I suppose it'll keep till Monday."

"Good. Sure. Okay." Why the hell couldn't he get rid of him? His eyes, which had been darting off in every other direction, at last settled on Joan, who had a hand clamped over her mouth and was doing her best to suppress a laugh. With a start, Jack realized he had not even withdrawn from her but was still standing there on his tiptoes, up to his scrotum in her bush.

"Oh . . . Jack?"

"Yes, Art?"

"Maybe we could get together on it tomorrow night. That is, if you don't mind talking shop . . . ?"

"*Tomorrow?*"

"Sure. Jan's party. You'll be there, won't you?"

"Yes. Fine. We'll talk about it then. So long." He hung up quickly, before Art could add another postscript to the conversation.

At last the laugh that Joan had held back exploded from her. She managed to whisper it out in kisses. He didn't quite know if he were expected to join in with her or feel angry at the interruption. Yet he was actually neither amused nor indignant. Simply relieved that the ordeal was over.

"You were *marvelous!*" she gasped out at last.

He didn't think she meant that. He knew he didn't feel marvelous. However, what he found surprising was that the ordeal of the telephone call had not dampened his desire. The receiver back on its cradle, he was ready now to finish what they had begun. He swayed back slightly and then pressed forward. Again. Again. Again. He grasped her by the knees and pulled her slightly toward him. Again. Again. Again. He was vaguely aware of the thumping that continued in accelerating rhythm against the desk. That was all he heard, for she had stopped laughing more than a minute ago.

They were late getting started. They always were. When at last Pat emerged from the bedroom, she came to him with an expression near desperation on her face and asked if she looked all right.

"Of course," he said. "You always do." And it was true; nothing spectacular but always all right. Tonight, for instance, she wore one of those shirtwaist dresses that went out with Jacqueline Kennedy. It fit well, it was neat, but certainly nobody would accuse her of overdressing for the occasion. At least the string of cultured pearls at her neck was a nice touch. He said as much.

"Well, if you're sure . . ."

He smiled and nodded. Be pleasant, he admonished himself. After all, it was easier that way. He called to the girls: "Hey, take a look at your mother. Doesn't she look terrific?"

They bestirred themselves. Carol turned away from the television screen and nodded. Nancy got up and lifted her arms, indicating she wanted to be kissed. This was done, the baby-sitter was instructed, and in three minutes more they were out in the car, ready to begin the drive to Van Dellen's place in Kenilworth.

Suddenly Pat turned to him. "You think this sweater is enough?"

"Well," he said, "you'd know that better than I would. If you think you'll be cold, why don't you run in and get your coat?"

"No. I mean, is it dressy enough?"

"Sure it is. Don't worry about it." He started the car, and they were on their way at last.

This uncertainty was something new with her. Or perhaps it had always been there and had only lately been aggravated. By him, he supposed. He blamed himself for most of what had gone wrong between them. Or perhaps "blame" was too strong a word—he *assumed* it was all his fault.

He took Sheridan Road north, winding along the old route along the lake shore with the radio on, exchanging a word now and then with Pat. He thought again about Joan and what had happened yesterday in the office. He literally found himself doubting that it really happened just like that then and there. It was so removed from all that had happened to him before that, even remembered precisely, the experience took on a kind of fantastic quality. Yes, that was it, of course. It was like a fantasy, wasn't it? Joan's silent entrance, the direct way that she had presented herself, the utter anonymity of their meeting. She had astonished him at the end by leaving just as she had come: silently, finger to her lips, backing out of his office. That was unreal. Only the phone call in the middle of it all from Art Carstens convinced Jack that it had all actually happened. Somehow that and that alone authenticated the entire experience.

"You certainly know the road. How many times have you been out to see Van Dellen, anyway?"

He frowned over at Pat. What was she getting at, anyway? "A couple," he said. "I guess twice with you to parties and once to deliver some stuff for his okay."

That seemed to satisfy her. "You sure know the way."

"I ought to," he said. "I drove this road out to Wilmette and Winnetka every Sunday afternoon for years so my mother could look at houses."

"Is that why you're so set against buying a house? Because your mother was all for it?"

"Maybe. Maybe that's part of it. I don't know."

"Jack, we've got the money. Or whatever we lack I could get from my family."

"I know. Let's drop it for now. Okay?"

Pat looked at him sharply. "All right," she said, "for now."

They continued on their way—out of Evanston now and well into Wilmette. His mind wandered back to Joan. It seemed to him he had thought of nothing and nobody else over the past twenty-four hours. He had called her three times during the day with no luck. Was this what it meant to be in love?

Two turns down two dark suburban streets brought them to Jan Van Dellen's place. He remembered the house from his earlier visits. It would have been impossible to miss anyway, because of all the cars thronged out front. Inside, it didn't seem nearly so crowded. It was the size of the place, Jack supposed. People wandered from room to room, drinks in hand, nodding and greeting again, in search of the party. There were rooms, alcoves, halls, all properly antiqued, leather-bound, and gilt-framed. Jack knew that this was what even moderate success in the ad business meant—Barton and Bradley was just a double-A agency with two big accounts—and while he was duly impressed, he was not in the least envious. He was so sure he would spend his money differently.

Jack had moved Pat through three different rooms, ostensibly in search of the bar but actually looking for Joan. He found the two not five feet from one another: the bar, served by a properly liveried young man whose two flashing hands kept the fifty or more guests well supplied; and Joan, who stood talking with Liz Meyer, watching the bartender hard at work. Jack parked Pat and headed off to get them drinks. The scotches he asked for took no more than seconds, it seemed. The young dark-haired man delivered them with a flourish and a wink and an "Enjoy your drink, sir." Style.

Jack wandered over to Joan and Liz—make it look casual—gave them a nod, and commented on the bartender.

"Isn't he terrific?" Joan exclaimed. "Liz and I have been watching him work. He's like a real old-time mixologist or something."

"Or something," Jack agreed. He turned to Liz. "Who's here?"

"Oh, about who you'd expect. All of us and all of them."

"Agency and clients?"

"And a few prospects."

"No matter what his many other virtues," Jack said with mock sententiousness, "our beloved president's not a very imaginative party-giver."

"Oh, I don't know," said Joan. "Wait until midnight when I pop out of the cake."

"I'll stick around for that." Jack looked from one to the other. "Well, I've got a drink to deliver."

"Come back when you can," said Joan.

Jack flashed her a smile as he turned away. "Count on it," he called back. Dodging his way back through the crowd that had gathered at the bar, he wondered just how plain it might be to Liz or to anyone else that there was something between them. Did it show? Did that matter?

When he got back to Pat, he found her talking to Art Carstens and his wife, Betty. "I was just hearing about your triumph," she said.

"You're so damned modest," said Art, "I have to toot your horn for you."

"Gawd, *modesty*!" crowed Betty Carstens, "that's not Art's problem!"

That got more of a laugh than it deserved.

"What about this Joan Bigley?" asked Pat.

Jack was suddenly tense. "What about her?"

"Well, I hear she's very good but sort of, well, pushy."

Jack looked at Art. "Is that what you said?"

"Oh . . . you know."

"Who is she?" asked Pat. "What's she like?"

Jack nodded across the room, daring her to look. "That's her over there with Liz Meyer. I was just talking to them."

"Oh," said Pat. "Oh, yes, she looks . . . interesting."

Jack studied his wife, trying to decide just what she meant by that. He would really like to know how Joan interested her, what she thought of her. But he decided it might be dangerous to dig.

Art Carstens clamped a hand on his shoulder. "Jack, boy, I wonder if we could have a word or two about that meeting. Now, Ray Dibble did bring up a point that I think deserves consideration, not exactly an objection, but . . ." Thus began a tedious, rambling discourse on yesterday's meeting, a conversation that should properly have taken place only in the office—but Art was determined. Betty Carstens wandered away first, followed finally by Pat. Yet Jack hung on doggedly, nodding soberly through it all, agreeing vocally when it was required of him, searching only for an opportunity to get back over to Joan.

When at last the chance came—Art flailing the air, declaring that he was sure that they would be able to work everything out in a day or two next week—Jack saw that Joan was then talking to, of all people, Consolidated's Calvin Ross. Well, there was his entrance, but how was he to get her away from him?

By the time he had gotten away from Art and over to the two of them, he had still not solved the problem. But Art handled it for him, blustering over behind Jack, thumping Ross on the back manfully, and boring in on him as he had on Jack a good half an hour before. Jack and Joan were able to shrink off to one side, smiling and nodding, just out of earshot.

"Whew," Joan whispered, "am I glad to get rescued!"

"Coming on strong?"

"Strong enough."

"I tried to call you a couple of times today," Jack said. He looked at her closely. She sipped at her drink and seemed to be staring over his shoulder. At what?

"I was out," she said, "all day."

"Somehow I got that impression," he said. "The telephone kept ringing."

"Oh, come on, boss," she said, fixing him with that brassy look, "give me a break. I was out shopping for this dress. Isn't it a killer?"

It was black jersey and it clung. She was right. It was a killer. He merely nodded. "Look," he said, "I've got to see you."

"I'm available," she said, "but are you?"

"I'll work it out. Is tomorrow afternoon all right?"

"Sure. Of course."

"Three o'clock?"

"Three o'clock."

They made no effort to talk after that, simply backed off in opposite directions, smiling pleasantly toward Calvin Ross, nodding to all around them.

He lost track of Joan after that until about an hour later when, looking across the living room, he happened to notice her deep in conversation with Pat. That surprised him, shocked him a little.

Although he had expected to hear something about it on the way home, his wife said nothing. Nothing at all.

"Take off your clothes," he said. "I haven't seen you nude."

"Is that so strange?"

"Under the circumstances, yes, I'd say it is."

Without another word, Joan did as he had told her. This was why he was here, Jack assured himself, in order to make love to her unhurriedly, as an act of discovery, to try somehow to define and measure what this thing was between them. For his part, he was sure he was in love. He had come this afternoon looking only for confirmation of that.

Leaning back on the sofa in the bare, bright room, he watched her expose herself. As he did, he was reminded of the strippers he had watched as a boy, as a young man. Not because she made an erotic performance of undressing—she went about it efficiently with her eyes fixed tightly on him—but because what she was doing was all part of the old stripper-fantasy, and it all fit perfectly, didn't it? The women of his daydreams had ever afterward been alternately aggressive and acquiescent. They were always bold enough to make the first move, as she certainly had been, yet were also willing to do whatever he wished. Could she have known that? Could she somehow have read his fantasies?

No matter. She herself was real enough. Nude from the waist up now, she was more slender and smaller-breasted than he had expected, almost frail, for in contrast her legs and hips were sturdy—a peasant from the waist down. She pushed out of her slacks, hooking her pants down with her thumbs, stepping out of the pile of clothing on the floor with a certain casual grace. Joan stood there before him then, hands on hips, framed in the windows of her apartment with all of the northwest side of Chicago as her backdrop. They were on the twenty-fourth floor, and such distance assured privacy. She could, of course, be seen with a telescope, but Jack was certain that would not have bothered her at all.

"Well?" she said to him.

"Well, what? I'm delighted."

"Well, I showed you mine. Now you show me yours."

He laughed, distracted, and she turned away suddenly and walked from his view. "Where are you going?" he called after her.

"To the kitchen to make a drink for us." There was a moment's silence, a hesitation, and then she added: "Get out of your clothes. It's unfriendly not to. It makes a person feel like an insect on a slide."

"Or an animal in the zoo?"

"Exactly. Do it."

Reluctantly, he did. He had no real intention of staying clothed throughout his visit, of course. But somehow the idea of exposing himself in daylight, as he had asked her to do, disturbed him more than a little. Could he walk around the way she did, with at least a pretense to casualness? He hoped to God he could. He heard water running and ice breaking—she was doing just what she said. He must now also, he supposed. Jack unbuttoned, unzipped, pulled, and tugged—and was finally free of his clothing, glancing regretfully down at the excess at his waist, wishing he had at least had the foresight to propose a nighttime visit. Next time he would know better.

She returned, a drink in one hand and a cigarette in the other. Her eyes flickered over his form there on the couch. "Well," she said, "that's better, isn't it?"

Jack smiled crookedly. "I'm not sure."

She offered him the glass. "Scotch," she said. He took it and sipped as she continued: "Sex—if I may say so without sounding as though I'm delivering a lecture—is mostly in the head. Or at least it is with me. It's sort of you-tell-me-your-dream-and-I'll-tell-you-mine."

"Oh?"

"That's right." She puffed deeply on the cigarette, then ground it out in an ashtray. She settled down on the sofa at a distance, facing him. "It's fun that way."

That word again. "Fun?" he echoed.

"Didn't anyone tell you it could be fun?"

"Well, sure. It's just that . . . " She waited, but he had no intention of finishing the sentence. He didn't know how. "Okay," Jack said, giving in, "you tell me your dream."

She grinned at him. He suspected for a moment she might giggle. "I thought you'd never ask." She moved herself back to her end of the sofa and rested her head on the arm. His eyes moved up her body as she stretched back languorously. It seemed to rise up topographically before him in hillocks and hollows, valleys and plateaus. Yet again and again his attention returned—instinctively, probably—to the place she intended it to go. Without quite staring, he managed to study it closely, a thing of puckers and crevices, all masked over with tiny tight ringlets of dark fur. He was almost ready to reach out and touch Joan there when she drew up her knees and spread her feet to the width of the sofa. "There," she said, "you get the idea?"

He got the idea all right, and it frightened him a little—a formless, primal sort of fear was what he felt settle over him. Not disgust. Fear.

"Well, I . . ."

"Oh," she laughed, "you're going to tell me you're not that kind of boy, is that it?"

"I . . ."

"Well, be that sort of boy, Jack. Be a different kind of boy. Be as many different kinds of boys as you can be." The tone of voice she used was soft, quietly demanding, exhorting. "That's it," she urged, "come closer. Come in there. I promise I won't hurt you. Why would I do a thing like that? Closer, yes, closer. Just a kiss. Go ahead. Give a kiss. What harm could there be?"

He did as she directed. She was talking to him as one might to a stubborn child or a skittish horse. He knew that, and he would have resented it if there had been the merest hint of derision in her tone. But there was none. She was sympathetic, more than sympathetic. She was pedagogically encouraging. He was her prize pupil.

Eyes open, he came up close and suddenly buried his face in the dark patch before him, breathing it in, tasting it. There was a deep, earthy smell to it, almost like newly turned humus, and the taste was tart and acid, almost metallic, from her sweat and probably from her urine, too. The fear he had felt left him. He simply knew that he had never been closer to any woman than he was at that moment to Joan.

He pressed his tongue inside, curiously at first, just to taste more of the tart, but then more urgently, giving himself to it as he understood better just what he was to do. And then he heard Joan sigh and shift, pushing down toward him, and he remembered her, hovering up there above him like some separate being. He felt her hands on the back of his head, caressing, her fingers combing through his hair, encouraging him to delve deeper. Her pelvis moved as he continued. The sound of her voice—praising, requesting, demanding, and finally crooning wordlessly—came to him as though from another room. Her fingers dug into his hair sharply. Her lower body went rigid for an instant, held by a passing spasm. He moved up and mounted her, kneeling at his work, driving into her with all the force he could draw from his upper legs, then grinding at her mercilessly as she thrashed along beneath him, and finally driving, driving, driving, as she moved to meet him time after time.

It ended in a mutual shudder. They lay back, panting—not side by side, for there was no room for him next to her—but in a kind of V, legs tangled, hands touching, resting.

"Well," she said after minutes had passed, "you see? You're talented in ways you never knew."

Jack said nothing. He wasn't sure he wanted to talk about it.

"One thing does surprise me about you, though," she continued. "Or maybe it shouldn't."

He turned to her. "What's that?"

"You struggle so."

"Struggle?"

"I guess that's what I'd call it." She thought a moment. "Struggle or fight or something. It's like you're always trying to win. I'm not your opponent, Jack."

"I . . . I never thought you were."

"Didn't you?" She studied him for a moment. "It's a game we play together. If we don't both win, then we both lose."

"You're quite the teacher, aren't you?"

"No." She grinned. "I'm a philosopher."

He reached down blindly to the floor and, groping carefully, found the scotch he had left there. He took a sip and passed it over to her.

"Tell me something," he said.

"Anything."

"I noticed you talking to Pat last night, my wife. What did you have to say to each other?"

"You mean, did we compare notes or something?"

"You know that's not what I mean."

"All right, sorry. We just talked about what women talk about in situations like that. She said, among other things, that she envied me."

"*Envied* you?" That did surprise him.

"Sure. Your wife's like a lot of other women, Jack—wants to be something on her own, something more than just a wife."

"Well, she never . . ." He left that hanging. On an impulse, he asked Joan suddenly: "How did you feel about that?"

"About her working, you mean?"

"No, no." He sounded annoyed, but he wasn't. Just trying to get to the point. "How did you feel about talking to her? I mean, here we are. Now. Like this. How do you feel about it now?"

"Well, I don't feel guilty, if that's what you mean. I don't feel anything particularly about it. She seems like a nice woman. You're a nice man. So what? I told you I don't believe in marriage."

"For yourself."

"Not for anybody else either. It just makes for messes like this one you've got yourself in now."

Somehow he never got around to telling her he thought he was in love with her. That was how he phrased it to himself: he *thought* he was. Tentative. Qualified. But in the hour that he remained there, the opportunity never presented itself, and so he kept his speculations private.

As it turned out, he was glad that he did. Having left Joan at last later than he had intended, and longer perhaps than she had wished him to stay, he traveled down the twenty-four floors in the elevator and stepped out into the lobby. There he met a familiar-looking young man—dark-haired, with quick eyes—who said nothing to Jack but nodded as he moved past him into the elevator. It wasn't until much later in the evening that Jack realized that the young man in the lobby had been the bartender at Jan Van Dellen's party the night before.

During the weeks that followed, theirs proved to be a difficult relationship to maintain. There were, of course, the usual practical problems inherent in any adulterous affair—the arrangements to be made, the lies to be told—and none of this came easy to Jack. It wasn't so much that it was contrary to his nature, but rather that it was contrary to his conception of his nature. He liked to think of himself as open, direct, frank, and basically quite honest. The many lies that he told his wife made it difficult for him to maintain this view—but not impossible. He solved the problem by assuring himself that it was all for her own good, and that if she knew what he was really doing those three and four nights a week he claimed to be working late at the office, then it would surely kill her. And so it became the kind of lie you told a sick friend—not really one at all.

That was the least of it. Joan herself was the problem. Mercurial, unpredictable, bold, she was difficult in all the same ways and for the same reasons that she had attracted him in the first place. In the office, she was a bit too ready to show affection, though probably no more so than before (it was just that he was more sensitive now to appearances).

Yet she was offended and angry, and she absolutely refused the only time that he had proposed that they spend their lunch hour in a hotel room. (Remembering Tommy Corcoran, he couldn't say that he was greatly disappointed.) On the other hand, she would act on impulse and with such abandon that she sometimes left him dizzy with embarrassment. There was that time, eating dinner side by side at a fairly posh restaurant on Rush Street, that she suddenly reached down under the napkin, unzipped him, and began working his penis. It was her idea of a joke—but not that merely. At the crucial moment, the waiter appeared, and Jack was forced to grit his teeth and fix a smile until the crisis passed. He wondered later what the busboy made of the napkin. Jack might never go back there again.

At times he thought he wouldn't put up with her at all if it weren't for the sex. That finally was what it was all about, wasn't it? Or was there something more? He was puzzled. How could she so successfully have reversed the regular professional roles of teacher and student that he had established? There was no doubt that at least in bed she had managed to do just that. A philosopher was what she had called herself, and he had to concede that she had evidently thought long, hard, and well on these matters. They were important to her, and she had convinced him that they should be important to him, too. As he got to know her better and came to know what was inside her, he understood that all that really mattered to her were her sexual pleasure, her work, and—what?—her independence, he supposed she would call it. To her they were closely related— or more than that: they were three separate aspects of the same reality. One night she had told him—they were lying together on her bed, the sweat and semen drying on them— that sex was limitless. "It will take you anyplace you want to go," she had told him, speaking more solemnly than she ever had before. "There aren't any boundaries."

"Well," he said, "there's death. That's one."

"Prove it."

She intimidated him. He admitted that to himself, though he would never have said as much to her. Somehow he had simply been unable to bring up to her that meeting with the young bartender in the lobby. What was he to think? That her calendar was so full that one sexual appointment followed so closely on another? That her life was a kind of intervaled gang-bang? That she maintained a male harem? He preferred not to think about that at all. The closest he had ever come to talking about it, she had laid it down as a dictum that exclusive relationships simply didn't work. Why? "For the same reasons marriages don't work. People don't own people." He had pushed the discussion no further.

And still, he told himself, he loved her. What other name could he give it? He was obsessed by her, had to force himself to think of anything else but her when they were apart, and, of course, he wanted to be with her all the time. They had done things together he had done with nobody else, certainly not with Pat. Therefore he must be in love with her. While Jack himself was aware that the logic of that was pretty shaky, nevertheless he knew what his feelings were, no matter what label they wore. The night she had talked so disparagingly of exclusive relationships, he had said to her later that they seemed to have a kind of fundamental difficulty in communication.

"How do you mean?" she asked.

"I don't know exactly. But when we have sex together, even when we talk about it, it's as though we were using two different dialects of the same language. You see what I mean? The same thing means one thing to you and something slightly different to me. The weight, the nuance, the connotation isn't quite the same. We *think* we understand each other a lot better than we do."

She looked at him oddly. "You know," she said, "that's true. I hadn't thought about it quite like that before, but it's true."

With all this, it was remarkable that their professional relationship continued as smoothly as it did. She didn't challenge him—at least no more often than before and possibly a little less—and she didn't ask for or receive favored treatment. In the office, except for the occasional hand on the arm, they were both quite businesslike.

A few weeks after their conference out at Consolidated, the print part of the "Solid" Girl campaign began to appear, paving the way for the television stuff that would begin in another month—if they stayed on schedule. It caught the industry by surprise. *Ad Age* and *Printer's Ink* both did features on the campaign, and Jack made sure that Joan got a good share of the credit. A good share was what she deserved.

It was a couple of weeks after the write-up in *Advertising Age* had appeared that Joan came by Jack's office late one morning and asked if they could have lunch together that day. That in itself was unusual. As part of Jack's keep-it-cool-at-the-office campaign, they usually lunched separately and got together only after working hours. Jack had no reason to suspect that there was anything special behind the request, but he found out soon enough that there was.

They had no more than settled at a table and ordered a drink when she said bluntly, "I've taken another job."

"You've *what*?"

She nodded soberly and looked him straight in the eye. "That's right," she said, "another job. I'm supposed to start in a month. That ought to give you plenty of time to find somebody else, shouldn't it?"

"I guess so, yes, but . . . Well, may I ask where it is you're going?"

"McCann-Erickson. It's all because of what we did on Consolidated. I mean, there's no question of that. They liked the campaign. They liked my part of it. They came after me and made me an offer."

"A pretty good one, I'll bet."

"Very good."

"It's a big outfit."

"Very big."

At that moment, the waitress appeared with their drinks. Jack was glad for the interruption. It gave him a moment to reorganize. He took a sip and then another and waited for his jumbled emotions—panic, anger, fear, sadness—to settle under control. "Look," he said to her at last, "I don't know if you're aware of it or not, but the usual thing in situations like this is to let your present employer know what the offer is so that he can meet it or better it. Now, when we get back to the office I suggest we sit down with Jan and talk this thing over. He's not exactly a big man with a buck, but he does know quality, and I think he can be made to see his way clear."

She said nothing, simply looked down at her drink and gave it a swirl.

"Well?" Jack prompted.

"Well, what?"

"Don't you think you owe us that?"

When at last she looked up at him, he saw that she herself was having problems holding herself in check. Her eyes glistened, and her chin was slightly puckered. "I suppose I do," she said. "I suppose I owe you a lot, Jack, but it's a debt that's just going to have to go unpaid for a while. Look, I've got to take this job. It's right for me, and I've got to get away from Barton and Bradley. I've got to get away from *you*. Can't you see that?"

"From me? What did *I* do?"

"Nothing. *We* did. What we've got going is a bad situation. It can't go anywhere except from bad to worse with us. As you said yourself, Jack, it's like we speak two different dialects."

"Well . . ." He hesitated, groping, grasping. "Well, I'm learning yours."

"It's no good, Jack. McCann-Erickson is a good chance for me, and I've got to take it. Don't you see? It's the only way we can keep on as friends."

He glared at her, so full of anger and unhappiness that he knew he would have to say something. But he really had no idea what would come out when he opened his mouth. "Friend?" Abruptly: "You won't need me for a friend there. You'll be too busy fucking your way to the top."

She didn't say a word to that. She simply shook her head in an emphatic negative, stood up, and walked out of the restaurant. When she didn't show up for work in the afternoon, he had to tell Van Dellen why.

"Oh, Jack," said Pat. "I like the area a lot."

"Me, too, Daddy," said Carol. "I like it, too."

"Lots of kids," said Nancy, pointing out the car window.

She was right, thought Jack, lots of kids. It was the truest, profoundest comment anyone could possibly make regarding this particular corner of Park Ridge—lots of kids. They were everywhere, whooping, running, falling, jumping up, and running again. It seemed no less than a community of children maintained by a small staff of adult servants. Why, they ought to have a ten-year-old mayor, he thought, and an eight-year-old chief of police—because clearly the kids were in charge.

He crept along down the street, both hands tight on the steering wheel, watchful, worried that one of the horde on either side might dart out into the middle of the road. At this moment he felt hopelessly outnumbered. That was why he was here, wasn't it? Outnumbered? Outtalked? Outmaneuvered? Well, not entirely. There was certainly another factor involved here. He had not even attempted to hide that from himself. Well, whatever the scenario and whatever the reasons, here he was, doing what he had hoped not to do—looking for that little house in the suburbs.

"That's it," Pat said, "right there, just ahead. Oh, look, Jack. Isn't it nice?"

He looked. Nice was what it was. Not beautiful. Not ugly. Not anything at all but nice. It was a kind of ranch-style house with a bungalow roof. He had passed three or four just like it on the way in. "Yes," he said, "it's nice." No need to gush.

He maneuvered the car over to the side of the road and eased it to a halt. The For Sale sign out in front confirmed what the address told them: this was the house they had come to see. The real-estate agent had promised Pat she would like it, told her it was the perfect house for them at this time. That was cute—*at this time*—the implied judgment that the John Gawlors were on their way up, a family with a big-income future. Well, Park Ridge may not have been Kenilworth, but Jack supposed it was a hell of a lot better than a walk-up in Rogers Park. He had resigned himself to buying someplace, and this looked like as good as any. As far as he was concerned, it was up to Pat.

The experience with Joan Bigley had brought him around to this. He knew that. If she had said the word he would probably have left Pat. If he had believed they had a future together, then he would have followed it—at whatever cost. One thing she had taught him, perhaps the most important, was that it was all right to be selfish and good to be reckless. And if her sudden departure had proved anything to him, it was that it did no good to put much faith in others. Except Pat, of course. He knew he could handle her, and he knew also that in a very real way she was necessary for the life he meant to live.

"Come on, Jack, let's go take a look inside." Pat was more excited than the kids were. They were taking all this more or less in stride. She could hardly contain herself. Her hand grasped him tightly at the arm.

"Sure," he said. "Why not?"

They all got out of the car and started across the narrow road together. The door of the house opened and a woman of about thirty-five stepped out. She was attractive in a routine way—tall, blonde, regular-featured. At first he thought she was the owner of the house, but then he noticed the briefcase under her arm.

"Who's she?"

"That's Virginia Jelinek," said Pat, "the real-estate woman I told you about."

She had a nice smile and no wedding ring. Well. Jack decided then and there to make a test case of Virginia Jelinek. He decided he would fuck her.

*

For once Klezek wasn't disappointed. With a lot of women, you could hump and pump away all night, and they would just lie there and take it. Oh, it was all very polite. They might say "please" and "thank you," and praise his Polish virility. But when it came to moving their asses, well, you could just forget about it.

That's not the way it had been with Liz Meyer, though. He did little more than touch her, and she was all over him. He liked that. There was no holding back, no pretending she was too much a lady to join in the fun. They went through his entire repertoire and then started on hers. He liked hers better.

As agreed upon, they had met after work at a place just off Michigan, ostensibly to talk a little more about Jack Gawlor. Klezek was on his own time, but what the hell, he wasn't just there on department business, after all. He knew that, and so did she. Well, one thing led to another—drinks to dinner, dinner to a "nightcap," and the nightcap—where else would you wear one of those things?—to bed. She was smart. She could talk. She made him feel good. He had an idea it was going to work out especially well with her when she felt the Colt Python he wore under his left arm and didn't make any fuss. Most women carried on about it some way or other. They either made him take it off that very instant, or haul it out and show it to them. When Liz felt it, he had just kissed her for the first time. Her arms were circled around him, and she happened to pass her hand over the holster and the butt of the pistol. She frowned up at him, groped it curiously, then realizing what it was, said simply, "Oh." Then she went back to kissing him. It was hard not to like a babe like that.

And he liked her very successfully in bed. It was as much fun as Klezek had had in a long, long time. When at last the two of them came up, gasping and giggling, they threw themselves down side by side on the pillows and simply panted together for a while, heaving along more or less in rhythm.

And then gradually they settled down, returning to themselves, finding their way back.

They talked desultorily of one thing and another there in the dark, their hands touching. Finally, Klezek turned to Liz, and even though he could make out only the outline of her face, he addressed her directly: "Hey, can I ask you something personal?"

"I guess now's the time to do it," she answered.

"Did you ever make it with this guy Gawlor?"

She was silent for a moment. Then: "That is personal. But I can understand that you'd want to know that. Besides, the answer is no. I never did."

"Why not?"

"Why not?" she laughed. "You are nosey aren't you? What do you mean, 'why not?' "

"Well, I mean, you two worked together for years, didn't you? I didn't have to hang around you that long to know I liked what I saw."

"That's very nice of you, of course, but as I said before, he kept his personal life pretty separate from work. Besides . . ."

"Yes?"

"I guess I never encouraged him. Oh, we were buddies around the office, gossiped a lot, and so on, but I never wanted it to go any further than that. Not even after he was divorced from his wife—maybe especially not then."

"Mind telling me why? Do you think he was queer then?"

"That depends on what you mean by queer. If it's homosexual, I have no idea, If you mean odd, then yes, he was queer. The last couple of years he had a kind of driven, desperate quality. Not about his work—somehow or other he managed to keep afloat at the office. But it was in his face, in his manner. There was that withdrawn quality I mentioned. One time I walked in on him, and he was talking to himself. Listening, answering—one whole side of a conversation. He didn't even notice me standing there in the doorway, so I just turned around and walked away."

Klezek said nothing for a long moment, and then, when he did speak, it was only to grunt, "Hmmmm."

CHAPTER SIX *1968*

By the last day of the shoot, the guard at the gate had gotten to know Jack by sight. He waved the rented Mustang through the moment he saw who was behind the wheel. That felt good to Jack. Was this what it was like to work in the studios? To be a part of all this? He drove slowly a short distance down the studio street to the visitors' parking lot, and, squinting all the while into the brilliant midday sun, managed to find a parking space. For the past week he had been meaning to pick up a pair of sunglasses. Somehow he had managed to live his life in Chicago without owning a pair. Out here they were a necessity.

He hurried the few steps across to the office building and, giving the receptionist a nod, went straight into the first-floor screening room.

"Ah, Jack. Good man." It was George Bertille, the in-house producer. That did him for hello.

"Sorry if I'm late. It was the damned traffic on the freeway." Jack took the seat beside him.

"It always is," Bertille said sympathetically. He glanced around the room. There were six or eight there ranged around them, most of them turned expectantly in their direction. "Are we all ready?" The only direct response he got was from Frank Pargiter, the director, who nodded. "Okay, then." Bertille called back to the projectionist: "You can roll it."

What they were about to see was the result of the second day of shooting. Three days was a hell of a long time to spend on a one-minute commercial, and the budget on this one was a killer, but this was to be a product announcement, and it would set the style and tone for the whole campaign to follow. Breeze would be marketing a brown-papered menthol cigarette in the fall—the company's answer to the cigarillos that were doing so well now. They were calling them "new Breeze Browns" and were pushing a strong masculine image, selling the brown-paper cigarettes as though they were phallic cigars. Jack had come up with the idea for the debut commercial. "What's more masculine than a gunfight?" he had asked, and getting no argument from Dick Raynor, the product ad manager, he had proceeded to blue-sky an entire miniature western in which the hero rides into town, blasts the bad guy, gets the dancehall girl, and then lights up his new Breeze Brown—all in the space of a minute. "Can we do all that in a minute?" Dick Raynor had asked. "On film," Jack had assured him, "you can do anything." But just to make sure, Raynor came out for the first couple of days of shooting. Finally, satisfied, and with matters pressing him back in Richmond, he had flown back east. Jack, in fact, had just returned from the airport where he had dropped Raynor off with a warm handshake and casual reassurance that everything was going just fine.

And it was. What Jack saw up there on the screen told him that. Pargiter was a pro, the best man available for the kind of mini-feature they were attempting. It was for him they had come out here to shoot it—and for the western set, of course. Hollywood was the logical place. A succession of images rolled by—the hero in closeup, the villain in closeup, the long shot down the dusty street—each of them repeated in take after take.

"Hey," someone said into the dark. "I like that back lighting. Looks good."

"Great stuff, Frank. Truly great." That from George Bertille.

Jack didn't know about great, but it was quality work, there was no doubt about that. He knew that, according to the word on the street, Jack Gawlor was not quite as sharp with television as he was with print—in short, a wordman, and as such, not altogether suitable for the creative-director spot he had just taken over at Barton and Bradley.

Well, he thought, the hell with them. He had been thinking concepts and selling concepts since he came into the business. It just so happened that he was also a damned good copywriter. If they couldn't handle that, then it was their problem. This Breeze Brown commercial would go a long way toward establishing him. Let them try to say he couldn't handle TV after they saw this.

The lights came on. George Bertille turned to him. "Well, Jack, what do you think?"

"I like what I see."

Bertille called to Pargiter, "Hear that, Frank? You're keeping the customer happy." Crass.

Pargiter simply nodded. Jack liked him better for that.

They broke up then, and a minute or two later Jack was walking down the studio street with Bertille, heading back to the western set. Bertille was doing most of the talking: "Well, listen, Jack, I felt that. I really felt that. I mean, all the time Dick Raynor was here on the set. I get really super vibes from him. You've got to be pleased with that kind of response."

"I'm pleased," Jack said. "I told you, George, I think it's going well."

Bertille gestured expansively. "I mean, Jack, you really ought to start thinking of us for *all* your work. After all, we're out here, man. This is where it's all happening."

"What's that supposed to mean?" Jack wasn't annoyed, just curious. "People out here are always saying stuff like that, and I'd honestly like to know. Just *how* is it all happening here?"

Bertille stopped and regarded him for a moment. "You're serious, aren't you? Well, look, what can I tell you? I mean, it's happening—right? This is the vanguard, the new consciousness, the wave of the future. You want to know what the rest of America's going to look like in ten years? Twenty? Look around you. This is where it's at—creatively, socially, politically, sexually . . ."

"Sexually? Come on. There's been nothing new since the Romans."

"It's all in the attitude, Jackie boy. Don't tell me Raynor

was taking up *that* much of your time. Surely you've noticed that people are . . . how shall I put it?—a little freer here? Look, if you'd like me to handle it, I'll invite somebody along for you at this little bash of mine tomorrow. Some-girl-body. What do you say?"

For some reason, Jack was slightly irritated at that. He knew that George meant well, but why did he have to act like some kind of pimp? Jack had been pleased when he had invited him to his home, but when George came on like this, he made it seem like it was all business—pimping for profit or something.

"No," Jack said after a slight pause, "I've got an old friend here. Somebody I've known since high school. I thought I'd bring her along—that is, if it's all right . . . ?"

"Are you kidding? Jackie boy, it's not all right, it's terrific!" They resumed their way. Jack was aware of the sidelong look given him by Bertille. At last George spoke: "High school, huh? A lot of years under the bridge, huh, Jack?"

"Not *that* many."

When at last they came out onto the western set, it took Jack a few moments to acclimate himself. It always did. Not that the frontier buildings and costumed extras made it all so realistic. They didn't. It wasn't. No, it was the little disorienting start it gave him each time he saw them there with the crew—the lights and reflectors, the big Mitchell cameras, and the sound equipment. *This* was Hollywood. *This* was movie-making. You could walk through the studio streets with sound stages looming up on either side and never get a hint of what was going on in them. It was only here with the process exposed to view that it came alive for him. He had to see it to believe it.

Pargiter had preceded them there by a few minutes, and already the set was alive with activity. He had been down squinting through the camera. Now he pulled himself up to his full five feet five inches and bellowed out in a voice so deep and commanding that it never ceased to surprise Jack: "All right, look, put a reflector in that doorway. Otherwise we're looking right into a black hole."

Details. It was all in the details. Jack knew that, but each reminder impressed him again what an artificial process the re-creation of reality was. And how tedious.

He settled down on a hitching rail beside an extra who was reading *An Actor Prepares* and spent the rest of the afternoon trying to look interested. He wasn't, really. Now that they were into the third day of the shoot, Jack's attention had flagged to the point that he wished only to see the thing through to the end. The dailies yesterday and today had told him that he was in good hands with Pargiter, that Jack's fundamental idea was being translated very smoothly to the screen, enhanced and enriched, as it should have been, by an experienced director. What more could he ask? Now especially with Dick Raynor gone, there seemed no need even to appear concerned. The situation was under control. So much so, in fact, that when Frank Pargiter boomed out, "That's it. That's a wrap," it was only four-thirty. An early end. There was handshakes and backslaps all the way around. Jack told Pargiter he was an absolute genius, which around here passed as no more than routine praise; for the third time he heard directions from George Bertille on getting out to the producer's place on the beach; and then he made a hasty exit, hurrying down the studio street to the parking lot.

Something unusual happened just as he jumped inside and started the engine. A car drove by only a few feet away, and Jack recognized the woman behind the wheel as Raquel Welch. There could be no doubt about it. In fact, she half-turned in his direction as she passed him by, as though to give him a better view of that million-dollar face of hers. But then she was past him, and was headed for the gate. Jack backed out of the parking space, and driven by a sudden urgency that he himself only half understood, he accelerated after her in brisk pursuit. He hoped to catch up with her at the gate, but by the time he got there, she was just passing through—the guard grinning in recognition and tossing her a two-fingered salute—and another car, a big Mercedes, had whipped in behind her. By the time Jack was clear of the gate, her car was nowhere in sight. He headed off down Ventura Boulevard in the direction he supposed she would have turned—and look! it was true, for ahead he spotted a car that was the right color. By the time he caught up with it, however, he saw that the right color was all that it was. The make was wrong, a Jaguar, and behind the wheel sat a fat, forty-year-old bald-headed man who looked as though he might be a salesman.

Raquel Welch. He looked upon the episode as a missed opportunity. Heading toward the freeway, he asked himself just what he would have done if she had been in that car he had pursued. Would he have followed her home? Would he have tried to catch her eye at a traffic light? And in response, as he headed up the ramp to join the thickening freeway traffic, Jack began to spin out for himself an elaborate fantasy in which he not only caught the attention of Raquel Welch but won her immediate interest, as well: A current passed between them. He pulled up beside her at one traffic light and then another and another. By the time she was ready to turn off Ventura, she had conveyed to him by licking her lips and other less subtle gestures that he was to follow her. He did just that, matching her skillful driving with his own road mastery as they wound up one canyon road and then down another. He was in full flight now, in hot pursuit, and ahead of him was both his prize and his competitor. He followed her so closely that they turned almost simultaneously down a side road that wound on up to her own cantilevered mansion in the sky. There she hopped out of her car and turned just long enough to determine that he was close behind, then skipped inside the house, leaving the door tantalizingly open. He would go in then, of course, approaching with a certain gravity to match the occasion, hitching up his pants in that old, masterful, masculine gesture, kicking the door shut behind with a solid, loud *bam*. Striding forcefully forward, he would listen for a signal, a hint of where she had gone—and it would come—a discreet cough, a low laugh, or, yes, the sound of music, soft jazz on the stereo. *That* was how he would find her. Nude? Not yet. He would help her undress—and she him. And then . . .

He was still working on "and then . . ." when at last he

turned off the San Diego Freeway and onto Venice Boulevard. He was headed for Marina del Rey, the new close-in private-boat dock where George Bertille had booked him at a hotel, promising him a "swinging scene." Jack wasn't so sure what that meant, and baby-sitting Dick Raynor he hadn't really had a chance to find out. All he knew was that it was pretty inconvenient getting from there to the studio each day. But where in Los Angeles was it *not* inconvenient? It wasn't a city; it was mass schizophrenia linked by a system of freeways.

Jack almost missed the girl at the corner because he assumed that she was waiting for the bus. But, no. She stepped out in his direction, her thumb hooked westward. He waved her into the car and onto the seat beside him. She was settled in and babbling on before he realized that tall, blonde, and well-developed though she was, his passenger was no more than sixteen years old, and probably a year or two less.

". . . and, like, I'm telling you, it really is true. I mean, here I am, you know? And this is it, you know? I mean, right away I could dig it. Far out, right?"

He thought she was telling him about the same thing that George Bertille was earlier that afternoon. But he wasn't sure. Glancing over in her direction, he sized her up, trying to guess her age, wondering if she were a runaway. He decided to ask: "How old are you, anyway?"

She shot a look in his direction, something between suspicious and hostile. "Are you into ages?" she asked. "Is that your trip?"

"No," he said. "I was just wondering. But why? What's your trip?"

"Love, peace, and happiness." Just like that.

"Well, I'm glad somebody's sure of something."

"Are you a cop?"

Jack hooted at that. "A cop? Me? Do I look like a cop?"

He glanced over and found her sizing him up. "I guess not," she conceded at last. "But you look pretty straight. What is it, you know, like—what do you do?"

"My job?"

"Yeah."

"I'm in advertising."

She turned away coldly. Jack got just a glimpse of that, but it was enough to annoy him. "Advertising's a shuck," she said at last.

"What's a shuck?"

"It's like, you know, a lie."

"All right, yes, I guess you could say that. Advertising is a lie. So what?"

"I believe in truth."

He had been wondering what it would be like to fuck her, a kid that young. Suddenly he was no longer interested. Glancing toward her, he found her still turned away from him, staring out the window. As his eyes returned to the road, they lingered over the space between them, and he happened to notice her feet, which were bare and propped up beneath her on the seat. They were filthy. His lack of interest immediately turned to revulsion. He swerved over to the side of the road and announced, "This is as far as I go."

She looked at him, surprised, evidently expecting an explanation or an apology or something. But Jack offered her nothing. He simply nodded to confirm what he had just said. And then obediently she jumped out and slammed the car door. The hell with her, Jack thought, and drove on to his hotel.

He had showered, shaved, and was buttoning up his shirt when the telephone rang. It was Pat, calling from home. She sounded troubled, upset. That made him feel guilty. He hadn't called her in three or four days. Whenever he talked to her long distance he felt guilty.

"Jack?"

"Yes, Pat?"

"I miss you."

"Well, I miss you, too."

There was a longish pause. During the silence he could

almost feel the tension and exasperation from the other end of the line pressing in on him through the receiver. This was an ordeal. He wanted it to be over.

Finally: "How long will it be?" she asked. "When will you be coming home?"

"In just a couple of days. They finished shooting today."

"Doesn't that mean it's all done?"

"No. I've got to stick around long enough to look at what they got today. Just over the weekend. I'll see it Monday."

Another pause. "All right. I guess." She hesitated. "Jack, I . . ."

"Yes?"

"We seem to be having some trouble getting through to each other lately, and I just want you to know that when you get back I'm going to make an effort to be more open. Jack, if we could just talk . . ."

"Well," he said, uncertain just what she wanted to hear, "all right."

"You know, it's never easy, but if we could both just try, I think it would help . . . a lot."

Jack frowned down at the floor, again unsure of what to reply, looking only for the magic words that would end this conversation.

"I think that sounds like a good idea, Pat," he said at last. "I'm . . . I'm willing."

That seemed to do the trick. "I guess that's all I can ask," she said, brightening perceptibly. "We'll leave it at that, shall we?"

In another minute, following a brief report from Pat on a drainage problem—Jack told her whom to call—they said goodbye and promised to talk again in two days.

Jack sighed and sat down on the bed the moment he had hung up. These telephone dialogues with his wife always took a lot out of him. More, somehow, than face-to-face encounters with her ever did. In person he knew he could read her better, allay her fears, and put her, if not at ease, at least into a more manageable state. He supposed he had accomplished that more or less just now on the telephone. He hoped he had. The trouble was, you couldn't really tell unless you looked her in the eye. That was how she was. You had to read her eyes.

He was aware, of course, that there was a certain irony to their present situation. Their roles had been nearly reversed. In the past, it had always been Jack who was trying to persuade Pat to talk to him—to confide her secrets, to open up. Well, he was convinced now that she had no secrets—and he wanted to hold on to his own. In fact, he wanted things to continue just about as they had. He had his own life now, and Pat was just a part of it. Suddenly, for her, that didn't seem to be enough. She wanted understanding, frankness. She thought they ought to see a marriage counselor. That'll be the day, he thought.

Let's see—he glanced around the room. Where had he put his cigarettes? He felt the need for one. The truth was, he could use a drink.

All the way back from Chasen's they were quiet, he and Stella, until they reached the creep-traffic on the Strip. They had talked freely over dinner, and it had been a kind of reunion for them, two old campaigners, veterans of their separate wars. They told stories. They laughed a lot. They kept it light. It was just the right tone for what was their first meeting since that lunch the day Tommy Corcoran died. Not that they had known one another so well before. But they had been close, physically close, and they knew things about each other that others did not. If not exactly friends—Jack had searched for the right phrase over coffee—he and Stella might accurately be described as intimate acquaintances.

The silence they had fallen into was in its own way just as easy as all their talk had been earlier. It was friendly. There seemed no need to speak at all until they hit that massive traffic jam west of La Cienega on Sunset. When they did, Jack turned to Stella, honestly puzzled, and asked, "What is this, anyway? Is it always like this?"

"Weekends it is. The Strip's been this way since they took it over."

"Who's they?"

"The kids. The hippies."

He looked around them and saw what she meant. The kids crowded the sidewalks, and at each corner they brought the flow of traffic to a halt begging for rides. Each one was more outlandishly dressed than the next. Cowboys jostled cossacks. There were grande dames in tea dresses and harlots in halters. Nobody wore clothes. Everyone was in costume.

"I could have routed you around most of this," Stella admitted. "But, to tell you the truth, I kind of like looking at them."

"You *do*?"

"Yes. Why should that surprise you? They're beautiful... young. The other night I did more than look."

Glancing over, he found her turned in his direction with an amused smile on her face. Was it directed at him, or was she simply remembering? "So?" he asked. "What happened?"

"I picked one of them up, a lovely boy. I just opened up the door and chose one at random. I don't know how I ever managed to get so lucky. He was, well, not boring at all—as some of them can be."

Jack's eyes swept the teeming gang of them at the corner, resting briefly on one face and then another. Some of them looked distinctly unpleasant, if not actually dangerous. It looked to him as though she might have been risking more than boredom. But that may well have been the fun of it. "How old was he?"

"Oh, God." Her hand fluttered indecisively. "Sixteen? Seventeen? Who can tell how old they are. He was *so* soft, though. Just like a baby, really." Suddenly she let out a husky, throaty laugh.

"What is it? What's so funny?"

"I was just remembering. He hardly needed to shave, and yet he was trying to grow a beard. There were long, single blond hairs growing in places around his face—and he was *so* proud of them." She laughed again. "They tickled."

"Oh? You got around to that, did you?"

"That was the idea, Jack. That was the idea."

He smiled. Really, she was shameless, wasn't she? He felt

like her co-conspirator, her partner in crime. "Go on," he urged.

"Well, you know, I had the darndest time getting the message across to him. It seems he was headed home to some godawful place out in the Valley—and was I headed in that direction? When it turned out I wasn't, he was all ready to jump out at the next corner. 'Now, wait a minute,' I said to him. 'I'd like to contribute to your education.' You know, he actually thought I wanted to give him money." She burst out giggling at that.

"You didn't, did you?"

"Give him money? Are you kidding? I'm not that hard up."

"You're not a bit hard up, as far as I can see," Jack offered gallantly.

"Why, thank you, sir. It's little remarks like that that brighten up a girl's evening." She hesitated, as though she were about to add something more to that, then she plunged on with her story: "Well, finally, when he was just about to jump out of the car, I just *grabbed* him—" In a demonstration, she reached across the front seat and under the steering wheel and grasped Jack firmly at the crotch, where he had already begun to firm up just listening to her.

She surprised him. "Hey!" he said, laughing. She relaxed her grip slightly but left her hand resting there.

"Anyway, I said to him, 'I'm going to teach you there are some people over thirty you really can trust.' And you know what?"

"What?"

"He *finally* understood what I was getting at."

They both roared at that. Stella laughed so long and hard that she was obliged to remove her hand at last from Jack's lap and search out a Kleenex from her purse to dab her eyes dry.

"And what happened then?" he prompted.

"What happened then was that we went to my place and had a very pleasant fuck, as I hope we two shall now do." Stella paused. "Turn right at the next corner."

Her hope was satisfied within a short while after their arrival at her apartment. Although they may have lacked the sense of almost desperate urgency that had possessed them during their first episode those years ago in Chicago, they nevertheless warmed to their work and managed with experience and expertise to accomplish what mere raw enthusiasm had driven them through before. And it was all done at greater length and with considerably greater pleasure.

As Jack lay on Stella's bed, his hand touching hers, he found himself comparing the two occasions and decided that getting older had its compensations. Then he found himself wondering just how he stacked up against Stella's visitor the other night. They probably fucked all night. Kids could do that. Well, he'd be ready to try again in just a little while.

Suddenly Stella gave his hand a squeeze. She took him by surprise. "Mmm," she said, "that was nice. You must have taken lessons."

"No. Just practice."

"You must have worn your wife out getting that good."

"I've had . . . other help."

"I supposed you had. Like to stay the night?"

"Why not?" He paused then, remembering George Bertille's party. He had meant to ask her about that earlier. "There's someplace I have to go tomorrow. Maybe you'd like to come along."

She turned on her side and looked at him. Even in the dim light that spilled in from the bathroom he was struck, as he had been long ago, by the beauty of her dark, dark eyes. "Come along where?" she asked.

"An afternoon party out in Malibu. Probably stretch into early evening."

"Advertising people?"

"Sort of. Film, really. It's the people who are doing this commercial I'm out here on."

"Not boring? My oil people are all boring."

"Well . . ." He made a great show of judgment and finally shook his head. "No, probably not boring. But no promises."

"Good. I can't stand promises."

The moment they hit Bertille's place out beyond Zuma Beach Jack knew that his sudden, reckless impulse to take Stella along to the party had been pure and perfect inspiration. She fit in beautifully—just different enough from the rest to seem interesting to them, and just enough like them to put them at their ease. It was instructive to him simply to stand back and watch her move through the party. If Pat had half her style and social grace she would be the toast of every party in Chicago. And who was this dark-haired woman with the deep, dark eyes who drew interested looks from the men and women around her, who spoke with such apparent assurance and ready wit, whose laughter seemed to resound through the room? Who was she? Why, she was Gus Karras's fat, big-nosed kid sister, that was who she was. Inside that great cocoon of a body had been a butterfly struggling to be let out. But perhaps not even she knew that back then. Stella was a self-creation, as much a work of art as any that hung on George Bertille's walls. No, far greater than anything he saw there. She was her own masterpiece, and he admired her for that. He more than admired her. He wondered what it would be like to be married to such a woman.

After a bit, when he came around with a refill on her drink, Jack discovered what Stella had found to talk about that fascinated them so: money. Or, money writ large: the economy. She was talking shop to them, and they loved it.

"Look," she was saying, "if you want to know the way I see it, then I'll put it very plainly—disaster lurks."

"Not a good time for the market?" Frank Pargiter asked.

"Are you kidding? Buy real estate. Or if you've got to gamble, go for grain futures, or pork bellies."

"You really mean that?" From a tall, silver-haired and terribly sensitive-looking man whom Jack had not yet met.

"Of course I mean it," declared Stella. "I not only mean it, I do it myself."

"Grain futures? Pork bellies?"

"Real estate."

The three of them—Bertille, Pargiter, and the silver-haired

man—exchanged looks. They were impressed. So was Jack.

"Let me ask you something," said Bertille.

"Sure," she said. "Go ahead."

"Why is everything so screwed up?"

"That's easy. It's the war."

"The war? Come on. In the past, war's always been good for the economy. That's the way it was with Korea, World War II. I mean, war might be immoral as hell, but it's always been good for business."

"Not this one." She was firm.

"Why not?"

"Because Johnson's been financing it with money that doesn't exist, money with nothing behind it. He just keeps printing it up and paying it out." She took a sip from the scotch Jack had just handed her and regarded George Bertille with a flat, direct gaze. "Why do you think the *Wall Street Journal*'s been saying we should get out?"

"Well . . ."

"In the beginning, it was on the very sound business principle that it's foolish to throw good money after bad. Now it turns out that even the good money we've been throwing is bad. The economy's being ruined—and all for the war."

Again the looks exchanged between the three. Bertille included Jack this time, raising his eyebrows, rolling his eyes. Very expressive, that one.

This time, Pargiter: "So the kids are right?"

"About the war? About getting out?"

"Yes."

"Sure, they're right. But, then, I think they're right about a lot of things."

"Look, could I interrupt?" asked Bertille. "I believe I see where you're going, and I just wonder if I could steer this whole group over to that corner of the room so my wife could get some of this. You see, we've got this problem with my son, sort of a generation gap I guess you'd call it, and I keep telling her . . ."

George Bertille succeeded in moving Pargiter and Stella over to his wife. The silver-haired man hung back and introduced himself to Jack as Bob Frankel and said he was a writer.

"Screenwriter?"

"Television, mostly. Like everybody else in the business, though, I started out in the studios. Junior writer—only a hundred and fifty per—but, oh, we had fun in those days."

"I'll bet you did."

Frowning, Frankel regarded his drink for a long time—so long that Jack found himself wondering if he had said something to offend the man or failed to respond in the proper manner to something that had been said. But, no: "You know, I've just been thinking about how different things are now. How did things get so much out of hand? All those things your wife was saying about the way things are screwed up. Hell, I know they're screwed up. I want to know how they got that way—and it's not *just* the war. Maybe it was all that fun we had in the old days. Maybe we shouldn't have had so much. Maybe we should've worried more and done more back then."

It was kind of a speech, but obviously very sincerely meant. People were saying things like this all the time now—especially out here. When they weren't lying around the pool, or screwing their brains out, they were beating on their chests, asking themselves where things went wrong.

"Well, I certainly can't argue with what you say," Jack responded at last with proper gravity. "I would like to clear things up on one point, though."

"Oh? What's that?"

' "She's not my wife."

Somebody else made the same mistake a little later on. A woman with whom he had been talking, the wife of an account executive at a local Los Angeles agency, happened to mention something Stella had told her about house prices down in Orange County—and she also referred to her as "your wife." Odd. Back in Chicago that sort of error would be commonplace, almost inevitable, for they assumed there that every couple over age twenty was lawfully wedded. Not here, though. There must be something about Stella and him, about the two of them together, that suggested permanence. In any case, this time he didn't bother to correct the woman—let her think them husband and wife, if she liked. In fact, it rather pleased him that she did.

Toward the end of the affair, George Bertille happened to catch Jack out on the deck where Jack had gone to admire the Pacific sunset.

"Freshen your drink?"

"No, it's okay. I know where the bar is." He paused, giving Bertille a chance to excuse himself, but his host stayed on. "Good party, George," he added at last. "Thanks for having me."

"Don't mention it. Thanks for bringing your friend, Stella. That girl's got a real pair of balls on her."

It happened that Jack was taking a gulp of watery scotch when Bertille came out with that. He sputtered and almost choked on it, trying with difficulty to suppress the laugh that suddenly tickled and tormented him. Clearly, Bertille intended what he had said as a tribute to her.

"You okay?" asked Bertille, clearly concerned.

"Sure," whispered Jack, then wheezed: "Don't worry about me."

"She was great with my wife. Really reassuring, you know? And she was saying basically what I've been trying to tell her all along—that the kids have got a point and maybe we should listen to them, you know?"

"I know," said Jack, finally recovered, though still a little hoarse. "Love, peace, and happiness."

"Right," agreed Bertille. "What the world needs now. I mean, they're showing the way. That kid of mine is no genius, and I personally think he was full of shit to drop out of Cal State Long Beach, but we owe it to him to listen, you know? He may even have something to tell us."

"And a little child shall lead them," Jack offered piously.

"What's that? Shakespeare?"

"No, the Bible."

"The Bible? No shit?"

It turned out that Stella and Jack were among the last to leave. It was dark. There was a chorus of goodbyes from the house. The host and hostess exchanged kisses and handshakes with them appropriately at the door. Jack found his car halfway up the driveway and beckoned Stella inside. And then moments later, they were out on Pacific Coast Highway headed south, on their way back to the city.

"Well," said Stella, once they were under way, "that wasn't so bad."

"Not boring?"

"Not boring."

"If you want to know," said Jack, risking a glance in her direction in spite of the heavy traffic, "you made quite a hit there. George Bertille said you had balls."

She laughed and snorted. "He would," she said. "No higher praise from him."

"And a number of people there thought we were married."

"*Married?*"

"Yes, Mr. and Mrs."

"Oh." She sounded positively glum.

He looked in her direction. She was turned away, staring out the window. Was she avoiding him? his eyes? Probably. "And why so great an 'oh'?" he asked at last.

"Because you might get the idea that was something besides funny."

"You didn't laugh."

"That's why."

They drove along in silence for a while. On the left side of the road the fast-food franchises rushed by in a blur of colors in which yellow predominated. On the right was the expanse of darkness that was the ocean. Even if he hadn't known it was there, he would have smelled it—not fishy or rank but simply moist and . . . deep.

Ahead of them, a traffic light turned red. He put on the brakes and brought the car to a comfortable halt. They were near the beach. A straggling line of pedestrians marched across the highway before them, illuminated by the headlights of the waiting cars. A single figure detached from the rest and moved up the shoulder of the highway toward their car. It was a girl, a slight figure all but lost in the folds of the long, white petticoatlike gown that she had on. As she came closer, Jack saw that unlike most of the girls her age, she wore her hair short. It was blond, cropped and curly, so that it ringed her head like a halo. That, and the plain, sexless appearance of her narrow features gave her a little of the look of a Renaissance angel. Jack also saw that the girl's arm was elevated slightly, and the thumb was out.

"Oh, my God," said Stella, "look at her. She's beautiful." Without another word to Jack, she waved the girl over and rolled down her window.

"Hop in," she said to her.

But the girl hung back. Unsmiling and serious, she bent down to the window. "How far are you going?" she asked. There was a kind of whine to her voice, as though she were near tears.

"All the way into town," Stella said reassuringly.

"Santa Monica?"

"We'll work it out."

Satisfied, the girl opened the back door of the car and jumped in. Stella turned to Jack and gave him a smile whose meaning he could only guess at. The light had changed. He stepped on the accelerator and concentrated on the road ahead, listening.

"What's going on in Santa Monica?" Stella asked.

"Free concert—out on the beach."

"Oh? Anybody good?"

"I don't know. It doesn't really matter too much. You just go, like, to see people."

"And it *is* free, after all."

The girl laughed as though Stella had made a joke. "Yeah." There was something spaced-out about her, as though she weren't quite properly plugged in.

But Stella laughed, too, rather mysteriously. They were cooking something up, weren't they? He glanced over at her and found her leaning back and facing the rear, concentrating eagerly on their passenger. She shot him a glance. Her dark eyes were gleaming with excitement. He realized that he had never seen her quite like this before. A sudden elation rose in him.

"Ask her," he said to Stella, "if she trusts anyone over thirty."

Stella giggled at that, just like a kid. "Well, how about it?" she asked the girl. "Do you?"

She hesitated, as though she weren't quite sure what the right answer was. And then, vaguely: "Sure, I guess so."

Jack tried to catch her in the rearview mirror, but it was too dark to see anything back there but a shape. "What's your name?" he asked.

"Lisa."

"Nice name," said Stella.

"Nice girl," Jack said. "Where are you from, Lisa?"

She was suddenly cautious: "Well . . . not from around here." Then she added hastily: "But it's all right with my parents. My mother knows where I am. I mean, I didn't just split from home or anything."

"Hey, take it easy," said Stella. "We're on your side."

"Well . . . okay. It's just that people are always hassling me about that, like, am I a runaway or something. I mean, one lady picked me up on Wilshire and was going to take me straight to a police station so they could just, like, check me out, or something. I mean, I *told* her I wasn't a runaway or anything, but she didn't believe me, I guess."

"What happened?" Jack asked.

"I jumped out at the first stoplight she came to, and, wow, did I ever run!"

Stella laughed as though she had been there herself. "I'll bet she was pretty surprised."

"Yeah," said Lisa. "I didn't wait around to find out, though."

"I'll bet you didn't," said Jack.

A moment's silence fell over the three of them. Nothing tense. Just a pause. They were all waiting to find out what would happen next.

Finally, Jack spoke up: "Say, I've got an idea. We haven't eaten yet, Lisa. Maybe you'd like to come along and have a bite with us."

"Gee, I don't know," she said. "A restaurant? I mean, you don't have to do that or anything."

"Our pleasure. I guess the concert will keep for a while?"

"Oh, sure. That's no big deal. Just, like, you know, a chance to hear some music and see some people is all."

"Well, listen," Stella put in, "if that's the case, maybe I've got an even better idea. Why don't we all go up to my place? We could send out for pizza or Chinese and just listen to records. I've got *everything*—Beatles, Stones, Big Brother, the Airplane."

Jack kept his eyes on the road ahead and waited quietly for the response. At last it came: "I really like pizza a lot."

When at last Lisa came out of the bathroom, Stella and Jack were waiting, tucked naked beneath the covers with just enough space between them for a girl her size to fit. They had been firm about it. As soon as they got that big, flouncy petticoat off her and saw those filthy feet and ankles, the next step was clear: she would have to take a bath. And so, in between kisses, heavy breathing, and compliments on her youth and beauty, the two of them edged her toward the bathroom and once they had got her inside it, switched on the water full-blast and pushed her oh-so-gently into the tub. There they left her, hoping she had the sense to take it from there. And as it turned out, she had that much at least, for she emerged as clean and fresh as the angel she resembled. Her curls, half-soaked with steam, were clenched even more tightly around her head, so that she was even more like a boy than Jack had expected—a boy without a penis. She had no breasts to speak of, just a chest with two nipples. Her body, slender and a little gawky, seemed just a little wider at the hips than at the shoulders, though no more so than an adolescent boy's might be. As he made his inspection, Jack felt just a little queer. He wondered how Stella felt.

Apparently just fine. She was sitting up, smiling, her big breasts spilling out over the covers, gesturing toward the girl. "Come on," she said. "Come on in. This is when the fun starts."

Lisa seemed a little uncertain. She looked from Stella to Jack, anxiously, a nervous smile fixed on her face, her hands hovering uncertainly in the vicinity of her hips. "I don't know what to do," she said with an embarrassed shrug. "I mean, like, I never did it before with more than one person."

Jack made it a point not to say that he hadn't either. He simply beckoned her toward them and said, "Don't worry about it, Lisa. Just let nature take its course."

She looked from one to the other, and reassured by the smiles on their faces, she jumped onto the bed and made for the covers on all fours. Jack later had time and opportunity to reflect that what happened after that had little or nothing to do with nature. And that was what he liked most about it.

They just fooled around for a while. A lot of kissing and touching and murmurs of encouragement. Lisa was the focus of their attention. Jack's fingers lightly traced a triangular pattern on her torso which found its corners at her nipples and navel as he kissed and nuzzled her throat, all the while breathing in the smell of soap and wet from the bath. While below, Stella devoted loving attention to Lisa's pubes, separating her lips, probing, searching, discovering. First the tip of one finger found its way inside and then another. The fingers moved gently, and regularly, and with assurance, all but hidden from view part of the time by the fuzzy fur cover that trimmed the girl's vulva.

"Oooh," said Lisa at one point, "does that ever feel cool."

And then, with no signal needed between them, Jack and Stella exchanged places—Stella moving up to lick and suck at those uncushioned nipples of Lisa's, and Jack going below to do the same at the third nipple there. The girl began to whimper and whine so that he thought for a moment he might be hurting her. Was she crying? He moved away and raised up so that he might see her face.

"Don't stop!" she whispered urgently. "Do you ever give good head!"

Jack smiled at that and began again, and then thinking better of it, he shifted and tugged at Lisa, bringing her upright in a kneeling position above his face. He continued to tongue, now pushing deep, pushing and straining from far back in his throat. Looking up from this queer perspective, he saw Stella above him, as well, her arms wrapped around Lisa, hugging her, the two of them locked deep in a kiss. And then a moment later Stella was lost from sight, though not gone, for he felt her below, straddling him at his hips, taking his penis with care, pushing it up inside her. Now he was inside them both, he the horse and they the riders. They posted in rhythm, calling out to one another and exhorting him to go, go, go, go. And like a good horse at their command, he went—until he could go no more. And then, spent, long past his orgasm and theirs, he went motionless, static, and felt comfortably near death. The two tumbled off him and snuggled up on either side. Stella pulled the cover up over them, and he slept.

Later he roused himself sufficiently to be aware that they had left him. He was wondering where they were until—when?—he heard their voices.

"You've got such nice big tits. Mine are so tiny." That was Lisa.

"I love them. I love everything about you." Stella.

And then a moment later—or was it an hour?—he heard a funny hum. Like an electric razor, only quieter. Afterward, he remembered thinking, "Oh, well, let them have their fun"—and then dropping off to sleep again.

So this was what it was like, Jack mused, what he had been dreading and fighting so ever since he came back from California. It really wasn't such an ordeal, was it? Just three terribly sensible and sane people sitting around a desk in a comfortable office, saying sensible and sane things to one another about relationships. About his relationship with Pat, about hers with him, and about theirs with David Zaslofsky, Ph.D. Zaslofsky was a clinical psychologist. His field was family relations. He was the marriage counselor whom Pat had been trying for months to get Jack to see.

Jack had been trapped into this visit by circumstance. He had returned from California with a case of gonorrhea. It had to be Lisa, or Stella, or maybe Stella's beautiful boy of a few nights before. But what did it matter? They all had it by the time he got back to Chicago, didn't they?

And wasn't that what Stella implied when he called her to break the news? "It's not a matter of blame, Jack," she had said. "It's just being in the right place at the wrong time. Call it a communicable accident." At any rate, this "communicable accident" had kept him in sexual quarantine for a period of two weeks until the penicillin did its job, and he was pronounced cured. He had to make some excuse to Pat, and so he pled impotence and managed somehow, through force of will, to make it stick. But this intended failure took away from him his last weapon against the marriage counselor. He had always argued that theirs was basically a sound marriage because the physical side of it worked so well—when you've got your health, you've got everything, was the idea—and Pat had offered no reasonable rebuttal for that. But now, of course, with Jack pleading sexual dysfunction, the prop was kicked out from under his argument. As Pat declared, they were in trouble—and it was up to David Zaslofsky, Ph.D., to do something about it.

For his part, Dr. Zaslofsky wasn't so sure about that. First of all, he admonished them, they were not to call him doctor. While it was true that he had claim to the academic title, he was not a psychiatrist, not a medical doctor, and he didn't want them thinking of him that way. He wasn't there to cure them. He was there to talk to them. They were all friends, right? Pat and Jack were to call him David.

It was on that basis—one-to-one, as David described it—that they proceeded. He asked each of them, first of all, to give his personal version of their marriage, to describe it from their separate points of view. They did that. Jack, naturally, liked his version better than Pat's. It seemed to him altogether more generous. According to him, theirs was basically a comfortable relationship, one based on trust and mutual understanding. If they had lately had a little difficulty talking to each other, the problem was only temporary. They would find their way out of this, just as they had found their way through all their difficulties in the past.

The past was what troubled Pat. In her version of their relationship, the two of them lived lives totally compartmentalized, apart from each other and apart from their daughters. Their troubles were cumulative. This last . . . difficulty, well, it was just the latest, not the worst. In her opinion, the worst was when they moved out to the suburbs. She felt that she had just been put in her little place to keep house and manage domestic matters while he made his way in the great world.

"Well, what's so wrong with that?" Jack asked her. "Women have been doing that for centuries . . . millennia. Why is that so bad—keeping house?"

"Because I'm better than that," Pat said to him. "Because I can be somebody myself. Because that's why you married me." She leaned forward, looking at him almost desperately. "Isn't it?"

Jack was shocked at her. All this intensity—and in front of a stranger, too. He sat and stared at Pat for a moment, then turned away suddenly and shook his head.

"What's the matter, Jack?" It was Zaslofsky. His voice was hardly more than a whisper.

"Nothing . . . well . . . I don't know."

"Are you embarrassed?"

"Well, I suppose a little. Yes."

"Does Pat often embarrass you?"

"No," Jack replied quickly. "She never acts like this."

"And it bothers you when she does?"

He turned to her. Her eyes were on him. Jack didn't understand what this was all about. "Yes," he said. "Yes, it does."

"Well, if you'll pardon my saying so, I think we three should set it as a goal in these talks to embarrass you as often as we can."

"What?" Jack was confused and a little angry. "What's this all about?"

"I think you need to get in touch with your emotions, Jack—and part of that is accepting the emotions of others. If that embarrasses you, then okay, let's embarrass you often, and maybe it'll stop embarrassing you so much."

Jack looked from Zaslofsky to Pat. They were both sitting forward and concentrating on him so closely that it seemed like a goddam conspiracy or something. "Look . . . David," he began at last, "I'm no dummy. And if I read you correctly, what you're telling me is that I'm repressed."

"I don't use that terminology," Zaslofsky said rather primly.

"Come on," said Jack, "if you don't level with me, how do you expect me to level with you?"

Zaslofsky smiled: he had been caught out. "All right. I guess you're right. There is a category . . ."

"And that's the way you see me? As repressed?" Jack forced a laugh at that. "If that's your version of me, then I think we can wind this up in a hurry, because if you'll pardon my boasting, I am probably one of the least repressed men in the world!"

*

He hung around late that night just to make the call. The office was all but empty. Klezek came and went, and finally only the new man, Aiello, was left, sitting in his corner, pushing papers. Melaniphy regarded him sourly. He thought him a fuck-off, a guy whose single talent was time-wasting. Melaniphy had been short on his roster for over a month, and they had been promising for longer than that to send a couple of men down from Eleventh and State. But if they were going to send him more Aiellos, then he would rather go shorthanded. Klezek was worth ten of this guy.

Melaniphy looked at his watch and, satisfied at last that sufficient time had elapsed for him to reach Stella Karras, he dialed her number in Santa Monica and listened to the phone at the other end ring twice before it was picked up.

"Hello?"

"Hello? Is this Miss Karras?" Whoever the woman was on the wire, she sounded younger than he had expected from the tone of those letters.

"No, but—"

"Could I speak to her please?"

"Well, I . . . sure. Who is this? Is this long distance?" There was a certain querulous quality to the voice.

"Yes, it's long distance. This is Sergeant Joseph Melaniphy of the Chicago Police Department."

There was a short pause at the other end. Then: "Oh. Just a minute." That usually got them.

A longer pause and finally: "Hello, I'm Stella Karras. What can I do for you?"

"Just answer a few questions, if you will, Miss Karras. It is Miss Karras, isn't it?"

"Yes, I . . . But what is this all about?"

"A person of your acquaintance has been the victim of a homicide, Miss Karras. We're proceeding with the investigation."

"May I ask who?" she asked a little stiffly.

"A John Gawlor. I believe you knew him as Jack."

"Jack? *Oh my God, no.*"
"*You're surprised, then?*"
"*Why, yes, of course I am. Why shouldn't I be?*"
"*Oh,*" said Melaniphy, "*something you said in one of your letters to him. Something about living dangerously. I believe you told him to watch his ass.*"
"*You've read those letters?*"
"*Yes, of course I have, Miss Karras. This is a homicide investigation.*"
"*Am I a suspect?*"
Jesus, thought Melaniphy, *these people read too many mysteries.* "*No, you're not a suspect, Miss Karras, unless you were in Chicago about ten days ago and are big enough to beat a man to death.*"
"*He was* beaten *to death?*"
"*That's right.*"
"*Oh, my God. Poor Jack.*"
"*That's what his wife said.*"
"*Has* she *seen those letters of mine?*"
"*No.*"
"*Could they be returned to me? I mean, there's no need for her to see them, is there?*"
Melaniphy sighed. "*I'll see what I can do—pending the successful completion of the investigation, of course.*"
"*I understand.*" *She paused, then:* "*Look, I don't know what I said in that letter about living dangerously. I was probably just teasing him or something.*"
"*No, I don't think so. You seemed to be warning him. Let's see if I can find it here . . .*"
"*No! Wait! I remember! He had written me this long letter on hustlers—how they were different and how they operated and so on, and—*"
"*Hustlers? Male? Female?*"
"*Male.*"
"*Oh.*" *There it was.*
"*We were pretty frank with each other. I guess you know that if you read those letters. Anyway, it was in response to that. I said something like, 'I can see you're living dangerously.' And I believe I added that they play rough.*"

"Yes, that phrase does occur. It had me interested. You weren't talking about anybody specific, then?"

"Sergeant, I haven't been back to Chicago for years. I couldn't *have meant anyone specific.*"

"I see." Shit, thought Melaniphy. "Just one more thing. Would you send me his letters to you? They're material to the investigation."

There was dead silence for a moment at the other end of the line. "I can't," she said, then: "I've destroyed them all. I only wish he'd shown the same consideration to me."

CHAPTER SEVEN *1974*

IT WAS ONLY AFTER he had been sitting in the room for a number of minutes—at least five—that he noticed that it was only half as large as he had supposed. He was at the bar and had already been served when he turned to survey the place, made a quick movement back for his glass on the bar, and caught that same movement made by the man directly opposite him—who turned out to be, of course, no more than his own reflection. There is that moment of truth, often remarked upon, when a man comes upon himself suddenly in a mirror and sees—what? In Jack's case, nothing more or less than a well-dressed man whose movements were made with assurance, one who was reasonably handsome, and still more or less young. In other words, a man whose appearance would have seemed totally unexceptional in the near-north-side bars that he usually frequented, but one who seemed just as completely out of place here.

This was Pepper's, a blues club on the near south side. Jack had come here because it was one of the few places left in the city where blacks and whites still might meet. What had brought him here? Whom did he expect to meet? In a way, he wondered that himself. It was just that he had been having this persistent fantasy, one that he supposed went back to his first sexual experience—ordeal?—down in that black whorehouse in southern Illinois. He remembered it rather vaguely and with a certain indulgence. It was hard for him to believe today that he had ever been as dumb and naïve as he certainly had been then. But the fantasy—how did it go? He reran it in his mind for the hundredth time, and he saw the tall black woman, walking straight toward him, stopping and staring. As it happened, her features were a little indistinct, for after all they could be filled in later. What he saw most distinctly were her eyes—deep, deep brown, call them black, and very fierce—and her hair, which she wore in a tight inch-long afro. They met. They mated in a fierce struggle, from which Jack eventually emerged the victor.

But why? Why this recurring daydream? He probably hadn't even *looked* at ten black women in the last ten years —but perhaps that was the reason why. Perhaps his unconscious was telling him that it was now high time that he did. He had learned to accept these messages, wherever they came from, and that was why he was here now tonight at Pepper's.

The band was tuning up. The kids were coming in. It wouldn't be long until the guitars were roaring and screaming, and Jack was wishing that he was home in Park Ridge. He had cooked up a phony story for Pat about a dinner meeting with a client just so he might have a shot at acting out this little head-movie of his. He had come to Pepper's to browse, to see if *she* were here. But no. No *she*: no fierce black eyes and no inch-long afro. All Jack saw around him were white college kids, some black men, and a few remarkably prim brown-skinned waitresses moving among them.

A black man settled at the bar one stool down from Jack and ordered a Chivas on the rocks. The man sported a huge, bushy afro and was dressed in a gaudy ensemble of purple and maroon. Jack didn't like his looks but felt obliged to smile when he got a nod from him. It wouldn't do to discourage contact, would it?

"Ain't see you in here before," the man began cautiously.

"My first time."

"You come for the music?"

"Oh . . ." Jack shrugged. "You know."

The man nodded and took a sip of scotch. "Maybe you here looking for somebody," the man suggested.

"I might be," Jack agreed.

"What this somebody look like? Maybe I know her."

"How do you know it's a her?"

The man looked at him and a slow smile spread over his face. He had bad teeth and had gray in that wiry bush that sat on his head. "I just took a guess. You tell me am I right because I know a lot of the womens, and I might know the very one you looking for."

Jack looked away from him, surveying the room. He wondered if he weren't unconsciously hoping to catch sight of her in some previously overlooked corner, or perhaps as a recent arrival just coming through the door from the street. But whatever he had hoped for, he went unsatisfied, for nobody even remotely like her was there to be seen. He turned back to the man with the big afro and nodded. "Yes, as a matter of fact you're right. I am looking for somebody, and she happens to be a woman."

"You know her name?"

"No."

"What she look like? She my color?"

"Just about."

"She tall? little? in-between?"

"Tall." Jack hesitated, wondering whether to commit himself. "And she's got an afro about that long," he added, holding his thumb and forefinger up about an inch apart.

The black man smirked at him. "Oh, you like a natural?"

"That's what she's got," Jack said severely and stared the man down.

"Sure. I can dig it. Well, now, it just so happens I do know that girl. But she ain't here tonight."

"I can see that."

"Why don't you come on along with me? I take you to her."

"Why don't you call her up and have her come here?"

"She need a cab."

"I'll take care of that."

The man with the afro shrugged, slid off the stool, and headed toward the back of the place—presumably to a telephone. Jack watched him go and silently mouthed the word "pimp" with a certain evident contempt. Then he turned to the bartender and ordered another drink.

By the time the girl got there, Jack had finished that one

and had started another. It was true he was drinking more, but he kept that a secret, as he did almost everything else in his life. And he carried it well enough so that nobody but Pat really knew. She knew altogether too much about him, it seemed to Jack.

The man with the afro had drifted away after making the call. The music started then, exploding through the room with a great scream and holler, filling it with sound so thick and substantial that it seemed palpable. Jack wanted to reach out and push it away. But instead he did no more than hang on miserably at the bar, following that bobbing afro as it moved around the room from table to table, glancing at the street door every time it opened, so that it became a kind of ritual. Fifteen minutes passed, going on twenty. Jack was telling himself it was time to go and the hell with the pimp, when at last the girl appeared.

He barely noticed her. In fact, he missed her entrance into Pepper's and would have overlooked her altogether if she had not gone to the table where Afro sat with a small crowd of white college boys. She bent down and whispered something into the black man's ear—and that was the first glimpse that Jack got of her. This had to be her, didn't it?

Yes, it did. When she came forward with Afro to Jack's place at the bar, he had to admit that she met his specifications—but, on the other hand, she failed completely to satisfy his expectations. She was tall. She had a natural of just about the length he had indicated. She was really a very pretty girl. And yet . . . and yet . . . where was the fury? where was that fierceness? With head slightly bowed, she approached. Was she embarrassed? shy? He regarded her curiously, half-expecting that eventually she would raise her eyes and stare at him in such cold anger that any lesser man would be stricken with terror—though not Jack, of course— and thus the fantasy would begin. But, no. When at last she did raise her eyes, though they were just as dark as he had hoped they would be, the anger he had expected to find in them was utterly absent. What he found instead was something rarer and more attractive. They were as deep and swift as the eyes of a doe. They moved all around her, darting this way and that, apprehensive and ready. It looked to Jack as though she might turn around and run out the door at any moment. He hoped she would not.

Afro was there to make certain she did not. He held her tight by the elbow and marched her straight over to Jack. "This here the somebody," he said, presenting her.

Jack saw she was not as young as he had supposed. She was in her midtwenties, at least, and perhaps over thirty. But she certainly looked scared. "Does she have a name?" Jack asked. Then, to her: "Do you?" It came out colder and harsher than he meant it to.

She glanced up and looked directly at him for the first time. Her face was narrow. Her eyes were almond-shaped. There was something oriental about her—but it wasn't her color. "Yeah, I got a name," she said, stiffening slightly.

"It's Molly," offered Afro.

"Molly? It's been a while since I've heard that one."

"It'll be a while before you meet another girl like her."

He looked from Molly to Afro, then nodded. She may not have been *her*, but she was interesting. He would put off the battle with Miss Supernigger until another night and see what Molly had to offer. "Would you like to have a drink with me, Molly?" he asked as politely as he was able.

"Uh, no. Maybe someplace else."

"All right, then." Jack tossed a few dollars down on the bar and pushed off his stool, weaving slightly. Had he had *that* much to drink? Evidently he had. "Let's get going."

"I paid her cab fare," said Afro.

"Well, let's talk about that outside," said Jack.

"Suits me."

And Afro led the way. Molly followed him and Jack stumbled after the two of them. His path took him past at least three tables of college boys. They regarded the three of them with interest, but what they showed Jack was hostility, nothing but hostility. So he was the villain? Afro and Molly the victims? Well, he thought, fuck you, college boys.

They made their way out to Michigan Avenue. A taxi waited at the curb right at the entrance to the club, probably the same one that had brought Molly there. Once out there,

Jack turned to Afro and focused on him blearily. "How much do I owe you?"

"For the cab? Twenty. She came from a long way off."

"Let's call it even at ten." He pulled out a bill from his wallet and, with a nod, stuffed it in the handkerchief pocket of Afro's suit. "Any complaints?" he asked.

Afro regarded him coldly. "If I got any, I take it up with her."

They left him there standing on the corner. And as the two of them hopped into the waiting taxi, Jack offered the driver the name of a Loop hotel he had used before.

About what happened after that he was not altogether certain. The three drinks he had had in quick succession at Pepper's must have hit him all at once, for he later remembered becoming suddenly dizzy. The lights of South Michigan Avenue swirled by crazily. The rocking and bumping of the taxi gave him the woozy and unpleasant sensation that he was floating on rough water. He began to sweat unexplainably in the cool, damp night.

"You all right?" the woman beside him asked.

He said he thought he was, but maybe they ought to get something to eat. And then to the driver he gave the name of a big restaurant near the hotel. It seemed safe because nobody ever seemed to go there.

The food might have helped if he hadn't ordered another scotch as soon as he sat down just to settle his stomach. It was then that the events of the evening began to jumble hopelessly. Did the steak he ordered ever come? He wasn't sure, but he did know that he had had at least one other drink. The waitress tried to talk him out of it, and he had had to insist. He kept a picture of the girl across from him, sitting silently, her eyes alternately concentrated on the table before her, then shifting uneasily around the room. Somehow he seemed to be talking a lot to her, although he couldn't remember afterward what he had said. And then in the middle of it all, the room began to spin, and because he suddenly found it impossible to retain his balance on the chair, it became necessary to take a seat on the floor. They must have left right after that because he remembered being offered firm encouragement toward the door. Yet in the middle of all this a face appeared that was vaguely familiar. Had he imagined this? A bearded face wearing glasses that somehow resembled David Zaslofsky. But it was all quite uncertain. He was now sure he had imagined that. And then out in the street, where the air felt good. Inside again where they were arguing—not Jack, but the girl, with someone else. And, well, that was all, wasn't it?

Gradually, he began to come around. He was unable to breathe through his nose, and his head was filled with such a desperate, angry pulsing pain that at first he was sure that some artery had exploded inside his head and that he had drowned his brain in his own blood. And so, suffocating, drowning, aching, sickening, he opened his eyes and pushed himself up to a sitting position in bed. Where was he? He had no idea and no memory of coming here. Whatever clear, consecutive recall he had of the night before had more or less ended when he left Pepper's with that black girl.

Oh, God, he thought glumly—*her!* Well, he had been rolled for sure. There was no point in even looking in his wallet. He only hoped she had left his credit cards so that he could settle up at the desk on the way out. He was surprised at himself, profoundly dismayed. You had to be a particular kind of fool to get drunk within arm's reach of a whore. He was acting like some boot in on his first leave from Great Lakes. Half in shame and half in pain, Jack covered his face with his hands. He sat that way for a moment, considering, and told himself sternly that he had better watch his step, or some morning he might wake up with more than a hangover—he might wake up dead.

It was only then, as he sat blindly brooding, that he became aware of the sound of deep rhythmic breathing in the room. He dropped his hands and looked—and there she was in the next bed. Or he assumed that long lump under the blankets was the girl. At the moment he couldn't even remember her name.

Jack got out of bed and noted that he was dressed in his shorts and nothing more. The rest of his clothes were nowhere to be seen. Moving carefully, for his head still throbbed brutally, he went around to the far side of the room near the windows so that he could get a better look and be sure about the identity of the next bed's occupant. Yes, it was she. Although her head was half-buried beneath a pillow, and only the lower two-thirds of it was visible, there was no mistaking the rich brown tone of the skin, nor the woolly texture of the black hair peeking out from beneath the pillow. There was a sweetness to the expression on her sleeping face, the hint of a smile on her lips. He stood for a moment to look, touched and fascinated; and then, shaking his head in silent tribute, he went into the bathroom to shower. Too bad he couldn't remember her name.

It wasn't until he was nearly dressed that she began to stir. He had found his suit and shirt hanging neatly in the closet, each piece on a separate hanger. And off to one side, hung with equal care, were the black dress and tan raincoat she had worn the night before. He touched the dress and let the silky artificial fabric slide through his fingers. Then he pulled on his pants, tucked in his shirt, and began knotting his tie. It was then that she shifted her legs and let out a long, deep sigh.

Jack was feeling better now, more in control. His head was clearer and was no longer pounding quite as it had. He glanced at his watch. He had time to stop off at the barber on Grand under Michigan for a shave before going into the office. His suit was a little the worse for wear, but he would buy a shirt and tie on the way in and would look quite okay for the people at the office. Luckily there were no client meetings scheduled that day. He didn't look all *that* good, and he didn't really feel up to talking to the boys from Breeze—or from anyplace else, for that matter.

The girl in the bed near the window let out a moan, and Jack decided he must do something about her before he left. He took out his wallet and inspected its contents.

"It's all there. Or most of it is. I had to pay to get the room, and I took it out of there."

Jack looked up and found her sitting up in bed, her breasts

covered by the sheet that she clutched close to her. "I owe you something," he said as he came over to her.

"Yeah."

"Thirty?"

"I get fifty for overnight," she said. "Only we didn't do nothin'. You want to now?"

"Can't. I have to go to work. Get shaved. Buy a shirt." Why was he making excuses to her? "Look, I gave that pimp ten. What if I split the difference with you?" He fished four tens from his wallet and tossed them down on the bed within her reach.

She simply nodded and left the bills lying on the blanket. Now that she was wide awake and Jack had another look at her, he found himself wishing he could stay, wondering what it might be like to get to know her better.

"He ain't no pimp," she said abruptly. "He's my uncle."

"He's *what*?"

"Yeah, well, he ain't got no regular girls or nothin'. Just kind of steers people. Meets them together. He knew I needed the money, so he met me with you."

He was intrigued, curious, suddenly fascinated. "Look," he said to her, "let me ask you something. If you needed the money, why didn't you just take my wallet and go on home? You certainly had the chance."

She raised her eyes to his. "I ain't into stealin'," she said. "Not just yet. Besides . . ."

"Besides? Yes—what?"

"Besides, if you had what I got to go home to, hotel room like this look pretty good to you."

Jack didn't know quite what to say to that. He was sure, however, that he wanted to get to know her better. "Okay," he said. "Why don't you stay here for a while then? Meet me for lunch. I . . . I won't put you through last night again."

She smiled at him, a grin really. "You was pretty drunk."

"I sure was."

He wrote down the name of another restaurant on the back of a card and passed it to her with directions from the hotel. She nodded seriously through it all, and he was struck again by that remarkable face of hers with its oriental cast. He ended with a shrug and: "Just one thing more."

"What's that?"

"I don't know your name."

"It's Molly. You forgot. Everybody call me Molly B."

"Okay, Molly B. I'll see you later on."

Jack left then and began trying to sort through things on the way down in the elevator. As he passed by, he got a queer look from the man behind the desk.

Sometime around midmorning, he got around to calling Pat. He called her at the office in Des Plaines. For a couple of years now she had been working for Virginia Jelinek at the same real-estate company through which they had bought their own house. It took Jack a while to get used to that. There was more involved than the occasional inconvenience caused him by having a working wife. "After all," Zaslofsky had urged him, "try to understand how important it is to her." Well, Jack did understand up to a point, and he made allowances. What bothered him, although he had said nothing about it, was that of all the real-estate people in the Chicago metropolitan area she had had to seek out the one whom he had fucked. Did she know? Was this her revenge? He thought not—though he was absolutely certain Virginia had hired Pat just to get back at Jack. Women were like that. It had all happened so long ago that he could hardly remember their little mini-affair. As he called it, she had come on to him when she was showing them the house; and then on the telephone, when they should have been talking about business, she had dropped certain hints to him, and he had picked up on them. In other words, she was the aggressor—and that had been the problem with her from first to last, for she was a very aggressive woman, competitive, emasculating—and, having discovered that, during a few nights spread over a number of weeks, he had decided to end it. And, of course, hiring his wife was Virginia's revenge. What more perfect act of emasculation? But if only that was intended, then even he had to admit something more had developed.

Pat proved to have a talent for the real-estate business—women often did—and she had done remarkably well in it. Jack had to admit that. If pressed (but who was to press him?) he might even have admitted that he wouldn't be tossing money around on whores and near-whores if she hadn't been nearly equaling his salary with her commissions. But what the hell, they had it, so he might as well spend it.

He had to ask his way through an operator-receptionist and a secretary just to talk to his own wife. Jesus, this was impossible, wasn't it? But at last she came on the wire, pert and professional: "Patricia Gawlor." She was certainly under control.

"I seem to remember the name, but not that tone of voice."

"*Jack!* Oh my God, Jack, where are you? Are you all right?"

"Oh, sure I am. Of course. I'm right here at the office. I just called to let you know what happened."

"Well, I'm glad you did."

"It's simple enough, honey. I got drunk. Those good old boys from Virginia drank me right under the table. Literally. When I woke up this morning I was tucked away in a hotel room with a hangover that just wouldn't quit."

"But why didn't you call us *then*? The girls and I were just out of our heads. We thought maybe you'd had an accident or been mugged or something. You know what's in the newspapers."

Jack held back for effect, biting his lip. "Well, I should have," he said. "I certainly should have. But I was late to the office, and I only had time to run for it. You understand."

"I guess so."

"And it's been such a busy morning that this is the first chance I've had to call you."

"Well, okay . . . But we were worried."

"I know you were, honey. And, Pat?"

"Yes?"

"I'm sorry."

Molly B.? Jack found out at lunch it was short for plain old Molly Butler. She said she was from "just outside of

Pascagoula, Mississippi." (Jesus, thought Jack, what's *outside* Pascagoula?) She was thirty, married and deserted, with two kids who were now parked down there with their grandparents. That was why Molly B. needed all that money. One of them, the boy who was the oldest, had some kind of disease.

"What kind of disease?" he asked her.

"I don't know. Some man's name. Hutchins?"

He thought a moment, and then it came to him: "Hodgkin's disease? Is it Hodgkin's disease?"

"That's it. I never can remember that. Prob'ly because I don't want to." She paused a moment and searched Jack's face. "That's a pretty bad disease, huh? Hotchin's disease?"

"It's pretty bad."

"That's what the doctor say." She paused and picked for a moment at the plate of roast beef before her. Then she raised her face and looked at him squarely. "I tell you one thing, though," she said. "It's an expensive damn disease. Ain't no way in the world I'm ever going to pay for that damn disease. Not with workin' a job, not with hustlin' on the side. Just ain't gonna happen." She returned to her food. A particularly tempting morsel of meat eluded two stabs with her fork. She picked it up quite unself-consciously with her fingers and popped it into her mouth. Jack turned to see if anyone were looking. Evidently not.

"You've got a regular job, then? A day job?"

"Don't I? I tell you I do. At that damn old dry-cleaning plant. I been working at that mess about as regular as you could do."

"Well, is today your day off, or what?"

"No, I just phoned in sick and went back to sleep in that hotel room." She looked up at Jack then and offered him a broad, comfortable smile. "It was nice."

She was obviously quite relaxed with him now. He couldn't help wondering about that. Last night, when she first appeared, she had looked plain scared. Jack wondered if that were the first time she had been out hustling. She certainly wasn't what you would call a hard-bitten professional.

He gave in to curiosity and asked: "Have you been at this long?"

"Since I been up here. Just six months. Tell the truth, I don't like it much. It's hard to breathe that damn cleaning fluid all day long."

"No, not the job. I mean, you know . . ."

"Hustlin'?"

He nodded.

She stopped eating and studied him for a moment. The smile had faded. This was serious business. "What you want to hear?" she asked him at last. "I been out a few times. I ain't too good at it, though. I get nervous."

"You were nervous last night."

"I sure was."

"Why? How come?"

"I ain't never been with no white man before."

"Well," he said, lowering his voice and leaning across the table, "you ain't never been with no white man yet."

She grinned. "I guess not."

"So why is everything suddenly changed? You're not nervous now, are you?"

"No."

"Well?"

She thought a moment and then began: "When I was a kid, all the time I worked for white folks taking care of their babies. I did it all. I fed 'em. I changed 'em. I must've wiped more little white asses than any ten white women. And I could handle those kids, you know? When I said move, man, they moved!"

Jack nodded, waiting for her to continue.

"And I don't know," she resumed, "with you last night, I stopped being scared when you started actin' drunk. I could see I was supposed to just take care of you the way I did those kids."

"Just another little white ass to be wiped? It that it?"

She grinned and shrugged. "Maybe. I don't know. I just knew I didn't have anything to be scared about."

"Well, you were right."

"Even when that friend of yours come up in the restaurant

and try to take you away, I wouldn't let him. I just said *I'd* take care of you. I could tell you didn't want to go with him, anyway."

Friend? Jack's mind reeled. He felt a sudden panic. Maybe he hadn't imagined Zaslofsky there, after all! "Wait a minute," he said. "What friend? Who was this? When?"

"I told you. At the restaurant when they was movin' us out. This friend of yours—David, some kind of long foreign name—he come up and say you should go with him. I just say, 'No way.' Real tough, you know? And you just tell him to go away. Don't you remember?"

"What did I say?"

She smiled and shrugged. "You tell him to fuck off." And then she started laughing. She laughed long and hard at that. Jack turned to see if people were staring.

So David Zaslofsky had seen him reeling drunk with a black whore. Well, why not? He was sure it must have given him immense satisfaction. Wasn't this what Zaslofsky had always suspected? Hadn't he hoped for just such a development? Of course he had.

Jack brooded over this on the drive home that night. Zaslofsky—David, as he insisted—occupied a curious place in Jack's life. He should have occupied none at all. It had been a couple of years since Jack had set eyes on the man. After he had broken off those Saturday morning sessions in Zaslofsky's office in Evanston, he supposed he had ended things with him then and there, that he had excised a major irritation from his life. But that wasn't how it had worked out—not at all. Pat had continued to see him. Jack had argued that they didn't *need* a marriage counselor's help, that things were now better between them—which was true—and that they owed it to themselves to work their way through their own difficulties just as they had in the past. Oh, he was very convincing—except that Pat was not convinced. "You may be right," she had said to him. "Maybe *we* don't need his help, but *I* do." And that, it seemed, was that.

Jack dated the more or less constant state of uneasiness that had overcome him from that decision of Pat's to continue seeing the psychologist alone. Before, those visits had merely been something to be endured, sometimes embarrassing, often annoying in their consequences—but limited in their effect upon him. But now? Now David Zaslofsky's influence seemed to settle over every aspect of Jack's life like some pernicious power. Face-to-face, Jack could deal with the man. At this distance, however, Zaslofsky was utterly unbeatable. Jack found that out first when the question of Pat's taking a job came up. Well, it didn't just come up, of course—Zaslofsky had almost certainly put her up to it. In any case, Jack had talked to the psychologist about it on the telephone, and he had been very cleverly maneuvered into declaring that he *wanted* her to take that job with Virginia Jelinek. The two had talked on a couple of other occasions after that, though always over the phone and never at length. Jack simply didn't trust him. Even so, Zaslofsky made his presence felt. Whenever Pat popped up with some opinion that astonished him, or some new idea that disturbed him—as she did increasingly often these days—Jack found himself wondering if perhaps she had gotten that from "David." He didn't like it, but he was afraid of digging too deeply, so he never asked. He really didn't want to know what his wife talked about to the man.

Well, he thought, now they'll have plenty to discuss. Zaslofsky had probably already been on the phone to her. In fact, as he turned down his street and began counting the houses to make sure he stopped in front of the right one, he found himself glumly assuming that by now Pat would know all about it and that he was in for a very bad evening.

That, however, proved not to be the case.

Before he could get his key in the door, his younger daughter opened it and greeted him briskly with a smile.

"Hi, Daddy."

"Hi, honey."

"Hear you had a bad night, huh?"

"Not good. And this morning wasn't so good, either. I believe you call it 'barf.'"

"*Yuk!*" Nancy shuddered appropriately, and he handed the *Daily News* over to her.

It was Carol's night for dinner, and she was fussing mightily in the kitchen. She hardly responded to his greeting, but he didn't take that personally—you never could with her these days.

And then there was Pat, setting the table, looking up, smiling. He saw her with an exactitude that was altogether new—as though catching his first glimpse of her after a long absence, or perhaps more accurately, seeing a movie image of her run in slow motion. This was really how she looked, wasn't it? That broad mouth turned wide at the corners, those blue eyes raised ruefully to him. Had she grown prettier while he was looking the other way? Perhaps she had. Or perhaps it was just the expression on her face. But it was a nice face. He had to admit that.

"Poor Jack," she said. There was no trace of irony there.

He nodded emphatically. "Poor Jack is right. I really feel like I've been had," he said. "You know what the boys from Breeze pulled after I talked to you?" He barely paused for her to respond because, of course, there was no way for her to know. "They decided to wind up early and go back home today. All Bucklew did was call up and say they'd decided to go with what we showed them yesterday." He had decided to stick to his story. If she challenged him with what she had heard from Zaslofsky, he would insist that the black girl was with Bucklew: You know how those good old boys away from home, etc. He was sure he could pull it off. He was a good liar.

"But isn't that good?"

"Well . . . sure. But if I'd known that I wouldn't have had to go out and hold their hands last night. I wouldn't have put you through what I did."

She shrugged. "You know what my father used to say."

"What's that?"

"It goes with the territory."

He bent forward and kissed her squarely on the mouth. Was this all there was to be? Maybe Zaslofsky hadn't gotten around to calling her yet. "Did I ever tell you I love you?" he asked.

"Yes, but I like hearing it."

"Well, I do." And it was true. There was nobody who could make him feel better, more comfortable, than Pat—when things were right between them. And somehow that's how they were that evening. There was such intimacy between them. He couldn't account for it. Time after time their fingers touched. Once when he was talking to Carol about the trip she was planning next month up to Ripon to look over the campus, he turned and happened to notice Pat studying them both—not anxiously but lovingly, as though she wished to fix the two of them, this moment, in her head. She smiled then, and nodded as though to affirm all this.

And then, later, as they sat watching television with the girls, she turned to him suddenly and asked if he might not like something to drink.

"Are you kidding?" he asked. "After last night? I'd do well to swear off completely."

"Well, I just want you to know I don't disapprove, or think you've got a problem or anything." She hesitated, then added, "Those things . . . misadventures like last night, well, they happen sometimes."

He turned and studied her for a moment, trying to discern what all she had meant by that. What was she trying to tell him? But Pat had addressed the television screen, and even now kept her eyes steadily on it. Her face was as nearly without expression as it could be. "No," he said, "thanks anyway. I'll take a pass. No drink."

"All right," she said, "just so you know how I feel."

They made love that night. They outlasted the girls, said good night to them, and a little while after Johnny Carson's monologue they went up the stairs hand-in-hand. Pat insisted on bathing, and so Jack knew just what she had in mind. Fine. He looked forward to it tonight, as he had not in a very long time. After all, this had been a good evening, hadn't it? And now they might make it even better, mightn't they? Whatever else this meant, it made Jack appreciate all the more what he had here with Pat and the girls. Home—nights like tonight—it was all so important to him, a kind of safe harbor, a castle keep against the world outside. And then he realized that was how his mother used to talk about her dream-with-a-white-picket-fence. Funny. He had just about come full circle, hadn't he?—except that in a funny way, Jack himself was that world outside as well. It was from himself he sought protection.

Molly B. was no trouble at all. All he had to do was tell her the time and the place, and he could count on her to be there. That was how it should be with a whore, of course. But was she more than a whore? A mistress?

He wasn't sure. There was something special about her. He had known that the moment he first saw her. And all the time that he had spent with her after that first disastrous night—time snatched in lunches and spare hours after work— had been conscientiously directed toward catching and isolating that special something, grasping it and examining it. And still that quality of hers had eluded him. He only knew he had to keep seeing her until he knew what it was. Was that so strange?

They had been going to the same cheap hotel just south of Roosevelt Road on Michigan. Almost as a joke the desk clerk, an old, toothless white man who spent all his time working crossword puzzles, kept assigning them the same room—third floor, right front. It was neat and clean enough, though it could have used a coat of paint. But it had a battered television set and a big old cast-iron dragon-footed bathtub, and these absolutely delighted Molly B. They were all the entertainment she needed during the long afternoon hours between lunch and dinner that Jack spent in the office. He could count on it—just let himself inside the door, take two or three steps inside, and look—there she would be, soaking in the tub, her long brown body folded at the knees, her legs spread as if for intercourse. And she would look up at him, those almond-shaped eyes wide with affection, and smile the very sunrise of smiles. Then she would raise her arms to him to be embraced and taken dripping from the tub, as all the while he heard the alternate bleat and roar of punch lines and canned laughter from whatever inane sitcom rerun she might have on at the moment.

And he would tumble her down onto the bed. Then, as he

studied the slender, dark, naked body, so unlike his own, that was stretched out before him, he would begin to undress. Unbuttoning, unzipping, tugging and pulling, doing indifferently whatever needed to be done, he concentrated wholly on her. Inevitably his eyes would go to those black, fuzzy patches around her body and to the short, tight ringlets of hair on her head that were so much like pubic hair. But there were other points of interest—her feet, for instance. They were so long and narrow, the soles so pink, and the toes as long as a child's fingers. So different from his own blunt, splayed white-man's feet. He was fascinated.

The first time they lay down together, he found her trembling a little and asked if she were cold.

"No, I ain't cold."

"Nervous?"

She nodded. "Ain't I a dumb nigger? Not like it was the first time or anything."

He smiled down at her, feeling oddly benevolent, then bent to kiss her first on the lips and then on each brown nipple. As he ran one hand through that tight tangle upon her head, he moved the other through the patch over her pubes. Her hair was as resilient and thick as he expected it would be, but it surprised him somehow by being a little softer than he would have supposed. Her bush seemed almost silky. He licked each armpit, tasting the salt of her sweat, glad to be spared the sour shock of some deodorant or other on his tongue. She stirred slightly, let out something between a moan and a sigh, and stretched her arms luxuriantly above her head. Encouraged by that, he began licking his way down her torso. When he reached her pubes, he buried his nose in the patch and rubbed lightly, expecting her to laugh or giggle. But no—she tensed, and he wondered why. With his two thumbs he opened her lips, marveling at the contrast between their livid brown and the pink of the soft flesh inside. He was about to insert his tongue when he was grabbed roughly at the ears, and he felt himself being tugged back up her body.

"Hey! Don't you do that woman-stuff to me," she said to him. "You fuck me like a man." She wasn't angry—just direct and terribly emphatic. And so he did as she demanded, finding her a little closer to his old dream of Miss Supernigger than he had ever expected her to be. It was strange to be given such orders by a whore, and stranger still to be caught in a sudden brute contest of the pelvises. Old-fashioned fucking. They heaved and bucked away at one another like a couple of athletic teenagers. He slowed the pace at least twice and stopped briefly once altogether when it seemed he was about to climax. Holding back, then, he proceeded to probe, building up a steady rhythm as he moved to kneel beneath her buttocks, taking great swinging thrusts at her, all but leaping into her from beneath, again and again and again. They went at it that way, moving together, panting, groaning, grinding away until at last there was nothing left to hold back, nowhere else to go but forward and down, down, down into the final sputtering fall.

When he fell away from her and rolled onto his back, he found himself puffing away, half-exhausted, and wondering how long they had been banging away at each other. Minutes and minutes, he supposed. Hours? But he had won, hadn't he? Hadn't he? A crooked, derisive smile spread over his face as he stared up at the ceiling.

"You smilin'," she observed, staring across at him.

"Am I?"

She nodded. "All you mens alike. Black or white. It don't make no difference. Ain't but one thing make you happy."

"And what's that?"

"You know."

"Yes, I know." He paused a moment, remembering, then, plunged on: "I was just thinking about the first time I ever did this, you know, with a woman."

"What about it?"

"She was like you."

"What you mean 'like me'? Ain't nobody in the world like me."

"She was black."

"Oh." She let that sink in. Then she glanced across at him rather shrewdly. "She sellin' her ass?"

He didn't like being seen through quite so quickly, but

she had him, didn't she? "Yes, she was," he said. "How did you know?"

"How you get together with a black woman unless she sellin' her ass? You tell me that."

This wasn't going in quite the direction he had intended. What was he supposed to say to that? He decided to meet her head-on. Heaving himself up on an elbow, the smile long since faded from his face, he looked down upon her and asked, "Does that bother you? That I was with a black whore? That I'm with you now?"

"Sheeeitt," she said. "How that bother me? Just because I'm sellin' my ass a little on the side? You think that make me a whore?"

"Well . . ."

"Ain't no way I'm a whore unless I do something I don't want to do. That's what my uncle tell me. He say a little hustlin' on the side don't mean nothin'. Just if you hold something back that belong to you, it's okay. You know? Everybody got to hustle sometime. Just if you let people pick all over you and take whatever they want, then you're really a whore." She paused, her face turned to him, staring, and asked, "You understand what I'm tellin' you?"

There was no way of avoiding those eyes of hers, was there? She sent him back over his own life, and for a moment had him considering his own standards, his own choices. And, yes, he had to admit that he had been hustling on the side for years, but that he had always held something back. Consciously? He couldn't say. He only knew there were lines that he drew, pieces of himself that he held back, and that he was no whore. He thought about this and wondered for a moment what she would have made of any of it. Not much, probably. At last he replied: "Yes, sure. I understand." And of course he did.

After a number of days spent just this way, his late arrivals home written off as overtime at the office, Jack found he was falling into a kind of routine with Molly B. Whether he intended it or not, she was becoming a part of his life. He found himself looking forward, mornings and afternoons, to the time he would be spending with her in that crummy hotel room. He realized this was so without quite knowing how he felt about it.

Late one afternoon he was stopped on the way up to the room by the desk clerk. The old man grinned up at him and nodded as Jack walked hurriedly by, but then called after him: "Oh, cap'n?"

Jack turned back, annoyed, and for some reason a little apprehensive. "Yes?"

"I was just wondering, you been using that room up there pretty steady by the day. Maybe you'd like to take it on by the week or even by the month. Give you a lot better rate on it." He blinked his watery eyes at Jack once or twice but continued to look at him steadily.

Jack thought about it a moment and nodded. "Maybe I would," he said.

They agreed on a price. Jack counted out seven tens and told the desk clerk to keep the change. That suited the old man just fine.

He didn't get around to telling Molly B. about it until an hour later when they lay side by side on the bed.

"I took it for a week," he said to her. "How does that sound to you?"

"What you mean?"

"Well, you said once you didn't have much to go home to. You can stay here if you want to."

She moved over onto her side and raised up so that she was half-sitting. "I can?"

"For a week, anyway. If you stay in the bathtub that whole time, though, you'll be as wrinkled and shriveled as an old woman." He smiled up at her so she would know he was just joking. Sometimes she seemed not quite so sure with him.

She smiled back at him, returning him ten for one, sweet pleasure for irony. "You somethin', you know that? How I get so lucky? Don't you worry. I ain't gonna look like no old woman for you. Don't you worry."

The familiar face loomed out over him like the visage of

some angry god. She made him feel like a child again. He didn't much like the feeling.

"Now, Mother," Jack said, "I'd just as soon we dropped it. This isn't the time or place to talk about that. Not in front of the girls."

"Oh, *Daddy!*" Carol—acting predictably put out.

He turned to Pat, silently appealing for help, but she offered none. She gave him a vague, rather opaque look, as though to tell him he was on his own.

It had all begun when Nancy quite innocently had used that favorite word of hers, "barf." Jack's mother had turned to her and told her rather sharply not to use such language at her table.

"But everyone says 'barf,'" Nancy objected. "Even Daddy did the other day."

The wide-eyed shake of the head he had given his daughter had gone unnoticed.

His mother leaned forward in sudden interest. "Oh, what was the occasion?"

"It was when he got sick with the men from Breeze."

"Breeze?"

"Cigarettes. They're *clients*." Nancy was proud of herself. She obviously had a few things to teach her grandmother about the working of the great world outside. "They all got stinko."

"Oh?" She thrust herself over toward her son. "Maybe you'd better tell me about that," she had said to him.

And it was then that Jack made that little speech about this being neither the time nor place to discuss such matters. And it was a moment later that Pat had let him down. He would talk to her about that—but not until he got her alone.

At last he managed to squelch his mother by threatening to leave if she persisted. He would have left, too, and simply gone out to wait for the others in the car outside. This was their little party, anyway. These women had no need of him here.

In the end nothing so drastic was necessary. He stared his mother down, and Pat at last introduced a new subject for discussion—Carol's trip up to Ripon. What had taken her so damned long? At any rate, the crisis was past. Minutes later the moment was all but forgotten, and they were once more awash in that sea of boredom where his mother was undisputed master of the ship. These weekly dinners with his mother were so damned trying. He had it in mind to quit coming altogether. But did he have it in him really to do it?

The trip home was a bit of a trial. Carol was quiet. All Nancy had to say was, "I'm really sorry, Daddy." And Pat? Well, she chose that time to rehash the whole day at the office—three difficult clients and a lot of half-baked philosophy from her boss, her friend and his, the one, the only, Virginia Jelinek. Well, okay. So what? It all helped pass the time, didn't it? Although he couldn't say he was really interested, it didn't bother him to hear Pat rattle on this way. It reminded him of the many times in the past that he had rattled on just as emptily to her. Turn about and all that, he supposed. He was nothing if not fair.

That was Jack's attitude, his position, when he went in to talk to Pat later that night: he was fair, tolerant, evenhanded, generous. Why should he be made to suffer embarrassment or worse by this cabal of women?

He found her in their bedroom. In one corner of it she had set up a small desk where she sometimes worked at night —though what she found to do there, he had no idea. She looked up and smiled as he entered the room. For a moment he was disarmed, but he managed to hold onto the grave expression that he had worn into the room. This wasn't the time to weaken.

"There's something I want to talk about," he began.

The smile faded. She nodded. "All right."

"It was that business at my mother's."

"What business, Jack?"

"Oh, come on, Pat. You know very well what I mean. When Nancy made that blunder and my mother began grilling me about the other night. Getting stinko."

"Well, Jack, she's just a kid. She said she was sorry. I know she is."

"I'm not blaming her. I'm blaming you."

"*Me?*" She seemed honestly shocked—or was putting on a pretty good act. "Do you really mean that?"

"You bet I do. Didn't you see that look I gave you? I was asking for help. And did I get it from you? It looked to me like you were lining up with her—and after that nice speech you made the other night about my 'misadventure.' That was the term, wasn't it? Very neat. Very literary."

"Jack, what is this all about?"

"Why, you were ready to throw me to the wolves!"

There was silence for a moment between them. Jack looked at her, staring her down as he had his mother. It wasn't hard. When Pat looked away, she seemed almost frightened. Well, he thought, let her quake a little. It might do her some good.

Still looking away—to be precise, down at her desk where she was nervously tracing an isosceles pattern with her finger—she began to speak, haltingly, carefully: "If I . . . made you feel that I was . . . indifferent to your situation with your mother, then . . . well, I'm sorry. I guess that if I didn't rush to your aid, it was because I thought you could handle it."

"Well, I *could* handle it," he fired back. "I had to."

She turned to him. "Yes, you did—though I must say you used a bit of overkill, threatening to leave like that."

"Drastic measures for a drastic situation."

Pat shook her head. "Honestly, Jack, sometimes I wonder if we're even perceiving the same reality."

"Oh? Philosophy!"

"Please," she said, "don't do that."

"Don't do what?"

"Ridicule me."

"I'm not ridiculing you. I'm just . . ." He trailed off, searching for words.

"Just ridiculing me. Look, this is very basic. The way you see your mother, why, it's way off. You see her as much more formidable than she is. Jack, she's an old woman. She depends on you. We're all the family she's got. You don't need to take her . . . her crotchets as seriously as you do. You overreact."

He looked at her suspiciously. "You mean I don't act rationally?"

"I didn't *say* that! Please don't put words in my mouth. You're always doing that."

"Oh? Am I?"

"Yes, of course you do that. I told David just the other day that that is the single most disturbing thing you do."

"You told him that? What else did you tell him?"

She raised her eyes. "Jack, David is my friend. I tell him everything."

"Everything?"

"That's right. *Everything*."

"In other words, I come up quite a lot—as a subject for discussion."

She looked at him, her lips pursed, her eyes narrowed. "Yes. You do come up from time to time."

"I'll bet I do. You know what I think? I think I ought to sit in on those sessions just to protect my own interests."

"Maybe you should. You were the one who broke off the visits—who was so sure they weren't doing any good."

"Yes. Well?"

"Well, maybe you were wrong."

"Maybe. And maybe the whole system stinks."

"What's that mean?"

"I think," said Jack, "that it should be obvious what it means. I really don't like having myself discussed by you and Zaslofsky like I was some sort of case or something. That's what you do. Even when I was there, it was like I wasn't—the way you two talked about me. I hated that. Why do you think I quit going?"

Pat rose and took a step toward him, but he moved back. He didn't want to be touched by her—not quite yet. "Jack, it isn't like that at all. We just . . . talk. We don't have these attitudes you seem to think we have."

"I suppose he doesn't have an attitude toward me." Jack hesitated—but only for a moment—then plunged on: "I suppose he didn't tell you a few things about me? About meeting me the other night and who I was with?" There. It was out. He didn't give a damn. He was glad.

"He . . . well, yes, he did tell me something about it." She spoke vaguely, almost evasively, as though she wished to get beyond all this as quickly as possible. "He was concerned about you, Jack. Don't you understand that?"

"I only understand that you people are treating me like *I* was the patient—humoring me, making allowances for me. *I hate it.*"

"Jack, there *is* no patient. We just talk."

"Well, if David only told you something about it, then he may have spared you the essential fact. I was with a woman when he saw me."

"Jack, don't."

"She was a black woman. A black whore."

"Don't."

"And you know all these nights I've been working late at the office? Well, I wasn't. I've been with her. And you know what? She doesn't think I'm a case at all. She thinks I'm a man—something you seem to have forgotten. And in a lot of ways, Pat, I really prefer her company to yours."

Pat put her hands over her ears. "Don't, don't, don't, don't, don't," was all she seemed to be able to say.

He had nowhere else to go, so he headed for Molly B. and that crummy hotel on South Michigan. At least the rent was paid up there for a couple of days more. When he showed up, suitcase in hand, the man at the desk looked at him and shook his head. Meaning what? He waited for an explanation of some sort, but none came. So Jack shrugged and, tugging his suitcase, marched up the stairs. He let himself into the room. It was empty.

Tossing the suitcase on the bed, Jack wheeled around and hurried out of the room, slamming the door behind him. He had no idea why he expected to find her there. Molly B. was probably out working the streets or the bars, he told himself. Why, he was lucky he hadn't surprised her there with a trick. That would have been a little messy, wouldn't it? But, after all, why not? She was a whore, wasn't she?

He really ought to remember that. In the future he would.

"Tell her I'm coming back," he called out to the desk clerk as he stormed past.

Once out on the street, he realized he had nowhere to go, no one to see, nothing to do. And as his bad temper subsided, he grew a little fearful—afraid of being alone, afraid of being bored, afraid of the void that he now saw opening up before him. He was in no condition to go for a drink. What he needed was some diversion.

It was by this process of induction that he arrived at those two blocks of bookshops, peepshows, and porno theaters that lined South State Street. They used to be strip joints and burlesque houses. He remembered his solemn attendance at the old Gem as a kid. Almost a religious experience for him then. It had taken him a long time to grow up, hadn't it?

He went indifferently into the first one he came to and regretted it in the first moment he sat down inside. There was a dank, rotten, unhealthy odor around him. Was it dead wood and ruined mortar he smelled, or the memories of a million wasted fantasies that had gone sour there in the dark? Maybe he would have been better off in a bar, after all. There was a certain amount of foot-shuffling and snuffling, so he knew he was not alone. As his eyes adjusted to the dim light flickering from up front, he saw he was one of about ten there in the small theater. The heavy breathing ahead of him turned out to be an old man asleep.

But as his attention focused upon the figures writhing and heaving up on the screen, he gradually became oblivious of his immediate physical environment and was once again engrossed in the ancient spectacle that never ceased at least to interest him. Jack was soon lost in the endless montage of pumping, grinding asses and closeups of viscous organs and matted pubic hair that looked peculiarly like the underwater pulsings of invertebrate sea creatures. There were come shots. There was fellatio. There was cunnilingus. And so on. But as time stretched on, there in the dark, Jack gradually became aware of a certain dull sameness to what he saw up there on the screen. This was no doubt due in part to a lack of inventiveness on the part of the director and cameraman. He had seen other porno films that were far more visually original than this one—more variety in the shots, better editing, more interesting lighting. And this one had not even a pretense of plot. For dialogue there were groans and moans and an occasional "oh, wow," while partners were mysteriously and suddenly changed from time to time without explanation. The only moderate surprise in all this came after Jack had been sitting there in the dark for about an hour. A sudden cut introduced an entirely new pair. After a bare minimum of nuzzling and panting, the two got down to business which, in this case, was soon revealed to be anal intercourse. There could be no doubt what they intended, for there was a great show of buttock-spreading with appropriate closeups revealing precisely the targeted area. The aperture was so puckered and tiny that Jack was frankly doubtful that a penis the size of the one that now filled the screen could be introduced into it. Evidently the woman was equally doubtful, for at one point her face was visible as she strained to see over her shoulder, and she looked quite honestly fearful. That look stirred Jack. It was the truest and realest thing he had seen in this whole hour of counterfeit ecstasy: she looked truly scared. And when the penis was pushed up tight against her, and the pushing and forcing began, they were suddenly offered another glimpse of the woman's face, and she was obviously in pain. They were faking nothing, those two, and Jack was suddenly leaning forward in his seat, absorbed, fascinated, almost palpably sharing the strain as the man pressed into her. They used nothing—no Vaseline, no lotion, no lubricant of any kind—and when at last it was all over, and the penis was withdrawn in dripping, detailed closeup, Jack noticed a smear of blood around the opening. And somehow, though he couldn't say why, he was profoundly moved by the sight of it.

He jumped up from his seat and left the theater in a great rush, heading straight for that hotel on South Michigan. He couldn't wait to get there. He flagged down a taxi there on State Street and gave the driver the address as they sped off, thinking all the while about what he had just watched and its strange effect upon him. You seldom saw anal intercourse in porno films. It was still the great taboo, wasn't it? Why? There was that business of the butter in *Last Tango*, but they had faked that. And so what did that mean? Absolutely nothing. Jack had to admit he had never tried it. Why not? A certain fastidiousness, he supposed. He was almost embarrassed that he had not.

All but running into the lobby, Jack found himself momentarily halted at the desk and staring into the grinning face of the desk clerk. He supposed that meant she had arrived at last. Well, it was about time. And as though to confirm Jack's understanding, the desk clerk nodded and pointed a finger up in the general direction of third floor, right front. It was all taken care of, wasn't it?

Jack bounded up the stairs two at a time and barely had the keys out when Molly B. threw open the door and grabbed him by the wrist and pulled him inside.

"What you doing here?" she asked him, smiling. "The man say I just miss you. Then I see your suitcase. You come to stay a while or something?"

"We'll see," Jack said huskily, pushing the door shut behind him. He looked around the room. There were little touches here and there—pictures out of magazines taped to the walls, bottles and jars, combs and brushes arranged symmetrically across the top of the dresser—so that it was obvious that she was settling in, making a home for herself here. That annoyed him. He couldn't, at the moment, have said why.

"You having trouble at home, ain't you? Well, never mind. Old Molly B. give you some loving and make you forget all about that." She circled his neck with her strong arms and pulled him close to her, continuing to smile into his expressionless face.

In another few moments they were on the bed together, she nude and he in socks and shirt, unwilling in his haste to strip further. She wanted to kiss, caress, and fondle. He wanted none of that. "Turn over," he told her.

She looked at him oddly but did as he directed. A few seconds later, feeling him against her, she exclaimed, "Hey, what you up to? That ain't the right place."

"Never mind," he said. "It'll be all right."

She twisted and tried to rise, but his full weight was upon her. He thought for a moment they were going to wrestle right there on the bed. But suddenly she was still. "You always trying to put things in the wrong hole, ain't you?"

"There's no wrong or right to it," he said coldly. "It's just what gives pleasure."

"Gives *you* pleasure, maybe, but it hurts *my* ass."

He leaned forward so that his mouth was just at her ear, and he began whispering: "What does it matter if it hurts a little? I won't make it any more painful than I have to. I promise."

"Get off me."

"No. Listen. I'll pay you more. I'll pay you a hundred."

"Get off. I ain't your whore."

"Two hundred. Think about it. Think about Hodgkin's disease. You could send a hundred home and keep a hundred for yourself."

There was silence for a moment—just the sound of the two of them breathing deeply, out of sync. Jack waited. At last Molly B. spoke up: "Get it over with."

*

It was a week and a day after Pat heard of Jack's death that the call came. She had been out showing a couple of houses —in fact, she had put in a pretty full day, since it happened to be a Saturday—and it was late in the afternoon, almost suppertime. Although she was tired, she practically flew to the phone when it rang, because Nancy had told her when she came in that a woman would be calling. "I think it's about Daddy," her daughter had said.

"Why?"

"She wanted to make sure that you were the Patricia Gawlor who was the widow of John Gawlor. That's what she said—the widow. I told her when to call back."

And this was the time. Pat reached the phone just after the first ring. She held her hand on the receiver and took a couple of deep breaths through the second ring in order to calm down, a trick she had learned from Jack. Only then did she pick it up.

"Hello? Yes?"

"Mrs. Gawlor? You're the widow of John Gawlor?"

"That's right," she said and then waited tensely.

Nothing came for a moment. She could hear some heavy breathing at the other end of the wire. An emotional moment. And then: "I have some information I'd like you to pass on to the police. You're in contact with them, aren't you?"

"Uh . . . yes. Only . . . why don't you tell them yourself?"

In answer, a funny laugh. Funny peculiar. "I don't think, in this case, it would be wise for me to do that. Let's try it my way."

"All right. Of course."

"I want to give you the name of the man who killed your husband—or ex-husband, I guess."

Now it was Pat's turn to do a little heavy breathing. There was something quite unreal about this, as though this phone call were coming to her from outer space or something. Finally, and very weakly: "Yes?"

"Do you have a pencil?"

Pat glanced around wildly, almost ran off to get one but then came back to the receiver: "No . . . I . . . It's all right. I won't forget."

"No, I guess you won't. His name is Carl Mossberg. That's C-A-R-L M-O-S-S-B-E-R-G, and he hangs out at a bar on State Street called Dizzy's. Have you got that?"

"Carl Mossberg, Dizzy's, State Street."

"Fine. I just want you to know that your husband was a friend of mine, and he always spoke well of you, Mrs. Gawlor. Always."

"I . . . well, thank you. Thank you for everything. I—"

Pat was interrupted by a click and a dial tone. Whoever was on the other end of the line had just hung up. Pat replaced the receiver and then went quickly to her desk to write down the information she had just been given. She looked up to find Nancy there, staring at her inquiringly.

"Who was that?" her daughter asked.

"It was . . . well, I don't know who it was. But it was somebody with some information."

"About Daddy?"

"Yes." Pat turned away, hesitating, frowning, then she looked back at Nancy. "Let me ask you something."

"What's that, Mom?"

"Are you sure that was a woman?"

CHAPTER EIGHT 1978

JACK MET DENNY by chance one night in a bar on Rush Street. You could talk to him. That was the important thing, the surprising thing, and that was why he never thought of Denny as a pimp. Quite some time after that first meeting, when they had been seeing one another regularly a couple of times a week, Jack got around to asking him how he got into the business.

"You really want to know?"

"I asked, didn't I?"

"Well, I was a very good customer. And I just figured, why not make it work for me, too?"

Jack laughed. You were never sure with Denny whether it was straight stuff or just a routine.

"No! Really! You think I'm putting you on, right?"

"Not necessarily."

"Well, good. Because you're such a terrific customer, Jack, I wouldn't want to lose you. But if I do, see, I don't want to get a competitor. I want a partner. I can just see it. With your advertising smarts and my merchandising, man, we'll clean up! Billboards on Michigan Avenue—just a picture and 'Wanda—332-1798.' Class, right? Or radio—'Tired of humping the same old inert form? Put some spice in your life! Try Gloria—289-2868.' And television? Man, with television, the possibilities are limitless. Just think about it!"

No, you were never sure with Denny. He was so glib and such a charmer, that he seemed to invite frank discussion, something on a more personal level. And yet you were never sure with him just how seriously you really ought to take him. Well, what did it matter? As long as they hit it off so well.

Denny was about ten years younger than Jack, good-looking in an unobtrusive sort of way and a good conservative dresser. This was his image. But it was more than an image—it was the man himself. He was one of them—an equal, a friend, a helper. And Denny helped Jack often and well.

Denny's Wanda was from West Virginia, though except for a certain pleasing softness in her consonants she had long ago lost any trace of a regional accent. She was tall, red-haired, and so professionally competent in manner that Jack found her a little frightening the first time they got together.

"Mmmm," she said, flashing a smile, "and what did you have in mind tonight? Anything special?" Every whore tries to affect an ironic style. But Wanda had it down cold.

He sat down on the bed and swirled the cubes in his glass of scotch. They clinked pleasantly as Jack smiled up at her. "That sounds like a dare," he said. "You've probably done things I haven't even thought of."

"Probably."

"What's fun from your standpoint?"

"Whatever turns you on."

If Jack had thought about it at all, he would have conceded that eventually it had to happen. And chances were, it would happen just the way it did that afternoon on Michigan Avenue. He was walking along, eyeballing the girls and thinking of nothing in particular, when suddenly he focused on one in particular who was coming his way, remarked to himself that she looked familiar, and realized almost simultaneously that the girl was Joan Bigley.

He was moved to run away and at the same time felt driven toward her across the space that separated them. What could he do? Where could he go? He hesitated an instant, then, resolved, moved swiftly forward with his right hand outstretched, a smile fixed on his face.

"Jack, is it you?"

"You bet it is. How are you, Joan? How are things at McCann-Erickson?"

"Oh, there? I wouldn't know. Haven't been there for ages. That was two jobs back."

"I'm sorry. I guess I did see something in *Ad Age* about you moving on. Onward and upward. That's the way."

"Well, onward, anyway." She smiled at him rather ruefully, and he found himself trying to remember what that Frenchman had said about all of us taking some pleasure in the misfortune of our friends. And she wasn't even a friend. Yet what was she?

"What's the matter, Joan? Unhappy with your job at—where was it again?"

"Mangram-Bailey."

"What accounts have they go you on?"

"Oh, Sniffs, Kitchen Delight."

"Is that the problem? You used to swear you'd never write that stuff."

"No, that's not the problem. It's . . . oh, I don't know. I feel like I'd like to get out of the business or something."

"Really? You must be discouraged."

"No, not discouraged. Kind of basically uninterested. I've gotten pretty good at something that just doesn't seem worth doing." She looked away, her eyes flickering momentarily at a passerby, then turned back to Jack. "I'm thinking pretty seriously of going to law school. I've even taken the LSATs and applied at Northwestern."

"You *are* serious."

"More than before." She smiled at him suddenly, as though she had just thought of something funny. "We were a couple of crazy kids, weren't we? Isn't that what people say in situations like this? You know, I always liked you, Jack. I always remember you with a lot of affection—except that it pains me there were such hard feelings at the end. There didn't have to be, you know."

"I suppose not." Hesitating, he ventured uncertainly forward: "Maybe we ought to have lunch and talk about that. I . . . I'm separated now, you know. My wife's filing. I've got a place of my own in Evanston now. It's . . . it's sort of a new experience for me." He looked at her hopefully.

Joan peered into his face then looked deep into his eyes for seconds without saying a word. And as she did, the smile on her face faded. It was as though she were reading him and didn't like the story written there. At last, she said, "I don't think we should get together again, Jack. It wouldn't be a good idea."

He gave her a hurried goodbye then and left her standing there on the avenue. He wasn't hurt, just angry—and also strangely apprehensive. Later in the day, while washing his hands in the men's room, he caught himself staring into the mirror, trying to see what she had seen in his eyes.

It was the kind of bar where, even after dark, you had to stand for a moment just inside the doorway to accustom your eyes to the light, or the lack of it, before proceeding farther. Jack always had the feeling he was entering a cave. He took that moment standing, waiting, peering, looking for Denny. And there he was, off in the corner where he usually sat, alone, waving Jack over.

Going to him, Jack exchanged looks with a few men sitting at the bar. He wondered if, like himself, they were all clients of Denny's. They seemed men without faces— well-dressed and pleasant, but without identities— like extras in a movie.

Denny had his hand extended when Jack reached him. They shook warmly, old friends together on a happy occasion.

"I got some good news, and I got some bad news."

"First the good news."

"No. First the bad."

Jack shrugged and nodded, practically in one motion. "Okay," he said, "first the bad."

Denny looked at him, still smiling, and said, "Wanda's got some bruises you-know-where."

"Oh?"

"Come on, Jack, don't give me 'oh.' This is serious business."

"Well, I'm not saying it isn't, Denny." He looked around him uncomfortably, wondering if anybody at the bar could hear them. Denny didn't seem to mind if they were overheard. "I . . . well, tell Wanda I'm sorry."

"You don't need to tell Wanda anything. Tell *me* you're sorry. Listen, that girl makes her own deals. She can look out for herself, believe me. She's not complaining. *I* am!" Denny trailed off in exasperation, as though words had utterly failed him. When he resumed, it was in a lighter tone: "That Wanda, she's a peach, right?" He wanted an answer.

Jack frowned in wry puzzlement: what was he getting at? "Okay, sure. Wanda's a peach."

"You buy a peach at the grocery store, and it's bruised so bad you don't want it, who do you blame?"

"Well . . ."

"You don't blame the peach?"

"No."

"You blame the guy who sold it to you, right? You begin to get the point? I'm the guy who's selling the peaches. If a guy gets bruised merchandise, then I'm the guy who gets blamed. He doesn't buy my peaches anymore."

"Okay," Jack said. "Okay, I understand."

"Good. Now for the good news. You forgot about that, didn't you?"

"Yeah, I guess I did."

"The good news is I've got Gloria for you tonight."

There were a number of good reasons for him to rent the place on Juneway Terrace that lay just on the Chicago side of the Evanston line. It was only a room, but a room was all he needed. After all, he wasn't going to live there, just carry on a few experiments, more or less. He thought of this as his laboratory, and it seemed a good idea to keep it separate from his living quarters in Evanston. Nearer, more orderly, somehow. Neatness mattered to him more and more these days. He wondered why.

With a place like this, he would also be less dependent on Denny. His regular routine with Wanda was costing Jack a small fortune. Besides, he liked it less and less that Denny knew so much about him—far too much, really. It got in the way between them sometimes.

Jack could bring women to the room. It was adequate for what he had in mind, suitable for the sort of women he wanted, and perfect in its bare particulars.

One night he was on West Chicago Avenue later than he should have been. Where was it, anyway? Afterward, he tried to fix the location with some exactitude—but, no, all he was sure of was that it was west of LaSalle. He knew he was taking a chance even walking along that stretch after dark, much less after midnight. But he was still playing the adventurer, still being the fool.

He wouldn't even have noticed the woman who emerged from the doorway ahead and careened down the stairs to the sidewalk if she had come out in the daytime. He would have thought, "Just another drunk," and he would have been right: one more unfortunate. But you notice things at night. Your perceptions are heightened. You see better. You hear better. At least Jack did, he was sure. It was as though he had been granted special physical powers to face the tests and crises of the night. That's the way he thought of himself, anyway—as a kind of nocturnal experimenter, a researcher into the dark places, a Faustus of the sidestreets.

The woman walked unsteadily along about twenty feet ahead of him. He heard her talking, something between a mutter and a mumble. As he gradually overtook her, he saw, first of all, that she was black. The red wig she wore had fooled him, but when she turned her head slightly, he caught a glimpse of her features, and they were unmistakably negroid. Also vaguely familiar. And then, coming up close behind her, he realized that the ceaseless stream of grunts and slurs that issued from her were obscenities. "Goddam, sonofabitchin', cocksuckin', asshole-bastard." And so on.

Finally, at the corner of LaSalle and Chicago, she stopped and rallied herself for the trip across the street. As she stood there sagging, illuminated by the bright streetlights on the corner, Jack recognized her at last as Molly B.

She turned suddenly and looked at him angrily. "What you starin' at, motherfucker?"

He didn't even reply. He backed off, turned, and crossed Chicago Avenue to get away. Had she recognized him? No, he was sure she hadn't. She was too drunk for that, too drunk for much of anything.

"You don't live here, do you?"

"No, I work here."

"What kind of work do you do?"

"I'm doing it now."

She burst out laughing. "*This* is your work?"

"Why not? Think of me as a social scientist—a *very* social scientist."

"That's funny."

"Good. It was supposed to be."

"Are you sort of, like, you know, a sex researcher or something?"

"Exactly."

"Far out! What have you, like, found out so far from me?"

"Not enough."

Annoyed with himself, irritated at Denny, Jack at last left the bar on Rush Street after waiting a full forty-five minutes for his friend. Friend? Hardly that. Pimp, procurer—what was the British word?—ponce. It was Denny's function to serve Jack, and it would be far better not to confuse the relationship with notions of friendship. Would a friend have kept him waiting? Would a friend have promised him new stuff, then fail to deliver? He had told Denny plainly that unless he could come up with something more interesting than Wanda or Gloria or their one-time-only replacement, whining Barbara, then Jack was simply no longer interested in doing business.

"Sounds like you're getting restless," Denny had observed.

"You might say that," Jack conceded tightly. "Or maybe I'm doing well enough on my own I don't need your help."

Denny looked around him. "We're sitting here talking, aren't we? You must need me for something."

There was a tense moment between them. Jack momentarily weighed the possibility of telling Denny off, of breaking with him completely. But then, almost in the instant that the thought had occurred to him, he dismissed it as a bad idea. He may not be dependent on Denny in the same way as before, but nevertheless he needed him—needed somebody who knew who he was and what he was and would still sit down beside him and talk as one human being to another. Maybe Denny knew that. Maybe he counted on it.

In the end Jack simply suggested that the two of them probably needed each other, and they let it go at that, agreeing to meet again the next night.

"I'll have a surprise for you," Denny promised. "A new girl. Nice. Not boring. Believe me."

"Been cruising Trailways and Greyhound again, eh, Denny?"

"Never mind where I get them. Just be glad I got an eye for quality."

That was what brought Jack back to the bar and what had held him there for forty-five minutes—or closer to an hour, as he saw when he glanced at his watch—the expectation that Denny would arrive with a girl who would solve all his problems, answer all his prayers, change his whole life. But, no: his problems went unsolved and his prayers unanswered.

Without quite expecting to or knowing why, Jack found his way into another bar on State Street, the kind of out-of-the-way place that he ordinarily avoided. He probably needed one more drink to simmer down—or maybe he was doing a little cruising on his own.

He took a place beside the only unattached woman there. Judging from the way she was decked out—all black net and clinging jersey—she was probably a hooker. But what did it matter? He preferred them. With whores things were neater, more on the up-and-up. You didn't have to come on to them.

When the bartender appeared, Jack turned suddenly to Miss Net-and-Jersey and asked, "What's that you're drinking?"

Not in the least startled, she looked at him with a slow smile. "This? Why, it's a brandy alexander."

"Looks interesting. I think I'll try one. You're about done. Would you like another?"

"Why, I'd love one. Thank you."

Jack nodded to the bartender, who had listened carefully to all this, and held up two fingers.

"That was nice of you," she said. She had a good voice—not exactly deep but with husky overtones—and a familiar ... attitude, as though she was at once mocking and trying hard to please. A whore's attitude. "And," she continued, "I thought it was very deftly done, too."

Ah, the lady has a vocabulary! "Deftly?"

"Well, you obviously wanted to talk. We're doing that now. And I thought you accomplished it rather well. Nice. Direct."

"Deft, in fact."

Her eyes flashed with amusement. "Exactly," she said.

Jack was curiously interested. By the time their drinks had come, he had hitched his stool over closer to hers and was well into an involved discussion of the inanities of barroom gambits. Gerry—that was her name—told Jack that the dumbest opener anyone had ever tried on her was spilling a drink on her dress.

"Wait a minute," Jack put in. "He did that just to talk to you? How do you know it wasn't an accident?"

"Because he told me later on."

"Then it worked?"

"I'm afraid so." The expression she showed him was one of sly chagrin together with a certain humorous self-deprecation. There weren't many who could have held all that together, but hers was one of those mobile and terribly expressive faces that with the lift of an eyebrow or the dip of a lip coud say quite separate, if not contradictory, things. She seemed to know it, too, for the truth was the lady did mug a bit. Jack wondered if perhaps Gerry weren't given to practicing in front of a mirror.

They talked on enthusiastically, playing out their parts with style and even, perhaps, a little grace. In transcription their conversation would have seemed no more than small talk, yet it shimmered with nuance and subtle emphasis so that words, phrases, even whole sentences seemed actually to mean a good deal more than they said. It was exhilarating, a kind of high for Jack. Finally, he broke off, leaned close, and said, "Look, why don't we leave?"

"And go where?"

"I've got a place."

"Why? What did you have in mind?"

"I'm sure we'll think of something."

She regarded him for a moment. "We probably will," she agreed.

Jack waved the bartender over and tossed a five down on the bar. Somehow the bartender seemed offended that they were leaving. "Aren't you staying for the show?"

Jack looked around and noticed for the first time that there was a small stage at one end of the narrow room. "No," said Jack, pointing at the five. "Will this cover it? If you're running a tab on her, I'll take care of that, too."

Without a word to Jack, the bartender picked up the bill and turned to Gerry. "Pam will be furious," the bartender said to her.

"Oh," said Gerry sharply, "just let her be."

The bartender shrugged grandly and walked away. Jack hadn't noted it before, but there was something rather effeminate about the guy. Faggots—Jack disliked them on principle. He turned to Gerry. "What was that all about?"

"Nothing," she said. "Personal stuff."

"Shall we go?"

Jack was tempted to take her home—that is, back to his place in Evanston—for he felt about her in a far more personal way than he had any woman he had been with for a while. In the end, however, he decided not to because, after all, she was probably a whore. Nothing had really been said, no prices had been quoted, but it seemed more or less understood between them that she had some interest in him other than purely social. Besides, she *looked* like a whore, and looks counted for a lot in Evanston.

And so Jack turned off Sheridan Road at Howard Street

and headed for Juneway Terrace, as he had so often in the past few months.

"Where are we?" Gerry asked, as he pulled into a parking space in front of the building. "Is this still Chicago?"

"Just barely."

"Do you live here?"

"No. Just a place I keep."

Gerry looked at him rather curiously but said nothing as she followed him out of the car and into the building. Predictably, the old busybody at the top of the stairs opened her door to look them over. She never seemed to miss. But when he turned back to give her stare for stare, the door banged shut—just as it always had in the past. One of these days he would catch her looking and—what? Stick out his tongue? Expose himself? It would serve her right if he did.

"This is it," he told Gerry as he stopped in front of the narrow entry and fished out the key. He unlocked the door and flipped on the lights.

She stepped inside and looked around, obviously unimpressed. "You spend much time here?" she asked.

"Some," he said. "Enough. Why?"

"This place needs something."

"A woman's touch."

"Something like that." Her eyes returned to him. "A human touch would do." She was trying to figure him out, wasn't she? Jack wasn't sure he liked that.

"Come here," he said.

She hesitated a moment, and that further annoyed him. There was something about her—good-looking in an overstated way, but in this light there seemed something oddly lopsided to her appearance. What was it? At last she took the two steps that separated them, found her way into his arms, and stared for a long moment into his eyes. She was tall, taller than he had realized. Even with flats on, she was nearly his height. Their lips fit together perfectly.

She was tense. He could feel the muscles of her shoulders and back tighten as he moved to encircle them. Suddenly she ended the kiss and pulled back from him. "Wait," she said. "I want to make sure you understand about me."

What was there to understand? That this was going to cost him some money? "We'll talk about that later," he said and kissed her again. His hands moved over her body, grasping at a breast, circling around the clasp at her hips, and then, slowly, deliberately, raising her skirt.

She broke away from him, pushing him off with two hands. Even though she had taken him by surprise, she seemed unusually strong. Confused and angry, he stared at her. "Look, what is this all about?"

"You know I'm a TV, don't you?"

"What do you mean?"

"A transvestite—in drag, darling." And then in a voice so much deeper that it shocked Jack: "Darling, I'm a man."

Jack said nothing for a long moment, trying with some difficulty to come to terms with this. Gerry began backing toward the door. He opened his mouth to speak, found he could think of nothing appropriate to say, and so he began laughing.

He laughed longer and harder than he had in years—perhaps ever. What might have seemed to him the worst moment in his life a year ago, maybe even a month ago, now struck him as merely funny. It was such an absurd surprise—almost surrealistic and at the same time so crudely, ridiculously funny—that he had no defense for it whatever: all he could do was laugh.

"Well, you seem to be taking it rather well." Gerry seemed slightly irritated at his reaction.

Jack gasped, trying to bring himself under control. Then finally: "It's . . . it's the surprise, I guess . . . the shock." He wiped at the tears in his eyes.

"Sometimes people get nasty when they get surprised that way."

"I'll bet they do." The thought set him chuckling again.

"It's not funny," said Gerry. "I got beaten up pretty badly once and slapped around two or three times." And then, sullenly: "Didn't you know what kind of bar you were in?"

"Gay?"

"Not just gay—TV. They've got a drag show there. My girlfriend dances in it."

"Pam?"

"You do pay attention, don't you? Yes, Pam." There was a pause. Gerry looked at Jack strangely and smiled. "Well?"

"Well, what?"

"Where were we before you were so rudely interrupted?"

Was she—he?—serious? Was Jack expected to continue? He almost burst out laughing again at that—but somehow the moment the thought occurred, there didn't seem to be anything funny about it. It was . . . interesting. Hadn't he carried this prejudice quite long enough? What was it they said? If you haven't tried it, don't knock it.

Jack stepped over and placed his hands on Gerry's hips, and then with the same care he had taken before, he began lifting her skirt. Once he had it up to her hips, Gerry swiftly hooked her thumbs into the nylon bikini panties she had on and flipped them down. Jack's hand groped the space that had been opened to him, and then he felt his hand encircle her penis. It was not fully erect but flushed and full, and he kneaded it gently with his fingers, thinking it strange as he did so that he had never held a penis other than his own in his hand. It was an odd feeling. There was a difference between them, wasn't there—his own and this one. Each organ distinctive in size and configuration—here narrower at the head, there thicker at the joint. This one filled Jack's palm like a fish, one about the size of a small trout.

The first time he heard one of the girls at the office say "Shit," he tried to get her fired. Her name was Karen. She wasn't his secretary or anything, just one of the pool typists. He was passing by her desk as she sat banging away intently on her Selectric—and she suddenly made an error. She hit the top of the typewriter in frustration and said it: "*Shit!*"

Jack was shocked. He looked at her a moment. The girl grabbed the sheet of paper out of the machine, wadded it up, and threw it down at the wastebasket at her feet, missing by a good six inches. He went straight to Liz Meyer and told her what he had just heard.

Liz seemed puzzled. "So?"

"Well," Jack said, "do you think that's proper?"

She shrugged. "I guess not. It's not polite conversation or anything, but does it matter?"

"What if a client should hear her?"

"Clients say 'shit,' too, Jack."

"Yes, but she's a woman. A girl. I think she should be fired."

"You may be a vice president," she said, "but we've got four vice presidents in this agency and only two good typists. And Karen's one of them. So please, Jack, don't push it."

He shook his head in disgust, got up, and walked away. Three days later, he heard the same girl refer to a job she had been given as "this fucking shit," and he walked right on by. It did no good to complain. Why should he bother? This, he supposed, was what they meant by the sexual revolution. He hated it.

Gerry's name was Gerald, of course—Gerald Gorman. He worked during the week as a clerk at a men's clothing shop in the Loop. Jack dropped by to check him out one day and hardly recognized him. It wasn't just seeing him dressed properly and stylishly in three-piece masculine attire. No, it went well beyond that. There was no trace of Gerry's weekend identity here. He didn't mince, he didn't drawl or hiss, he was at least as thoroughly and successfully male as he was female. Jack was deeply impressed: Gerry managed to be two different people.

There could be no doubt, however, which of them was the real one. Gerry was more sincerely and truly a woman than any Jack had ever known. Gerry, the ex-seminarian, had told him of a phrase out of Catholic theology—"baptism of desire"—that roughly summed up his situation. It seemed that when somebody truly wanted to be a member of the One True Church and yet was barred for whatever reason or difficulty—should such a person then die outside the Faith, then he could be considered for all intents and purposes Catholic, for he had achieved baptism by virtue of his intense desire. Thus Gerry. If, God forbid, he would die without having achieved technical womanhood, then he would have made it anyway because nobody wanted it the way he did. He had, in fact, even made arrangements with the only gay undertaker in town to be buried in a full-length gown, no matter what he should happen to be wearing when he was brought in. Until that day should come, he would go right on playing the part for all he was worth from Friday night to Monday morning, and even a few days during the week. He hustled a little, it was true, though more for the excitement of it than for the money he was able to make at it. But he put all he earned this way, as well as whatever he could save from his job at the clothing store, into a fund for what Gerry referred to as "a sex reassignment procedure." He had made inquiries. He knew who could best handle the operation and roughly what it would cost. "It's just a matter of time," he told Jack cheerfully.

In a sense, though, time was of the essence. Jack had never been unkind enough to ask Gerry's age, though it must have been somewhere around thirty. For the life he had planned for himself, Gerry had only a few good years left—five at the outside. Yet he refused to recognize that, refused to acknowledge anything but the demands of the moment. Jack had never known anyone before quite so obsessed with the present. But, no, that wasn't quite accurate, because through Gerry he began to meet a whole group of people who lived just as Gerry did, who were just as obsessed with the possibilities of the passing moment. They were homosexuals of some persuasion or other (Jack found out there were many), and their entire lives were defined and determined by their sexual identities. But wasn't Jack's?

For instance, he discovered that Pam traveled in every weekend night all the way from Wheaton just for the grand pleasure of pretending she was a stripper—or, rather, of stripping to G-string and pasties and pretending she was a woman. Then she drove back to a wife she despised and a child who now seemed a disastrous mistake, long since convinced that the only future for her was the sex-change operation that Gerry kept urging. And after that? Well, neither Pam nor Gerry nor any of the rest seemed to worry about what might happen after that.

Jack tried to think of himself as a bisexual. It was difficult. Since in the beginning his only experience was with Gerry and Pam (Gerry pushed the two of them together, then pumped them both for details), and they were so manifestly female, there seemed no need to alter his personal perspective appreciably. After all, Gerry gave head as well or better than any woman Jack had known. And to have anal intercourse with Pam or Gerry was not all that different with having it off with Molly B. or any of the rest. Only the problem of the penis remained, and that problem was one that rather interested him. It seemed such an anomaly that Jack found himself ignoring it at times just to see if it could successfully be overlooked (it could), and at other times—like that first time with Gerry—giving it his full attention.

Jack was not at all sure, though, that he could make it with any one of the butch guys who drifted in and out of the bar. Not the johns, who tended to be droopy and furtive and held no interest for him at all, but the macho hustlers, sleek and tough, who challenged him with their masculinity. They said, in effect, "Look, buddy, I'm just as much a man as you are, and I'm ready to fuck you to prove it."

One night one of them elbowed aggressively in beside him at the bar and introduced himself as Carl. He looked at Jack boldly and asked him if this were his first time in the place.

"No," said Jack, "I've been in here before."

"You like the atmosphere?" Which meant: Which way do you swing?

"I like it fine."

"There's more action down in the next block. You know the place? Dizzy's?"

"I know the place."

Carl was wearing tight jeans, a dirty white tee shirt, and a black leather jacket replete with studs and zippers. A walking cliché. He hooked his thumbs into his thick brown-leather belt and looked Jack rather coldly in the eye. "Maybe you'd better forget about it," he said. "It might be a little more than you can handle." With that, he turned and walked out of the place.

Gerry was over immediately. She squeezed Jack's arm sharply at the elbow. "What did he want?" she demanded.

"I guess he wanted me to go with him to Dizzy's."

"Stay away from that place. And stay away from him. Listen, darling, if you want more trouble than you can handle, then just get yourself involved with Carl."

"Oh? So you know him?"

"You just bet I do, and I've got the lumps to prove it."

Jack shrugged and looked away. He suddenly felt angry at Gerry—and really for the first time. They had gotten on remarkably well during the couple of weeks they had known each other.

Gerry's hand slid down and covered Jack's on the bar. It was a remarkably large hand for a woman. There would be no operation to take care of that. "You know, Jack," she said to him, "I worry about you."

"Don't bother."

"Well, I do." Gerry hesitated, and then plunged on: "Listen, every time I think of you in that crummy room by Howard Street it makes my skin crawl a little. How you can spend time there I really don't understand."

"I told you, I don't live there. I . . . I work there."

"Work?" she echoed and looked at him disbelievingly.

"Well, I don't see that I should have to defend myself to you," Jack said primly. "But I think of it as a sort of laboratory."

"Jesus," she said. "Call it whatever you want to, but the whole thing smells of death. Don't you understand that?"

He was beginning to hallucinate. He found that out from the superintendent of the building in Evanston one morning when he rode down on the elevator with him. The super, a harmless sort whose only fault was his tendency to extend simple greetings into short conversations, looked at Jack knowingly when he stepped out of the car with him and then asked, "Did you get that settled last night?"

"What settled?"

"Don't ask me. But you was having a big argument with yourself about something. Something about not using that kind of language in public. Oh, you was all excited, believe me."

Jack looked blankly at him a moment, then made a quick recovery: "Oh, yes, I remember what I was thinking about now—though frankly I had no idea I got quite so noisy about it. I guess I'd had a little too much to drink."

"Everybody does sometimes. I do every Saturday night. You hold it pretty good, though, except for that talking to yourself."

"Well, I'll hold it even better next time. So long!" Jack hurried away and out the door of the building before the super could even say goodbye.

He hadn't had a thing to drink the night before—all right, *one* scotch after work while he was waiting for Karen, the foul-mouthed typist at the office. But had he met her at that bar around the corner? Had he taken her back to his place and taught her a lesson as he swore to himself he would do? Now he wasn't so sure. And he did have to admit that his memory of the evening seemed to end rather abruptly. Yes, he remembered lecturing her on the way up to his apartment on just why it was impossible for her to continue using the kind of language she did around the office—and, yes, he even remembered them hurrying by the building superintendent in the midst of it. Inside, he remembered graphically pulling the clothes off her, pissing on her, kicking her, and finally fucking her as she whimpered gratefully to him. And that, oddly, was all he remembered. He didn't remember driving her home. He didn't even remember her dressing and letting herself out of the apartment alone. Nothing at all. It had just suddenly ended like a movie reel run out, or a TV show switched off at the commercial break. It made Jack wonder.

That morning, in the office, he studied Karen carefully for any sign from her of what had happened the night before. But none came. She said hello to him with the same indifference as before. There was no secret look passed from her to him. There was nothing. She was either a terrific actress or had a very bad memory.

The other possibility, of course, was that it had not taken place in any specific, literal sense at all. That possibility seemed more a probability the longer he considered the question, and it disturbed him just a little. On the way home that night he asked himself about a few other things that had been happening to him recently. Had he really seen Molly B. that night a while ago—or just a black woman who reminded him of her?

An odd smile spread over his face. More than anything else, he felt embarrassed.

It was the first time the whole family had been together, by Pat's reckoning, in more than a year. And having said that, she immediately glanced guiltily around the table at Carol and Nancy and Jack, having obviously just realized that the last occasion that had united them was the funeral of Jack's mother. Poor Pat! She all but clapped her hand over her mouth.

Jack decided it was up to him to rescue her. "And it feels just great, doesn't it?"

She smiled at him gratefully. "It surely does."

"Daddy, why did you ask for lamb this Easter?" asked Nancy. "We always have ham."

"It's a tradition," Carol put in. Most of the time she could hardly contain her scorn for traditions of any kind.

"Well, yes," said Jack, "I guess it is. But so's lamb—*agnus dei*, lamb of God, and all that."

Carol made a face. "What's that? Sounds Catholic."

"Well, all right. I'll have to confess that I got all this from a friend of mine who went to the seminary." In answer to Nancy's blank look, he explained: "He was studying to be a priest."

"Oh."

"*Is* he a priest?" Carol challenged.

Jack laughed. "No, just a friend." And then for Pat's

benefit: "But you can see what pious people I'm hanging out with these days." His little joke.

"Somebody you work with?" Pat asked.

"No. Just somebody I met."

"At a party?" she persisted. Why was she so interested? Did all wives—even ex-wives—have a sixth sense about such matters? What could she suspect about Gerry?

"Yes," Jack said finally, "at a party."

It had gone well up to that moment. Now suddenly Jack was uncomfortable. He looked uneasily around the table at Pat and his two daughters and asked himself why in the world he had agreed to this Easter dinner with them. It was grotesque. He had so little in common with them these days that he was really like a stranger to them. Only they didn't realize that, and somehow that made him feel even more completely a stranger. What was the point of all this? To pretend they were still a family? To pretend they all still cared about one another? Jack was all alone now, and he knew it.

But still, the girls seemed to get something from it. Maybe it was worth it for them. Nancy and Carol had both brightened up since his arrival an hour before. He decided to play the role for them. "You girls have certainly grown," he said.

"Oh, Daddy, we haven't," protested Carol. "Not for a couple of years, anyway."

"Not up, maybe," Jack said.

"And not out!" Nancy insisted. "I've taken off five pounds in just the last month."

"All right, all right," he laughed. "Not up and not out, but what I mean is, you've both matured so. Look at you. Nancy getting ready to go to college and Carol almost out. Tell me, Carol, what have you got in mind for afterward?"

Carol looked around the table a little apprehensively, it seemed to Jack, giving him cause to wonder. "Well," she said with a tentative smile, "I've interviewed for Pan Am stewardess school, and I've got my application in at a couple of other airlines."

Jack was silent for a moment. He looked at her rather darkly. "At Consolidated?" he asked.

"No, not that one. Pan Am's where I really want to go, Daddy. It's international."

He sighed. "Look, Carol, I don't know quite how to put this without sounding kind of old-fashioned, but do you think that being a stewardess is really . . . suitable?"

"Oh, I know what you're thinking," she said, "and I get this all the time at school. Everybody thinks it's kind of a joke, a girl with my marks winding up as a stew. I mean, stewardesses *do* have kind of a lightweight image. But I tell them it isn't forever. It's just to give me a chance to see some of the world before I settle down and really try to do something with my life."

Jack exchanged looks with Pat. Hers told him that the two had talked it over and that Carol had at least Pat's tacit approval. He could see he would get no help in this from her. Sighing, he began: "Well, honey, the *lightweight* image isn't the one that bothers me. I don't know if you're aware of it, but stewardesses also have a reputation for being, well . . . fast . . . easy."

"Oh, *Daddy!*" Carol was monumentally indignant; she clearly wanted to hear no more.

"No, let me finish. I realize that with all those Consolidated Girl ads I worked on, I'm at least partly responsible for this . . . image. But, look, honey, all we were doing was trading on an attitude that was already well established. Whether it's true or not, people have thought that—"

"You don't understand," she interrupted him.

He halted, annoyed, and looked at her for a moment. "All right," he said quietly, "what don't I understand?"

Looking around the table, including her mother and sister, she then leaned forward and said earnestly to her father, "People don't *care* about that stuff anymore. That whole thing of who's a nice girl and who isn't is just something that nobody *bothers* with. It went out . . . well, it went out with the pill."

Jack sat tight-lipped for a moment, fighting the anger he felt welling up inside him. At last, under control, he cleared his throat and spoke up: "I believe I'll have another helping of that lamb," he said. "Pat, you really outdid yourself this time."

Denny really seemed glad to see him. He grabbed Jack's hand and pumped it hard, using the two-handed grip favored by Irish politicians in Chicago. In that gesture he summed up himself and his elusive style: Denny himself was something of a pol, a ward-heeler, a man dedicated to keeping happy a select constituency of males, providing special services and nailing down their votes. And right now he was after Jack's vote.

"Jack, me boy!" he boomed out. "Where've you been keeping yourself? It's been months, hasn't it?"

"Well, weeks maybe."

"Far too long, anyway. Sit down, sit down." He called out to the bartender: "A perfect rob roy on the rocks with a twist for my friend." To Jack: "I never forget a man's drink. I might forget a name, even a face, but I'll never forget a man's drink."

Jack laughed. It was probably true. "Sometimes you forget appointments," he needled.

"Ah, Jack, *mea maxima culpa*. Forgive me, please. Listen, I know how it must've looked to you, but, believe me, I *didn't* forget. I just had, well, *terrific* difficulties that day."

"What kind?"

"Well, let's just say that Barbara has got a problem."

"She always did, as far as I was concerned."

"Now she has a problem of a very specific nature—and she's free to work it out on her own. I hope, for her sake, she manages to do just that."

Jack studied Denny for a moment. Was this a put-on? You never knew with him. "What sort of problem?" he asked.

"The girl sticks needles in her arm."

"Oh."

"That night I was supposed to meet you she OD'd, and I had to get her in the hospital. What a mess that was! And then I also had to pay off the people there, so it doesn't get entered as drug-related, which it very obviously is. So, anyway, by the time I got it all taken care of, I was already an hour and a half late to see you, and I hadn't even gotten in touch with the girl I was going to bring by for you."

"Well, those things happen."

"You always were one to take things philosophically, Jack. A gentleman and a scholar."

The bartender brought Jack's drink. Jack took it with a nod, then raised it in salute to Denny.

"Cheers," said Denny.

Jack took a sip. It was made right, so that it had that nice nutty taste that the best of them always do. He came up with a smile, then leaned over toward Denny rather confidentially. "You know," he said to him, "I'm sorry for Barbara's trouble, but in all honesty I have to say one thing."

Denny nodded soberly, his blue eyes full upon him. "What's that?" he asked.

"The girl was a lousy fuck."

The two of them burst into laughter at that. And when they had finally calmed down to giggles, and with every face in the bar turned toward them, Denny nodded and said, "You know, I think that was her big problem." And that set them going again. It was the best laugh Jack had had since he found out Gerry was a man.

At last, Denny: "Come on, Jack, fun's fun, but let's talk business."

"All right."

He leaned forward and lowered his voice: "Have *I* got a girl for you."

"Oh, Denny, that's what you always say."

"Don't I always deliver?"

"Well . . . usually."

"Except for Barbara?"

"Okay. Except for Barbara."

"Got anything against black girls?"

"Not a thing."

"This one knows you."

It took a while, the night that Jack and Molly B. got together, for them to know quite what to say to one another, quite how to approach each other across all that separated them. There was so much that did.

Jack began by telling her how nice she looked—and it was true, she did look wonderful. Remembering that disastrous first night of theirs, it had been Jack's idea to take her to dinner. He was delighted to see the heads turn as she walked by, almost regal in black velvet, her head high, her eyes straight ahead. He wondered disinterestedly what it would be like to be with such a woman permanently. Married, or something. The question nagged at him all through dinner. What would it be for him? for her? He tried to imagine it and couldn't. Nothing would come.

Together they ranged over the rather pitiful store of memories they shared, taking care to avoid the obviously painful. He asked about her uncle. There wasn't much to tell: he was still around, "still taking care of business." She told him how it happened she had met Denny and gone with him. Nothing special: she was working a hotel bar on her own one night when in came Denny, zeroed in on her immediately, and took her upstairs. Afterward, he proposed an arrangement, and she accepted.

Jack studied her for a moment. Her face, her eyes, had taken on a kind of opaque quality, so that she was now rather difficult to read. He remembered those half-wild eyes of hers shifting uneasily around Pepper's as she marched down the bar toward him, and as he looked now at this beautiful mask across the table from him, he asked himself where that country girl had gone. "Has it worked out for you?" he asked. "With Denny, I mean?"

"Oh, sure. He's a pretty nice man. He's fair, you know?"

"Good."

"Not like some of them."

Her speech was improved. She seldom messed up her verbs, and there were now little conversational niceties sprinkled through her talk—"so to speak" and "very definitely" recurring most frequently. Quite the lady. But Jack found that he missed that country girl.

"How're your children?" Jack asked.

"Well . . ."

"I really mean the boy. The one with Hodgkin's disease."

"He died."

"I'm sorry," he said quite automatically. But as he thought about it, he meant it. He was terribly sorry.

"Oh, it was a nice funeral, though. Very definitely a nice funeral. It was out of the best funeral parlor in Pascagoula, the one where only the white people got buried from when I lived there. Things change. Even down there." Molly B. was silent, remembering. For a moment the mask softened. It was no longer a mask. There were tears glistening in each eye as she continued: "The AME Church choir, they sang 'In the Garden,' which was for my mother, and then they sang 'What a Friend We Have in Jesus,' wnich was for me. There were flowers, just a whole truckload of flowers, so to speak. Oh, it was very definitely a nice funeral." She looked full at him and smiled.

"I'm sure it was," he said.

"I paid for it all myself," she said proudly. "Every bit of it."

By the time they got to Jack's place on Juneway Terrace, the two of them had loosened up and were old friends again. He had tidied the place up for her and changed the sheets. Still, it looked rather dingy. As he switched on the lights he felt rather embarrassed by it. "Look," he said to her, "we could go to my place in Evanston. Maybe we should."

She touched his arm lightly. "It's got a bed, it's fine. It's a little bit like that old room on South Michigan. You remember that, don't you?"

"I remember it," he said. "I certainly do."

"Well, then," she said. That was enough for her.

They made love. Fucking wasn't the word for what they did. Jack had not felt so tender toward anyone for years, perhaps not since the last good time he and Molly B. had been together. There was, he knew, a kind of valedictory quality to their meeting. They both seemed to perceive that. It was all in the moment—this moment. They had not seen one another for a few years, and there was something that told them both that they might not see one another for many more. Yet there was no hint of desperation to their labors.

They were metered to an easy schedule that left time and opportunity for them to delay and improvise along the way. And afterward, as they lay side by side, quiet, both more or less overcome by the spirit of the occasion, Jack told Molly B. it had never gone so well for him. And she simply smiled.

Then, as they drifted together into sleep, something occurred to him. He roused himself to ask her, "Have you ever been drunk?"

"Huh? What you talking about? I ain't no saint. 'Course I been drunk."

Jack sat up in bed. "No, I guess what I mean is, have you ever been drunk on Chicago Avenue—you know, on the street at night? Could I have seen you?"

"No, I ain't. No time I can remember." She settled down again, ready to let sleep come.

"Then I must have had a dream about you."

It wasn't that the hallucinations had actually ceased, it was just that Jack had brought them more or less under control. He was able to sort them out, to convince himself of what was real and what was not. This wasn't really so difficult once he had come to recognize it as a problem. He did have an upsetting moment, however, when he was least expecting it. It was on his way home from work one evening on the elevated. He had left his car that day to be serviced and was rather enjoying his rides on the el. Coming from Evanston, he was assured of a seat into the Loop, and he had made it a point to leave the office late enough—around six-thirty—so that he could have one going home. On that kind of schedule, he was able to read to and from, and he wondered why he didn't do it that way every day.

Where did it happen? Somewhere between Wilson Avenue and Bryn Mawr, he supposed. Jack had been reading the paper, almost drowsing at some dull article on inflation when he happened to glance up from it and look around him in the car. It was fairly full, although nobody was standing in the aisle. He had a full view of the passengers up and down and on either side of him. Most of them seemed as drowsy as he was. But not the boy who sat across the aisle and just ahead of him. Because of the arrangement of the seats, the kid was facing him. Jack was in position to get a good look at him.

There was something familiar about the kid. He sat swaying with the motion of the train, but he was alert, attentive, looking all around—looking everywhere, in fact, except directly at Jack. He wore a letter jacket—was it Jack's old high school?—into which he had both his hands thrust. The realization came gradually: It was not what the kid wore. It was not his haircut, which was surprisingly short for this day and age—almost a crewcut. It was . . . what? His eyes, first of all. They were as dark as Jack's and as restless. In fact, they were very much like his own. The shape of the face, too, was very much like his, though not as full. But there is was, all of it: the long nose, the thin lips . . . Why, thought Jack, he's me! It's me, the way I was back in senior year of high school. Not *like* me. But, *me*!

Jack was torn between terror and curiosity. He didn't know whether to jump up and start screaming, or to reach over and touch the boy to see if he were real. Could the others who were seated around them see what was so plain to Jack? If not, why not? He needed a witness, an objective observer who could assure him that he saw what he saw. He turned to the man next to him—well dressed and about ten years older than Jack—solid, conservative, absolutely perfect for such a purpose. Jack tapped him lightly on the arm. "Excuse me, sir."

The man looked up, startled. "Yes? What is it?"

"Could you tell me if . . ." Jack turned back to point out the other, his double, to the man beside him and found himself no longer there. The seat was not empty. Instead, it was now occupied by a much younger boy who looked not a thing like Jack. Had Jack simply imagined it?

"Yes? What was it you wanted me to tell you?" his seat companion prompted.

"Uh, could you tell me what the next stop is?" Jack finished lamely.

The man glanced out the window to orient himself, then said simply, "Bryn Mawr."

"Thank you."

Jack stared at the boy across the aisle, trying to decide just what it was about this puffy little eighth-grader that had set him going. Why had Jack been unable this time to distinguish false from real? Why had his defenses failed him so completely in this bizarre instance?

It was very troubling. No two ways about it.

Just to show Gerry that he was quite capable of running his own life, Jack began making it occasionally on up the block to Dizzy's. He couldn't really say he liked the place. It was much less congenial, even seemed a little threatening. Although there always seemed to be a few empty stools around the large horseshoe bar, men were jammed in separate groups and clusters around it, their backs outward, making walls of themselves against him. Jack came to understand that they were bunched together like this according to sexual preference—the leather boys here, the sparrow hawks there, and so on around the bar.

From time to time he would steal in, grab a stool between the groups, and stay the length of a single drink. Occasionally he saw someone he recognized from down the street—though never Gerry or Pam or anybody else in drag. That seemed to be an informal house rule. No doubt there were others. Once in a great while somebody would detach himself from one of the groups around him and come over to talk to Jack.

"Hi, you look familiar."

"I've been coming in here."

"But not for very long."

"Not long enough, I guess."

They were looking him over, he supposed, trying to decide about him. Was he a cop? a tourist? or just a shy john? Where did he fit in? Jack was beginning to wonder about that himself.

This treatment kept up until one night when Carl happened in, walked by, and recognized Jack immediately. He stopped and stood for a moment staring at Jack, his hands in his jeans. "Well," he said at last, "so you finally decided to come and play with the big boys."

Jack shrugged. "Here I am. Can I buy you a drink?"

"I thought you'd never ask."

Carl edged in beside him at the bar, ordered a straight shot of Wild Turkey, and stayed just long enough to toss it back. The two of them exchanged no small talk but simply regarded one another with detachment there at the bar.

"You look pretty straight to me," said Carl appraisingly.

"That's all right with me. I feel pretty straight."

"Just curious, huh?"

"You might say so."

"I just did." Carl said it with no special emphasis, but that ended the conversation. He pushed away from the bar and walked off.

It wasn't an especially friendly meeting, neither on Jack's side nor evidently on Carl's, but it did have a remarkable effect. It rendered Jack immediately acceptable to the bunch there at the bar. Smiles were sent his way. Groups opened up to him. And when the curious came to call, they stayed a little longer and talked far more affably than before. If Jack was all right with Carl, then clearly he was all right with the rest of them.

As a result of all this, he left Dizzy's one night with Hal, so delicate-featured and wispy in manner that he might just as well have been in drag. But he wasn't, so Jack allowed himself to count Hal as his first official homosexual experience. So what? When Jack came, it felt the same with Hal as it did with anyone else of whatever sex. And afterward? Well, afterward Jack found out that Hal was a computer programmer and as dull as the dullest whore he had ever talked to. He considered stopping by to see Denny the next evening after work. Maybe something with Molly B. would come of that.

But instead he looked in on Gerry. He felt a little guilty, as though he had deserted her or something. Which was silly because neither of them owed anything at all to the other. Jack owed nothing to anyone. And if Gerry had any real attachment at all, it was to Pam. Still, there was that little discomfort there between them the moment they caught sight of each other. He found her where he had expected to

—huddled in one corner of the TV bar with the rest of the girls. Settling down near the door of the place, he waited —and again as he expected, Gerry came over to him.

"Hi."

"Hi, darling. Long time no see." Her voice was, in a way, her greatest accomplishment, the most feminine thing about her. It aroused him a little just listening to her.

"Not so long. A week?"

"Something like that, I suppose. But I worry about you."

"You shouldn't. Nobody should worry about anybody."

"That sounds like your philosophy. Is it?"

"You might say that."

"Well, forget about it," Gerry said. "It's phony philosophy." She sat there, searching his face. She made him a little uncomfortable.

"Can I buy you a drink?" he asked abruptly.

"No," she said, "I've got one going. But thank you, anyway."

He nodded curtly.

"It's you over at that place—Dizzy's," she resumed. "That's what bothers me. I do wish you wouldn't go there, darling. They're not a bit gentle over there." She paused, hesitated. "Or maybe you've found that out already?"

Jack turned to Gerry in exasperation. "Look," he said, "I haven't found anything at all. Why do you keep after me this way, like some mother hen or something? God, Gerry, I can hardly wait until you get that damned operation. But you know something? You're practically there already. You've got the nagging down cold. The plumbing doesn't amount to shit compared to that. And no woman I've known —including the one I was married to for seventeen years— can nag the way you can."

Gerry stood there quietly, taking it all, waiting for him to finish. And then, when at last he had: "You can say anything you like to me. But I want you to promise me one thing."

"What's that?"

"I want you to promise me you'll stay away from Carl."

When Jack came bursting into Dizzy's, he suddenly realized he was moving practically at a run. Was he so eager to get inside? No—to get away from Gerry. Embarrassed, he slowed down a bit too abruptly, trying his best to effect a casual saunter as he moved down the bar, looking for Carl. In the end, however, it was Carl who found him. And wasn't that the way it had always been in the past? The Carls of this world always seemed to know just where to find him, didn't they?

Jack had settled at the bar, ordered a drink, and taken a sip when he felt a hand heavy on his shoulder. Without even looking, he knew who it would be.

"I was hoping you might be in tonight," said Carl.

"Really? Why?"

"I've got something that's going to interest you."

Jack frowned, annoyed. There was such a presumption in what he said—and not just in the words alone. The tone of voice, the expression on his face, everything in his manner, seemed to suggest that Carl knew Jack better than Jack knew himself.

"All right," he said, "let's see."

"I haven't got it here. It's out in the car." Carl inclined his head toward the door. "Come on. Take a look."

For a moment Jack hesitated, restrained in spite of himself by Gerry's warning. What was this all about? Would Carl get him out in some dark alley and knock him over the head just for the money Jack might have on him? He was probably capable of it. But would he do it? No, Carl was too smart for that. He would have Jack figured for a long-term investment paying off at a high rate of interest. Whatever else he was, Carl was street-smart.

"Where's your car?"

"Over on Cedar. Not far."

Jack nodded and followed him along the bar and out the door of the place, noting that heads were turning as they passed by. What was it in their eyes? envy? apprehension? contempt?

Out on the street, the two moved along quickly, heading

west toward the dark side of town. Neither of them spoke for nearly a block, and in the silence Jack could feel the excitement rising in him. It wasn't anticipation, for he had no specific idea what lay ahead. But *that* was it, of course—*not* knowing, just flying blind.

Carl tapped him on the arm and pointed across the street. "It's down there," he said. "I told you it wasn't far."

Jack followed him over, suddenly finding it necessary to take a few deep, steady breaths to calm himself down. He hoped Carl wouldn't notice.

"I get the feeling with you," said Carl over his shoulder, "that you're sort of shopping around."

"What do you mean?"

"Looking for something that'll turn you on."

Jack had caught up with him. He looked over at Carl but got nothing from him. Nothing at all. "Look, what am I supposed to say to that? You got me out here, didn't you? I'm curious."

Carl stopped. They had evidently reached their destination. Jack glanced at the old beat-up Buick that was squeezed in at the curb but saw nothing inside.

"Okay, this is it. See, a lot of guys wouldn't have the balls for this. You know, they'd say it wasn't their thing and all—but, bullshit, they just don't have the balls for it. If it's that way with you, then just say so. You'll save yourself some money and me a lot of grief. Fair enough?"

Carl banged on the back window of the car. Jack peered inside, and for the first time saw dimly that there was a shape stretched out across the back seat. Carl banged again, and the shape stirred.

"Hey, come on," Carl called quietly. "Open the fucking door."

Somebody sat up in the back seat, pushed over to the door, and looked out. The face at the window was all eyes and looked scared. Carl pointed down to the lock on the door. A pair of fingers appeared and pinched it up. The door came open, and out tumbled a boy of about thirteen or fourteen. He was a good half-a-head shorter than Jack or Carl, dressed in jeans and a soiled flannel shirt. He looked from one to the other and blinked rapidly. Jack couldn't tell if he were still sleepy or about to cry or what.

Carl fixed a hand on the kid's shoulder. "This is Ronnie," Carl said, "and he's a great little fuck."

The boy was from Arkansas—Blytheville, "up around Missouri and right near the river." Jack got that from him, though not much more, during the long drive to Juneway Terrace. At one point, somewhere along Sheridan Road, Ronnie turned to him and asked, "What kind of car is this here?"

"A Seville."

"A Cadillac, ain't it? That's who makes it?"

"That's right."

"I'm going to get me a car like this here. I'm going to get me a car first thing."

Jack glanced over at him. Ronnie had his eyes on the road ahead. He wasn't an especially attractive kid—frail, sharp-featured, weak-chinned, so that in profile he had a kind of rodent look as he leaned forward and squinted through the windshield. Maybe he needed glasses. Maybe that's what all that blinking was about.

If he felt anything at all for the boy, he felt sorry for him—but not *too* sorry. No, that wouldn't do at all. Carl was selling meat and Jack was buying. It was best to keep it at that level. Otherwise things got messy. He had found that out a long time ago.

"I hope you get that car, all right," Jack offered at last. Somehow it seemed important to keep the kid talking—to reassure him, he supposed.

"Oh, I'll get it. Carl said so."

"You like Carl?"

The kid hesitated, as though trying to decide what answer Jack wanted to hear. Then: "He's all right. He's . . . sort of showing me the ropes."

And that was all he got from him. Finally Jack turned on the radio to fill the silence.

It had not been easy getting him away from Carl in the first place. Carl expected to come along and wait for the kid downstairs or something. Jack had to start walking off down the street before he was finally able to convince him he would not put up with such an arrangement. Then Carl called after him, half-consenting, bringing him back to talk some more. In the end, it was agreed that Jack would return Ronnie to an all-night coffee shop on Rush when he had finished, and Carl would pick him up there.

And when would that be? Jack had no idea, really. This might take five minutes or five hours. It might not happen at all. Carl was wrong when he said that all it took was balls. Something like this, something altogether new, required a certain inspiration. And as of the moment, that inspiration simply had not come. Here he was turning down Juneway, looking for a parking spot, and he still hadn't quite felt his way into it.

He got the kid upstairs without incident. For once he managed to elude the old bag in second floor front. Maybe she was having one of her bridge nights with the girls.

"In here." Jack unlocked the door and threw it open. Ronnie held back a moment, then, apparently reassured by a nod from Jack, he went inside.

"Get undressed," he told him. Keep things simple. Be firm. Give him the idea you know what you're doing. So much of what happened next would depend on that understanding between them. "You want to use the bathroom?"

The boy looked at him and blinked. "No."

"Well, I'll be right out." Jack went in and relieved himself, watching his urine boil white in the bowl, planning his moves. If the kid needed a bath, Jack would insist on it, might even give it to him. That might get him in the mood. A shower? Why not? He caught an image—not a fantasy, just the beginning of one—with the two of them together, the water jetting down upon them, the steam billowing around, the lather thick on their bodies. Touching. Jack held it, feeling the first faint stirrings from his penis. He tugged on it two or three times, milking the last drops of urine from it, feeling it grow, subtly but perceptibly, in his hand. Maybe this was going to work out after all.

Jack flushed the toilet and undressed quickly in the bathroom. With an approving glance in the mirror above the wash basin, he tossed his clothes over his arm and threw open the door to the next room.

He was there—not the kid, not Ronnie, but himself, the boy he had seen on the el just ten days ago. Yes, there, standing by the bed, now looking at him calmly, more in possession than that poor, rat-faced kid could ever have been, was the specter of his seventeen-year-old self that had sent Jack into such panic when it had caught him by surprise somewhere between Wilson Avenue and Bryn Mawr. Well, this time Jack wasn't so surprised. What he felt was not panic but a sense of urgency, a pressing need to get through, to communicate with this pseudo-self.

"You're thinner than I remember you." It was true. The nude body he now saw was less manly, more adolescent than he had supposed his had ever been. Conceit in retrospect, he guessed—but it was hard to believe he could have played football with a build like that.

"Huh?"

The face was unmistakably his own, however. The light might not be especially good here, but it was bright enough to give him a clear view of those familiar features. Give or take a few wrinkles, minus a few ounces of flesh, they were precisely the same as those he had viewed fleetingly in the mirror a minute before. "You know what they say—" Jack tossed it off casually as he advanced toward the bed. He was now close enough to reach out and touch the other, but he made no such move. "You know what they say," he resumed. "The child is father of the man. Is that what you are? My father? Crazy idea, isn't it?"

"Mister, what're you talking about?"

He smiled slowly. "Of course," he said, remembering. "You hadn't come across that yet, had you? It's Wordsworth."

"Who?"

"They kept you pretty illiterate in high school, **didn't**

they? 'The child is father of the man. And I could wish my days to be, bound each to each by natural piety.' "

Jack was brought up abruptly by that. Natural piety, was that it? There was irony for you. So this seventeen-year-old was father of this forty-three-year-old? Then and there, whatever warmth, whatever generosity he might have felt a moment before was suddenly replaced by a sense of rage—anger and resentment that he found it hard to disguise. It was rage at his life and the direction it had taken—or perhaps that it had taken no direction at all, perhaps that was the problem. It was true, wasn't it? All those years of desperation that separated them—they all began with him, didn't they? Jack's whole shitty life came right back to this kid with his face that stood before him now. It was one of those truths that, once perceived, simply could not be denied. But who would deny it? Not Jack. He wanted only to set things right.

"Why don't you lie down?" he suggested as offhandedly as he was able.

Mysteriously, and without a word, the other one did just that. It was almost as though he were reassured that things were now as they should be. He took a position on his stomach, his face turned away from Jack.

Backing off to a chair that stood against the wall, Jack set his clothes down carefully, his pants on top. From them, he slipped his belt, looped it quietly through the buckle, and went over to the bed. He drew the fingers of his left hand slowly along the naked back, down the entire length of the torso, in a caress. And with his right, he brought the belt loop to a position just above the head.

EPILOGUE

After paying a protocol visit to Captain Quigley, whom he had known when they were both up at Eleventh and State, Melaniphy looked in on Chicago Avenue Vice and got all they could give him on Carl Mossberg. He was a pretty rough boy. Originally from Duluth, he had done time at Stillwater on aggravated assault before drifting down to Chicago. Since he had arrived in town four years ago, he had been booked three times, even held a week once in County when he couldn't make bail. But for one reason or another he had never been brought to trial on any of the charges. Which were—Melaniphy looked over the sheets—assault, assault, and (here was something interesting) pandering. He pointed that one out to Sergeant Bissell, who had dug the file out for Melaniphy, and asked him about it.

"He had a kid, a thirteen-year-old boy, he was trying to sell to every queer on the near north side."

"When was that?" Melaniphy shuffled back through the documents to see.

"A couple of years ago," said Bissell. "It's down there." Melaniphy saw it was a date in 1975. Probably not the same kid. "The way I remember it, Bissell continued, "the kid got out of juvenile home and just took off. Nobody ever saw him again around here. No kid, no case. So they dropped charges."

Melaniphy nodded sympathetically. The policeman's lot is not a happy one.

"That's the only time we even came close to nailing him. But he's been at it off and on ever since with some poor kid or other. Always boys, of course."

"That son of a bitch," said Melaniphy. "He's my man, all right. No doubt about it. But how can we nail him?"

"I don't know. Get an informer, I guess."

"We got an informer but no witness. Nobody who can even put Mossberg and Gawlor together that night."

"You got a problem."

Melaniphy thought a while. "Tell me something. What's this bar like, the one where Mossberg's supposed to be all the time?"

"Dizzy's? Oh, it's a fag bar. You know what they're like. You used to be on Vice."

"Yeah. The way I remember it, they're just like fucking sorority houses. A lot of jealousy and rancor and all that shit."

Bissell grinned. "That about says it. The way this one is different is that it's a little rougher than some. A lot of butch hustlers, like your boy, who kick ass just for fun. Some fairly heavy S-M operators hang out there, too."

"So a lot of old scar tissue, huh?"

"Yeah, and some fresh bruises, too."

A smile spread over Melaniphy's round face. "You know," he said to Bissell, "the way you describe it to me, Dizzy's sounds to me like a very disorderly place."

"Think we ought to raid it? It's overdue."

"I don't want to tell you your job, sergeant, but you never know what you might turn up. Could be *very* helpful to me."

As it happened, the raid on the bar turned up three individuals who admitted seeing John Gawlor depart Dizzy's on the night in question in the company of Carl Mossberg. That was good. What was even better was that after a lot of screaming and yelling by Melaniphy—what he called his intensive-interrogation technique—he got some little fairy of a computer programmer to say that he had checked out Gawlor's place on Juneway for Mossberg the night before the murder and passed the address on to him. A couple of them said they were aware of Mossberg's relationship with the boy. They said his name was Ronnie, and that was all they knew about him.

Melaniphy got signed statements from all of them, and with these, a warrant to search Mossberg's room on West Huron. He sent Klezek over to do the job. Then he sat down in the squad room with Bissell and smoked a cigarette, gathering strength for what lay ahead.

"You've had a big night," Bissell observed. It was meant as congratulations.

"So far pretty good," Melaniphy conceded. "Now comes the hard part."

"You think Mossberg's going to hold out? You got a case already."

"Circumstantial—but not bad. Remember, the guy's beaten three raps already. Besides this is murder. What has he got to lose holding out?"

"I see your point."

All in all, Melaniphy was not looking forward to the interview with Carl Mossberg. As he marched back to the interrogation room, he decided that the part he liked least was just being in the same room with the creep. It was as though even limited exposure to him might contaminate Melaniphy. But what the hell, he told himself, he'd been exposed often enough before, maybe even contaminated two or three times—and he had survived. Hadn't he? Of course he had. So he would survive Carl Mossberg, too.

What surprised Melaniphy most about him was that Carl was really kind of an attractive guy—not just handsome (he would have expected that, considering he was a hustler), but possessed also of a certain rough charm, evident intelligence, and something like wit. All this emerged gradually during the first hour of the interrogation. It took only a minute or two for Mossberg to grasp what it was Melaniphy wanted from him, and why it was that, of all those hauled in that evening from Dizzy's, the cops had chosen to talk to him last of all. He would have suspected, of course, but from the moment that his suspicions were confirmed, he began playing a very cagey game, trying to find out just what they had on him. And that Melaniphy didn't want him to know—not just yet.

Bits and pieces did come out, though. When, for instance, Carl boasted that he had two guys who would swear he was drinking in Dizzy's all night that night, Melaniphy couldn't resist countering, "That's funny. I've got three who've already signed statements saying they saw you leave with Gawlor, and that you didn't come back that evening."

"Well, I guess it's my guys against your guys, isn't it?"

"That's the way it looks, Carl."

"Then we both lose. Juries never believe queers."

"Who said anything about a jury?" Melaniphy asked, making a great show of injured innocence. "I thought we were just discussing the night in question."

Carl stood up. "You mean I can go?"

"No. Sit down. We haven't finished discussing."

No, they hadn't finished. Melaniphy took Carl through the entire story once again, getting him to admit for the first time that, well, maybe he did know who Gawlor was, after all. He may even have taken a walk with him on that night—the one Melaniphy was so interested in—but, anyway, it was just around the block, and you meet so many guys in a place like Dizzy's that you can't remember them all. "Maybe your guys just didn't see me come back in," Carl suggested. "I'm a pretty quiet guy. People don't notice me sometimes." He flashed a smile. Self-deprecating or ironic? Melaniphy could take his pick.

But he declined to choose. Instead he jumped up and walked around briskly to a point just behind Mossberg. He bent over then and, with his mouth six inches from Carl's right ear, he yelled as loudly as he could, "CUT OUT THIS FUCKING SHIT!" He stepped back then and saw with satisfaction that Carl had stiffened in response, probably waiting for a blow to follow. Good, thought Melaniphy, let him wait.

He began next on Carl's relationship with the kid. About this he found him strangely willing to talk. Carl didn't deny knowing the kid, didn't deny Ronnie was a runaway and that he had let him move in with him. But, he insisted, he was acting like a big brother to the kid. "I liked him," Carl declared. "I really did! I bought him stuff and gave him money. We were buddies."

Melaniphy got the idea, listening to him, that Carl had thought this all out carefully beforehand, that this somehow was to be the very essence of his defense. He had the feeling, too, that it wouldn't be easy to shake him. Still, he would give it a try. He was just taking him back over the territory—how had he met Ronnie? where?—when he was interrupted by a knock on the door. It was Klezek, beckoning him out into the hall. Without a word to Carl, Melaniphy stepped out and closed the door after him.

"Yeah? What did you turn up?"

"I thought you'd be interested in these." Klezek held out three credit cards. Melaniphy took them and looked them over. They were from Shell, Visa, and American Express. All three were made out to John F. Gawlor.

"From Mossberg's place?"

"Taped under a drawer."

Melaniphy nodded, relieved.

Klezek continued: "I also got what I think are the boots he used to do the number on Gawlor. I found a pair in the closet, freshly shined. Now the place is a mess, see. The clothes in it are mostly dirty and dirtier. I asked myself why these are so nice and shiny and tucked away in a corner, and so I looked them over—and what do you know? He was lazy. He just put the polish on over the dried blood. I even spotted bits of hair and what might be flesh tucked in the space between the soles. Before I came back here I dropped the boots off at the lab. That's why I took so long. They said they'd have the report by the morning."

Sighing, nodding, now giving in to the numbing exhaustion that he had been fighting for the last couple of hours, Melaniphy said to Klezek, "You didn't take so long. I would have waited all night for this."

Klezek glanced at his watch. "You have, just about."

Melaniphy left him with a single pat on the shoulder and went back into the interrogation room. Briefly, and with unusual detachment, he outlined to Carl what they had against him and concluded by asking if he would like to make a statement. "I'd say we got you for Gawlor. Give us another day or two, and we'll have you for the kid."

"I didn't kill the kid!" Carl said with surprising vehemence.

"What do you mean? What're you telling me?"

"I'm telling you I didn't kill him. It was all set up for me to come in after about fifteen or twenty minutes, when they'd be at it. The kid took care of the door. I thought this guy was a straight, and I could shake him down, you know? But when I come through the door, the kid is there on the bed with this belt around his neck, and just looking I could tell he was dead. And here's the guy, see, sitting at the foot of the bed with his head in his hands. Well, I went fucking *wild*. I knocked this guy down, and I started working him over, and I guess I got carried away."

"I guess you did." Melaniphy studied Carl, trying to decide how much truth there was to the story. He had to admit that it had a certain ring.

"That was no bullshit, what I told you before," Carl said earnestly. "I liked that kid. He was practically a kid brother to me, you know? When the jury hears what Gawlor did, they'll give me a fucking medal!"

"You're counting on that, aren't you? You've got it all thought out, haven't you? Maybe you can fool them, you son of a bitch, but you can't fool me. I'm going to nail you for that kid, too. I promise you."

Carl shook his head in agitation and practically screamed at Melaniphy, "Why should I kill the kid? He was a fucking gold mine for me!"

And suddenly Melaniphy understood that Carl was telling the truth: it was Gawlor who had killed the kid.

He got the statement. It wouldn't take long to get Mossberg booked and over to the Eleventh and State lockup. Melaniphy asked Klezek to handle it and went home to grab a couple of hours sleep.

The sun was just coming up over the lake as Melaniphy hit the Outer Drive at Oak Street. Jesus, this is a pretty city, he thought, this part of it is, anyway. He tried thinking about that, tried thinking about anything at all except what he had just walked away from—because that made him feel guilty. It was bad detective work. He had closed his mind absolutely to the possibility that it might have been Gawlor who killed the kid. Why? Because of Gawlor's wife, he supposed—or worse yet, because in some half-assed way he thought he understood the guy. He didn't. He probably never would. But he was going to work on it.